–The–
Hidden
Jewel

Trailblazer Books

Also by Dave and Neta Jackson

-The-
Hidden
Jewel

Dave & Neta Jackson

Story illustrations by
Julian Jackson

BETHANY HOUSE PUBLISHERS
MINNEAPOLIS, MINNESOTA 55438

Published by Bethany House Publishers
A Ministry of Bethany Fellowship International
11400 Hampshire Avenue South
Minneapolis, Minnesota 55438
www.bethanyhouse.com

Printed in the United States of America by
Bethany Press International, Minneapolis, Minnesota 55438

Library of Congress Cataloging-in-Publication Data

Jackson, Dave
    The hidden jewel / Dave and Neta Jackson.
        p.   cm. — (Trailblazer books)
    Summary: While traveling in the south of India, fourteen-year-old John and his mother encounter the Irish missionary Amy Carmichael and find themselves drawn into helping the work of the Dohnavur Fellowship.

    [1. Missionaries—Fiction. 2. Carmichael, Amy, 1867–1951—Fiction. 3. Dohnavur Fellowship—Fiction. 4. India—Fiction. 5. Christian life—Fiction.]
    I. Jackson, Neta. II. Title. III. Series
PZ7.J132418Hi   1992
[Fic]—dc20   91–44062
ISBN 1–55661–245–1   CIP
                                                                AC

This glimpse into the life of Amy Carmichael and Dohnavur Fellowship is based on the true story of an Indian girl named Muttammal, called "Jewel," and the young man, Arul Dasan. Many real people, events, and details have been worked into this simplified version of their story. However, the Knight family and the role they played are fiction.

DAVE AND NETA JACKSON are a husband/wife writing team who have authored or coauthored many books on marriage and family, the church, and relationships, including *On Fire for Christ: Stories from Martyrs Mirror*, the Pet Parables series, and the Caring Parent series.

They have two children: Julian, an art major and illustrator for the Trailblazer series, and Rachel, a high school student. They make their home in Evanston, Illinois, where they are active members of Reba Place Church.

CONTENTS

Chapter 1

Incident on the Cog Train

THE INDIAN SERVANT went first, loaded down with an assortment of baggage. Fourteen-year-old John Knight followed him out of the station, then stared at the strange train puffing at the edge of the platform. "Father!" he called back over his shoulder. "What kind of a train is this?

TRACK 2

It's so small—almost like a miniature train. And look!" John pointed. "The engine's on backward!"

John's mother and father emerged from the station doorway, each wearing a *topee*, or sun helmet, to protect themselves from the intense Indian sun. Sanford Knight smiled at his son's confusion. The tall English government official had only been in India for six months himself and understood how different everything must seem to his wife and son.

"This is a cog train," he said, "the only way to get up the steep hills to Ootacamund. The engine is placed at the back of the train so it can push the cars up the hills. And look between the tracks."

John squinted as he focused on the shiny tracks. A row of spikes ran like a third rail between them.

"A wheel beneath the engine grabs those cogs and helps pull the train. Now, come on, Leslie," he said to his wife. "In you go." Mr. Knight opened the door to the first-class car and assisted his wife into the train. Azim, their Indian servant, followed with the bags, stowing them in the overhead racks.

Laughter and girlish shouts caught John's attention. A flock of young Indian girls dressed in brightly colored long skirts were climbing into the third class car, along with a woman dressed in a pale blue *sari*. *That's strange,* he thought. *That woman looks English—or white, anyway. I wonder why she's wearing Indian clothing?*

The conductor, dressed in a blue coat and white turban, was calling "All aboard!" and the steam engine let out a mighty *whoosh*. There was a flurry of doors opening and people scrambling onto the cog train. John leaned an arm out the open window as the train jerked and made its way slowly out of the station. The Nilgiri hills rolled brown and dry on every side. His father said it was greener and cooler at Ooty—as Ootacamund was usually called—a resort town called a "hill station" nestled in the foothills of the Western Ghats.

The Knights were heading for Ooty to enroll John in the British school there. As the train lurched and groaned up the hills, he wondered what the school would be like. "All the English families come to Ooty for their holidays in the hot season," his father had explained. "It's a good place for a school. You'll feel right at home; the town is very British."

John wasn't sure he wanted to feel at home—not if that meant England. India was the most exciting place he had ever been. He and his mother had recently arrived from England to join his father, the new junior magistrate in the Tinnevelly District of south India. The senior magistrate was scheduled to retire in 1910, and the British government was giving his father one year of preparation to take over the civil duties of judge and magistrate.

From the moment John walked down the gangplank of the ship, India shouted adventure. Crowds of people swarmed in the streets, competing with bicycles, horse-and-buggies, and ox carts for the right of way. Donkeys loaded with bundles plodded slowly between village markets. Majestic banyan trees provided some shade and relief from the dry heat in

Palamcottah, the large town where the Tinnevelly District Court was located. Temple elephants paraded in the streets; monkeys scolded from the tall grasses in the countryside. John had been warned that sometimes leopards came down from the hills, though he hadn't seen any.

John sighed. Just the thought of entering the spit-and-polish corridors of an English boarding school, even if it was in India, was enough to bore him to tears. There was so much to see and do here.

Nevertheless, after a week of settling into their new home in Palamcottah, Sanford Knight decided they must get John into school without delay, and combine it with a short holiday in Ooty. They had already taken the regular train as far as it would go, traveling in the relative comfort of a first-class car with their Indian servant. The cog train was the last leg of their journey.

As John leaned on the window ledge, a movement toward the back of the train caught his eye. He leaned farther out. "I can't believe it!" he exclaimed. "There are people on the roof of the train!"

Mrs. Knight peered out the window and looked up. "Oh, my word. Someone could get hurt!"

Mr. Knight glanced up from the newspaper he was reading. "Mmm, yes. The lower castes are hopping a free ride. It's not legal, but tolerated."

Just then the cog train pitched as it rounded a curve, shaking the railroad cars severely. John glanced up just in time to see a poorly dressed Indian man slip and fall from the top of the train, landing soundlessly in the brush and rocks beside the tracks.

"Stop!" John yelled. "A man just fell from the top of the train!"

"Sanford, how do we stop the train?" cried Mrs. Knight. "He fell head first!"

Mr. Knight jumped up and pulled on the emergency brake chain. Nothing seemed to happen at first. "John!" Sanford Knight yelled, and John pulled on the chain with his father. A few moments later the cog train groaned and stopped, the steam engine belching smoke in protest. The Indian conductor came running to their car, obviously upset with John's father. "You stop the train? What is the matter, *sahib*?"

John pointed. "Back there! I saw him! A man fell off!"

The conductor turned and hurried back along the track. Other doors were opening in the other cars and people peered out. John scrambled after the conductor, with his father and mother following.

The train had gone several lengths beyond where the man had fallen. He was motionless and appeared to be unconscious. Dirty rags barely covered his gaunt body; he had no hat or turban. The conductor pushed aside the noisy crowd that was gathering and looked the man over closely; then he began waving and shouting at the other passengers in an unfamiliar language. It was obvious to John that he was telling everyone to get back on the train.

"What is it, conductor?" said John's father, who came up just then with Mrs. Knight and Azim.

"Nothing, nothing. We can do nothing. He is *pariah*—untouchable."

"I see," said Mr. Knight.

"What do you mean?" demanded Mrs. Knight. "We can't just leave an injured man lying beside the railroad tracks."

Mr. Knight pulled his wife aside. "Leslie, my dear, you don't understand. The Indian caste system is very complex—we mustn't interfere with their beliefs. Hindu religion, you know."

"I don't know!" protested John's mother. "But I do know that as a Christian and an Englishwoman, we must—"

"You are entirely right, madam," said a calm woman's voice. "Would you help me?"

To John's astonishment, the white woman in the pale blue sari walked right past the conductor and bent down beside the injured man. Her hands felt

14

over his body gently. "Nothing broken," she said. "But he has hit his head. We must get him into the train."

"Miss Carmichael!" protested the conductor. "It is not done!"

The woman ignored him. "Would you help me?" she said again, looking at the Knights.

John wasn't sure what was going on, but he liked the woman's gutsy attitude. "Yes, ma'am!" he grinned. His mother also stepped forward. Azim looked shocked and backed away. Reluctantly, Sanford Knight assisted his wife and son and the woman in the sari as they picked up the injured man and carefully placed him inside the third-class car. John tried to ignore the smell of the dirty body.

A loud cheer went up from the freeloaders on the roof of the train, and John waved to them in response.

Once back in their first-class compartment, John's father looked displeased. "I say, I will not have my wife and son getting involved in the messy little affairs among the Indian social classes. You cannot solve their problems with misguided sympathy. My job as an official of the British government is to rule and bring order to the country, while letting the natives take care of their own social affairs."

"Oh, Sanford," said his wife. "Don't look so dark. It was the Christian thing to do. We couldn't let the man die, could we? I wonder . . . who is that Carmichael woman?"

Mr. Knight sighed. "I have heard about her—a

troublemaker, they say. She is an Irish missionary, I am told, who refuses to follow the customary missionary methods. Instead she has gone about 'rescuing' girls, of all things, who belong to the temples, or something like that. All I know is that she has made a lot of Hindu holy men very angry."

"Don't those girls have families?" John asked, not understanding again.

"I don't know. It's really none of our business," said his father. Mr. Knight snapped open his newspaper. He had heard quite enough of Miss Carmichael.

"Hmm," mused Mrs. Knight. "I'd like to meet her properly. My curiosity is up. It's unthinkable that those young girls might have belonged to a temple."

I'd like to meet her, too, thought John. He'd especially like to meet some Indian young people. Boys would be nice, but even Indian girls would be better than getting stuck in an English boarding school.

A whistle blew. The brown grasses had given way to rich green trees and brush on the hillsides. Then the first red-tiled roofs of Ooty appeared.

Chapter 2

Reprieve From School

THE HEADMASTER of Kingsway School for Boys did not blink, but sat solid and unyielding behind the big desk.

"What do you mean, we can't enroll John because the term has already started?" The veins in Mr. Knight's face and neck were beginning to stand out. John watched his father with interest; he knew Sanford Knight was used to getting his way.

The Knights had gone directly to the school after arriving in Ooty. His father had been right—it looked very much like his old school back in Brighton, except, instead of the English Channel sparkling in the distance, the Western Ghats rose like a misty wall out of the foothills. Boys in blazers and school ties looked at him curiously and poked each other as the three Knights walked down the cool corridor. Once they had been ushered into the school office, however, it did not take them long to realize they had bumped into another type of wall: the headmaster.

"We have our rules, Mr. Knight," the balding man said patiently, his wire-rimmed glasses perched on the end of his nose. "Our winter term began in mid-January; we are now already four weeks into the term. It would be quite upsetting both for the class, and I believe for John, to try to enter at this time. My recommendation is that you wait until the summer term."

John, trying not to slouch in the uncomfortable wooden chair, held his breath. *Not have to go to school?* Was it possible that he wouldn't have to enter this English prison for a few more months? That would mean he could get acquainted with India—the India that lay out there on the plains, back in the Tinnevelly District!

"Sanford . . ." said John's mother, touching her husband's sleeve.

"Not now, Leslie," said Mr. Knight impatiently. He scowled at the headmaster, then went to stand by the window. "This is quite inconvenient, Mr. Bath. I have responsibilities; I must travel. I had hoped that John could settle into school so that my wife might join me. And I don't like him getting behind. Are you sure—?"

"Quite sure," said the headmaster. "However, since you have made the trip to Ooty, why don't we complete our interview and do the paperwork necessary to enroll John for the next term. That will be at least one thing out of the way."

And so it was done. An hour later Mr. Knight hailed a *tonga*, a two-wheeled horse carriage, and gave the name of Willingdon House to the driver. As the horse clipped along toward the inn, he stared moodily as they passed the stately Ooty Club and St. Stephen's Church.

"Sanford," Mrs. Knight tried again, "maybe it's all for the best. This gives us some more time to be together as a family, to adjust to our new surroundings. And don't forget that I have my teaching certificate; I could tutor John in most subjects."

"That's right, Father," said John. So far he had said little, hoping not to betray the wild happiness within that wanted to hoot and holler with joy. "I'll study with Mama; that way I won't get behind."

"Humph. Not exactly the same as a proper school. But I guess we'll do what we have to do."

Their bags had already been delivered by Azim to the large rambling inn, nestled among stone paths and flowering bushes. "This is lovely!" said Mrs. Knight, taking off her *topee* and walking through the airy sitting and sleeping rooms. "Let's put disappointment behind us and just enjoy our holiday!"

John felt a little guilty. He wasn't disappointed, and he was for sure going to enjoy the holiday!

The next day Leslie Knight dressed in comfortable walking clothes and shoes and set out for a hike with John; there were many walking paths from Ooty into the hills. Sanford Knight chose to go to the men's club instead to get the news.

"John, stay with your mother," he ordered. "Remain on the paths and don't go far. There are snakes and wild animals in the hills; you can't be too careful."

"Yes, Father."

The path soon left the town behind them and went up at a steep slant. The mountain forest was cool and shady under the lush cover of leaves. "Oh, lovely," murmured Mrs. Knight, stopping now and then to get her breath.

Mother and son walked in silence for half an hour, then the trees thinned and the sound of water grew louder. Rounding a bend, they were confronted with a marvelous waterfall, surrounded by outcroppings of rock overhead.

It was a few moments before John realized they weren't alone. The woman from the cog train sat on a boulder watching several of her girls splashing in the water at the foot of the falls. She was still dressed in the pale blue sari, one of the smaller children cradled in her lap.

"Why, Miss Carmichael," John heard his mother say. Mrs. Knight approached the woman and held out her hand. "I had been hoping to meet you. My name is Leslie Knight, and this is my son John. I was wondering whether the man who fell off the train had recovered."

The woman shook Mrs. Knight's hand and smiled at John. "My name is Amy Carmichael. Won't you join us? We are soaking up God's beauty, aren't we,

Blossom?" The Indian child on her lap giggled and then reached out a chubby arm.

"I think the man will be all right," the woman went on. "He has a bad concussion and is resting at the guest cottage where we are staying."

"I must admit our chance meeting yesterday has left me curious," said Mrs. Knight. "Tell me about yourself and these girls—if I'm not being too bold."

Amy Carmichael's eyes rested fondly on the girls who had tucked their skirts up and were still poking around in the water, casting curious glances in their direction. Miss Carmichael had brown eyes, surrounded by laugh wrinkles and skin tanned by the sun. John guessed she was at least forty.

"There is not much to tell," the woman said. She seemed suddenly shy. "We live just outside the village of Dohnavur in a place we call Dohnavur Fellowship. It is home to me, several godly Indian women, a few English volunteers, and many more girls like Blossom here whom God has rescued from the evil practices of the Hindu temples. A good woman here in Ooty—a Mrs. Hopewell—has made her cottage available to us so that we might have a place of retreat. Right now many of the children at Dohnavur are sick; I have brought these girls here to escape the fever.

"Now," she brightened, "tell me about yourself."

Mrs. Knight chatted briefly about their recent arrival, her husband's position as junior magistrate in Palamcottah, and their coming to Ooty to enroll John in school.

"Ah," said Miss Carmichael upon hearing that John could not enter school at mid-term. "No doubt you are deeply disappointed." She winked at John; he grinned. He liked this Amy Carmichael, whoever she was.

"You say you are a teacher, Mrs. Knight?" continued Miss Carmichael. "We have a great need for teachers at Dohnavur."

"Oh, I don't know if I could teach," John's mother said. "We are still so new to India. I have no idea what life will be like in Palamcottah, or what Sanford will expect of me as the wife of a magistrate. And, of course, I need to be tutoring John until he can start the summer term."

John wandered away from the two women toward the waterfall. The mist felt cool on his face and hair. He wondered if any of the girls playing in the water beneath the falls spoke English. "Hello," he said, standing on the bank.

The girls in the water fell silent, pressed their palms together, and bowed their heads toward him in a little *salaam*, or greeting.

John held his hands together and salaamed right back. This brought giggles from the girls, but they still kept their eyes lowered.

John wondered what to do next. How could he tell them he wanted to be friends when he could not speak their language? Then he had an idea. He sat on the bank, removed his walking shoes and socks, and stepped into the water. It was cold! He took a few more steps away from the bank; he would walk across on the stones and small boulders that dotted the mountain stream. Maybe he could show the girls how it could be done. But he was not prepared for the strength of the rushing water, and without warning a slippery rock sent him under in a big splash.

Before John knew what was happening, several small, strong hands had grasped his arms and pulled him up out of the water. Then, just as quickly, the

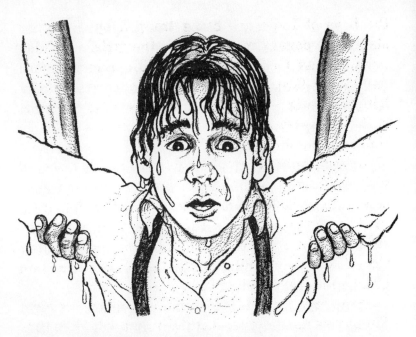

Indian girls had scrambled up the bank and were running toward Miss Carmichael and his mother, leaving a dripping John to make his way out of the stream.

He was embarrassed. But all his mother said when he approached the group clustered around Miss Carmichael was, "Better sit in the sun and dry off; it's quite cool in the forest."

John sat at a little distance from the group, shivering in his damp clothes and trying to regain his pride. But he could still overhear the conversation.

"You must at least come to visit us soon," Amy Carmichael was saying. "Dohnavur is only twenty miles south of Palamcottah. Bring John with you if you like! We haven't any boys—though God knows the boys of India are being trapped by the same slavery of paganism that holds the girls. Someday ... someday God will provide. Oh. Except Arul. Arul is our first boy, a few years older than John, I believe. He is a great help and blessing, and has suffered dearly for his faith in the Lord Jesus. He could show John around. . . ."

John forgot his damp clothes. Oh! If only he could visit Dohnavur Fellowship and meet this Arul person. But . . . would his father allow it? He didn't seem too pleased about John mixing with the Indians socially, much less being friendly with Amy Carmichael, who dressed like a native, rescued little girls, and made the Hindu holy men angry.

But, then, he knew his mother was on his side. There was no way that Leslie Knight would be content to sit around sipping tea with other English ladies when an opportunity to get to know the real India—and even help its children—was being offered to her.

Chapter 3

The Money-Begging Elephant

THE HOLIDAY IN OOTY lasted two weeks. The weather in late February was sunny and moderate during the day, but downright chilly when the sun sank behind the hills. One day Mr. Knight took his wife and son to a polo match at the Ooty polo grounds. They also went riding in the hills on hired horses, dined at the Ooty Club, and poked around the Nilgiri Library. Each day's activities usually ended with tea served on the open porch of Willingdon House.

John and his mother also enjoyed several hikes into the mountain forest with Amy Carmichael and her little band. (Mr. Knight, not keen on hiking, preferred the more dignified company at the club.) As the Indian girls scampered along the trails, John thought they looked like wildflowers with brightly colored ribbons of yellow, rose, blue, and green braided into their beautiful thick black hair.

The Irish missionary and her girls left Ooty a few days before the Knights. "Forgive me if I'm being forward, but why do you travel third class?" Leslie Knight asked Miss Carmichael as they said goodbye on the Ooty train station platform.

"Because there isn't any fourth class!" Amy Carmichael laughed, and swung onto the cog train. The girls, all chattering like magpies, leaned out the windows waving goodbye until the little train disappeared.

As they turned to walk back to Willingdon House, John asked his mother, "What did she mean?"

Leslie Knight brushed away a pesky flying insect. "I'm not sure, son. She seems to think it's important to identify with the people of India, to live as they live and travel as they travel. 'All are one in Christ Jesus,' she told me. I also imagine money is limited, caring for as many children as she does. But imagine—traveling third class on those hard benches! So crowded and uncomfortable."

John silently agreed. Even traveling in first-class compartments, the trip "home" to Palamcottah was tiring. After the cog train took them down the mountain, the trip took several more days by regular train. At every station water carriers would run alongside crying, *"Hindu tunni!"* or *"Mussulman tunni!"* ("Water for Hindus and water for Muslims," Azim, their Indian servant, explained.) Food could also be purchased from vendors who prepared curries and rice dishes right on the station platform. At night, Azim let down an overhead berth on which John slept, while his parents slept on the cushioned seats below.

From the train station in Palamcottah, they were carried to the junior magistrate's house by *palanquin*—individual chairs resting on two long poles carried on the shoulders of Indians wearing only *dhotis*, loose loincloths wrapped between the legs and tucked in at the waist.

It was hotter in Palamcottah than in Ooty, but the heat was dry and bearable. The house with its walled courtyard was open and airy. Servants seemed to appear out of nowhere to unpack their bags, bring water for baths, serve four o'clock tea on the porch, and deliver *chits*—letters sent between households for communication, including several invitations from British army wives who wanted to meet Mrs. Knight.

"Do we really need this many servants, Sanford?" Mrs. Knight asked, as first one, then another appeared to do small, simple tasks.

Mr. Knight laughed. "*We* don't, but *they* do," he chuckled. "You will soon discover that the caste system in India is worse than any trade union back in England. If a servant is from the farming caste, he will weed the vegetable garden, but he won't clean the toilets—you will need to hire a sweeper to do that. On and on it goes!"

True to her word, Leslie Knight obtained a variety of schoolbooks and started John on his lessons—

three hours each morning. But they had only been back in Palamcottah for a few days when Sanford Knight, home for lunch as was his custom, announced that he had to travel on government business to Bangalore, a major city in south India about three hundred miles to the north.

"I am afraid I shall be gone for several weeks," he said to his wife. "I would like to take you with me, Leslie, but with John not in school . . . well, I simply don't have time to make the necessary arrangements to bring you both along."

"It's quite all right, Sanford," Mrs. Knight assured him. "We'll do fine. John should keep up with his lessons, and perhaps we'll have time to explore the countryside a bit."

John was disappointed at being left behind. Bangalore! He was sure a large city would be mysterious and exciting. Then he realized his father was still talking.

" . . . don't want you going about alone, Leslie. You must take one of the servants with you at all times. Azim is a good man; I will leave him here with you. One of the other servants can go with me."

Two days later Mrs. Knight and John waved goodbye as a two-wheeled *tonga* with Sanford Knight, a servant, and the luggage headed for the Palamcottah train station. But it only took a couple of days for John to grow restless. Azim fixed up an old bicycle for him to ride, but his mother felt uneasy letting him go very far on his own.

Leslie Knight was restless, too. Once lessons were

over, there was very little for an English lady to do. She went over the menus with the Indian cook, arranged the cut flowers that appeared fresh from somewhere each day, and accepted visits from bored Army wives eager to get a look at the junior magistrate's wife. But John knew his mother was uncomfortable with the endless gossip that accompanied these visits.

Then a letter arrived from Dohnavur Fellowship. "It's from Miss Carmichael, John!" Mrs. Knight exclaimed. "A note inviting us to visit Dohnavur. Why, that's the very thing. She said Dohnavur was only twenty miles from Palamcottah. We can hire a carriage or even those funny chairs on poles . . ."

"*Palanquins*, Mama." John grinned.

" . . . And your father will be gone several weeks. This would be a good time to go since I doubt he would be interested. It will be our chance to explore the Tinnevelly District, and see the villages on the way."

Mrs. Knight lost no time in sending a return message to Dohnavur that they were coming on March 10. John was hoping his mother would forget about lessons, but he saw the schoolbooks go into the bags. Azim arranged for a two-horse carriage that would take them part way; then they would have to find local transportation to take them on to Dohnavur.

They arose early, but the cook would not allow them to depart without doing justice to the large breakfast he had prepared: papaya slices, porridge, fish cakes, boiled eggs, and toast and marmalade, washed down with tea. John slid the fish cakes into his napkin when he thought no one was looking—ghastly things for breakfast, he thought.

The carriage arrived a bit later. There was a flurry of activity while the servants piled the luggage on one seat, then helped Mrs. Knight and John into the other. Azim climbed up with the hired driver.

As the horses threaded their way through the crowded dirt streets of Palamcottah and then headed south into the countryside, John had a delicious sense of freedom. The courtyard walls around their house in Palamcottah were confining; they seemed designed to keep India out. But now the road was beckoning him toward unknown adventures.

The carriage passed field after field of muddy rice paddies, where farmers were preparing the soil for planting in April and May. Some farmers guided plows behind single oxen; others used crude hand tools to break up the clods of dirt. John noticed that each paddy was surrounded by a little dirt dike. "They keep water in when the monsoons come, young sahib," Azim explained.

Most of the villages along the road were small and poor. Ragged children ran alongside the carriage crying, *"Buckshees! Buckshees!"* holding out their hands for money. Azim shouted something at them in the Tamil language and they scattered. Women crouched over fires and cooking pots outside their mud-wall and thatch-roof huts, or carried waterpots on their heads as they returned from the village well.

Noon had passed when the carriage came into a larger town called Four Lakes. John noticed a Muslim mosque with its twin minarets not far from the ornate gold dome of a Hindu temple. "The carriage must return to Palamcottah before dark," said Azim. "It is only five or six miles to Dohnavur. We can hire a bandy." Mrs. Knight and John got down from the carriage near the marketplace, and Azim paid the driver. Azim then disappeared into the market to find an ox cart for hire.

While they were waiting for Azim to return, John heard a commotion coming from the direction of the Hindu temple. A magnificent elephant decorated with richly embroidered fabric and flowing tassels came into view. Shouting and laughing, children danced about dangerously close to its enormous feet. The driver of the elephant sat on its neck and guided it toward the marketplace.

At a nearby booth, the elephant stopped and stretched its trunk into the booth. John noticed that the vendor placed something into the trunk, which the elephant swung up to its driver. Then the trunk swung back toward the vendor and rested a brief moment on the man's head.

The elephant came nearer, and suddenly the great trunk reached out toward John and Mrs. Knight. He heard his mother stifle a cry; John too felt a little frightened. What was he supposed to do? *Buckshees! Buckshees!*" shouted some of the children. John dug in his pocket for a *four anna* Indian coin and placed it in the pink, sloppy wetness of the tip of the

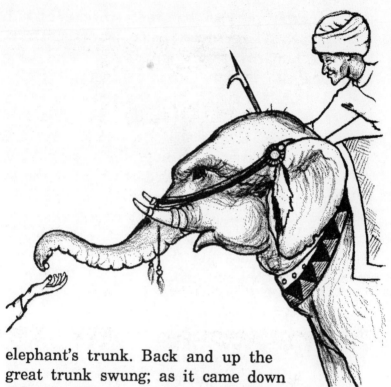

elephant's trunk. Back and up the
great trunk swung; as it came down
John thought it was going to smash into
him. But instead the elephant rested its trunk gently
on John's head in blessing, then lumbered on.

"Hindu elephant," said Azim's voice in John's ear.
"Collects money for the temple."

The fear had passed but the excitement remained.
John decided not to ask his mother whether giving
money to a pagan temple was a good thing for an
English Christian to do; he would never forget the
feel of the elephant's trunk resting on his head.

Azim had not been able to locate an ox cart for
hire, but they were hungry. The servant unpacked

the lunch that the cook had sent—vegetables with rice wrapped in large green banana leaves, and fruit. They ate hungrily, sitting on their luggage, using their fingers to scoop the food into their mouths. Mrs. Knight started to giggle, then she and John nearly choked as they burst out laughing. If only Sanford Knight could see them now!

Azim finally located a bandy, which was nothing more than a covered cart pulled by two oxen. But by now the afternoon sun was beginning to slide down the western sky when they left Four Lakes and headed toward Dohnavur. The oxen were slow, barely covering three miles an hour. For a while John and his mother got out and walked alongside the cart.

As they neared the village of Dohnavur, John noticed that a young Indian girl was following them. But she seemed frightened when she saw John looking in her direction, and darted into the brush.

"Did you see that girl, Mama?"

"No. Where, dear?" said Mrs. Knight absentmindedly. John didn't bother to reply. The girl was already gone.

In the village of Dohnavur, Azim dismounted from the cart to ask directions to the home of the Irish missionary. John thought he saw the same girl again, inching close to Azim's elbow as he talked rapidly in Tamil with an old man. John looked closely at the girl. She was maybe twelve years old and wore many gold bangles on both arms and around her ankles. But he had a hard time getting a look at her face; she looked this way and that as if afraid someone would see her, and she held a corner of her scarf over her nose and mouth.

The old man pointed west of the village, and when John looked again, the girl had disappeared.

"Just outside the village," said Azim, hopping onto the cart. Sure enough, as they left the village, they soon approached a large, walled compound. The bandy driver drove up toward an arched gate made of bricks. A small sign at the side of the gate had strange black scratchings on it, which John supposed was in the Tamil language. Underneath the scratchings were the English words, "Dohnavur Fellowship."

They had arrived.

Chapter 4

Refuge!

Azim pulled the rope and rang the bell to announce their arrival as the bandy driver unloaded their bags. Soon the iron gates swung wide and a young Indian man greeted them with a big smile.

"Mrs. Knight! John Knight! Welcome! My name is Arul Dasan. *Amma* is expecting you."

"*Amma*?" John whispered quizzically to Azim.

"*Amma* means 'mother' in Tamil," said the servant.

Arul looked about eighteen or nineteen years old, John thought, as they followed the young man into the compound toward a one-story house with a wide porch. Amy Carmichael was sitting on the floor of the porch with several Indian women feeding a one-year-old baby with her fingers. When the little party came close, Miss Carmichael jumped up to greet them.

"Leslie! John! I am so delighted that you have come! And this is . . . ?"

"Azim, our . . . er, servant," said Mrs. Knight.

"We are all servants here!" smiled Miss Carmichael, shifting the baby to her hip and giving Leslie Knight a hug to take away the awkwardness of the moment. "Come and join us for our meal."

She introduced the other women workers. "These are our *accals*, big sisters to the children." The *accals* beamed big smiles and greeted them with their palms pressed together in gentle salaams.

John and Arul sat with their plates of food on the steps to the porch a little way from the women. Azim accepted the food but walked away from the house to eat. John looked around at the other small houses scattered about the compound. All the buildings were turning a deep blue as the sky reddened in the west. Some had wavy red-tile roofs, others had straw thatch, though they looked more sturdy than the ones he'd seen in the villages along the way. He wondered where the girls were . . . then the sound of children singing came floating through the twilight.

Arul nodded toward the music. "The little ones are singing praise to God!"

John swallowed the last of his rice. "Arul," he said, "how did you come here? I mean, there are no boys . . . just girls."

Arul grinned. "I heard the Word of God and

wanted to follow Jesus. But my family was very upset. They beat me and threatened to rub pepper in my eyes. So, I came to my new home with Amma."

"How old were you?"

"Ten or eleven. I forget." The grin flashed again. "This is my new family. I work hard to help Amma; she lets me stay."

John sat staring out into the deepening twilight. Birds twittered their good nights from the tamarind trees. It felt strange to hear someone talk about being beaten just because he wanted to be a Christian. In England, everyone John knew was a Christian . . . well, at least they went to church on Sunday. It was the expected thing to do, like honoring your parents and the British flag. John believed in God, and of course he knew that Jesus was God's Son . . . but what did it mean to "follow Jesus" in the way Arul was talking about? Would he be willing to call himself a Christian if his family threatened to rub pepper in his eyes?

A bell rang.

"Someone's at the gate," said Arul, getting up. "We aren't expecting anyone. I wonder who . . . ?" He walked quickly toward the outer gate. John followed him at a trot.

The bell rang insistently, and as Arul and John got closer, they could hear the faint sound of fists beating on the gate and urgent cries. Throwing back the bar, Arul pulled on the gate and it swung in. A frightened young girl took a step backward, as if afraid of being struck. Then she threw herself at the boys' feet crying a single word over and over.

John stared, his mouth open. It was the girl who had been following them on the road to Dohnavur!

"What is she saying? What does she want?" John asked anxiously as Arul bent down and lifted the girl to her feet.

"Refuge! She wants refuge," the older boy said. "Quick—shut the gate!"

John hastily barred the gate again, then caught up with Arul and the weeping girl as they made their way toward the main house where Amy Carmichael and John's mother were sitting with the Indian women. As the group on the porch heard the commotion, Miss Carmichael handed the baby to one of the Indian *accals* and came rushing down the steps.

"Dear child!" she said, drawing the girl into a warm embrace in the folds of her sari.

"There, there, you are safe here." The "mother" of Dohnavur Fellowship brought the unexpected visitor onto the porch and sat down, holding the girl, big as she was, on her lap. The girl's dark arms went around Miss Carmichael's neck and clung to her tightly.

Arul tapped John on the shoulder. "Come. We will say good-night. Let us leave them."

John looked at his mother, who was similarly being drawn away by the Indian women. She nodded at him and gave him a little smile as if to say, "I'm sure it's all right. Go with Arul." So he followed the older boy through the compound, which was dark now, except for the light of the moon.

Arul took him to a small thatch-roofed cottage with a little porch made of cane. Inside Arul lit a lantern. It had only one room, which was quite bare except for a writing table, a chair, a cupboard in one corner and three wooden bed frames. Woven rope within the frame served as the sleeping surface.

"*Charpoy*," Arul said, pointing at the wooden frames. "Beds. For you, me, and Azim."

Arul disappeared for a few moments and came back with John's bag. "Azim says he will sleep outside." Arul shrugged.

The *charpoy* looked rather uncomfortable, even with a blanket covering the woven rope. But it had been a long, exciting day, and within moments John was sound asleep.

❖ ❖ ❖

John awoke to the sound of birds in the tamarind trees. At first he didn't know where he was, but then the events of the previous day came flooding back. He was at Dohnavur Fellowship, sharing a small cottage of sun-baked bricks with an Indian boy.

John sat up. The room was empty. He dressed quickly and stepped out into the bright sunshine. Azim was waiting for him on the little porch.

"Young *sahib*, your mother waits for you at the main house," said the servant.

John heard childish laughter. He saw several Indian women and older girls taking several babies for a walk along one of the paths, either pushing buggies in which two or three babies sat or holding older tots by the hand.

Leslie Knight and Amy Carmichael were talking on the porch as John and Azim approached. "Ah, there you are, John," said Miss Carmichael. "I was just discussing our young visitor last night, and my idea affects you as well. Please, help yourself to a little breakfast and join us."

A plate of sliced fruit, some muffin-like cakes, and a pot of tea were laid out on a little table, along with plates and cups. John helped himself, then sat on the floor near his mother.

"I was just telling your mother that it is obvious this young girl is from a very high caste, and it may be difficult for her to mix with the other girls here at first. I don't know her story—she was too exhausted last night to tell me. But . . . why, here she is!"

John had heard no one, but there, standing in the

doorway was the girl, a shy smile on her face. Miss Carmichael held out her arms, and the girl went straight to her. She shook her head no when offered some food, but stood leaning against Amy Carmichael.

"Come, child," said Miss Carmichael, "we must know more about you." She took the girl's hands in her own and said something in Tamil. The girl then spoke rapidly, the smile disappearing and her eyes once again looking like a frightened rabbit. She pointed several times to the south and once she pointed to John and his mother.

While the white woman and the nut-brown girl talked, John studied the girl. Her face was heart-shaped, framed by jet-black hair pulled back into a braid. She wore jeweled earrings and a gold neck-lace. Her sari, a delicate rose color, was edged with gold and green. Her feet were bare, but as he had noticed before, she wore gold bangles on her ankles, as well as both arms. She was the most beautiful girl he had ever seen.

Finally Amy Carmichael spoke in English, al-most to herself. "We shall call you Jewel, for God has plucked you out of the dirt into His kingdom of light, and longs to polish your heart to shine for Him."

Then she turned to Mrs. Knight and John. "Jewel comes from the merchant caste; her father, a wid-ower, was quite a wealthy man. But he died last year, leaving Jewel in the care of her uncle. In his will, the father named Jewel as his heir, to be inher-ited when she becomes eighteen, or when she marries, whichever comes first. Her uncle wants to get hold of her money, so he has arranged for her to be married to a distant relative of his—an old man of fifty!"

"Oh, no!" cried Mrs. Knight. "Why, she can't be more than twelve years old!"

Amy Carmichael shook her head sadly. "Oh, if only it were forbidden! But child-brides are quite common in India—young girls of twelve and thirteen, married and having children before they are even out of their teens. If the husband is old and dies, a girl becomes a widow who is blamed for her husband's death and abused as a household slave for the rest of her life by his relatives."

"She followed us—from Four Lakes, I think," John said. "I saw her twice before we arrived last night."

Miss Carmichael smiled. "You did not know you were leading her to us, but all things work together in God's plan. She is from Vallioor—that is the town where the post office and telegraph are located. She had only heard of the white *Amma* and the big home 'where children grow up good.' She ran away as far as Four Lakes when she saw white people traveling by bandy and decided to follow, hoping that you would lead her here."

Just then Arul came running up to the house. "Amma! There is a man at the gate—very angry! He has come for the girl!" Then he spoke rapidly in Tamil.

The effect on the girl was electric. She immediately cried out and threw herself at Amy's feet. Miss

Carmichael lifted her up and hushed her in Tamil.
John could now hear the bell ringing furiously at the
gate.

"Arul, let the man in," said Miss Carmichael
calmly. She drew the girl down upon the bench she
was sitting on and placed a protective arm around
her. Some of the Indian women workers and girls,
hearing the commotion, gathered at a distance to
watch.

In a few minutes Arul came back with an Indian
man who strode angrily up to the house. He was
wearing a *topi*, a cloth hat with no brim, a long tunic
and tight leggings, and carried a stick.
Azim seemed to appear from nowhere and stood in the man's
way; Arul also turned
around on the steps
and faced the ad-

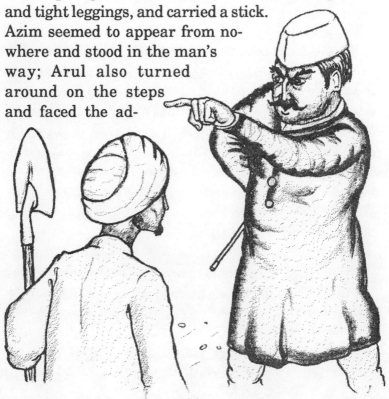

versary. The little group on the porch—Amy Carmichael, Jewel, Mrs. Knight, and John—stood up and faced the man, though Jewel hid her face in Amy's arm.

The man's eyes were narrowed and his face hard. He spoke rapidly in Tamil and pointed at Jewel.

"What is he saying, Arul?" John whispered, standing slightly behind the older boy.

"He says she is his niece, his legal ward, and she must come home with him at once."

Miss Carmichael said nothing at first, but gently turned Jewel and encouraged her to lift her face and look at her uncle. Then she spoke to the man in Tamil. Arul quietly interpreted for John.

"Amma asks if the child is to be married; the uncle says yes, it is all arranged. . . . Now Amma is asking Jewel if she wants to be married." John saw Jewel shake her head and she spoke a single word forcefully; even without knowing Tamil, John knew it was no. "Now Amma is asking Jewel if she wants to go with her uncle. . . . Jewel says no, she wants to stay here. . . . The uncle says, 'So? She is only a girl; it is not for her to decide.' . . . But Amma says it is her choice; she will stay here."

This made the uncle furious. He shook the stick first at Jewel, then at Amy Carmichael, and let loose a torrent of angry words. Azim took a step forward, and the man backed off. With a few more words and threatening gestures, he turned on his heel and strode back toward the gate.

"What did he say?" breathed Mrs. Knight, whose

face had suddenly turned quite white.

"He said we are guilty of kidnapping, and we haven't heard the last from him yet," said Miss Carmichael. "Arul, be sure the gate is locked. We will need to take extra precautions for a while." As Arul ran off, Amy walked over to the little cluster of girls who were watching, gave a few reassuring hugs, then sent them off to their tasks.

Amy Carmichael returned to the porch and said, "Leslie, I believe God has sent you and John for this very time. Let me tell you my idea. . . ."

Chapter 5

Good Friday Comes on Easter

AMY CARMICHAEL'S IDEA was simple: she wanted Mrs. Knight and John to stay several weeks to help care for Jewel. "The *accals* and I have our hands full with the other children—we have over thirty right now, and many are babies! Jewel will need special care because of her caste. Until God breaks down the barriers, we should respect her caste restrictions as much as possible. But she will be lonely not mixing with the other girls and will need a companion. And, given the danger, it would be helpful to have Azim and John around the compound to assist Arul."

"But we don't even speak her language!" protested Mrs. Knight.

Amy smiled. "Arul can interpret when needed.

But love is the same in any language."

Mrs. Knight had a good many objections. They had only planned to visit a week. What if her husband came home while they were away? What about John's schooling? Was she neglecting her duties at Palamcottah?

"Those are reasonable concerns, Leslie," said Amy Carmichael. "Seek God's will. He will show you what to do. But I believe that your arrival on the same day Jewel found us is not a mere coincidence."

Later Mrs. Knight and John went walking by the stream that ran alongside the west wall of the Dohnavur compound. "I hardly know what to think," confessed his mother.

John shrugged. "You can tutor me here as well as at home, Mama."

"Well . . . I suppose that's true."

"And what would you be doing in Palamcottah? Sipping tea with the colonel's wife and having all those servants hovering around doing everything except your thinking!"

Mrs. Knight laughed. "When you put it *that* way . . ." Then she sighed. "But I would hate to be gone when your father returns. That seems unfair."

John picked up a stone and sent it skipping into the stream. "Send Father a message. Just ask him to let us know when he's coming home. We can at least stay *until* then."

"I guess you're right." Mrs. Knight was silent for a few minutes. "I've never really thought of seeking God's will when trying to make a decision. I mean, we keep the commandments and go to church faithfully, but—"

"Why, you are a good Christian, Mama!"

"Hmm. Maybe. But Amy Carmichael lives as if Jesus Christ were right here in India, and she were one of His disciples."

That afternoon Mrs. Knight told Amy they would stay until her husband returned from his business trip. Miss Carmichael immediately held a little prayer meeting to praise God. Azim was sent to Vallioor to telegraph a message to the household at Palamcottah and another to Sanford Knight in Bangalore. Jewel moved in with Mrs. Knight in the Guest House.

The days settled into a routine: Mrs. Knight tutored John in the mornings while the Dohnavur girls were busy in their schoolrooms. Jewel sat near Mrs. Knight weaving on a hand loom. Sometimes Arul sat in on the lessons between chores. At these times, the Guest House schoolroom often degenerated into a language swap.

"How do you say 'I'm hungry'? . . . 'Good morning'? . . . 'Go away'?" John would pester Arul. The English boy's efforts to say things in Tamil often triggered a giggle from Jewel. But the language swap intrigued the girl; she crept closer, and soon began to try out a few English words.

In the afternoons, John helped Arul with the maintenance work on the Dohnavur grounds. *Amma*— as everyone seemed to call Amy Carmichael—wanted a new garden to help feed the growing Dohnavur family, so Arul and John spent days digging up a new plot and hauling stones away. The older girls could often be seen in the other gardens weeding around the new green shoots and hauling water from the wells to keep the ground moist. At other times John would see them heading for the Weaving Shed or the Milk Kitchen.

In the evenings, the Dohnavur "family" gathered in the House of Prayer for worship and prayer, led by Amy or one of the older Indian women. John patrolled the compound with Azim or Arul, making sure the gates were secure. He loved to hear the girls sing; their clear voices seemed to rise in the hot, still air and hang like a canopy among the leaves of the tall palm trees.

Several weeks passed; March melted into April. On the Saturday before Easter Arul handed John a bucket with a murky brown mixture in it. "The babies are gone today; the *accals* have taken them on an outing. We need to put new floors in the nurseries."

New floors? Whatever did Arul mean? John followed the older boy to one of the thatch-roofed cottages that housed the babies. The simple furniture and sleeping mats had been hauled outside. Arul showed John how to slop the wet mash onto the floor and spread it evenly with a brush.

"What is this stuff?" John asked. It felt like warm mud.

"Cow dung."

"*Cow dung!*" John dropped the brush and leaped

to his feet. His stomach turned as he thought of his hands in the sloppy mess. "I won't do it," he muttered and stalked to the doorway. This was too much, he thought. It was one thing to dig a garden and haul stones for Dohnavur Fellowship, but he drew the line at sticking his hands in a mess of manure. He was a guest, a volunteer, for heaven's sake!

A woman's gentle voice at his side startled him. "May I have that bucket?" Amy Carmichael said. She picked up the bucket he had abandoned and joined Arul on hands and knees, spreading the thick liquid on the floor. John reddened and watched awkwardly from the door.

When the floor was covered, Amy straightened her back and stepped outside. "At Dohnavur Fellowship, John, all work, great and small, clean or dirty, is done for God." She smiled, handed him the bucket, and disappeared around the corner of the cottage.

John sighed.

"But . . . why cow dung?" he finally asked Arul.

"The cow is a useful animal." Arul grinned. "Dry cow dung makes good fuel. And when it's dried, dung has no smell. On the other hand, fresh dung is mixed with water and spread on the floor. When it dries, it makes a soft floor—much more friendly than hard English floors! Soft to the feet, warm in the cool season."

John picked up the brush and bucket and followed Arul to the next nursery. He'd try not to think about it.

When both baby nurseries had new "floors," the two boys washed up at one of the wells, then walked toward the main house. As they approached, they saw a two-horse carriage and driver standing inside the compound. A tall white man wearing a sun helmet stood talking with John's mother on the steps of the porch.

"Father!" yelled John, dropping the bucket and running the last few yards.

Sanford Knight smiled and gave his son a manly handshake and a clap on the shoulder. "I see you've been busy, John."

John blushed. "I . . . I need to change my clothes. Been doing a little dirty work."

"I can see that," said his father. "Get changed; I'd like you to join your mother and me for a talk . . . at the Guest House, did you say, Leslie?"

John quickly changed his clothes in Arul's cottage, then found his parents. "Didn't you get the message about my arrival home, Leslie?" his father was saying.

"I'm afraid not, Sanford, or I would surely have been back in Palamcottah. Someone here has to pick up the mail in Valioor. Your message is probably sitting there now. I'm terribly sorry you had to come all this way for us."

"What is this about helping to care for a runaway girl—Jewel, is that her name? Really, Leslie! You know how I feel about interfering in the domestic affairs of the Indian people."

"I know, Sanford. But it's different when a child runs to your arms because she is terrified of being married to a man five times her age."

Sanford Knight frowned. "Miss Carmichael means well, Leslie, but there are legal consequences to her actions. I don't want my own wife and son *breaking the law*. After all, I am junior magistrate for the Tinnevelly District!"

John sat on the steps of the porch while his parents talked. Maybe his father was right on this . . . he hadn't thought that they could be breaking the law. He wondered what would happen to Jewel when they left. He knew already that he would miss Dohnavur Fellowship.

Azim, on the other hand, was visibly relieved that they were going home. Things were too mixed up at this place, in his opinion. White women and boys did servants' work; servants were invited to sit and eat; caste distinctions were being lost, he complained frequently to Arul.

Sanford Knight agreed to wait until after the Easter celebration the following morning to begin the journey home with his family. Just before dawn the three Knights, with Jewel clinging sadly to Leslie, joined the crowd of excited girls and their *accals* in front of the main house.

"He is risen!" people greeted one another in English and Tamil.

"He is risen indeed! Alleluia!" came the response.

The crowd made their way along the paths, around the school and girls' cottages, through the round brick gateways that marked each section of the compound, to God's Garden.

"Why do they call it that?" John asked Arul.

"Babies are buried here who became sick and died. But there are no markers; just flowers and trees. The babies are in heaven—God's Garden."

In the garden Amy led them in singing Easter hymns in both English and Tamil. The sun rose red and glorious, bathing the sky in pink, shimmering light. The birds set off a joyful racket. *Was it something like this on the day Jesus broke out of His tomb?* John wondered.

The group finally wandered back toward the main

house for an Easter breakfast picnic. Jewel shook her head no when offered something to eat; she would prepare something later. As they sat on the ground enjoying the fresh fruit and breads made especially for the occasion, the front gate bell began ringing. Arul trotted off to answer it.

"Probably the carriage," said John's father. "I told the driver to be here early."

But it was not the carriage. Two men walked resolutely into the compound behind Arul. One of them was Jewel's uncle; the other, an Indian police-man.

Amy Carmichael rose to meet them. Leslie Knight drew a protective arm around Jewel, who was shiv-ering with fright.

Jewel's uncle waved a paper at Amy and sneered a few brief words in Tamil. John heard Arul suck in his breath. "Police orders," Arul said quietly to the Knights. "Jewel must return with her uncle."

Amy was about to say something when Sanford Knight got to his

By Order
of the
District Police

feet and approached her.

"Miss Carmichael," he said. "I realize I am a guest here. But I am also a court official of the Tinnevelly District. And I must tell you that you have no legal right to keep this girl, no matter how tragic you think her situation. The penalty for ignoring a police order could be prison."

"I don't care for myself," Amy said quietly.

"But you must think of all the persons in your care. If you wish, you could file a counter suit in court and let a judge decide what should happen."

All voices fell silent. Only the birds in the tamarind trees continued their racket. Then, slowly, the "mother" of Dohnavur walked over to Jewel and bent down. She spoke first in Tamil, then in English. "Jewel, the paper says you must go with your uncle. But we will fight. I will go to court and ask if you can come here to Dohnavur to live—permanently. In the meantime, Jesus your Friend will be with you."

The uncle, realizing no one would stop him, strode over to Jewel and pulled her roughly by the arm.

Suddenly Jewel began to scream and kick. The Indian policeman took her other arm, and the two men half carried, half pushed the girl toward the gate. John heard Amy gasp, "Have mercy, Lord!" and his mother broke into sobs. John took an involuntary step, but his father laid a restraining hand on his shoulder. He watched helplessly as the trio disappeared through the gate. But Jewel's loud wails could be heard for a long time.

John jerked away from his father's hand and walked quickly away from the picnic area. Hot tears stung his eyes. Easter? Resurrection? It felt more like a crucifixion.

Chapter 6

Swami-Lover

THE TRIP HOME to Palamcottah was tense. John knew his father was probably right—legally. But it seemed so *wrong* to just stand there and let that evil man drag Jewel away against her will.

His mother cried off and on all the way home. "There, there, my dear," Sanford Knight tried to comfort her. "You can't possibly rescue all the girls whose relatives arrange a child-marriage. Admittedly, it's a bad custom, but it is legal."

"Then change the law!" snapped his wife. She blew her nose on his handkerchief. "I'm sorry, Sanford. I know it's not your fault; you're just the magistrate. But even one child forced into that kind of legal slavery is . . . is a *sin!*"

The month of May was the dry hot season at its

worst, with temperatures soaring over one hundred degrees. Mr. Knight wanted to send his wife and John up to Ooty to escape the heat, but she declined, saying the family had been apart too much already. John was going to start school in June; they would travel to Ooty then.

The monsoon rains came right on time in June, bringing joyous dancing in the streets as the rice paddies filled with water and the parched earth received its yearly drink. But it made for miserable traveling by train as the Knights headed for the Kingsway School for Boys in Ooty. The train compartments had to be closed up and the humid heat was stifling, even in first class. But as they switched to the cog train for the last climb up the Nilgiri Hills, John leaned out the train window, letting the cooler moist air bathe his face.

The cog train was packed with boys returning to school and their families. John looked around, wondering if he'd be able to make a friend. He had been lonely in Palamcottah and missed Arul's friendship, even if the Indian boy was several years older. John sighed. Well, it was school now and he'd have to make the best of it.

He was assigned a room in the dormitory with two other boys from his class. After Azim deposited John's luggage, Mr. Knight steered John's mother away quickly. "He'll get on better if we don't wait around," he murmured to her.

The boys seemed friendly enough as they shook hands and picked bunks. "You're the new boy, eh?"

said one, a tall lanky fellow. "I'm Jim; this is Torry. Irish, he is!" Jim gave the red-headed Torry a friendly poke in the ribs.

"Isn't Ooty a hoot?" said Torry. "'Course it's school, but it beats sitting out the monsoons down in the towns. What a steam bath!"

"Beats rubbing elbows with all the swamis, too," snorted Jim.

John was puzzled. "Swamis? You mean *swami*, the Hindu holy men?"

Jim laughed. "Swamis, wamis, it doesn't matter. All the native boys and their ugly gods. They give me the creeps. Never know what they're thinking."

John was silent, unsure how to respond. Finally he said, "Not all Indians are Hindu or Muslim; some are Christian."

"Or pretending to be," said Jim, "just to get on with the British."

"No, really," said John. "I have a friend—his name is Arul Dasan. He became a Christian and his family threatened to rub pepper in his eyes."

"There, you see?" Torry said. "Totally barbaric. These people are not at all civilized."

John shut his mouth into a thin line. The conversation was going in a direction he didn't like. He busied himself lining up his books on the little shelf above his study desk.

"Hey, what about this Arul fellow?" Jim persisted. "He is actually your friend? How did you meet him?"

"At Dohnavur Fellowship," John said reluctantly, stuffing his suitcases under the bed. "My mother and I stayed there a month, helping to take care of a girl who was going to be married as a child-bride." The moment it was out of his mouth, however, John was sorry he said anything.

"Ooooh. A *girl*," Torry hooted.

"Not just a girl—a *native* girl," said Jim, rolling his eyes. The two boys flopped on their beds, laughing.

John straightened up and marched to the door. He had to get out before he said something he would regret.

"Hey, don't go away mad, old man," Jim laughed. "It's just that we've never had a *swami-lover* for a roommate before." And the two boys punched each other's arms gleefully as John escaped into the hallway.

Miserably, John loosened his Kingsway tie and pushed his hands into the pockets of his blazer as he made his way down the stairway to the first floor. He walked over to the school office and asked to see the headmaster. After a fifteen-minute wait, John was ushered into the office.

"Hmm, young Knight is it?" said Mr. Bath, the headmaster.

"Yes, sir."

"Settling in all right?"

"Yes, sir. I guess. But what does Kingsway offer in languages?"

"Why, all the classical languages, of course: Latin, Greek; and French, German—"

"Any Indian languages? Tamil, for instance?"

The headmaster just looked at John. "Indian languages? Why, no, it's hardly necessary. Most high-ranking Indians in British India speak English."

"But not the people, sir. I realize that India has many languages and dialects, but Tamil is the most common language of this area of south India where my father is commissioned as magistrate. I am interested in learning Tamil."

The headmaster pursed his lips and tapped a pencil on his desk. "Interesting . . . interesting. Well, I'm afraid we can't help you, Mr. Knight. We have no Indian teachers at Kingsway. British for the British, Indian for the Indian, you know. But, hmmm . . ." Mr. Bath got up from the big desk and looked out the window over the town of Ooty nestled in the folds of the Nilgiri Hills. "There is a young Indian lawyer who speaks both English and Tamil who lives here in Ooty. He might be able to tutor you. Here . . ."

The headmaster scribbled a name on a slip of paper and handed it across the desk. Then he shook his finger at John. "But I warn you, Mr. Knight, learning Tamil is a hobby, to be done in your spare time, which is rare at Kingsway. If I hear that you are neglecting your regular studies, you will be ordered to stop, do you understand?"

John nodded and backed out the door with the slip of paper. He looked at the name: "Mr. Rabur, Woodcock Lodge." Pocketing the paper, John made a vow: he would certainly not mention language lessons to Torry and Jim.

John was kept busy with his lessons at Kingsway and only got to see his mother and father, who stayed on at Willingdon House for a one-week holiday, on the following Sunday afternoon. But after having supper at the Ooty Club with his parents, John refused a *tonga* ride back to the school and said he'd like to walk.

Woodcock Lodge was not far from the club, a charming rooming house for single men doing business in Ooty. Mr. Rabur was a little surprised to be paid a visit from an English schoolboy, but seemed pleased at John's request for tutoring in Tamil.

"Most unusual, young *sahib*," chuckled the young Indian lawyer. "I am honored. What do you say—

Sunday afternoons? It is not enough; Tamil is a difficult language. You will have to study during the week as well."

"Yes, sir," grinned John. "I will work hard."

John managed to get along reasonably well with Jim and Torry, in spite of their constant teasing. "Hey, swami-lover, we need a goalie for soccer"; "Ah-ha, swami-lover has a letter! Must be from his native girl!"

The letter in question was from his mother, dated July 2, 1909. "My dear son . . ." it began.

> *The rains keep us indoors much of the time. I imagine it is the same for you. (Better for studying!) But unfortunately the soccer field will be soggy. Never mind the mud; play hard!*
>
> *I heard from Miss Carmichael. She has petitioned for a court hearing this month to receive custody of Jewel until a trial date can be set to resolve her situation. Your father feels she has embarked on a hopeless task. And it may be so; she desperately needs a sympathetic lawyer. . . .*

Lawyer! John could not get his mother's letter out of his mind the next time he went to Woodcock Lodge for his Tamil lesson. Even though he had only known Mr. Rabur a few weeks, he found himself telling the young Indian lawyer the whole story of meeting Miss Carmichael, the trip to Dohnavur, and Jewel pounding on the gate crying, "Refuge! Refuge!" and her uncle dragging her away on Easter.

Mr. Rabur listened quietly. When John was finished he said, "Hmm. An interesting case."

John grew bold. "Could you help Miss Carmichael, Mr. Rabur? I don't know how I could pay your fee, but . . ."

The Indian lawyer stood at the window of his

sitting room and watched the clouds wrapping the hills in a thick fog. "I have to go to Palamcottah next week. I may inquire into the case; I'll see what I can do. But, young *sahib*, I promise nothing."

John grinned. He fairly flew off the porch of Woodcock Lodge when the lesson was over . . . and nearly crashed headlong into Jim and Torry, who were standing on the stone-lined path outside.

"So, what's this?" hooted Jim. "Our friend mysteriously disappears every Sunday afternoon—and here he is, visiting a rooming house of the local variety."

"A girl, Mr. Knight? Are you dating?" teased Torry.

"Very funny," said John. He started walking rapidly back toward the school. He didn't want to explain to these two rascals about Mr. Rabur and Tamil lessons. But the two boys badgered him all the way back to Kingsway, so finally John said, "My father's a magistrate, right? So I got a letter from my mother about some legal business; she asked me to deliver a message to a lawyer here in Ooty. Now, is that all right with you?"

It wasn't exactly the truth, but close enough, he thought.

"Oooh, touchy, touchy. Why didn't you say so in the first place?" said Jim. He messed up John's hair and ran off laughing with Torry. John sighed. Jim and Torry were all right some of the time, but he wished he had some real friends.

Mr. Rabur was gone to Palamcottah the next

Sunday, so John had to wait two weeks before he heard if anything happened. Borrowing a schoolmate's bicycle, he splashed through the Ooty streets to Woodcock Lodge in a downpour. He was getting tired of the monsoons—even if it was "just like home" in rainy England.

"Come in, young *sahib!*" smiled Mr. Rabur. "You will need to dry yourself by the fire."

John accepted a cup of hot tea and stretched his wet feet toward the fire in Mr. Rabur's sitting room. Then he said: "Did you meet with success in Palamcottah?"—in perfect Tamil.

Mr. Rabur threw back his head and laughed. "You have been working! I am proud of you. And yes, I have news."

The young Indian lawyer had gone to the magistrate's office in Palamcottah and arranged to meet Miss Carmichael before the hearing. Mr. Rabur offered his services free of charge—a favor "for a friend," he said. "At the hearing—"

"Did my father hear the case?" John interrupted. "He's the junior magistrate in Palamcottah."

"No . . . this was an older gentleman, due to retire this year," said Mr. Rabur.

"The senior magistrate," said John. "Well, go on."

At the hearing, both lawyers presented their clients' petitions. The other lawyer said his client was the legal guardian of his niece, and the marriage was all arranged. Mr. Rabur said the child was violently opposed to the marriage and had run away once. She wanted to live at Dohnavur Fellowship and go to school. His client, Miss Carmichael, was petitioning the court for temporary custody until the matter could be decided by the court. Mr. Rabur argued that the child's interests should be taken into account and the custody allowed to give time for a proper case to be prepared—by both sides. If the child remained with her uncle, what was to prevent the marriage from taking place before the case could be decided?

"I am most happy to report that the magistrate ruled in favor of Miss Carmichael—for now," said Mr. Rabur.

"That's it?" said John. "Just like that? Jewel went home with Miss Carmichael? Wahoo!" he shouted.

"It's not quite that simple," cautioned Mr. Rabur. "Because the matter has still not been decided, the magistrate respected the relatives' wishes that Jewel be required to 'keep caste'—that is, she may not eat food prepared by others outside her caste or eat with others not of her own caste; and further, she may not change her religion. This was spelled out in a *yadast*, or agreement between the parties."

John frowned. "That means she will have to cook and eat alone; she is the only one of her caste at Dohnavur. And—pardon me, Mr. Rabur—but it is hard to be at Dohnavur Fellowship and not desire to be a Christian."

"No pardons needed, young *sahib*," Mr. Rabur smiled. "I, too, am a follower of Jesus. It is for that reason I have agreed to help Miss Carmichael prepare for the upcoming trial."

Chapter 7

Fire!

SCHOOL WAS OUT by mid-October for "winter break" and John managed the train trip from Ooty to Palamcottah by himself. The "cool season" had eased the temperatures to seventy or eighty degrees on the plains, and the fully ripened rice fields beside the train tracks waved gently in the path of the harvesters.

After four months in very British Ooty, John had almost forgotten the crowds in the Indian towns. As he waited in line at the station to get his ticket, four or five people crushed behind him, waving *rupees* over his shoulder trying to get their own tickets.

He had done well in school—a report which pleased Sanford Knight. John answered questions about classes, sports, teachers, and other students over lunch on the porch of the big house in

Palamcottah. He decided to say nothing about being heckled by the other boys.

John was glad to see his mother looking well and rested. "It's the cool season," she smiled. "This is India at its best!"

After his father had returned to court, John asked, "What is happening at Dohnavur? When is the trial? Have you seen Jewel or Arul or Miss Carmichael?"

His mother laughed. "One question at a time! No, the trial date keeps getting delayed. The uncle's lawyer keeps filing this motion or that complaint—I don't understand all the legal issues. And yes, I have been going to Dohnavur about once a month to volunteer for five or six days. Jewel is blossoming, although she complains about having to cook and eat alone. Amma tells Jewel it is her 'cross to bear' for Jesus right now. And Arul always asks about you."

"He does?" John was pleased. "Can we . . . is it all right if I go along the next time you go to Dohnavur?"

John's mother nodded. "I think so. Your father says I am too involved in Amy Carmichael's work, of which he doesn't fully approve. And I must say, he is not alone. I have heard both British and Indians criticize her. But he agreed to the once-a-month visits as long as they don't conflict with the social obligations that come along with being the magistrate's wife."

A few days after John's arrival back home, a letter arrived from Dohnavur Fellowship.

"Several of the *accals* and many of the children are sick," Leslie Knight said, reading the letter quickly. "And Jewel's uncle tried to snatch her when

70

she went to the market in Four Lakes with the other girls. Fortunately, she eluded him and got back safely. But Amy Carmichael wants to know if we—you and I, John—could come and help them for a few days."

Mr. Knight reluctantly agreed, providing Azim went with them. And so once more John found himself on the way to Dohnavur. He remembered that first trip into the countryside six months ago—and the temple elephant that "blessed" him with its trunk!

At Four Lakes, they once again let the rented carriage return to Palamcottah and took a *bandy* the last few miles. As the covered ox cart drew near to the arched brick gate of Dohnavur Fellowship, John thought he saw two figures slink into the trees and underbrush. But the late afternoon sun shone in his eyes and he couldn't be sure.

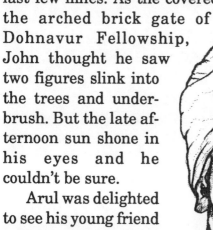

Arul was delighted to see his young friend and laughed aloud when John said, "I am glad to see you again," in Tamil.

Azim looked startled when John spoke Tamil. John

had given away his little secret; he had enjoyed picking up a few things that Azim said in Tamil when the servant thought he didn't understand.

Jewel came running to meet them, all smiles. When she saw John, she stopped and shyly pressed her hands together in a *salaam*. Then her smile broadened. "*Annachie!*" she said.

"*Annachie?*" John asked, turning to Arul. He had not learned that word in Tamil. "What does she mean?"

Arul grinned. "*Annachie* means 'elder brother.' You and me—that is the name Jewel calls us: *annachie*."

A strange warm feeling gripped John, and for a moment he couldn't speak. Brother. Yes, that is how he felt about Arul: an older brother. And Jewel seemed like a younger sister.

"How do you say 'younger sister' in Tamil?" he finally asked Arul.

"*Tungachie.*"

"*Tungachie.*" John rolled the word on his tongue. Then he pointed from himself to Jewel, pressed his palms together in a *salaam*, and said, "Jewel, *tungachie.*"

Jewel clapped a hand over her mouth, suppressing a giggle. Then she flew on bare feet back to the group of older girls playing with several babies under a large tamarind tree. That was when John noticed that the bangles were gone and Jewel's arms and ankles were bare.

"What happened to all of Jewel's jewels?" he asked

his mother as they made their way to the main house to see Amy Carmichael.

Azim muttered something under his breath in Tamil about a woman's jewels showing her family's status and attracting a suitable husband. John pretended he hadn't heard.

"I'm not sure," said Mrs. Knight. "The last time I was here, the bangles were gone. I think she became aware that the Indian women here have laid aside their jewels to show that they love Jesus more than wealth. And one day Jewel just took them off."

Amy Carmichael smiled and welcomed them warmly, but her eyes were tired and her face pale. That was when John and his mother realized Amy herself was sick. Leslie Knight stayed with Amy while John went to unpack in Arul's little cottage. As before, Azim refused a bed inside.

Then Arul showed John around the compound. The garden they had dug last March had produced many vegetables to help feed the Dohnavur family. In God's Garden, little bouquets of flowers decorated a new mound of fresh dirt.

"One of the babies died last week," Arul said quietly. "A temple child. It often happens. A child is snatched from living death, but Satan attacks with sickness. But death has no power here. We go to live with Jesus."

As they passed the baby nurseries, Arul teased, "You are just in time to help spread new floors!"

John gagged and made a face. Arul laughed.

"Don't worry. We did it last week. But . . ." The older boy pointed to the thatch roofs. "Amma wants to rebuild the nurseries. Termites are eating the walls, and—"

"Didn't I hear the children singing a little song about termites 'trying to be good' by working hard?" John laughed. "But my Tamil is not very good yet!"

Arul laughed, too. "Yes, yes, you are right! Amma wrote the termite song for the little children!" Then Arul's smile faded. "But we are worried. Jewel's uncle makes many threats to burn these houses. Thatch roofs are very dangerous. Every night we must watch."

As it turned out, John, Arul, and Azim patrolled the wall surrounding the Fellowship each night and slept during the day. Mrs. Knight insisted that Amy Carmichael go to bed while she nursed the Indian *accals* who were sick. A temporary clinic was set up in the main house for the babies and children who were sick. The older girls moved into the nurseries to help take care of the healthy babies.

Several days passed, and no more children became sick. Amy grew stronger and became impatient with Leslie Knight's strict orders to "take it easy." One day she called Arul and John and asked whether they had seen or heard anything during their nightly patrols.

"Nothing, Amma. All is well."

"Hmm. I feel easier when Jewel's uncle is visible and noisy. All this quiet makes me uneasy. Arul, I know this may sound strange, but I would like you to organize all the *accals* who are strong enough, and all the older girls, to fill every bucket and pot you can find with water from the wells. Place as many as possible by each house with a thatch roof."

What Amma said, the others did. But it took the entire day to gather all the pots not being used, draw water from the wells, and distribute the full pots to the thatch-roofed cottages. John tried to carry a full pot of water on his head like some of the *accals*, but he nearly got a soaking. After that he settled for carrying pots on his shoulders.

When they were done, everyone was tired and aching. "Surely we can sleep tonight," John said, stretching his sore muscles. But Arul insisted that they walk around the wall, just as they had done the previous nights.

John could barely keep his eyes open. But he plodded the length of the east wall from the main gate to God's Garden until he met Azim, who was walking the north wall. Then each went back the way he had come.

Once John thought he heard a branch snap on the other side of the wall, and suddenly all his senses were alert. He barely breathed as he stopped and listened. But even though he stood there for ten minutes, he heard nothing. Finally he started to walk again.

Then out of the corner of his eye he saw it: an arch of flaming light came flying over the wall and landed on the thatch roof of one of the nurseries!

At that same moment, another torch came flying over the wall and landed on the thatch roof of a second nursery. "Fire!" he yelled. "Help! Help! Fire!"

He rushed into the first nursery and shook the form of the *accal* sleeping by the door. "Get out! Everyone out! Fire!" he screamed.

In a split second, girls and *accals* were awake and scooping up the little ones. John grabbed a baby and rushed outside. He handed it to an *accal* who was already holding an infant and trying to gather the others around her. Without stopping to think, he ran over to the second nursery. The fire was now leaping from the roof ten feet into the sky.

He ducked into the dark door. The place was filled with smoke. "Get out! Get out! Fire!" Then holding his breath he felt around the room, shaking the *accal* and older girls. "Get out! Fire!" he hissed. He grabbed two small bundles cuddled up together on a grass mat and stumbled out the door. The *accal* and other girls were coming out now, each holding one or two babies.

John grabbed one of the waterpots they had filled earlier that day and threw it on the burning cottage. It would never be enough! he thought in despair. Then he realized that others had come running and were grabbing the water pots.

Suddenly Jewel was by his side, her face twisted in panic. "*Annachie*! Baba!" she cried, pointing toward the nursery.

What did she mean? *Another baby still in there?* He looked at the flaming roof. No one dared go in the cottage now. He looked around frantically. Where was Arul and Azim? They would know what to do!

Jewel was shaking him. "*Annachie! Annachie!* Baba inside!" John looked into Jewel's face, her eyes wide with fear. Then suddenly she ripped off her scarf, dipped it into a pot of water and gave it to him. *Now,* he thought. *Now or never. God help me.*

Tying the wet scarf around his face, John dove into the door of the cottage. He couldn't see anything. He dropped to his belly and crawled across the floor. He kept feeling grass mats. Empty. Nothing in the corners. The smoke stung his eyes and his lungs hurt when he breathed. Where was the baby? Maybe

77

there was no baby. Maybe . . . wait. Feeling for the storage cupboard, he reached underneath. His hand felt a soft lump. Reaching in with both hands, he pulled out a small child.

Hugging the baby to his chest, John pulled himself along the floor until he found the door. As he stumbled out, he heard someone yell, "His hair's on fire!" and a wall of water hit him full in the face. John was so shocked he just stood there dripping wet.

Someone took the baby from him, and someone else led him over to a tree and pushed him to sit down. For the next few minutes John just sat with his eyes shut, hugging his knees, coughing and choking. The night was filled with shouts, people running, the sounds of flames crackling.

"John, are you all right?" It was Arul. John opened his eyes. His friend was crouching on one knee in front of him.

"The baby," he whispered. He realized he could hardly speak. "Is the baby dead?"

Just then Jewel's face appeared next to Arul. "Baby safe," she said in Tamil. She reached out and touched John's singed hair and smiled. "*Annachie.*"

A spasm of coughing gripped John so he could hardly breathe. He looked first at Arul, then Jewel. "*Annachie. Tungachie,*" he whispered. "My brother. My sister."

Then John dropped his head on his arms and cried.

Chapter 8

A Bloody Nose and a Black Eye

As soon as John had arrived back at Kingsway
School after the New Year, he had borrowed a
bicycle and pedaled over to Woodcock Lodge to ask
Mr. Rabur if he could continue his Tamil lessons.
The lawyer had heard rumors of the fire and insisted
that John sit down and tell him the whole story.

Mr. Rabur listened quietly as John told him about
the fire at Dohnavur Fellowship.

"The Lord Jesus protected you, young *sahib*,"
said the Indian lawyer. "What about the two nurseries? Were they destroyed?"

John nodded. "In spite of all our pots of water!
But Amma said that God works all things for good. It
was time to replace all the mud-brick and thatch
houses with regular brick and tile."

"But rebuilding the cottages would take a lot of money and labor!" said Mr. Rabur. "Did Miss Carmichael appeal for help?"

John shook his head. "That's what I would have done. But Amma has never asked people for money. She believes they should only ask God to supply their needs. So, the women and girls at Dohnavur just started to pray." He smiled sheepishly. "Well, I prayed too, but I grew up with the idea that 'God helps those who help themselves,' so I was rather skeptical. But special money gifts began to come in the mail—from England, the Continent, even America—people who couldn't possibly have heard of the fire that quickly. Not only that, but many of the villagers from Dohnavur, Four Lakes, and even Vallioor showed up to help them rebuild!"

"Amazing!" chuckled Mr. Rabur. "Praise God. But . . . how did your father respond?"

"He was very upset, of course, and wanted us to come right home. He thought the whole situation was getting much too dangerous. Mama wanted to stay and help take care of the babies who had lost their houses, but Amma encouraged her to respect Father's wishes. However, I did stay on for a couple of weeks to help with the building. Somehow it was important. . . ." John hesitated. "You see, I was having nightmares every night about the fire. Mama thought building the new nurseries would help heal the bad memories."

"And?" prompted Mr. Rabur.

John smiled. "It worked. No more nightmares."

"Well! We have used up all our lesson time for today. You need to get back to school before tea or they will send out a search party."

"What about the trial? What's going to happen to Jewel?"

"Patience, young *sahib*," said the lawyer. "These things take time."

"All right," John said. "But I have one more request."

"Yes?"

"Will you call me John instead of 'young *sahib*'? All my teachers at Kingsway call me John."

Mr. Rabur looked very pleased. "Of course. John it is."

John had been assigned to the same dorm room with Torry and Jim again this term, so he braced himself for the inevitable teasing. He gritted his teeth when they made stupid remarks about the Indians and kept his mouth shut about how he'd spent his winter break. But the more he refused to talk about his friends Arul and Jewel, the more Jim and Torry made up their own stories.

"Lover boy must have had a good time with his native girlfriend over winter break," taunted Jim. "He's so secretive."

"Lay off."

"Maybe she lives here in Ooty," said Torry. "John always disappears on Sunday afternoon."

"It's none of your business."

The boys laughed. But one Sunday afternoon as John pedaled back to school on his borrowed bicycle after a language lesson, Jim and Torry were suddenly running alongside.

"So! She lives at Woodcock Lodge! That was some story last term about you going there to see a lawyer."

"Shut up. You don't know what you're talking about."

"Come on, Johnny boy. We're your buddies! You can tell us!"

Jim and Torry badgered him all the way back to Kingsway. Finally John had had enough. "Look, it's no big deal. I'm taking lessons in Tamil from an Indian lawyer, all right? I . . . I'd like to become a lawyer here in India, so I need to know the language."

It just came out, but suddenly John knew it was true. He *was* interested in becoming a lawyer, and he wanted to be a lawyer here in India.

"Oooh, Johnny boy wants to become a swami-lawyer—" Torry started in, but Jim cut him off.

"Really? Say, we don't know any Indian lawyers. Look, John, could you introduce us? I mean, maybe Mister—what's his name? Rabur?—maybe Mr. Rabur could come speak to us over at the school."

John looked at Jim suspiciously. "What do you mean, speak?"

"Well, you know. The Careers Club sponsors speakers telling about different occupations. Mr. Rabur could come and talk about being a lawyer."

"What's the catch?" John wasn't sure he trusted Jim. On the other hand, he thought the boys at

Kingsway should get to know some Indian professionals.

"No catch. Will you ask him?"

And so it was arranged for the first week in March. John was nervous about having Mr. Rabur come to the Careers Club, but Jim's whole attitude seemed to have changed. He stopped calling John "swami-lover" and checked with John several times to be sure Mr. Rabur was coming.

On the scheduled day, John met Mr. Rabur at the gate to Kingsway School and escorted him to the schoolroom where the Careers Club met. John was surprised; the room was packed. As they entered, all voices fell silent. He walked with Mr. Rabur to the front of the room. Something felt wrong, John thought, but he couldn't put his finger on it. Maybe he was just nervous. Then he realized what it was. At Kingsway, the custom was for the boys to stand when a teacher or visiting speaker entered the room. But everyone remained seated.

John brushed the uneasy feeling away. Maybe a club was different than the classroom. He introduced Mr. Rabur, and the Indian lawyer began speaking on law as a profession. He spoke of the many difficult legal issues created by the centuries-old caste system still existing even under the British Crown. He had just begun giving some case studies as examples, when suddenly all the boys rose silently as one person, turned their backs and filed out of the room.

Mr. Rabur stopped uncertainly in mid-sentence. John was astonished. What was happening? He leaped up and grabbed Jim by the arm. "What's happening?" he hissed in Jim's ear. "Why is everyone leaving?"

"Oh, pardon me," Jim said loudly, turning around. "Did we forget to tell you? We double-scheduled by mistake. There's chocolate cake for supper. Really don't want to miss it, you know." And with that Jim sauntered into the hall to a thunder of laughter and clapping.

Something exploded inside John. In three running strides, he tackled Jim and slammed him up against the wall. "You snake!" he cried, and slugged Jim in the jaw as hard as he could with his fist.

"Fight!" someone yelled and arms reached out to grab John. But he tore himself out of their grip and swung at Jim again. But Jim, who was bigger and heavier than John, blocked his arm and threw him to the floor. John felt Jim's fist smash into his nose and

warm blood spurted into his mouth. Then he was jarred by two more blows to his face.

Somewhere in the far distance, nearly drowned out by the shouts and whoops of the boys in the hall, John heard Mr. Rabur commanding, "Stop it! Stop it!" Then he felt himself being hauled up and pushed through the jostling crowd of boys.

"He started it!" he heard Jim yelling behind him. "Did everyone see that? John started it!"

The headmaster restricted John to the dormitory for a month, except for classes and meals. When John tried to explain how rudely Mr. Rabur had been treated by the Careers Club, the headmaster said, "It was just a prank, John. Hardly worth fighting about. Fighting is absolutely against Kingsway rules, and you need to learn a lesson." However, he did move John out of Jim and Torry's room.

John's eye was nearly swollen shut. When the swelling went down, it turned black and blue, causing the other boys to put up their fists mockingly every time he came around. It wasn't so bad until Sunday rolled around and he couldn't go into town for his weekly lesson with Mr. Rabur. John wanted very much to talk with his lawyer friend about what happened, even though Mr. Rabur had said, "Never mind, John. I appreciate your going to bat for me, but it's all right. Fighting doesn't really change people like Jim and his friends."

On Monday a sealed letter was delivered to his room. He unfolded it and looked at the signature. It was from Amy Carmichael.

"Dear John," it said. "We have come to Ooty on . . ."

Ooty! Amma and some of the girls were here in Ooty right now? John felt like bashing his head against the wall of his room. He'd give his right arm to see them, and here he was confined to the dormitory!

He continued reading. "We have come to Ooty on holiday and are staying at Mrs. Hopewell's cottage. March 10 is Jewel's Coming Day. Could you come to help us celebrate? She would very much like to see her *annachie*."

March 10. John looked at his calendar. That would be Thursday. He had no idea what a Coming Day was, but he was going to be there, even if they kicked him out of school.

The door to Mrs. Hopewell's cottage opened in answer to his knock.

"John!" Amy Carmichael said joyously. "You came after all! When we didn't get any reply to our note we thought . . . John! What happened to your eye? And whatever are you wearing?"

John felt silly. He was wearing white leggings, a rumpled tunic, and a *topi* on his head. He told Amy what had happened with Mr. Rabur as briefly as possible. "The only way I could come see you and the girls was to sneak out. I talked one of the Muslim boys who works in the kitchen to loan me some clothes, so . . . here I am!"

"For all the world looking like a pagan! And acting like one, too!" Miss Carmichael said, shaking her head. "Fighting, indeed. Well, come on out to the garden. The girls are having a party."

She led John through the lovely English cottage and through the double glass doors that led into the garden. The girls in their colorful saris were tossing a ball back and forth, trying to keep it away from Jewel, who was dancing about in the center.

John stared. Jewel's head was wreathed in flowers and her dark hair hung loosely about her shoulders. She was wearing a sky blue sari with silver edges and a necklace of flowers hung about her neck. He realized that in a year she had grown from a twelve-year-old girl-child to a thirteen-year-old young woman.

87

Jewel caught the ball and turned to show Amy. "*Annachie!*" she cried when she saw John. All the girls came running, and they all made clucking noises when they saw John's black eye. Amy shooed them away and soon had them shrieking with laughter in a game of Follow the Leader.

"You are hurt?" Jewel said to John soberly in Tamil. John felt a thrill, realizing he could understand her.

He shook his head. "I'm all right now. But what is a Coming Day? Your birthday?"

Jewel's eyes lit up. "Don't you remember? March 10—Jewel's Coming Day!"

Suddenly it dawned on John. It was exactly a year ago that Jewel had come pounding on the gate of Dohnavur crying, "Refuge!"

Amy Carmichael plopped down beside the English boy and Indian girl. "I'm getting too old for games!" she wheezed. Then giving Jewel a hug, she said, "At Dohnavur we don't always know when a child was born. But we do know the glad day God brought them to us. So instead of birthdays we celebrate Coming Days!"

John grinned. "Then I guess it's my Coming Day, too! Come on, Jewel, let's go play Follow the Leader!"

The party lasted into the twilight. They laughed and sang, and ate wonderful treats Amy had prepared for the occasion. John hated to leave, for he knew that he wouldn't be able to sneak out again—if he hadn't been discovered already. Before he left, he had a talk with Amy Carmichael.

"Amma," he said, as they stood on the stoop in front of Mrs. Hopewell's cottage, "would you pray for me?" The words sounded strange to John. In all his fifteen years he had never asked anyone to pray for him before. "I have so many feelings about India and its people—people like Arul and Jewel and the other girls and Mr. Rabur. But I get so angry at people like Jim and Torry and others. And I feel confused when I'm with my father. He's a good magistrate, and is careful to apply the law justly. I admire him. But sometimes . . ." John stared into the deepening twilight at the moon rising above the Nilgiri hills. He didn't know how to say that he felt lonely—especially here at school, but also in Palamcottah. Everywhere except Dohnavur.

Amy Carmichael walked him to the cottage gate. She nodded. "I will pray, dear John." She clasped both his hands in hers. "Go in peace, my son. Someday, I know, you will do great things for God and for India."

As he trotted off into the darkness, he heard her call out after him, "But no more fighting!"

Chapter 9

On Trial

JOHN PAID A COUPLE RUPEES to the Muslim boy in the school kitchen for the leggings and tunic and kept them. The clothes had helped him out once; who knew when he might need them again?

By October of that year, 1910, John had completed his public school education at Kingsway School for Boys. After graduation, Sanford Knight began making preparations to send his sixteen-year-old son back to England for further education.

"But, Father," John reasoned, "you know I'm interested in law. I'd like to observe some of the court proceedings in Palamcottah—especially now that you are the senior magistrate. I know I would learn a lot."

Sanford Knight rubbed his chin thoughtfully.

"And besides," John went on, "if I wait to begin college until next June, mother and I can spend Christmas with you here."

"He's right, Sanford." Leslie Knight eagerly embraced the idea. "Once John goes back to England, visits will be few and far between. Let's enjoy a few more months together before being separated."

"I know I'm in trouble when you both gang up on me," Mr. Knight smiled, shaking his head. "All right. We'll wait until March to book passage on a ship. Leslie, it's been two years since you've been home to England. Why don't you travel with John, see your family in Brighton, and get him settled in school? That way you'll miss the monsoon season altogether."

John breathed a sigh of relief. The family discussion had gone just the way he wanted. But he had other reasons for wanting to stay. The trial date to decide Jewel's fate had been set for September 3, then postponed to October 8, then October 28, and now Mr. Rabur had just informed him that it had been set back to December 21.

Leslie Knight guessed what was going on in John's head. "This could be very difficult, John," she said gently when they were alone. "The case may very likely end up in your father's court, meaning he will have to rule in the case."

John hadn't thought of that. "But Father is just; he will surely rule in Dohnavur's favor."

"Yes, your father is just. But we—you and I—see this situation from a very personal viewpoint. Your father sees it as an issue of law and local tradition."

A visit to Dohnavur in early December was a joyous reunion with Amy Carmichael, Arul, Jewel, and the others. John was amazed at the nurseries and other new buildings with their sloping red-tile roofs. "You not only rebuilt the old ones," he said, "you've built some new ones."

"God keeps sending us little Lotus Buds." Amy smiled. "And someday God will send us men workers—and then we will open our doors to little boys whose families sell them to the temples and pagan acting groups."

While John was at Dohnavur, Amy received word from Mr. Rabur that the trial had been postponed once again—indefinitely.

Christmas passed, then the New Year, then February. No new trial date had been set. John's heart sank. He and his mother had tickets sailing from Colombo, Ceylon, the big island off the tip of southern India, on March 24. How could he go to England without knowing what would happen to Jewel?

John was in this frame of mind when he came frowning into the courtyard in Palamcottah one day in early March, only to discover that his mother had a guest.

"John!" she called. "Come meet my old school chum, Mabel Beath. Mabel has heard all about Dohnavur Fellowship in my letters and wants very much to visit there." Leslie Knight turned back to her friend. "All visitors to Dohnavur somehow become volunteers, however, so be warned!" she laughed. Then her smile faded. "The situation with the girl named Jewel is very serious. Miss Carmichael has risked prison several times standing up to the uncle's claims on the girl."

John didn't want to hear any more. He felt too upset. But in the next few days he came to like Mabel Beath despite his bad mood. The motherly lady had a way of coaxing a laugh out of him, and she seemed genuinely interested in Jewel's story.

Mabel Beath left for Dohnavur on the same day John and his mother took the train for the coast. Both mother and son gave letters of farewell to Mabel to deliver to their friends at Dohnavur Fellowship.

"Take care of your mother, John," Sanford Knight said, firmly gripping John's hand. "You shouldn't have any trouble. There's a ferry across the gulf, then another train will take you to Colombo. I have reserved rooms in a hotel there for you until the ship sails."

John stared out the compartment window as the train rattled through the countryside. Oxen were plowing up rice fields; farmers were setting out new shoots. Women beat clothes on rocks in the rivers; *mahoots* sat on the heads of their elephants as the beasts pulled logs out of the forests or paraded through the villages in temple dress.

He was leaving India. Would he ever see Arul and Jewel and Amma again?

A telegram was waiting for them at the hotel in Colombo. It was from Mr. Rabur, the lawyer.

TRIAL SET FOR MARCH 27 *STOP* PRAY FOR US *STOP* GOD'S WILL BE DONE *STOP*

John and his mother stared at each other.

"I can't believe this!" John said furiously. He kicked one of their bags sitting on the floor.

"Maybe it's for the best," his mother started to say.

"No, it's not!" John interrupted. "I can't leave India without knowing what's happening. It'll be months before we hear. . . . Where's that sailing schedule."

John ran a finger down the sailing dates.

"Mama," he said, straightening up. "This is the biggest favor I'm ever going to ask of you. Don't get on the ship. There's another ship that sails in two weeks. We'll take that one."

"But, John! The tickets . . . your father . . . what are you going to do?"

"I'm going back to Palamcottah. I'm going to be there for that trial!"

John only had four days to get back to Palamcottah. Without reservations, he ended up going third class most of the way. Eight to ten people were crammed in each compartment, some sitting on the sleeping berths overhead. The Indians in third class stared at this English boy traveling by himself. They stared even more when he said, "May I sit down?" or "When is the next train?" in Tamil.

Several times an Indian woman, carrying food for her family in a woven basket and seeing he had none, would share some rice or curry with him. But at least twice he felt stealthy fingers reaching into his pockets; he was glad the money his mother had given him was tucked safely in a pouch under his shirt.

The first night he slept very little. The heat, strong body odor, and fear of being robbed kept him awake. But by the second day he was so exhausted he fell asleep on the floor of a train station, using the small bag of clothes he was carrying as a pillow.

As the train wheels clicked loudly between towns, John kept praying, "O God, please let me get there on time."

John was in a daze when he got off the train in

Palamcottah at noon on Monday. It was March 27. But was he in time for the trial?

He went straight to the courthouse and made his way up into the crowded gallery where the public was allowed to watch court proceedings. He stationed himself as close to the railing as he could, using a rather fat man as a shield, and looked down.

Amy Carmichael and Mr. Rabur sat at a table on one side of the courtroom. Jewel's uncle and his lawyer sat on the other side. John stretched his neck. Jewel was nowhere to be seen. *Where could she be?* he wondered.

Back at Dohnavur? Then he heard a familiar voice say, "Will the clerk please read the judgment?"

It was his father, sitting on the judge's bench.

John frowned. The judgment already? He had missed all the arguments! What had happened? Was it going well for Jewel staying at Dohnavur or not?

An Indian clerk stood up and began reading from several pages. John strained to hear, but couldn't catch what all the complex, legal language meant. Then after several minutes the clerk read something that caused a stir in the gallery.

"Quiet!" said Sanford Knight, banging his gavel. "Will the clerk read the judgment once more?"

The clerk raised his voice. "The court hereby orders Amy Carmichael, of Dohnavur Fellowship, to surrender the child in question to her legal guardian by April 4, and to pay all court costs of these proceedings."

Pandemonium broke out in the gallery, with cheers, shaking fists, hugs and laughter. John realized he was standing in the midst of the uncle's relatives and friends. But he felt as though someone had slugged him in the stomach. Jewel had to go back to her uncle within a week, then be forced into a marriage she didn't want?

On the main floor the uncle was vigorously pumping his lawyer's hand up and down. John's gaze shifted to Amy Carmichael who sat quietly on the other side of the room. Her hands were folded on the table in front of her, her face tilted slightly up and her eyes closed. Was she praying? Then John saw her smile; a look of triumphant peace and joy seemed to radiate from her face.

The crowd was moving out of the gallery, and John let it carry him down the stairs and outside. Should he go in and see Amy and Mr. Rabur? What about his father? But he felt numb, incapable of making a decision or talking to anyone. Instead, he found himself walking back toward his father's house, his bag of clothes slung over his shoulder.

As he walked into the courtyard through the small gate at the rear of the house, John had no idea what he was going to do. His bicycle, the one Azim had fixed up for him, was leaning against the cookhouse, a one-room cottage separate from the main house where all the cooking was done.

John stared at the bicycle. He looked around; no one had seen him yet. Then, suddenly, he knew what he had to do.

Chapter 10

Disappeared!

JOHN PEEKED INTO the cookhouse. Empty. He slipped inside, rummaged through his bag and pulled out the leggings, tunic, and topi. Taking off his shirt, shorts, and shoes, he put on the native clothes. Then he noticed his white hands and feet, and his heart sank. Wait . . . he snatched up a coffeepot and looked inside. There was a thick brown paste at the bottom; the cook often left the pot on the fire too long. He smeared the thick coffee on his hands. They stained a nice nut brown. Perfect! He quickly covered all his exposed skin, remembering at the last minute to do his ears and the back of his neck.

The courtyard was still empty. The servants often rested during the hottest part of the day, espe-

cially when the family wasn't at home. John picked up the bicycle, stuffed his bag in the basket, and wheeled it out the gate.

The road to Dohnavur had the usual traffic: farmers in their slow-moving ox carts, women walking with pots on their heads, a few bicycles, a string of donkeys with their drivers. But John barely noticed. At first he pedaled furiously, but then realized he had twenty miles to cover and finally settled into a steady pace.

The shock of the court judgment wore off and anger rose in its place. How could his father rule against Jewel? *How could he!* Didn't he realize what returning Jewel to her uncle would mean? A child bride . . . John's stomach turned at the thought of Jewel being forced to go through a pagan wedding ceremony and becoming the wife of an old man who didn't even love her. She was only fourteen!

Well. He was *annachie*, Jewel's "older brother." And he wasn't going to let it happen.

What he was going to do once he got to Dohnavur, he had no idea. But something inside drove him on. He had to let them know what the court judgment was. They had to save her.

He turned off the main road at Four Lakes and headed for the village of Dohnavur. Only six miles to go. In Dohnavur he spun through the dirt streets, scattering chickens that got in his way. Finally he could see the compound wall and main gate of Dohnavur Fellowship.

John got off his bike, and suddenly his legs felt wobbly. Four exhausting days of train travel with little sleep and a twenty-mile bicycle ride was catching up with him. He pushed the bike to the side of the road and sat down, head between his knees, chest heaving.

He sat for some time, trying to catch his breath, when a shadow fell over him.

"Are you ill?" said a gentle woman's voice.

John looked up. "Miss Beath?" he said. It was his mother's friend, the one who had come to visit Dohnavur.

"Wha—who are you? How do you know my name?"

John struggled to his feet. "It's me—John Knight."

"My word!" the lady exclaimed, then started to laugh. "I never would have guessed. But I thought you and your mother—"

"Miss Beath! I can't explain it all now. But the court—my father—ruled against Dohnavur. Jewel must be returned to her uncle next week!"

"No! Oh, dear God."

"I must tell Jewel, and Arul, and the *accals*. It's urgent!" John picked up his bike and started for the gate.

"John, wait!" Mabel Beath put her hand on the boy's shoulder. "Does anyone know you are here? Does your father? Or Miss Carmichael?"

"No . . . I only got back to Palamcottah this morning. No one saw me at the trial."

"Then no one here must see you, either."

"Why?"

"Come, let's talk."

Reluctantly, John hid his bicycle in some bushes and walked with Miss Beath into the brush and a stand of tamarind trees where they couldn't be seen from the road.

"When I came to Dohnavur," said Miss Beath, "my spirit immediately felt at one with Amy Carmichael and her work here. I understood when she promised Jewel that, whatever happened, she would not return her against her will to her uncle. Jewel has entrusted her life to us; Amma could not fail her."

John nodded. Yes, he understood that, too.

"The night before Miss Carmichael left for court, she came to me and looked into my eyes," Miss Beath continued. "'If everything fails,' Amma said, 'are you willing to help save Jewel?' 'Yes,' I replied. 'Even if it

102

means seven years in prison?' she asked. Again I said yes."

They had stopped walking and just stood looking at each other, the dusty boy dressed in Muslim clothes and the middle-aged English woman.

"I was walking outside the wall praying when I saw you," the woman said. "And now I know what we must do. *But we must do it alone!* No one must know—not Arul or Miss Carmichael or any of the others—because they will be questioned. It will look like they have disobeyed the court judgment. But if they know nothing, if Jewel has simply disappeared . . ."

"Stupid oxen!" muttered John as he pulled at their halters and tried to get the bandy turned around. Miss Beath had told him to come to this side gate after dark and wait.

When the oxen were finally turned around and facing toward the village, John climbed up into the bandy. "Wait how long?" he wondered.

He had hidden in the bushes until dusk, as Miss Beath instructed. Once he fell into a deep sleep and awoke with hunger pangs gnawing at his stomach. Why hadn't he grabbed some food from the cookhouse back in Palamcottah?

When darkness settled, he had trotted into the village looking for a bandy to rent. John hoped the darkness would help cover his disguise. He was careful to speak only Tamil, but he had a hard time convincing the bandy owner that he needed the oxen and bandy *without* a driver.

A monkey screeched nearby, and for a few minutes there was a general hubbub out in the brush. But he heard nothing from inside the compound walls. What was happening in there?

It was so hard to sit outside the compound, knowing Arul was inside. How he wished he could talk to the older boy! He wanted to see him again, tell him all about getting the telegram and the crazy train trip back to Palamcottah . . . the trial . . . the furious ride by bicycle all the way to Dohnavur. What would Arul think of Miss Beath's idea? John wished Arul could come with them! Arul would know what to do. Arul could . . . no, Miss Beath was right. Arul must not know anything so he could honestly say, "I don't know," if the police questioned him.

Thinking of the trial made John feel angry all over again. But what was it that Miss Beath had said just before she left him in the brush?

"John, don't be angry with your father. He did what he thought was right according to the law. I'm sure Amma is not angry; she knew the ruling might not be in her favor. If the judgment went against her, she intended to stay and appeal, to continue to fight for Jewel. And now we must do what seems right to save Jewel. Be very certain of that, John. If a Christian breaks the law to honor Christ, that person must also be willing to suffer the consequences."

John's thoughts were interrupted by a creaking

sound. The gate was opening. Instantly all John's senses were alert. A young boy stepped through the gate and looked around uncertainly. The gate closed behind him.

John was confused. He was supposed to wait for Jewel. Was it Arul? No, the boy was much too young.

The boy, who was carrying several small bundles, saw the bandy and scurried across the road toward John. "*Annachie?*" said a familiar voice in Tamil. "You have come for me?"

John stared in disbelief. *It was Jewel!*

"But your hair—it is all cut off," stammered John, saying the first thing that popped into his mind.

"And you look like an Indian boy!" said Jewel,

scrambling into the back of the bandy. She handed John one of the bundles. "Food for you. Mabel friend says you are very hungry." She pointed at the other bundles. "More food for the journey."

John smacked the whip on the backs of the oxen until they started moving down the road, then opened the bundle. He shoveled handfuls of the warm vegetable-and-rice curry into his mouth until his stomach was satisfied. Then he looked back into the bandy.

Jewel was sitting at the opening in the rear, looking back toward Dohnavur Fellowship, already hidden among the trees. "Goodbye, Amma," he heard her whisper in Tamil. "Goodbye, Arul *annachie*. Goodbye, sister friends. Goodbye, *babas*. Goodbye, Mabel friend."

Suddenly John felt very alone. He shivered, even though the March evening was hot and still. Jewel was now in his care. No one was coming with them; no one except Mabel Beath even knew where he was—and she was leaving Dohnavur before it was discovered that Jewel was gone.

"Oh, God!" he cried out silently. "Help us!"

Jewel crawled up beside him at the front of the bandy. "*Annachie*, where are we going?"

John glanced at the girl beside him, hair cut short and dressed like a boy. Then he looked at his own coffee-stained hands, dark against the white leggings he wore. Then he looked at the dark road that stretched out in front of them. Two "Indian boys" on their way to . . .

"Ceylon," he said. "We're going to Ceylon."

Chapter 11

Discovered

JOHN KEPT THE OXEN traveling east by back roads all through the night while Jewel slept in the back of the bandy. Toward morning they came to a village called Saltan's Tank, where they found a boy who was willing to return the bandy to the village of Dohnavur for a few rupees. But by this time John could hardly keep his eyes open, so he lay down to sleep under a tree just outside the village while Jewel kept watch.

In the late afternoon, the two young people set off on foot for the Town of Siva's Son, a Hindu town with a large temple right on the eastern coast of southern India. They covered the fifteen miles in four hours. As they wandered through the streets of the town at dusk, John felt anxious—what were they going to do?

"Annachie, look!" said Jewel. The girl was pointing to a simple house with a Christian cross painted on the wall beside the door. With his heart beating fast, John knocked at the door. It was opened by a woman who was not wearing the Hindu red dot on her forehead.

John pointed to the cross, then to themselves. "We are Jesus believers," he said in Tamil.

The woman smiled. "Come in, come in." She called to someone who sat outside behind the house in a small courtyard. "Pastor husband, two boys to see you."

A smiling Indian gentleman greeted them with the customary salaam; John and Jewel returned the greeting. "What do you need?" the man asked kindly in Tamil.

"We are going to Ceylon to find my mother," John said truthfully. The rest of the story did not need to be told. "But we need food and a place to sleep."

The man looked at them silently for what seemed a long time. Finally he smiled. "You boys are welcome to what we have."

They spent the night with the man and his wife, who had a small congregation of five Christian believers in the Town of Siva's Son. John was grateful that they did not ask many questions, but he worried that his disguise did not hold up under close scrutiny. In the morning the woman packed some more food in their bundle, but the man was nowhere to be seen.

"Wait. He will come," said the wife.

John was anxious to be on their way, but they waited. Soon the man arrived with a bandy and two oxen. "I will drive you as far as Tuticorin," he said, naming the next largest town about twenty miles up the coast. "There other Christians will help you."

John looked uncertainly at Jewel. A ride and someone to help them on their way would be wonderful. He hadn't said anything to Jewel, but he was worried about robbers on the road and an escort would provide some safety. On the other hand, maybe their greatest safety lay in keeping to themselves. If they got too familiar with people—even helpful ones—someone would soon guess they were not two Indian boys at all.

But the pastor was waiting. So John said, "Thank you," and gave Jewel a hand up into the wagon bed.

In Tuticorin, the pastor took them to the house of another Christian couple. He spoke privately with the man and woman, who nodded, glancing at John and Jewel from time to time.

Before he left, the pastor took John aside. "Trust our friends. Do not go alone until you get to the train. No questions will be asked. But," and the man smiled, "let the woman help you be an Indian boy."

John was startled. What did he mean? But the man salaamed and then waved goodbye, slapping the rumps of the oxen as the wagon headed back down the road to the Town of Siva's Son.

He soon found out. Jewel came to him with a strange brown paste and a length of white cloth. "Woman friend says to help you be an Indian boy," she said, grinning at him. She made him take off the tunic, while she rubbed the brown paste all over his chest, back, arms and hands, neck and face. John did his own feet and legs. Then Jewel wound the white cloth around his hair, making a small, neat turban.

John felt humiliated. How many people had seen through his hasty disguise? But Jewel looked at him approvingly. Maybe it was better now.

John and Jewel were taken to the next town, then the next, and each time handed over to local Christians. Very few questions were asked and they said little, only that they were on their way to Ceylon to find "mother." Their food bundle was refilled several times, and when they arrived at the train station that would take them to the Ceylon ferry, their stomachs were full.

On an impulse John bought a postcard, addressed it to Amy Carmichael in care of Dohnavur Fellowship, turned it over and printed in English: "The eyes of the Lord run to and fro throughout the whole earth, to show Himself strong in behalf of them whose heart is perfect toward Him." It was one of Amma's favorite Bible verses; he had heard her quote it many times when calming the fears of the little ones. He left the card unsigned. No one must know who wrote it, or why. But would Amma read between the lines, that Jewel was safe?

Two tickets to Colombo used the last of John's money strapped in the pouch around his waist. As he and Jewel collapsed on the hard bench in a third-class compartment, a strange feeling of weariness and peace seemed to consume his whole body. He had no idea what they would do once they got to Colombo. But hadn't God been with them each step of the way ever since they left Dohnavur Fellowship at night in the bandy? God would provide for Jewel . . . somehow.

The hotel room door opened and Leslie Knight stood looking at the two Indian boys with a strange, confused look on her face. Her hair was mussed and her face was strained.

"Mother! It's me—and Jewel."

Mrs. Knight's eyes widened and her mouth fell open. Reaching out, she pulled them into the room and shut the door. "John! Jewel! Oh, thank God!" she cried, clasping both of them to her, crying and laughing at the same time.

"Whatever in the world!" she finally gasped, holding them at arm's length and shaking her head. "I have been frantic with worry. When ten days went by and I still hadn't heard from you . . ." Her eyes filled with tears. "Tell me! Tell me everything!"

So John told the whole story from start to finish, while Jewel snuggled in the comfort of Leslie Knight's arm around her. His mother wouldn't let him leave out any detail. Finally she said, "But Amy Carmichael has no idea where Jewel is or who took her?"

"No. Miss Beath said no one at Dohnavur should know for their own protection."

Mrs. Knight was silent for a long time. Finally she said, "John, you know I don't like doing anything behind your father's back. I cabled him that we had an unexpected delay and would get the next ship. I told him not to worry, that we would enjoy our enforced holiday."

John felt alarmed. Had his mother's cable given them away? "Did he . . . ?"

"I got a reply yesterday. He sent money to help cover our additional expenses and expressed regret that he could not join us due to the number of court cases there in Palamcottah."

John breathed a sigh of relief. So far so good.

But Leslie Knight frowned. "Now that Jewel is here, what are we going to do? We can't stay in Ceylon indefinitely—and we can't leave Jewel here alone!"

Mother and son decided that John should scrub off the brown stain and resume his own identity, but that Jewel should stay hidden in the hotel room. Leslie Knight had meals sent up, and either she or John stayed with Jewel at all times.

In the next few days they discussed various plans: find a Christian church in Colombo and ask for protection for Jewel; take Jewel with them to England; send John back to England as planned, but Mrs. Knight would stay and continue looking for a safe place for Jewel. Each plan, however, had problems.

Nonetheless, John went down to the ship to see if there were any more tickets available for the next voyage. As he stood in the line, he noticed a large Englishman looking at him closely. John pretended not to notice. When it was his turn, he started to ask about another ticket, but noticed that the big man was standing close enough to hear his request. Abruptly John said, "I've changed my mind," and left the line.

He tried again the next day, but was told that there was now a waiting list. Did he want to add a name to the list in case someone canceled? John shook his head. Frustrated, he walked back to the hotel. As he entered the lobby, he saw the big Englishman talking to one of the Indian servants. He ducked behind some of the potted palms and hurried up the stairs to their room.

"What's the matter?" said his mother as he entered out of breath.

"I'm not sure. But there's a man—English—I

think he's been following me."

"Oh, surely not—" began Mrs. Knight.

Just then there was a knock at the door.

"Jewel!" John hissed. "Quickly! Hide!"

John grabbed Jewel's hand and pulled her into the sleeping room she and his mother shared. He pushed her under the bed—a real English bed with a ruffle covering the mattress and legs—then returned to the other room just as he heard his mother open the door.

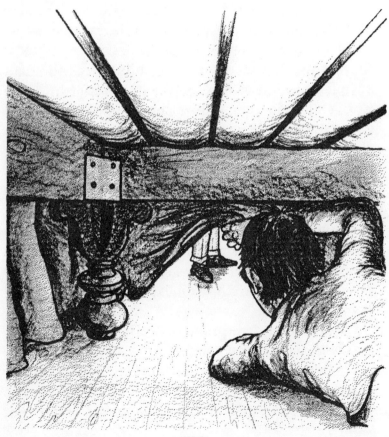

A man's deep voice said, "Mrs. Knight? My name is Handley Bird, formerly of England, now God's servant in southern India. I believe you have a little bird who has fallen from its nest and needs safekeeping?"

Reverend Handley Bird wore a rumpled white suit and a straw hat, which he twisted in his hands as he talked. Leslie Knight had ordered tea from the hotel and invited the caller to sit. John stood off to the side as his mother poured the tea. Was he a friend or an enemy?

"What is it you want, Reverend Bird?" asked Mrs. Knight, handing the visitor a cup.

The man smiled. He had ruddy cheeks and white bushy eyebrows that twitched up and down as he talked. "I was on holiday in Ooty when I ran into an old friend of my wife's, a Miss Amy Carmichael. She had come to Ooty to confer with her lawyer, a Mr. Rabur—I believe you know him?" The man looked at John.

John nodded slightly.

"She is very concerned over the plight of a girl named Jewel, who has disappeared. After telling me the story, and knowing I was on holiday, she asked for my help in locating her. I said I would, with all my heart."

"But why did you come to us?" John demanded. "Why do you think she is here?"

"After hearing as much as I could from Miss Carmichael and Mr. Rabur, I made a trip to Palamcottah to talk to the judge in the case—your husband, I believe, Mrs. Knight."

"That's right."

"I must admit I did not tell him I was acting on Miss Carmichael's behalf! In fact, Jewel's case only happened to come up as we talked about other legal matters of interest affecting the Tinnevelly District. While I was there a telegram arrived—"

"My telegram?" asked Mrs. Knight.

"Yes. Only later, as I was mulling over the whole affair, did the pieces seem to fall in place. A sailing date delayed . . . a girl disappears. Miss Mabel Beath, who left Dohnavur Fellowship on the day of the trial, was followed, but the girl was not found. Let me assure you that I told no one of my hunch— not even Miss Carmichael. After all, I knew nothing for sure."

"How do we know you are here as Miss Carmichael's friend?" John challenged. "Why should we trust you?"

"John . . ." reproved his mother gently.

"It is all right, madam," said Reverend Bird. "If this young man has spirited away our little bird through untold adventures and hardships, he has a right to know whom he should trust."

The stocky man drew a postcard from his coat pocket and handed it to Mrs. Knight. "Miss Carmichael gave me this."

John's mother took the postcard. "Why, John, this is your handwriting!"

"Ah!" said the man. He seemed satisfied.

John walked over to his mother and took the

card. "I only wanted to let Miss Carmichael know that Jewel was safe. I . . . I didn't mean to leave a trail that could be traced."

"Oh, my boy, you have done a very good job covering your tracks. To this day no one suspects— except me. And I assure you I am a friend, and have promised Miss Carmichael I will not rest until Jewel is safely out of the country."

"Out of the country?" John and his mother said together.

"Yes. China. I have reason to believe that Jewel's relatives have hired detectives to find her. They will stop at nothing to get her back. She is not safe here— it is only a matter of time before they follow everyone who has had anything to do with Jewel. I believe Jewel and I must leave immediately—today. I will deliver her to missionary friends in China where she can stay until she comes of age. Then she can inherit her father's land and choose to marry whom she will."

Mrs. Knight and John stared at Reverend Bird in stunned silence. It was all happening so fast.

"Er, by the way, where is the little bird?" the missionary asked.

"Oh, no! Jewel!" John remembered. He ran into the sleeping room and pulled Jewel out from under the bed.

"*Annachie* forgot Jewel," the girl pouted.

John led her into the other room. The bushy white eyebrows raised, and John realized Jewel did not look like a girl with her hair cut short and still wearing the boy's leggings and tunic. In halting Tamil, John tried to explain to Jewel what Reverend Bird had told them, and that he wanted to take her to China to keep her safe from her uncle.

Jewel looked at the man with her dark, trusting eyes. "If Amma sent Bird man to take care of Jewel, then I will go," she said in Tamil. She turned to John and Mrs. Knight. "If *annachie* and Leslie friend say Bird man is Amma's friend, then I will go."

Mrs. Knight, not understanding, looked at John for help.

John took Jewel's hands in his own and swallowed hard. "Yes, *tungachie*, sister. The Bird man is your friend. You must go."

Chapter 12

The Bride of Dohnavur

ALONE HORSEMAN rode south on the road from Palamcottah toward Dohnavur. It had been six years since John Knight had stood on the train station platform in Colombo, Ceylon, waving goodbye to the Indian girl he knew as Jewel. The young man, now twenty-two, could still remember the scene as if it had been yesterday: Jewel, her hair chopped short, leaning out the train window, smiling and crying at the same time; behind her, the ruddy face and bushy eyebrows of Reverend Handley Bird.

The rider was lost in his thoughts, and the horse veered around a slow-moving ox cart, keeping up a steady trot. John knew Reverend Bird and Jewel made it safely to China after a dangerous journey that took several months. He had practically memo-

rized the letter he had received from Amy Carmichael
in late fall that year after he had entered Oxford . . .

*. . . Reverend Bird just disappeared and I had
no idea what was happening. Then in October
I received a letter from China. Our precious
Jewel is safe! I have since heard the whole
story, and I am astounded at the great risks
you took to save her. But I thank you, John,
from the bottom of my heart.*

*Waiting to hear for so many months with
no word about Jewel's fate was a real challenge of faith for me. But even when the judgment was pronounced against us that day in
court, the Lord gave me an overwhelming sense
of victory! Jewel belonged to Him! . . .*

Since that time, John had heard little news. He
spent the next six years studying law at Oxford near
London. His mother, after getting him settled at
school, had returned to India to be with his father.
But after a severe illness brought on by drinking
some unboiled water, she never fully regained her
strength. Eventually both Leslie and Sanford Knight
had returned to England.

The meeting with his father had been strained at
first. Once Jewel was safely away, Leslie Knight had
felt compelled to tell her husband of their role in the
affair. John knew his father was angry. After all, the
magistrate's son had deliberately interfered with a
ruling of the court!

John had been angry with his father, too. The court judgment had seemed so heartless! So calloused!

But on one of John's visits home from the university, Sanford Knight had called him into the library. "Son," he said, clearing his throat, "your mother and I have talked about what happened many times. I can accept that you did what you thought you had to do. Even though I was angry when I discovered you had helped Jewel disappear, I have to admit I felt somewhat relieved. I ruled as I thought right based on the laws that concern India's family system and religious traditions—but I did not enjoy returning Jewel to her uncle."

John accepted his father's outstretched hand. Maybe father and son could respect, if not agree with, the action taken by the other.

The young man on horseback reached for the canteen hanging from the saddle, unscrewed the cap and drank. When he told his mother that he was returning to India, she was quick to say, "Don't forget to boil the water!"

He chuckled; his horse's ears twisted backward to catch the sound. That was India, all right: everything one took for granted in England—clean water, soft beds, a proper roof over your head—was a challenge in India.

As he rode into Four Lakes, John reined in his

horse at a food stall in the marketplace and bought two mangoes and some freshly baked flat bread for his lunch. Mounting once more, he turned his horse toward Dohnavur.

A feeling of excitement grew as John kicked the horse into an easy canter for the last few miles. Through the six long years he had been away, John had never once lost sight of his goal: to return to India and be an advocate for the people. But when he arrived, the first thing he had done was buy a good horse and set out for Dohnavur Fellowship. Before anything else he wanted to see his friends.

John slowed his horse to a trot. There was the village . . . cows creating traffic jams in the middle of the street, as usual . . . children running after him . . . spicy smells rising from the cooking fires in front of the mud houses. And there, through the trees, the mud-brick walls of Dohnavur Fellowship. John's heart seemed to beat faster.

Dismounting, the young man pulled the bell on the gate.

After a few minutes, the gate swung open. John stared at the familiar man who stood before him.

"Azim!" he cried. "What in the world are you doing here!"

His father's former Indian servant looked startled.

"It's me—John Knight!"

The man's eyes lit up. "Yes, yes! Young *sahib*." And Azim pressed his hands together in the familiar *salaam*.

John shook his head and laughed. "No, not *sahib*," he said. "We are friends! John and Azim!"

John led his horse into the compound, following Azim to the main house. What was Azim doing here? Why didn't Arul open the gate? Maybe he should have written that he was coming. But he wanted to surprise Arul and Miss Carmichael.

As he tied his horse to a nearby tree, John noticed that something seemed to be happening. Brightly colored streamers fluttered from the porch roof. Older girls, dressed in their colorful skirts and scarves, were setting baskets of freshly picked flowers from the gardens around the yard. Groups of younger girls sat on blankets under the trees, stringing jasmine flowers into necklaces and long ropes. Oil-soaked rags had been tied on thick sticks and stuck in the ground, making a line of unlit torches all the way from the gate to the house.

John stood looking around, somewhat bewildered, then he heard his name. "John! John Knight! I can't believe it!" Amy Carmichael came whirling out of the house and before he realized what was happening, had thrown her arms around him in a motherly hug.

The next moment she was holding him at arm's length. "Let me look at you. You have grown up into a proper young man! What a wonderful surprise." And she gave him another hug.

John was so happy to see her he couldn't even say anything.

"But why didn't you write that you were coming? What are you doing back in India? How long are you staying?"

John had to laugh at her long list of questions. But there was something he had to know first.

"Where is Arul? I came to see you—and Arul."

Her eyes widened. "You don't know? No . . . of course you don't. Oh, John, Arul isn't here!"

Disappointment rose in John's throat. Not here? He had come all the way to Dohnavur and Arul was not here?

"But . . . where—?" he began.

"Time for that later," said Miss Carmichael briskly. She took him by the arm and bustled him into the house. "The others will want to see you."

The faithful Indian staff women were decorating the inside of the house as well. Each one expressed surprise and delight upon seeing John, after which there was much whispering among the women.

"And Azim?" he managed to ask as she propelled him out the door once more.

"Oh, yes, Azim! When your mother and father left Palamcottah, Azim had no employment. He had been so helpful when he came with you and your mother that I asked if he would like to come and work for

Dohnavur. He gladly accepted. And," she lowered her voice in a secretive tone, "he is *almost* convinced that all men are brothers, just as Jesus taught, in spite of his long dedication to the caste system." The two laughed.

Amy took him around to the groups of children and introduced him. Some of the older girls remembered him, lowered their eyes shyly, and bent their heads in gentle salaams. To the younger ones, Amy said, "Little Lotus Buds, this is John—Jewel's *annachie*, as I have told you in the stories."

Lots of giggles and finger pointing came from the wiggly bundles on the blankets.

John worked up his courage as Amy took him back to sit on the porch and got him something cool to drink.

"What has happened to Jewel?" he asked. "Has she returned? Have you seen her?"

Amy's mouth twitched. Was she about to cry—or smile? He couldn't tell which.

"No," Amy said. "No, I have not seen Jewel since the day I left her to go to court that fateful day six years ago."

John was silent. He watched the streamers flutter in the slight breeze. Something strange was going on. Arul was not here . . . Amma seemed reluctant to talk about him, or Jewel. Had something bad happened? And yet, what about the streamers and flowers? On the other hand, he remembered Arul telling him that funerals at Dohnavur were great celebrations as a much-loved child or *accal* moved from this life into eternal life with Jesus.

"You look like you are getting ready for a celebration," he hinted finally.

Amy nodded, but said nothing. Then suddenly she jumped up. "Well! I have things I need to do. Just sit here and rest. I am sure you are tired after your journey. We will talk again when I am done with my duties. We have so much catching up to do!"

She disappeared into the house. In a few minutes, John heard much commotion and laughter inside.

He got up and paced the length of the porch. His riding boots thumped on the cane floor. He was very glad to see Amma . . . but his disappointment that Arul wasn't here was deep. He ran his hand through his hair. Why didn't Amma tell him what was going on?

The sun began to slip below the palms and tamarind trees in the west, making the mountains in the distance stand out in purple silhouette.

The normal time for supper came and went, but no one gathered to eat. Instead, most of the girls and some of the *accals* wandered down toward the gate. A few of the girls climbed up on the gate and peered over.

The crowd at the gate got larger and larger. John got up from the porch and had just decided to go see what was happening when he heard a shout raised in Tamil, "They're coming! They're coming!"

Who's coming? John wondered. Just then Amy Carmichael and the others in the main house came running out. "Come, John!" Amy called, grabbing his hand and pulling him along. "You will want to see!"

Several of the older girls lit one torch from a cooking fire, then lit all the other torches. Soon a blaze of light danced in the twilight. Azim had swung open the gate and the flock of girls surged into the road outside.

At first John couldn't see anything. Then he saw a bandy coming slowly up the road. But . . . it wasn't an ordinary bandy. White lotus and jasmine flowers had been woven all over the curved straw roof. The oxen that pulled the bandy had brightly painted horns and flowers tucked in their bridles and tied to the yoke.

A man and a woman dressed in white sat in the front of the bandy. All the girls were crowding around, jumping up and down, shouting, laughing, and throwing flowers.

John hung back and watched curiously as the bandy came closer. It looked like a wedding. The oxen stopped and the man leaped to the ground, then turned and helped the young woman to the ground. She was dressed in a snow-white sari, framing her heart-shaped face and large dark eyes. Amy reached them and gave the young couple a big hug, and there was much laughter. The next moment the young woman and man turned toward John, and a flash of recognition surged through his body.

It was Jewel and Arul!

The couple saw John at the same time.

"*Annachie!*" Jewel cried.

"John! My brother!" said Arul. And the three friends clasped one another in a big bear hug, with little children hugging their legs and others still throwing flowers into the air.

In a few moments, they were pulled apart by the excited children, and the bridal couple was escorted through the flaming torches toward the main house.

John was bursting with questions, but a grand celebration was in full swing. Grass mats were laid on the ground for people to sit on; bowls and bowls of food and sweets and fruits were brought out on the porch. As the bride and groom were given plates of food, the girls gathered into a choir and sang a gentle Indian love song, followed by several beautiful hymns in Tamil.

John sat on a grass mat and watched the festivities. Every now and then Arul looked his way and flashed a grin as if to say, "Soon, my brother. But right now, Jewel comes first."

Amy sat down beside him on the mat.

"You see, John, I always knew Jewel belonged to God, and that He had a new life for her. How we missed her, so far away in China! But we knew she was in God's hands. Then . . . one night I had a dream. In the dream I saw Arul and Jewel getting married. When I awoke, I could not shake the feeling that God had shown me His vision for Jewel. So I talked to Arul. As you know, it is not uncommon in India for marriages to be arranged. But I didn't want it to only be my plan. I wanted it to be God's plan. So I prayed that if this is what God wanted, both Jewel and Arul would feel in their hearts that this was right."

Amy glanced fondly at the couple, each with an adoring child in their laps.

"Letters went back and forth between Jewel and Arul. And soon they both agreed: yes, they believed God would have them marry. But, even though Jewel is now of age, it seemed better for Arul to go to meet Jewel and be married in Ceylon, and then return. Now there is no question of her uncle's claim on her."

John nodded. Yes, it was right. He had never thought of it, because six years ago Jewel had still seemed like a child. But now she was a young woman of twenty. Who better for her husband than his dear friend and brother, Arul?

Amy touched his hand. "John? I have another dream. I have spoken of it to you before. There are so many boys, lost in the temples, sold to the traveling acting groups, abandoned by their poverty-stricken parents. They need Dohnavur, too. But we have been waiting for the men, men who can teach them. . . ."

John looked at Amy Carmichael.

"You have come back, John. You know the language. You are part of our family here. Will you ask God if this is why He brought you back to India? But I don't want it to be my idea. If it is God's idea, you will feel in your heart that it is right for you to do."

Just then several of the girls grabbed John's hands, pulled him up and led him in a merry chase of Follow the Leader behind the laughing bride and groom. Helplessly John looked over his shoulder at Amma and gave her a smile.

Yes, he would ask God about the boys. . . .

More About Amy Carmichael

AMY CARMICHAEL WAS BORN on December 16, 1867, in the seacoast village of Millisle in Northern Ireland. Her father, David Carmichael, and his brother William were respected mill-owners from a God-fearing family with a well-deserved reputation for integrity and generosity. The eldest of seven children, Amy was headstrong and full of mischief, but with a tender heart for all living things. It was a happy, secure childhood.

When Amy entered her teen years, she went away to a Wesleyan Methodist boarding school in Harrogate, Yorkshire, for three years. While away from home, the vital truths from the Bible that she learned at her mother's knee took root in her heart and she opened her life to Jesus as her Savior and Lord.

But things were not well at home. Financial difficulties took the family to Belfast and Amy had to return home from school. The strain on her father may have contributed to the pneumonia that took his life in 1885; Amy was only seventeen years old.

For the next several years she helped care for her younger brothers and sisters, and at the same time began holding Sunday classes for the "shawlies"—the girls who worked in the mills and wore shawls instead of hats. These meetings soon grew to such numbers that Amy decided they needed a building. In faith she prayed for five hundred pounds to put up an "iron hall" that would hold five hundred girls. Her faith and vision were contagious, and soon the mill-girls were meeting in a new hall named "The Welcome," where they met for Bible study, singing and band practice, night school, sewing club, mothers meeting, as well as a monthly Gospel meeting open to everyone.

Amy's experience at "The Welcome" helped establish many spiritual principles that she followed throughout her life, such as looking to God alone for financial needs and receiving help in her ministry only from God's people.

At age twenty, Amy was invited to England in 1888 to begin a similar work for factory girls in Ancoats, Manchester, and moved there with her mother and a sister. In England she met Robert Wilson, one of the founders of the "Keswick Convention for the deepening of spiritual life." Attending her first Keswick convention at Wilson's invitation,

Amy committed her whole life to God. Wilson became a great friend of the whole Carmichael family, who always referred to him as the Dear Old Man ("D.O.M." for short). When illness and overwork forced Amy to quit her work in Manchester, she accepted Wilson's invitation in 1890 to come to his home, Broughton Grange, as a daughter and companion.

Amy thought God's plan was for her to care for the D.O.M. until his heavenly home-going—but on January 13, 1892, she heard God's unmistakable call to "Go ye" as a missionary and take the Gospel to foreign lands. Both Amy's mother and Robert Wilson released her to follow God's will, even though it was a great sacrifice for them.

But where was she called? Amy's missionary adventures took her first to Japan in April, 1893, but ill health forced her to return home a year later. No mission board would pass her for a foreign field; but, recommended by leaders of the Keswick Convention, she was accepted by the Church of England Zenana Missionary Society and sent to India in October, 1895. When she set foot on Indian soil, little did anyone know she would never return home again.

Amy threw herself into language study of Tamil so that she might share the Gospel directly with the people of south India. Her poor health took her to the hill-station of Ooty, where she met Reverend Thomas Walker and his wife, missionaries in the Tinnevelly District. Reverend Walker became her language coach, and as the relationship grew, the

Walkers invited Amy to join them in their evangelistic work in the Tinnevelly District. She called Walker *annachie* ("elder brother"); he called her *tungachie* ("younger sister").

With the Walkers' support, Amy gathered a band of Christian Indian women called the Starry Cluster who traveled from village to village in a bullock bandy, preaching the Gospel. One of these Indian women was Ponnammal, a young widow who became Amy's assistant until she died of cancer in 1915. Another young girl, Arulai, only eleven, was drawn by the love of God to this white woman in Indian dress. Arulai's boy cousin, Arul Dasan, also became a Christian in spite of persecution from his family. Both Arulai and Arul Dasan became valuable co-workers with Amy for many years to come.

It was while traveling with the Starry Cluster that Amy Carmichael first became aware of the "temple children," young girls who were "married to the gods" in the Hindu temples, a practice that included prostitution. Preena, age seven, was the first temple child to run away to Amy's protective arms in 1901. To provide a home for these girls, Amy established Dohnavur Fellowship near the village of Dohnavur in the Tinnavelly District. Soon Amy Carmichael became *Amma* ("mother") to dozens of little girls.

But Amma's heart also ached for the boys, some sold into temple service, others sold to acting troupes that traveled from town to town—a life that made it nearly impossible for these boys to grow up good and pure. The first two boys arrived in 1918; when Godfrey Webb-Peploe arrived at Dohnavur Fellowship in 1926 to help with the boys' work, there were seventy to eighty boys already!

The work at Dohnavur Fellowship followed a spiritual pattern that grew out of the Word of God and Amy's heart, represented in the key words: *love, loyalty, unity,* and *service*. She believed that co-workers in the Gospel should first and foremost love one another. Amma asked no one to do anything that she herself was not prepared to do. All work was considered a service of joy and love to the Lord. All needs were taken to the Lord in prayer, looking to Him alone for their provision, rather than letting their needs be made known to others. No money was borrowed; no debts incurred. God's will was often tested by the precept: "As God provides."

In October 1931, at the age of sixty-four, Amma fell into a pit, breaking her leg. She never fully recovered, and spent the next twenty years confined to her room. Yet new leadership was being prepared: Godfrey and Murray Webb-Peploe on the "men's side," and May Powell to replace Arulai, who was ill, on the "women's side." But Amy Carmichael continued to impart her faith and vision to both the children, who loved to visit her, and her co-workers. She wrote thirteen books after her accident, in addition to updating her earlier books. These books capture many stories of the lives of boys and girls, men and women, whom God brought to Himself through the work of Dohnavur Fellowship.

Amy Carmichael died on January 18, 1951, and was buried in God's Garden. No stone marks her grave; she is with Jesus. But her spirit lives on in the work of Dohnavur Fellowship in south India, still going strong today.

For Further Reading

Carmichael, Amy, *Gold Cord: The Story of a Fellowship* (London: Society for Promoting Christian Knowledge, 1932).

Elliot, Elisabeth, *A Chance to Die: The Life and Legacy of Amy Carmichael* (Old Tappan, N.J.: Fleming H. Revell Company, 1987).

Houghton, Frank L., *Amy Carmichael of Dohnavur* (Fort Washington, Penn.: Christian Literature Crusade, 1979, 1985).

Series for Middle Graders*
From Bethany House Publishers

ADVENTURES DOWN UNDER · by Robert Elmer
When Patrick McWaid's father is unjustly sent to Australia as a prisoner in 1867, the rest of the family follows, uncovering action-packed mystery along the way.

ADVENTURES OF THE NORTHWOODS · by Lois Walfrid Johnson
Kate O'Connell and her stepbrother Anders encounter mystery and adventure in northwest Wisconsin near the turn of the century.

AN AMERICAN ADVENTURE SERIES · by Lee Roddy
Hildy Corrigan and her family must overcome danger and hardship during the Great Depression as they search for a "forever home."

BLOODHOUNDS, INC. · by Bill Myers
Hilarious, hair-raising suspense follows brother-and-sister detectives Sean and Melissa Hunter in these madcap mysteries with a message.

JOURNEYS TO FAYRAH · by Bill Myers
Join Denise, Nathan, and Josh on amazing journeys as they discover the wonders and lessons of the mystical Kingdom of Fayrah.

MANDIE BOOKS · by Lois Gladys Leppard
With over four million sold, the turn-of-the-century adventures of Mandie and her many friends will keep readers eager for more.

THE RIVERBOAT ADVENTURES · by Lois Walfrid Johnson
Libby Norstad and her friend Caleb face the challenges and risks of working with the Underground Railroad during the mid–1800s.

TRAILBLAZER BOOKS · by Dave and Neta Jackson
Follow the exciting lives of real-life Christian heroes through the eyes of child characters as they share their faith and God's love with others around the world.

THE TWELVE CANDLES CLUB · by Elaine L. Schulte
When four twelve-year-old girls set up a business doing odd jobs and baby-sitting, they find themselves in the midst of wacky adventures and hilarious surprises.

THE YOUNG UNDERGROUND · by Robert Elmer
Peter and Elise Andersen's plots to protect their friends and themselves from Nazi soldiers in World War II Denmark guarantee fast-paced action and suspenseful reads.

*(ages 8–13)

-The-
Queen's
Smuggler

Trailblazer Books

Also by Dave and Neta Jackson

Hero Tales: A Family Treasury of True Stories
From the Lives of Christian Heroes (Volumes I, II, & III)

-The-
Queen's
Smuggler

Dave & Neta Jackson

Story illustrations by
Julian Jackson

BETHANY HOUSE PUBLISHERS
MINNEAPOLIS, MINNESOTA 55438

Published by Bethany House Publishers
A Ministry of Bethany Fellowship International
11400 Hampshire Avenue South, Minneapolis, Minnesota 55438
www.bethanyhouse.com

Printed in the United States of America by
Bethany Press International, Minneapolis, Minnesota 55438

Library of Congress Cataloging-in-Publication Data

Jackson, Dave and Neta
    The Queen's smuggler / Dave and Neta Jackson ; illustrated by Julian Jackson.
        p. cm. — (Trailblazer Books)
    Summary: Sarah tries to smuggle a New Testament into England in order to save the life of William Tyndale, a man imprisoned for translating the Bible into English.

    [1. Bible—Translating—Fiction. 2. Tyndale, William, d. 1536—Fiction. 3. Great Britian—History—Henry VIII, 1509–1547—Fiction. 4. Smuggling—Fiction. 5. Christian life—Fiction.]
I. Jackson, Neta. II.Jackson, Julian, ill. III. Title. IV. Series.
PZ7.J132418Qs   1991
[Fic]—dc20   91–4952
ISBN 1–55661–221–4   CIP
                                                                          AC

The majority of characters in this book were real people. The events involving William Tyndale, King Henry VIII and Anne Boleyn, Sir John and Lady Anne Walsh, John Frith, Thomas Poyntz, Humphrey Monmouth, and Henry Phillips are historical.

However, Sarah Poyntz, the "accident," and Sarah's role in trying to help Tyndale are fictional. Also, Miles' apprenticeship to his relative Thomas Poyntz is conjecture.

DAVE AND NETA JACKSON are a husband/wife writing team who have authored or coauthored many books on marriage and family, the church, and relationships, including *On Fire for Christ: Stories from Martyrs Mirror*, the Pet Parables series, and the Caring Parent series.

They have two children: Julian, an art major and illustrator for the Trailblazer series, and Rachel, a high school student. They make their home in Evanston, Illinois, where they are active members of Reba Place Church.

CONTENTS

Chapter 1

The Letter

SARAH GLANCED AT THE TWO empty places at the end of the large table. Why weren't Papa and Cousin Miles home yet? Their ship was supposed to come in today—Mama had said. The voyage to England and back across the North Sea with merchandise to sell should only take a week at most, unless . . .

"Miss Sarah!" boomed a voice. She looked up startled into the round face of Humphrey Monmouth, one of the English merchants who often stayed at her parents' boarding house here in Antwerp, Belgium. Her face turned red, but he was smiling at her.

"You don't have to worry about your father," Monmouth said, shaking his knife in her direction. "Thomas Poyntz is not only one of the best merchants England has the good fortune to call her own, but a smart seaman as well. He may have waited a day because of weather. Winds are a bit unpredictable in October. Or maybe business took longer than he expected."

"Or delayed by English customs?" suggested Mrs. Poyntz with a slight lift of her eyebrows. Sarah shot

her mother a quick look. Customs? Had the searchers found the books that her father so carefully concealed in the barrels of grain and wine bound for English markets? Although her parents had never spoken of it, her cousin Miles had told her about the bundles of New Testaments Thomas Poyntz regularly smuggled from Belgium into his native England.

"New Testaments in *English*!" sixteen-year-old Miles had said gleefully. "Translated by Master Tyndale himself!"

Sarah had often heard about the man who had once been her cousin's tutor back in England. She was glad when Miles had come to live with them here in Belgium to learn the merchant trade. When he wasn't traveling with her father, Miles often spent time with Sarah, and didn't seem to mind that she was three years younger. But where were her cousin and father now?

"Ah, customs," nodded Humphrey Monmouth. "A minor concern, Mrs. Poyntz. Thomas is a well-respected businessman on both sides of the strait with friends in high places. A minor concern." The stout merchant pushed back his empty plate and beamed at his hostess. "An excellent supper, Mrs. Poyntz! Excellent, indeed."

Just then Sarah heard the front door open and boots stamping. She turned excitedly toward the front hall.

"There, you see?" Monmouth exclaimed. "The seafarers have arrived!"

Sarah didn't wait to be excused from the table but flew into the hall. "Papa!"

Thomas Poyntz wrapped his arms around his only child, then soundly kissed his wife who was close on Sarah's heels. "Sorry we're late, my dear," he said to his wife, shrugging off his cloak. "Business always takes longer than we expect, right Miles?"

Sarah smiled at her cousin who was also taking off his wraps. "Mama told Cook to keep supper hot. And Mr. Monmouth arrived yesterday."

"Humphrey!" Thomas walked with his wife back into the dining room with its wooden beams and inviting table. "Should have known you'd be here warming your britches at my table."

Sarah started to follow her parents, but Miles pulled at her sleeve. "Your father has a letter for you."

"A letter? For me?" Sarah stared at her cousin. "Don't tease me, Miles."

"Honest! And it has the queen's seal on it." With a grin Miles headed for the dining room.

A letter from the queen? Queen Anne? Sarah followed quickly, but Cook was already serving up the empty plates, and everyone was talking at once. She sat at her place and toyed with a half-eaten roll. Finally she could stand it no longer.

"Papa!" she interrupted. "Miles says you have a letter for me."

The voices suddenly were quiet. "Why, yes, I do," said her father, drawing a letter from the leather pouch he wore around his waist. He looked at his wife, then handed the letter to Sarah. "Why don't you read it aloud?"

Sarah turned the folded parchment over. There was a red wax seal, with the queen's crown in the center. Picking up her table knife, she gently loosened the seal and unfolded the page. The letter was dated September, 1534. She looked up at her mother who smiled encouragingly.

The letter was written in a beautiful flowing script, and the first thing Sarah looked for was the signture at the bottom. It said: "Your friend, Anne Boleyn." Sarah's heart was thumping so loudly that she thought others could hear it as she began to read the letter.

My Dear Sarah,

I have often thought of you since our short visit at Little Sodbury Manor a few years ago. You must be a young lady now. And I am now Queen!

Now that you are older, I wonder if you and your parents will reconsider my invitation to come to Court and be one of my maids-in-waiting. There are several other young ladies your age. Please assure your parents that your education in music and literature will continue—I will see to it personally. And of course Court life is an excellent finishing school for young ladies.

I would very much like to see you again, Sarah. After all, you saved my life! But even more than that, you have a refreshing spirit that I value. I am sure we would be good friends. Give my highest regards to your parents. I hope to hear from you soon.

Your friend, Anne Boleyn

Sarah looked up. Mrs. Poyntz was smiling, but her father looked grave.

"How about that, Sarah!" Miles blurted. "A letter from the queen!" Humphrey Monmouth winked at Sarah, but then busied himself filling his pipe.

"Thomas?" Mrs. Poyntz said to her husband. "What do you think?"

Thomas Poyntz frowned. "The same thing I thought three years ago. It is a kind invitation, and I have no disrespect for the queen. She is a dear friend of my cousin, Miles's mother. But I do not want my daughter exposed to all the shenanigans that pass for court life. Look at what happened to Queen Catherine! Look at how Anne herself became Queen!"

"True enough, Thomas!" Humphrey Monmouth lit his pipe, puffed a few times, then exhaled a fragrant cloud of smoke. "But in spite of its weaknesses, an invitation to court is a great opportunity for a young lady. She would meet everyone in English society sooner or later. I have sometimes wondered whether you do your wife and daughter a favor living here in Antwerp away from England for so many years."

Sarah rose, clutching the letter, and slipped out of the room as her father said, "Spoken by anyone else, Humphrey, I might take offense. But I know you are my friend and mean well. It is business only that brings me to Antwerp, and I want my wife and daughter by my side. Sarah is still young. . . ."

The voices in the dining room faded as Sarah ran up the stairs to her bedroom. She shut the door quietly, went over to the window seat and sank onto the cushion. Pressing her cheek against the cool window pane, she looked out into the dark city street. The lamplights were shrouded with an evening fog.

She had often thought of Anne Boleyn—she hadn't been Queen then. But she'd never expected to receive a letter from her! After all, that was three years ago, when Sarah had only been ten years old. . . .

Chapter 2

The Accident

SARAH REMEMBERED meeting Anne Boleyn as if it were yesterday.

On one of his business trips to England, Thomas Poyntz had decided to visit his cousin's family in Gloucestershire, a good hundred miles from London. His cousin Lady Anne Walsh and her family lived on a lovely estate in the country.

Thomas Poyntz had taken Sarah along. "Some time at Little Sodbury Manor will do you good," her father said as their rented carriage clipped along past the fields and hedgerows, green with new spring growth. "If you can put up with your two cousins, that is," he teased. "Johnny should be about fourteen now . . . Miles a year younger."

Maybe it was because Mama had decided to stay home in Antwerp and Papa didn't keep reminding her to "act like a lady." Or maybe it was all the room to explore and all the new and wonderful things to do in the country. But Sarah had no trouble "putting up with" her cousins. The boys let her help feed and brush their ponies and taught her how to hold her hand flat while velvety lips nibbled a carrot from her hand. Johnny pointed out the various green shoots sticking up through the dirt in the gardens, naming the flower or vegetable each would be. Miles showed her the tree that had fallen over the creek in the last storm and cheered when Sarah walked across the trunk to the other side. She felt frightened when she looked down at the creek, swollen with spring rains, rushing beneath the tree. But Miles yelled, "Keep your eyes on the other side!" and in no time she was jumping off on the far bank.

Best of all, the boys took her exploring in the woods and meadows and showed her some of their secret places. Sitting under a natural canopy of brambles and vines one day, eating some bread and cheese the boys had smuggled out of the kitchen, Sarah wished she could stay at Little Sodbury forever and ever.

"We better go back," Johnny said, crawling out from under the canopy and standing up. He was nearly as tall as his father. "Mother is expecting company today and wants us home in time to clean up."

"Company?" Sarah asked. She didn't want the Walshes to have company. She wanted her cousins to herself.

"Just a childhood friend of Mother's—Anne Boleyn. She's a lady-in-waiting in the king's court."

Miles snickered. "For *now*. But King Henry has finally divorced his wife, and everybody knows he's got his eye on Anne."

"You shouldn't talk like that about Mother's friend," Johnny scolded. "Come on; we better go back."

But when the three young people walked up the lane toward the house, they saw two fine carriages standing in the drive, the horses still in harness and several servants unloading bags from the boot.

"Uh-oh," said Miles. "She's already here."

Sarah looked at her dirt-smudged hands. She couldn't wipe them on her dress . . . and there were leaves and stickers caught in her petticoat. She brushed at her dress, then tried rubbing her hands with some wet grass. That was a little better—but not much. If Mama were here, she'd be in big trouble.

But the grownups were busy talking and directing the servants where to take the bags. "Ah! Here are the children!" exclaimed Sir John Walsh as they came into the main hall. "Lady Anne, you remember our sons, Johnny and Miles. And this is our niece, Sarah Poyntz."

Two Lady Annes? This was confusing. Her papa's cousin was Lady Anne Walsh, and Anne Boleyn was Lady Anne, too. Then she realized everyone was looking at her, so she dipped her head and tried a curtsy.

"Sarah!" said Anne Boleyn. "You are just what I need in this household of handsome but awkward men. Mrs. Walsh has gone off to oversee dinner preparations, and I need a friend to help me unpack." She smiled and held out her hand.

Sarah looked at the two maids hovering nearby. What did she know about helping a lady unpack?

But she took Anne's hand and went with her to the large guest chamber where numerous gowns were already laid out on the bed. Only after Anne let go of her hand did Sarah remember that her hands were still dirty.

"*And* you have a smudge on your nose," Lady Anne teased, reading her thoughts. The elegant lady nodded toward the hand-painted china basin and pitcher on the washstand. Sarah felt her face go red, but she dutifully poured some cool water into the basin, used some of the lavender soap to scrub her hands and face, then dried them with one of her aunt's embroidered finger towels.

When Sarah was done washing, the maids were already hanging the gowns in the wardrobe. Sarah studied her aunt's guest. Anne Boleyn's dark hair was smoothed back from her face in the English fashion, covered by a pleated headdress rimmed with pearls. The square low neck of her rich red gown was also trimmed with pearls. Small red lips made her dark eyes stand out in the pale, clear face. Anne Boleyn wasn't exactly beautiful, but she was stunning and . . . exciting.

"So. You've cleaned up," said the lady, the same teasing smile playing about her lips. "Now let's go get dirty again."

Sarah looked at her quizzically. "I beg your pardon?"

"Help me choose a good dress for walking. You children have obviously been having a good time. I would love to get away from all the hovering and pampering of these silly servants. Would you take me for a walk and show me some of the sights, Sarah?"

Sarah laughed. "All right, if you'd like."

This is a very curious lady, she thought. Together they chose a simple brown dress with a high neck, with only a touch of lace at the throat and wrists. One of the maids removed Anne's headdress, then caught up the rich dark hair in a net at the nape of her neck.

Sarah's own hair was light brown, with curls and wisps that wouldn't stay tucked under anything. *Oh, to have that rich mane of thick dark hair,* she thought enviously.

Anne sent one of the maids to inform her host and hostess that she and Sarah were going on a walk . . . alone. The two maids protested, but Anne waved them off. "Come along, Sarah. We're a hundred miles from London, and I want some real fresh air!"

At the end of the lane, Sarah held open the gate into the meadow, then latched it behind her new friend. The Walsh boys' two ponies lifted their heads and ambled over curiously.

"Miles is going to teach me to ride!" Sarah said, scratching behind a pony's ears. "Do you know how to ride, Lady Anne?"

Anne Boleyn was feeding a wisp of grass to the other pony. "Yes . . . yes, I learned as a young girl in France."

"Are you French?"

Anne smiled. "No, but I was a maid-in-waiting to Queen Mary when she went to France to marry the French king."

"A *maid*-in-waiting? How old were you?"

"Just twelve. How old are you, Sarah?"

"Ten. How old do you have to be to be a maid-in-waiting?"

"Ten's a bit young," said Anne. "Sometimes I wish . . ." But she fell quiet as they started walking again.

Wish what? Sarah wondered, but did not ask. They walked in silence through the meadow, going through another gate and into the cool woods.

"Would you like to see the tree that fell in the storm? Come on!" Sarah grabbed Lady Anne's hand and skipped along the path. Anne laughed as she trotted to keep up, stopping now and then to unhitch her skirt from a pesky briar.

The massive tree lay on its side across the angry-looking creek. Its bare roots saluted the sky, still draped with clumps of dirt. Most of its branches lay on the other side, though a few trailed their arms and leaves in the rushing water.

"Can we go across?" asked Lady Anne.

"Sure. I walked over once with Miles and Johnny, so I'll go first."

Sarah gathered up her skirt with one hand and reached up with the other to grab a sturdy root. She stepped on the roots and knots which let her scramble to the top side of the fallen tree. "See?"

Reaching down, she helped to pull Anne up the same way she had come. Because she was laughing so hard, Anne had to try two or three times before she stood alongside Sarah.

"I feel ten years old again. If only my maids could see me now!" she grinned. "And what would King Henry say!" Then she really laughed.

Sarah giggled, too. She couldn't imagine Mama or "Auntie Anne," as she called Lady Anne Walsh, walking along a tree trunk. She edged out ahead, keeping her eye on the farthest branch as Johnny had told her. The trunk in the middle was about a man's reach around, and still narrower as it reached the other bank. But then there were branches to hold on to. Sarah had just reached them when a cry cut the still air.

"Sarah! I'm falling!"

Sarah turned around just in time to see Anne Boleyn hit the water, her neat brown dress swirling up around her waist. Anne's head disappeared for a moment under the foamy water, then she appeared gasping.

"Help! Help me! I can't swim!"

Chapter 3

The Visitor

SARAH STARED IN HORROR. Anne Boleyn's arms were flailing helplessly in the stream as her feet tried to find the bottom, only to have the rushing water tumble her against the tree trunk. There was nothing to grasp but the broad trunk which rested nearly six inches above the foaming water.

Without time to think, Sarah scrambled back the way she had come. There, about six feet from Anne, one of the tree's branches was sticking into the water.

"Anne!" she screamed. "Grab the branch!"

But Lady Anne didn't seem to hear. She went under again and reappeared spluttering.

There was only one thing to do. Sarah jumped.

The water was *cold* and rushing faster than it looked. Her clothes felt heavy and seemed to be pulling her down. Shaking the water out of her eyes, Sarah looked frantically for the branch. There it was. She grabbed a handful of leaves, then got a stronger grip with both hands. Now, where was Anne? Sarah looked behind her. Anne was trying to

grasp the tree bark with her fingers, but except for
her head and shoulders, the rapid waters seemed to
be pulling the rest of her body beneath the tree.

Even without letting go of the branch, Sarah
knew Anne was beyond the reach of her arm. But,
maybe . . .

"Anne!" she screamed again. "Grab my foot!"

Sarah held on to the branch with both hands,
letting her body float toward the frightened lady.
Anne grabbed the girl's ankle, and for a moment the
extra weight made Sarah think she would lose her
grip on the branch. But Anne pulled herself along
Sarah's leg until Sarah could reach out a hand. Then
Anne also got a grip on the branch, and the two of

them huddled in the water holding tightly to the branch and each other.

After a few minutes Anne's white-knuckled grip began to relax slightly. "Sarah, I think I can touch bottom," she said through chattering teeth. Her body sank slightly until her chin rested barely above the water.

Sarah was trying to think what they should do next when they heard, "Hullo! Sarah! Lady Anne!"

That was Johnny's voice!

"Johnny!" Sarah yelled. "We're in the water!"

In a moment Johnny and Miles were scampering along the tree trunk. They paused briefly above the two shivering females, then hurried over to the other bank. Johnny waded in first, pulling himself along by the branches, and grabbed Anne; Miles was right behind and reached out for Sarah.

In a few minutes all four were catching their breath on the bank. "What happened?" Johnny said.

Suddenly Sarah was scared. It was all her fault. She had taken Lady Anne across the fallen tree. Now there she was soaking wet, shivering and muddy. One of the king's ladies-in-waiting! What would Auntie Anne and Uncle John think? What would Papa say? And Anne Boleyn? Was she angry?

To her astonishment Lady Anne began to laugh. She'd lost her hairnet in the water and her dark hair lay plastered to her head and shoulders. The lace at her throat was muddy and limp. But she was laughing.

"Oh, dear children!" she gasped. "If I hadn't been so scared, that would have been the most fun thing that's happened to me in years!"

The foursome made quite a sight as they straggled up the lane to the manor house. But Anne Boleyn simply said she'd foolishly fallen into the stream, and if Sarah hadn't bravely jumped in to help, she would have been in a fine pickle indeed. And wasn't it good of those boys to come looking for them and help them out?

Baths were filled with heated water, muddy clothes rinsed and bundled off to be washed on the morrow, and dry garments provided. Now the three children and their fathers were gathered in the great hall by the stone fireplace waiting for the women to appear for dinner. Sarah thought the crackling warmth of the fire was especially comforting this cool spring evening.

A butler appeared. "Sir John? There is a gentleman at the door. . . ."

"Gentleman nothing," said a voice, and a tall young man dressed in traveling clothes appeared.

"John Frith! My dear young man!" boomed Sir John, and grasped the newcomer by both shoulders. "Come in, come in. We were just about to have our dinner, and you shall join us!"

"I apologize, Sir John, for not informing you of my arrival. There has been some need of secrecy concerning my return to England at this time. . . . Oh, excuse me. I did not realize you had other guests."

"No, no. Come in. You are welcome in our home any time." Sir John turned to Sarah's father. "This is John Frith, a good friend of William Tyndale, of whom I was telling you. John Frith . . . my brother-in-law Thomas Poyntz."

"John Frith!" said Lady Walsh as she came into the hall. "How glad I am to see you! We shall have a magnificent dinner party tonight. And this . . ." she indicated her friend, dressed in a rich blue gown, her damp hair caught once again in the jeweled head-dress, ". . . is an old friend: Lady Anne Boleyn."

John Frith looked a bit startled, but he took each lady's hand with a bow. "I am delighted to meet you, Lady Anne. Am I right that you may soon be our next queen?"

"I see the court gossip spreads far and wide," Lady Anne replied with a small smile.

Sarah blinked. Anne Boleyn to be queen? She had walked a fallen tree trunk with the future queen of England? Sarah tried to catch Miles's eye, but the boys were following the adults to the long table set with fine china, candles, and crystal. When all had taken their places, Sarah was glad Miles was sitting across from her.

When the food had been served and the servants were no longer lifting lids and pouring wine, Sir John beamed at his guests. "Frith, dear fellow, what word do you have of William Tyndale? It has been too long since we have heard any news, and we are eager to know how his translation work goes."

John Frith cleared his throat uneasily. "I should like to share what I know, but, uh, perhaps it is not fitting conversation for this present company." His glance rested momentarily on Anne Boleyn, then back to his host.

Sir John smiled. "My dear fellow, have no fear. Anne Boleyn is an old friend of ours. Whatever happens in this house is for our ears alone and will not become gossip for the court. Is that not true, Anne?"

Lady Anne did not seem offended by Frith's discomfort. "I too have heard the Walshes speak of William Tyndale and would like to know more," she said graciously.

Sarah was impatient with this talk. After her dunking, she felt weak with hunger. The juicy lamb on her plate smelled especially good; even the vegetables were swimming in a rich sauce. Miles was attacking his plate with gusto, so Sarah took a big bite of the sweet meat. *Heavenly.*

". . . So you see, dear brother," Sir John was saying to Sarah's father, "we engaged Tyndale as the boys' tutor, and learned much ourselves from his scholarly study of the Scriptures. Whenever we had other guests, he felt compelled to share his desire to translate the Scriptures into our English language. He wants all people—you and me, even these children—to be able to read the Scriptures for themselves in our native tongue, not just hear it read in Latin."

"But surely this was not a popular idea among the clergy," Thomas protested.

"Hardly!" laughed Sir John. "More than one or two left our table with a bellyache—and it wasn't from the food!"

"Yes," said John Frith, "the priests wish to keep the people ignorant so they can continue their wicked and evil practices."

"Father," spoke up Johnny, "remember when the abbot was here and Master Tyndale said, 'If God spares my life, before many years pass I will help the boy that drives the plow to know more of the Scriptures than you do!'"

Sir John laughed even harder. "Oh, yes! The plowboy's challenge!" But then his laughter subsided and he sighed. "Not long after that we realized it was no longer safe for William to remain in England. So he went to Europe to continue his work. We have not seen him since."

"He was a good tutor!" Miles said. "I wish I could see him again."

Lady Anne Walsh turned to John Frith. "But what has happened? Has he been able to print his English Bible?"

"Yes, he has completed the New Testament," nodded the young man, "though not without difficulty. The English authorities have followed him and he has had to move many times. But printed copies of the New Testament are regularly coming into England." A smile tugged at the corners of Frith's mouth. "The bishop has been buying up as many copies as he can lay his hands on and burning them . . . but the money goes straight back to Tyndale to finance his work on the Old Testament!"

Sir John Walsh roared with laughter again, and Anne Boleyn's eyes twinkled. "I would like to meet this Tyndale," she said. "I like his spirit! I myself would like to read the Scriptures in English. It is so tiresome to hear the priests go on and on in Latin, when I understand nothing."

The adults soon retired from the table and continued their conversation around the fireplace in the great hall. Sarah drew Miles aside.

"Is your Master Tyndale in danger?"

"If they catch him," said Miles. "When I was little, Master Tyndale told me about a family who taught their children the Lord's Prayer in English. The priests were so angry that they burned the parents at the stake. They said it was a sacrilege for the common people to speak God's Holy Word in the common language."

Sarah covered her face with her hands. *How horrible.*

"Cousin Sarah," Miles whispered, "I know the Lord's Prayer in English. Both Johnny and I. Our parents taught us."

"But . . . Miles!" Sarah was afraid. "What if the priests find out?"

"Don't worry. My parents are respected by all the nobles and clergy. And we only say it at home when we're alone."

Sarah was silent for a few minutes. Then she said, "Would . . . would you say the Lord's Prayer—in English—for me?"

Miles grinned. "If you wish. Fold your hands; it's a prayer, you know."

With the adults' voices and the crackling of the fire in the background, Sarah folded her hands and closed her eyes while Miles's voice softly chanted the words.

> *Our Father which art in heaven,*
> *Hallowed be Thy name.*
> *Thy kingdom come; Thy will be done*
> *In earth, as it is in heaven.*
> *Give us this day our daily bread,*
> *And forgive us our debts,*
> *As we forgive our debtors.*
> *And lead us not into temptation,*
> *But deliver us from evil.*
> *For Thine is the kingdom, and the power,*
> *And the glory forever. Amen.*

That night, tucked into the trundle bed which pulled out from beneath the big bed her father slept in, Sarah kept saying the words over and over again in her mind. *Our Father which art in heaven . . . Thy kingdom come, Thy will be done . . . Forgive us our debts . . .* As she drifted off to sleep, she thought she had never heard anything as beautiful as the Lord's Prayer.

Chapter 4

In Hiding

SARAH SLEPT LATE the next morning. When she awoke, noises inside and outside the house told her everyone else was up and about. She quickly washed, wiggled into a simple dress and pinafore, brushed her unruly hair as best she could, and stole down the stairs.

There were voices in the great hall and she heard her name. Peering around the great wooden door, Sarah saw her father and Anne Boleyn in earnest conversation.

"Your invitation is very kind, Lady Anne," her father was saying. "But I must firmly decline. Sarah is too young to leave her mother and me. . . ." He held up his hand as he saw Lady Anne about to say something. "And even if she were older, I do not wish my daughter to be exposed to all the stresses and temptations of court life."

"I would take utmost care of her . . ." Lady Anne said. Sarah sucked in her breath as she listened.

"Your intentions are no doubt most noble," said Thomas Poyntz. "But your own situation is as yet unclear. Will King Henry be able to marry you as he wishes? He is determined to have a male heir, which the poor queen was unable to give him. But a legal divorce is questionable."

"You don't approve?" Lady Anne's voice was mild.

"That is not the point," said Poyntz. "But I am concerned that my daughter not be caught up in political events beyond even your control."

"Caught'cha eavesdropping," teased a voice in Sarah's ear. Sarah jumped and looked up into the laughing face of John Frith. He took her hand and marched into the great hall.

"It is time for me to leave, Mr. Poyntz, Lady Anne," said the tall young man. "I came to say goodbye."

Poyntz looked relieved to have the conversation interrupted. He shook Frith's hand warmly. The young man had obviously impressed Sarah's father.

Frith then turned to Anne Boleyn.

"My lady, you said you would like to meet Master Tyndale. I don't know whether that will be possible in this life. But you may get to know the man if you read his writings." Sarah saw John Frith draw a slim book from his traveling pouch and place it in Lady Anne's hands. The cover was elegant, decorated with a beautiful script.

"*The Obedience of a Christian Man*," Anne read slowly.

"I wish it were a copy of the New Testament in English," Frith said, "but the latest copies have become ashes in the bishop's bonfires." He smiled wryly.

"But here you have Tyndale's thoughts about the importance of obeying God's Word—which is more important than the traditions of the Church or the decrees of the pope."

Anne laughed. "King Henry would like that! He's not overly fond of the pope's decrees, especially when he wants to divorce a wife." Then, more seriously, "Thank you, John Frith. Your gift will be read and treasured."

A few minutes later the Walsh family joined the goodbyes. As they watched Frith ride out of sight, Sir John Walsh sighed. "I fear for young Frith, as I fear for Master Tyndale. These are intolerant times."

Then abruptly he turned to Sarah's father. "There is a matter I wish to speak to you about, Cousin Thomas. Johnny is, of course, heir to the estate and has taken a keen interest in its management. But Miles," he nodded toward his younger son, "is of a different mind. He has expressed much interest in the merchant trade."

Miles was grinning at Sarah.

"I was wondering," Sir John continued, "if you would be willing to take him as an apprentice for a few years?"

Sarah's eyes widened. She had always wished for an older brother or sister. Was it possible? Would Cousin Miles really come to live with them for a while? Her head was swimming. Overhearing Anne Boleyn's invitation to be her maid-in-waiting . . . her father's refusal . . . all of John Frith's talk about Master Tyndale and people and Bibles getting burned . . .

and now Miles was coming to Antwerp to learn how to be a merchant trader like her father. She felt like she wanted to run away to the special place under the vines in the woods just to think it all over.

As it was, Anne Boleyn would graciously return to the royal court a few days later without Sarah. But when the carriage carrying Thomas Poyntz and his daughter Sarah pulled away from Little Sodbury Manor, Cousin Miles's luggage was stowed in the boot and Miles himself was waving goodbye to his brother Johnny.

That had been three years ago.

Now, sitting in the window seat of her bedroom in Antwerp staring at the fog swallowing the street lamps, Sarah remembered how Miles's mother had kissed her son goodbye, then turned to Sarah's father. "Cousin Thomas," she had said, "I know you will take good care of my son. If God gives you opportunity, will you also give a hand to our dear brother in Christ, Master Tyndale, should your paths cross?"

"I will, dear cousin," her father had said. "I am persuaded that his work is a God-given task. I will do what I can."

After one of their trips to England with a shipment of wine and fine silks, Papa and Miles had brought news that King Henry had finally obtained his divorce and married Anne Boleyn. But Sarah assumed she would never hear again from the lady who had fallen in the creek at Little Sodbury.

Now Lady Anne's letter lay in her lap.

Queen Anne's letter.

A light tap at her door interrupted her thoughts. The door cracked open. It was Miles. "Your father sent me to ask you to come down to the parlor."

"Am I in trouble?"

"No, goose," Miles grinned. "But he wants a family meeting about something." His grin faded, replaced by a small frown. "Your father kept disappearing on this last trip to England—even today after we unloaded ship. That's why we were late. But mum was the word to me. Guess we'll find out now."

Tucking the letter under her pillow, Sarah followed Miles to the parlor. Her mother and father were drawn close to the fire, and Humphrey Monmouth sat nearby, puffing on his pipe.

"Come sit down, Sarah . . . Miles," said her father. "There are some matters you must know about." Sarah sat on a footstool by her mother.

Thomas Poyntz took a deep breath. "Both of you, I am sure, remember John Frith, the young friend of William Tyndale—and your own family, Miles—whom we met during our visit to Little Sodbury several years ago. He has been a strong supporter of Tyndale's translation work, traveling between England and Belgium on Tyndale's behalf."

Poyntz paused and looked around at each person. "But I have learned on this recent journey that young Frith has been burned at the stake by Tyndale's adversaries."

"Thomas! No!" cried Mrs. Poyntz.

Miles looked stricken. Sarah buried her face in her mother's shoulder. *Not John Frith! Why? Who could . . . ?*

Then an awful thought crossed her mind. She raised her head and stared wide-eyed at her father. "It wasn't because Queen Anne . . . that book he gave her . . . oh, Papa!"

"No, no, my child," Poyntz assured his daughter. "I am sure Anne Boleyn had nothing to do with it. There are many enemies of the Gospel who desire to keep God's Word out of the hands of the people."

In spite of the horrible news, Sarah felt relieved. Of course Anne Boleyn would never betray a friend. But her father was still talking; she tried to pay attention.

"Not long after we met John Frith at Little Sodbury," he was saying, "Humphrey, here, good fellow, helped me to locate William Tyndale in Germany. He had given Master Tyndale a safe place to stay many years ago in England and has tried to keep track of him since."

Sarah looked at Humphrey Monmouth puffing on his pipe off to the side. What other secrets did the jolly merchant hold?

"Since that time," her father continued, "I have been helping to deliver Master Tyndale's New Testaments to England on our merchant ships—"

"Smuggling, Thomas—call it what it is!" chided Humphrey Monmouth. "This is not the time to shade the truth. Sarah and Miles are not babes."

"Yes, smuggling it is called by those who fear it," Poyntz admitted. "I have not spoken of it much here at home to protect you and Sarah, my dear, though Miles has shared the risk. But with the news of poor Frith's death I have come to a decision."

"Of course," nodded Mrs. Poyntz, relief easing the worry lines in her pale forehead. "It is much too dangerous to ship Tyndale's books at this time. No one will blame you if you stop for a season."

Her husband shook his head. "That is not the decision I have come to. If they have burned John Frith, they will double their efforts to capture William Tyndale. I have decided that he must be given safe refuge—here, with us, at the English Merchants boarding house."

Sarah could hardly believe her ears. She kicked Miles lightly with her toe.

"Oh, Thomas," said her mother.

Thomas Poyntz laid a hand on his wife's arm. "Only if you agree, my dear. There is risk, of course, but we have many friends among the nobility and clergy both in England and also here in Belgium. I would not do this if I did not think the risk worth taking."

Mrs. Poyntz sighed. "You are right, of course, Thomas. But—what of the other merchants who come in and out? Will not the word get around that Master Tyndale is here?"

Humphrey pulled the pipe from his mouth. "Most of our fellow merchants are like me, Mrs. Poyntz—in sympathy with Master Tyndale's desire to place God's Word in the hands of the common plowboy. In my mind there is no safer place for him to be than here."

Thomas Poyntz glanced around at his family. Mrs. Poyntz nodded slowly. Miles was grinning broadly. Sarah smiled and nodded, too.

"Then so be it. Because—uh—he will be here tonight."

"Tonight!" the group chorused as one.

"Yes. In fact . . ." Poyntz raised his hand for quiet. There was a light knock on the front door out in the hall. "That may be our guest now. Miles?"

Miles got up and went to the front door. Sarah jumped up and followed him. Unbolting the door, Miles swung it open.

There, outlined against the fog, a pack on his back, holding a packet wrapped in oilskin under one arm and a bag by the other hand, stood a man with a small beard and kind eyes.

"Master Tyndale!" exclaimed Miles. "It's really you!"

Chapter 5

The Tutor

AFTER A FEW WEEKS, it seemed to Sarah as if Master Tyndale had been part of the family for a long time. He settled quickly into a spare room on the top floor of the boarding house, his few clothes hung on the wall pegs and his books lined up neatly on the writing table.

The contents of the oilskin packet were laid out on the table along with an inkwell, several quill pens, and a knife to sharpen them. Here Master Tyndale sat, hour after hour, consulting one of his books, then writing on page after page of fresh paper.

He rarely went out, except on Monday afternoons and Saturdays. Sarah didn't know where he went, but when he returned he often looked sad and tired, and the purse that hung from his belt was limp. Mrs. Poyntz was always anxious when he went out and bustled about nervously until he was safely back in the English Merchants boarding house.

Sarah knocked on his door one mid-afternoon in November carrying a tray with a pot of hot tea and some fresh bread from the kitchen.

"Come in."

Sarah pushed open the door and laid down the tray. "You missed the noon meal, Master Tyndale. Mama says you are to stop and eat something."

The lanky man ran a hand through his limp brown hair and smiled wearily. "You are right, Miss Sarah. I get so caught up in my work, I sometimes forget to eat. That bread smells heavenly." He pushed the papers out of the way, broke off a hunk of bread, and poured himself a cup of tea.

Sarah glanced curiously at the many sheets of paper on the table. "What are you doing?"

"Ah!" Tyndale said, swallowing his bite of bread and washing it down with the tea. "I am translating the Psalms from the Hebrew Old Testament into English. Can you read, Sarah?"

"Well, yes," Sarah stammered, "but not very well."

"Try," he urged, handing her the parchment.

Sarah squinted at the words in the tiny script, and began to read.

The Lord is my shepherd;
I shall not want.
He maketh me to lie down in green pastures;
He leadeth me beside the still waters.

She looked up. "It's beautiful. But . . . what is it talking about?"

Tyndale raised his shaggy eyebrows. "This Psalm was written by King David, who was a shepherd in his youth. He is praising God that He takes care of us just as a shepherd watches over his sheep."

Sarah laughed. "I like that! Will you teach me some more about what the Bible says?"

Master Tyndale smiled. "It has been a while since I have had a student to tutor—not since I taught Miles and his brother Johnny many years ago at Little Sodbury. Oh, they were little rascals—always playing jokes on me." Master Tyndale chuckled. "I could hardly believe it was Miles when he opened the door the other night. Why, he is practically a grown man!"

Sarah waited impatiently as Tyndale finished his bread and tea. Didn't he hear her question? She watched as he carefully set the dishes back on the little tray.

"Sarah," he said, eyes twinkling as he handed her the tray, "I would be honored to be your teacher—in the Scriptures, English, Latin, history—whatever you want to learn! It would be one way I could repay your parents for their great kindness. But you must ask them for permission."

Thomas Poyntz was delighted with Tyndale's offer to tutor Sarah. Though some girls in England attended private schools, most were taught their letters and the fine arts—painting, needlework—at home. Living in Belgium, Sarah's formal education had been somewhat spotty.

And so the young girl and the scholar began each day that damp winter of 1534 and '35 with two hours of study. When Miles wasn't working with her father, he, too, joined the little class in Tyndale's attic room.

Sarah was fascinated with Tyndale's books. Some were written in Greek and German. And of course there was the big Latin Bible. But her favorite book was the English New Testament.

"Would you show me the Lord's Prayer?" she asked Master Tyndale one day as she and Miles sat on the bench which had been added to the small room for their lessons.

He opened the New Testament to the Gospel of Matthew, the sixth chapter. "There," he pointed, "verse nine."

And there it was: "Our Father which art in heaven, hallowed be Thy name," she read. Beside her, not looking at the page, Miles joined in: "Thy kingdom come, Thy will be done in earth, as it is in heaven . . ."

When they had finished reciting, William Tyndale was smiling. "You know it by heart," he said gently. "That is good, very good. My dear young people, hide

God's Word in your heart where it can never be taken away from you."

Their lesson that day was from Matthew twenty-five. First it was Miles's turn to read, which he did in his deepening man's voice:

> "I was hungry and ye gave me meat; I was thirsty, and ye gave me drink; I was a stranger, and ye took me in; naked, and ye clothed me; I was sick, and ye visited me; I was in prison and ye came unto me . . ."

"Who is it talking about?" Sarah interrupted. She knew she asked too many questions, but how else could she understand?

"When the Lord Jesus returns in His glory, this is what He will say to those who will inherit the kingdom of heaven. He is talking to you and me."

"But . . . we never did those things for Jesus. How could we?" Sarah felt dismayed. The Bible was so hard to understand!

"Ah. But read here," Tyndale pointed. So Sarah picked up where Miles had left off.

> "Inasmuch as ye have done it unto one of the least of these my brethren, ye have done it unto me."

"Do you see?" said Master Tyndale. "When we feed the hungry and visit the poor souls in prison, it is just as if we are doing it for Jesus himself."

"Then," said Miles thoughtfully, "it is not enough to know what God's Word says, we must *do* as it says."

Master Tyndale smiled broadly. "Exactly." He went over to the window and looked out over Antwerp's rooftops. "There are many poor souls out there who need the love of God," he mused. Then he turned back to Miles and Sarah. "I have an idea. How would the two of you like to go with me next Saturday as part of your lesson?"

"Where?" Sarah felt an odd excitement.

"You'll see. Now," he said, clapping his hands, "that's enough Bible study. Let's talk about geography. We have a whole new world map since Christopher Columbus discovered America in 1492—the same year I was born; that's how I remember it. . . ."

Sarah suspected that Papa had had to overrule Mama's objections to the Saturday outing. But she didn't care. She was just glad to be tramping through the narrow Antwerp streets with Miles and Master Tyndale, tugging her warm cloak tighter against April's chilly air. Belgium's damp winter had not yet given way to the warmth of spring.

"We're heading for the riverfront, aren't we, Master Tyndale?" she guessed after a few twists and turns.

He chuckled. "You're right, Miss Sarah."

Indeed, they were heading for the Schelde River on the north side of Antwerp, the largest and busiest port in Belgium. The river port was only fifty miles from where the Schelde flowed into the sea. To the south of the river's mouth lay the English Channel; to the north was the North Sea.

The trio turned into the narrow street that stretched alongside the docks. The sight of the big three-masted ships straining at their ropes never failed to take Sarah's breath away. Her father's ships—the *Red Queen* and the *Black Princess*—were out on buying trips to Spain, Italy, and northern Africa, and would come back laden with olives, almonds, cheese, grapes, and cut marble.

A tall Englishman wearing a red cloak seemed about to hail them, but Master Tyndale marched steadily past the docks and entered the maze of dense buildings and alleys at the far end. As they passed a baker's shop, he purchased four loaves of bread and gave them to Miles and Sarah to carry.

Two of the loaves were given to a young woman who came to the door of a shabby apartment with three youngsters pulling on her skirt. "Oh, thank'ee, Master Tyndale," she said. "I don't know when me Harry will return from sea. It gets mighty meager when he's away."

Sarah thought she saw the man with the red cloak following behind them. But her attention was distracted by Master Tyndale who was giving the third loaf of bread to an untidy man leaning unsteadily against a building and smelling like liquor. "Get yourself home, my dear man," Tyndale said firmly. "Take this bread to your wife. It may serve to

49

redeem your poor excuses of what has happened to your money."

A short way further, Master Tyndale went down a short flight of steps and knocked on a dingy door. Even though there was no answer, he lifted the latch and pushed the door open. When Sarah's eyes adjusted to the gloom, she saw an old woman hunched in a bed in the corner.

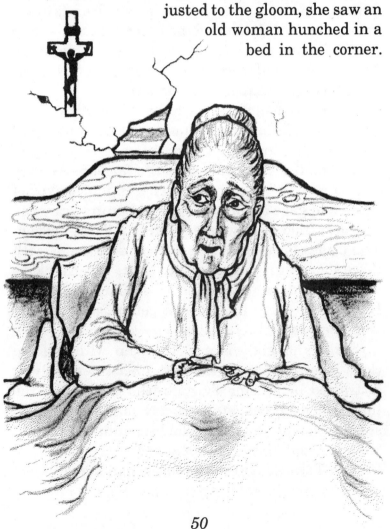

Instantly, Sarah's excitement seemed to drain away.

"Mistress Gilly," Tyndale said cheerfully in Dutch. "You have visitors today." He looked around for a candle, lit it from the not-quite-dead coals in the hearth and soon a soft glow eased the darkness. The old woman smiled wordlessly and clutched Tyndale's sleeve.

Master Tyndale patted the old gnarled hand as he looked around. "Miles," he ordered in a low voice, "build up that fire in the hearth and fetch some water to heat for bathing and tea. Sarah, see if you can sweep up and put some order to the room."

"Can't build a fire without tinder," muttered Miles. But he rummaged some sticks and lumps of coal from the corner, got a blaze going, then disappeared with a pot to find a rain barrel, which the poor often used to collect water.

Sarah found a broom—just old straw that was bound clumsily to a stick—with which she attempted to sweep. In the meantime, Master Tyndale was gently removing the woman's soiled garment and bedding. He rolled the stinking cloths into a bundle, bounded out the door and was back within ten minutes with a fresh bundle.

"See here, Mistress Gilly," he said cheerfully as he rolled the old lady gently from side to side, slipping the clean bedding beneath her, "Mrs. Leerdon did the laundry, just as she promised."

Not for nothing, I'll bet, thought Sarah.

Miles returned with the water and hung the pot over the fire to heat. After a few minutes Master

Tyndale dipped out some of the lukewarm water and gently bathed the old woman's thin body. Miles looked away discreetly, but Sarah helped dry the flabby skin.

Soon the old woman was propped up, wearing a fresh garment, drinking tea, and eating some of the soft bread as best she could with the few teeth she had. As she ate, Tyndale took a Testament from his pouch and read to her, translating into the Dutch language as he went along. Tears glittered in Mrs. Gilly's eyes and the pinched smile never left her face.

"Now, my young friends," said Tyndale, "we must go. But, Mistress Gilly, we will come again." On impulse, Sarah gave the old lady a quick hug. Miles stirred down the fire so it would make good coals, then shut the door behind them.

Sarah pulled her cloak around her once more against the chill as they climbed up the few stairs to the narrow alley. She was still thinking about Mrs. Gilly, and didn't see the stranger who stood in the shadows, not until he spoke.

"William Tyndale, I believe?"

Master Tyndale stopped short and Sarah ran into him. Tyndale half turned and with his arm kept Sarah and Miles behind him. But she peeked under his arm and saw the well-dressed Englishman in the red cloak. He was smiling, but a shiver of fear made her feel cold under her wraps.

Chapter 6

The Stranger

"THE NAME IS HENRY PHILLIPS," the man said, lifting his hat in greeting. He was cleanshaven and handsome. "I am a student at the university. I have often heard of your amazing work and have been eager to meet you."

"Yes?" said Tyndale cautiously. "What is it you want?"

"Simply to meet you, and talk. I have long felt frustrated with the Catholic Church, its petty squabbles and meaningless rituals. But until I heard about your efforts to put the Scriptures into the hands of the common people, I felt there was no one I could talk to about the desperate need for reform."

The man fell into step with Tyndale, and Miles and Sarah followed close behind, looking at each other uneasily. They could hear snatches of the conversation, with the man who called himself Henry Phillips doing most of the talking.

". . . was a student at Oxford—yes, your own school . . . unfortunately, I had a quarrel with my father . . . You have heard of Richard Phillips? Yes, he was a member of parliament . . . I decided to pursue a degree in law here in Belgium . . . heard you were in Antwerp . . . am intrigued by the German reformer, Martin Luther, and his ideas of salvation by faith alone and would like to discuss . . ."

The little party had retraced their steps along the riverfront and were turning toward the heart of the city when Tyndale stopped.

"My dear sir," he said to the man in the red cloak, "I am a guest in someone else's house. I would invite you to supper but I cannot presume on my host's hospitality. Perhaps we can meet again."

"By all means," said Henry Phillips graciously. "Ask for me at the Boar's Head Inn. That is where I stay when I am not at the university." He tipped his fine velvet hat to the two young people and walked quickly away.

"Master Tyndale!" said Miles. "I thought for a moment that you were going to walk back to the

English Merchants boarding house with this Mr. Phillips in tow, giving away your hiding place!"

William Tyndale was thoughtful. "It may be as he said—he is sympathetic to my work."

"But no one has introduced him; all we have is his word!"

"I don't like him," Sarah blurted.

"And why is that?" Tyndale teased.

"I don't know. He was following us. I saw him earlier."

"Did you now?"

Everyone talked at once at the supper table. Sarah told her mother about Mrs. Gilly and asked if she could pack a basket with jellies and cakes to take along the next time. Miles told about meeting the man in the red cloak. William Tyndale said Miles and Sarah had made his visits to the poor easier, and seeing the young people had brought a smile to old Mrs. Gilly's face.

"A good lesson in practical Christianity!" said Mr. Poyntz. Then he stroked his short beard thoughtfully. "But I am not sure I trust this Henry Phillips, William."

Tyndale nodded patiently. "We can neither trust him nor mistrust him until we get to know him. If he is seeking God's truth, how can I turn my back on him?"

"Yes-s, but . . ."

"And haven't you said yourself, good Thomas, that the Scriptures in our own language will open the eyes not just of the peasant but the nobleman's son?"

"Well, yes . . ."

"But," Tyndale acknowledged, "it would be best to see for yourself. Will you give me permission to invite Henry Phillips for a meal? Then we can talk together."

The next Saturday Miles was busy helping Mr. Poyntz inventory the new shipments brought by the *Black Princess*. The *Red Queen* was still at sea. But Sarah once again accompanied Master Tyndale as he visited the riverfront slums, this time with a basket of goodies from the Poyntz pantry for old Mrs. Gilly. She also brought some rose-smelling soap, a clean towel, and fresh candles. The old lady was delighted to see her. With great difficulty she half-whispered, half-croaked her name: "Sarah."

On their way home, Tyndale located the Boar's Head Inn and left a message for Henry Phillips to dine with them the following Wednesday if he was in town.

Phillips showed up promptly at five on Wednesday at the English Merchants boarding house with a gift of exquisite Belgian lace for the lady of the house. Mrs. Poyntz was a bit flustered, but accepted the gift and invited Mr. Phillips into the parlor. Sarah hung around but soon grew bored with the conversation and was glad when a servant announced supper.

The table conversation was lively. Phillips showed a keen interest in the merchant business, giving Thomas Poyntz an opportunity to tell about his adventures. "We are planning a trip to the West Indies soon—a whole new market for trade, thanks to that Spanish adventurer, Christopher Columbus."

"I hear you have discovered a market for, well, many new things the English want," said Phillips.

Sarah nearly choked on her meat. Did he mean the New Testaments her father continued to smuggle?

But Thomas Poyntz just chuckled. "Oh, yes, we English seem to want every new thing that can be found."

Phillips entertained them with the latest gossip from London and the king's court. "And the king has a new child—a girl again. Elizabeth they call her."

Sarah's heart seemed to skip a beat. Anne Boleyn had a baby girl? What was she like, this princess? Did she have Anne's rich dark hair and saucy smile?

After supper, Tyndale showed Henry Phillips his translation work on the Old Testament. Phillips admired several books in Tyndale's small library. The talk drifted once again to the "Lutheran reforms" in Germany. . . . Sarah yawned and reluctantly went to bed.

Tyndale seemed to enjoy talking theology with young Phillips. The law student came several times to dinner, meeting some of the merchants who stayed at the boarding house, and quickly engaged them in discussing the need for reform in England.

Everyone seemed to like Henry Phillips—except Sarah. "He's too friendly," she complained to Miles one night after supper, sitting on the stairs while the adults continued their debates around the hearth in the parlor. Even though April's chill had given way to sunny May, evenings still begged for a fire. "He talks to everybody—except us."

"Aw, that's the way university students are," Miles said. "They think they're so important with all their learning. Don't mind Henry Phillips."

Miles wandered off to see if Cook had some leftovers to snitch, but Sarah just sat on the stairs feeling gloomy. She was still sitting in the semi-darkness when the double oak doors leading to the parlor opened and her father came into the hall with Henry Phillips.

"Thank you once again, Mr. Poyntz, for a fine evening," said Phillips, buckling his cape around his shoulders and settling the velvet hat on his head. Then he lowered his voice. "You do know that there is a price on Tyndale's head."

"Yes, I do."

"A man who values money might be tempted to turn him in."

"But God's damnation would rest upon his soul!" said Mr. Poyntz. "Thank you, Henry, for the warning, but we are well aware of the dangers. We will look out for William's safety."

Phillips cleared his throat. "Well! I'm glad of that! It puts my mind at ease. Once again . . . goodnight."

The door closed behind him, and once again Sarah was alone in the shadow of the stairs. Was Henry Phillips warning her father? Or testing him to see if he might be willing to betray Master Tyndale?

Henry Phillips was gone for several days, which was fine with Sarah. She worked hard on her Latin verbs and memorized the Ten Commandments. Pleased with her progress, she went looking for her father who was spending a few days at home before an extended business trip to the south. She found him sitting on the front stoop of the boarding house, enjoying the afternoon sun.

"Papa! Listen to me recite the Ten Commandments!" she coaxed, sitting beside him on the stoop.

"What? And disturb my afternoon nap?" he teased. "Oh, all right, let's hear them."

"Listen, now, Papa, and don't fall asleep. 'I am the Lord thy God . . . thou shalt have no other gods before me. Thou shalt not make unto thee any graven image . . .'"

She was on the ninth commandment, "'Thou shalt not bear false witness against thy neighbor,'" when a shadow fell across father and daughter.

"Excuse me," said the young man who stood with the sun at his back. "I didn't mean to startle you. I am Henry Phillips's servant, and he sent me to inquire if William Tyndale should be in today or tomorrow, as he would like to have lunch with him."

Mr. Poyntz stood. "Yes, I believe he is in. But I hope your master comes today, else I won't get to see him. I am leaving tomorrow on business in southern Belgium and will be gone for several weeks."

"I will tell him!" said the servant. "I am sure he will come as soon as he can."

But Henry Phillips did not arrive that day, and the next morning Thomas Poyntz and Miles left for the city of Barrows. It wasn't until the next day that Sarah answered a knock to find Henry Phillips upon the stoop.

"Good day, Miss Sarah!" said Phillips. "Is Master Tyndale in? I would like to repay his many kindnesses to me by taking him to lunch at the inn."

Sarah left him standing at the door and went running up the stairs to Tyndale's room. When she returned with Master Tyndale close behind, her mother was just inviting Mr. Phillips to stay for lunch.

"I appreciate the invitation, gentle lady," Phillips smiled warmly. "But I am determined to take your house guest to lunch at my expense—though your food would undoubtedly be better than that at the Boar's Head Inn! Ah, Master Tyndale! You are good to interrupt your work for a friend. How about it—will you allow me to take you to lunch? I don't have much time in the city today, but have several matters I would like to discuss with you."

"Why . . . that would be kind of you," Tyndale said. "Mrs. Poyntz? Will it upset your table if I absent myself?"

Mrs. Poyntz shook her head with a gracious smile and went off to supervise the servants in the day's tasks. Phillips and Tyndale took their leave and were disappearing into the first narrow street when Sarah made her decision.

She was going to follow them.

Chapter 7

The Ambush

EVEN THOUGH THE STREETS of Antwerp were narrow and the crowded buildings often kept out the sunshine, Sarah had no need for her cloak. The late May temperature was mild, and at high noon, the sun reached down to warm the cobblestones.

Sarah wasn't sure which way the two men had gone, but she remembered that Phillips had said something about the food at the Boar's Head Inn. She quickly set off for the riverfront along the familiar route Master Tyndale took when they went to see Mrs. Gilly.

As she turned into the first street beyond the boarding house she was rewarded; Phillips and Tyndale were just ahead. There was no hiding; she could only follow undetected if they didn't turn around.

Sarah managed to keep the two men in sight as they turned into first this street, then that. In some places the narrow streets became little more than dark alleys. Phillips and Tyndale turned into one such alley, so narrow that they couldn't walk side by

side. Sarah saw Master Tyndale politely motion
Phillips to go first, but the younger man insisted that
Tyndale go ahead.

When Sarah reached the alley, it took a while for
her eyes to adjust to the dark shadows. Up ahead she
could see the two men reach the far end which
opened up into a wider street. Suddenly she heard
Tyndale shout, "Phillips! Run! We have been seized!"

Sarah froze. What was happening? She heard
grunts and scuffling. Her heart
pounded, and she pressed
her back against the
alley wall. She
half-expected
Phillips to come
running back
toward her,

but his tall shape just stood silhouetted in the opening of the alley. Then she heard him say, "This is your man. Take him to Vilvoorde Prison!"

Prison? The word sent a cold shiver down Sarah's back. Her mind was spinning. Tyndale had been captured . . . Phillips had betrayed him!

Then she heard Phillips speak once more. "You, officer. Take two of your men and go to the English Merchants boarding house. Get Tyndale's books and papers."

Sarah didn't wait to hear more. She dashed back down the alley and out into the street. Her feet seemed to fly over the rough cobblestones. Into this street; up that alley. Would she make it in time? She had to get there first!

She rounded the corner of the boarding house just as the pain in her side began to grow intense. But she couldn't stop now. In the door and up the stairs she darted. One flight, two. Up one more to Tyndale's little room.

Bursting through the door, Sarah looked around wildly. Where was the oilskin packet? There, beside the table. She grabbed it up, fat with the pages of Tyndale's translation work. There were more papers on the table but she had no time! From the shelf she grabbed a copy of his English New Testament . . . but where was the copy of the five Old Testament books? Her heart was pounding so loud it sounded like footsteps on the stairs. There—on the stand beside the bed. She snatched it up, and with books and packet clutched to her chest, she flew back down the stairs, ran down the hall to her bed chamber, and slammed the door shut behind her.

She hardly had time to think, yet everything seemed to be happening in slow motion. Throwing back the coverlet of her bed, she arranged the packet and books side by side, smoothed back the cover, then threw herself down upon the bed.

Downstairs she heard pounding on the door and her mother's startled cry. Heavy footsteps ran up the stairs. She heard shouting and furniture crashing. Sarah squeezed her eyes shut: *Oh, God. Oh, Papa.* Then she heard her mother's voice protesting, "What are you doing? What's happening?"

The heavy boots clattered once more down the stairs. One flight, two, three. The door slammed, and all was quiet except for her mother's sobbing.

Sarah got up and opened her door. Her mother was sitting on the stairs crying, and the frightened servants were beginning to come out into the hall to comfort her. "Oh, Sarah!" cried out Mrs. Poyntz. "You're all right! I—I don't know what's happened. Those soldiers went right up to Master Tyndale's room and took all his papers and books. He—he went out with Mr. Phillips, and your father isn't here, and . . ." Her shoulders shook with new sobs.

Sarah went over to her mother, fighting back her own tears. "Mama," she said, sitting down on the stairs and feeling her mother's arms come around her. She had to swallow twice to get the words past the lump in her throat. "Master Tyndale's been captured—taken to Vilvoorde Prison. It was Henry Phillips. Phillips betrayed him!"

Mrs. Poyntz looked at her daughter in shock. "Mr. Phillips betrayed Master Tyndale?"

Sarah nodded, then took her mother's hand and led her to the bed chamber. "But see?" She threw back the coverlet, and there lay the oilskin packet and two bound books.

Thomas Poyntz and Cousin Miles arrived back home as quickly as they could after receiving the urgent message from his wife. Surveying the ransacked room, Mr. Poyntz was furious. "I should never have left! If I ever get my hands on Henry Phillips . . . Tyndale should never have brought that imbecile into this house! He was too trusting."

Miles sat stunned on the little bench in Tyndale's room watching Mr. Poyntz pace back and forth. "How dare the authorities lay a hand on this man!" Sarah's father fumed. "What right did they have? Who was Phillips working for?"

Mrs. Poyntz tried to calm her husband. "Come, Thomas, let's sit down and think what we are to do."

The little family gathered downstairs in the parlor. "Come, Sarah," said her father, "tell me specifically what happened." So once more Sarah told her father and Miles about following Master Tyndale and Henry Phillips as they went off to have lunch, coming to the dark alley, hearing Tyndale's cries and

Phillips' command to take him to Vilvoorde Prison. Then she told of her flight back to the boarding house to rescue his papers and printed Testaments.

Miles looked at her with open admiration in his eyes. "You did a wonderful thing, Sarah," he said.

"I was frightened!"

"Of course you were," Mr. Poyntz said, taking her hands in his. "Anyone would be. The important thing is, you acted when every second counted. I'm proud of you."

Sarah still worried. "But I didn't get the papers on the table. I don't know how much work was lost."

Her father nodded thoughtfully. "Maybe it was just as well. The soldiers think they got something. Maybe they don't know how much they *didn't* get!"

Mr. Poyntz sat quietly for a few minutes, rubbing his beard. "I must get in touch with all the English merchants in the Low Countries to write letters of protest to the government. This is an outrageous breach of our traditional privilege as merchants in a friendly country. And I must try to see William Tyndale at Vilvoorde. . . ." A cloud passed over his face. "What a disgusting, vile castle that is! How could they put such a gentle man in that dungeon?"

Weeks passed, and Thomas Poyntz wrote many letters. He rode the twenty-five miles to Vilvoorde Castle but wasn't permitted to see William Tyndale. Discouraged but determined, he visited all the officials he could think of who might have influence to release Tyndale. Each effort was rejected. The Emperor of the Low Countries, which included Belgium, was turning against anyone with "reformation" sympathies. England's King Henry VIII, after declaring himself "head of the Church" in order to make his divorce legal, was now trying to prove he was still a "good Catholic." So, the Church's "enemies" were his enemies, too.

May turned into June, but the Poyntz family barely noticed. Fearing that Tyndale's unfinished translation of the Old Testament might never be published, Thomas Poyntz took the oilskin packet Sarah had rescued and disappeared for a few days. When he returned, he no longer had the packet, and all he would say was that he had passed it along to friends for safekeeping.

"The less you know, the safer you are," he said.

"I'm worried about your father," Miles said to Sarah as they sat together on the bench in Tyndale's room, which they often did now. "He is letting his merchant business go; all he does is try to get Master Tyndale released."

"I know." Nothing her father did seemed to work. Even Humphrey Monmouth, the portly merchant who was Thomas Poyntz's closest friend and ally, couldn't cheer him up. Just last night she had heard them talking in the parlor.

"If Tyndale is executed, it will greatly hinder the Gospel," her father told Humphrey. "His scholarship and good name are outstanding! The king never had a more loyal subject, except in one thing—Tyndale believes the Bible must be in the language of the people."

"I agree, dear Thomas," Humphrey had said. "But you are driving yourself beyond reason. You can't tackle the whole British Empire single-handedly. You must give some attention to your work. You have a wife and child to care for."

Her father sighed. "You are right, Humphrey. But there must be *something* we can do—something we have not thought of yet. If only King Henry could read a copy of the English Bible! He might be persuaded it is not 'heresy' but would benefit the people. Then the charges against Tyndale could be dropped."

Now as Sarah sat on the bench with Miles, an idea began to dance about in her mind. When she told her cousin her idea, he looked at her as if she were crazy. "You've got to be out of your mind, Sarah! Only a fool would do such a thing!" Seeing her hurt look, he softened his words. "It's just that . . . it would be dangerous, Sarah."

"But I want to ask Papa anyway. Will you come with me?"

Miles sighed. "If you insist. But I still think it's a crazy idea."

Sarah went to her bed chamber and opened the wooden chest where she kept her treasures. She took out the letter from Queen Anne and Tyndale's copy of the English New Testament. With Miles following, she hunted up her father who was sitting at a writing desk doing accounts. Her mother sat at a nearby window sewing.

Sarah cleared her throat. "Papa, I have something to say." She laid the letter and the New Testament on the writing desk.

"What is this, Sarah?" Thomas Poyntz glanced at the letter. "You know we have refused Anne Boleyn's request."

"I know, Papa. But just listen to me. You have tried everything to get Master Tyndale released. Last night you told Humphrey Monmouth that if King Henry could read a copy of the Bible in English, then he might see for himself that it isn't heretical." Sarah took a deep breath. "If I accepted Queen Anne's invitation to be a maid-in-waiting, I could take this copy of the New Testament and give it to her. *She* would surely show it to King Henry."

Mrs. Poyntz had come to stand beside her husband. A wordless fear was etched in her face.

"No!" said Mr. Poyntz. "I can't let you do that, Sarah. It's too dangerous."

Mrs. Poyntz laid a hand on her husband's arm. When she spoke her voice sounded strange, even faraway. "Thomas, Sarah's right. It's the only way."

Chapter 8

The Storm

THOMAS POYNTZ AND HIS WIFE talked about Sarah's idea for two days. Back and forth they went. But finally they agreed: Sarah could go. When her parents announced their decision, Sarah didn't know if the goose bumps on her arms were excitement or fear.

A letter was sent by messenger to Whitehall Palace in London. One week went by, two . . . But in the third week, a letter returned from Queen Anne. Sarah could come at once.

But there were many things to do to get ready. Who should go with Sarah? Mrs. Poyntz often became ill traveling by sea. Thomas had been cautioned by the other merchants to lie low for a while after his many attempts to speak to the authorities on Tyndale's behalf. It was finally decided that Miles should go with Sarah and accompany her to the palace. Thomas Poyntz informed his captain that the two young people would go on the next scheduled voyage of the *Red Queen*, along with a cargo of olives, wheat, and Belgian lace for the English market.

Mrs. Poyntz hired a seamstress, and the two of them sewed for days so that Sarah could have crisp new undergarments, a traveling outfit, and two new gowns. The traveling dress was a rich green, but simple in style. The other two dresses had the low square neckline common among English ladies, plus a split skirt from waist to hem in front revealing the wonderful embroidery on the underskirt. On one, the sleeves were split in the current fashion to show the puffed undersleeve, gathered with ribbon at several points down the arm. On the other, the sleeve was long and loose, with embroidery all around the wide cuff.

A new cloak and several new caps, including a fashionable "gable" headdress, completed Sarah's new wardrobe. When she tried on the new clothes, Cousin Miles gave a long whistle. "Queen Anne won't even recognize you as the same girl who jumped in the creek after her!"

Miles and Sarah took Mrs. Poyntz to visit Mrs. Gilly. A tear slid down the old lady's face when she heard that Sarah was going away. "I will see to Mrs. Gilly," Sarah's mother said when they got home. "It's one thing I can do to carry on Master Tyndale's work."

"Oh, thank you, Mama," Sarah said, throwing her arms around her mother. She knew it wasn't an easy promise for her mother to make, since Mrs. Poyntz did not feel at home in Antwerp and in the English Merchants boarding house.

There was one last thing that had to be done. Mrs. Poyntz made a pocket on the inside of Sarah's petticoat, where the fullness of the skirt at the hip would hide the bulk of the New Testament Sarah was smuggling into King Henry's court.

The day of the voyage was cloudy and gray. It was high summer, but Belgium's climate was mild and moist. The tide was in and the *Red Queen* rode low in the water as the last of the cargo was stored in her hold. Poyntz had decided that no other New Testaments should be smuggled on this trip; if searchers came aboard they would find nothing and would be more likely to leave Sarah and Miles alone.

Cargo ships had only a few cabins—one for the captain and one or two for passengers. The crew bunked wherever they could. Mr. Poyntz brought Sarah's trunk and traveling bag below deck to the tiny cabin reserved for passengers; Miles bunked with the crew.

Mrs. Poyntz set a basket of food on the small table wedged into the cabin. "The crew may be able to eat the ship's fare, but it isn't very appetizing," she whispered in Sarah's ear as she gave her a hug.

"Tide's going out, Uncle Thomas," said Miles, appearing at the cabin door. "Captain says all ashore."

On deck Mr. Poyntz gave Miles last-minute instructions for dispersing the cargo at the London docks. "Cooperate in all ways with the authorities. You don't want any unnecessary attention. But your main responsibility is to get Sarah safely to Whitehall Palace and into the care of Queen Anne. Here is Anne's letter to serve as your introduction."

All too soon the goodbyes had been said and Sarah's parents stood down on the dock. The ropes were cast off, and as the small sails on the bow and at the top of the foremast were loosed, the ship moved out into the Schelde River to ride with the tide. Sarah was on her way to become a maid-in-waiting to Queen Anne of England, and there was no turning back.

The wind was light, and the *Red Queen* moved slowly down the river channel toward the sea. Traveling at five knots, the fifty-mile trip to the mouth of the river took most of the day. The overcast sky was growing dark when the shore shrank back and the river merged with the North Sea.

Sarah and Miles stood near the stern watching the Low Countries retreat behind them. All the sails had been loosed and stood out full from the three tall masts. Sarah shivered and pulled her warm cloak closer about her as the ship leaned with the wind. Her hair was damp from the spraying mist and escaped in moist curls from the cap she wore.

Miles gripped the bulwark. "This is a crazy idea, Sarah," he said, squinting against the wind and

mist. "But I can't bear the thought of Master Tyndale just sitting in that dungeon—or worse. So I'm hoping your crazy idea works."

Sarah had her own doubts. It had seemed like an adventure at first, but as the land disappeared in the fog and darkness, she suddenly wanted to be back home with her mother and father around the parlor fire.

The waves seemed to be getting higher, and Miles and Sarah had to hold tight to the bulwark to keep their balance. Suddenly a voice startled the two cousins. "Miss Sarah!" A ship's crewman was at their side. "A storm is rising fast. The captain says to get below."

Miles helped Sarah down the steps to the lower deck, then went off to see if he was needed to help batten down the ship against the storm. The lantern was swinging from its hook in her cabin and Sarah wondered if she should blow out the candle, but its small light was comforting. She decided against getting into her nightgown and just lay down on her berth. She could feel the hard lump of the New Testament sewn into her clothes and squirmed until she wasn't lying on it.

It had been a long day, and Sarah soon fell asleep to the creak of the ship and the whine of the wind.

The next thing she knew, Sarah was flying through the air. Her head knocked against something hard, and it took a minute or two before she realized she'd been thrown out of her berth and had hit her head on the table leg. The cabin was dark; her candle had gone out. The ship was pitching wildly, first to the left, then to the right as if it were hitting the waves broadside. She thought she could hear shouts somewhere, but they were drowned out by the high-pitched howling of the wind and the loud groans of the ship.

Holding on to the table leg, Sarah pulled herself up and crawled back onto her berth. But there was no sleep now. She had to hold on just to keep from being pitched to the floor again. What was happening? Was Miles all right?

Suddenly the small porthole burst open and a rush of water poured into her cabin. Sarah tried to push it closed again, but it was wrenched out of her hands again and again, water pouring in each time. And then abruptly the *Red Queen* turned, lifting Sarah's side of the ship into the air and away from the waves; Sarah slammed the porthole and twisted the latch just seconds before the ship righted itself.

Sarah was soaked; so was her bedding. Holding on to the table, she opened her cabin door and looked out into the passageway. There was no one in sight. Bracing herself, she made her way toward the steps leading to the deck and crawled up toward the hatch.

Sarah lifted her head above the deck. Her heart nearly stopped. A huge wave broke over the bow of the ship, sweeping a sailor off his feet. As she watched in terror, the man slid helplessly toward the side, then was catapulted into the raging darkness.

She opened her mouth to scream, "Man overboard!" but the wave reached the hatch and poured through the opening, knocking her down the steps.

Just then a dark form tumbled through the hatch and nearly fell on top of her. She couldn't see who it was in the dark, but an unfamiliar voice cursed. Then the voice snarled, "Get back in your cabin, girl! Come on!"

"But a man . . ." she spluttered as strong hands pulled her up and roughly pushed her back into her cabin. "A man just fell overboard!" she cried. But the sailor pulled her door shut muttering, "Passengers! Ain't no place for passengers on a cargo ship." A key clicked loudly in the latch.

Sarah lunged back to the door. Locked. *What if . . . what if it was Miles who had been knocked overboard?* She pounded on it with her fists. "Let me out! Let me out!" But the sailor was gone. Frightened, Sarah returned to her berth shivering. Pulling her knees up under her chin, she held on tight to a post. Twice she returned to the door, pounding on it, but it was indeed locked. Finally, back on her berth she laid her head down on her knees and cried. And there she sat throughout the terrible night. Sometimes sleep overtook her, only for her to be jerked awake by the pitching of the ship.

Then someone was shaking her. "Sarah? Sarah, are you all right?"

She opened her eyes and looked into Miles's face.

"Oh, Miles!" she cried, throwing her arms around his neck. "I was afraid you . . . I saw a man go overboard!"

"I know," said Miles soberly. "A new man . . . he didn't answer roll call when the captain took count after the storm."

"The storm is over?" Sarah untangled herself and stretched her cramped legs. Then she realized the sun was streaming in through the little porthole.

Miles laughed ruefully. "Yes, just before dawn. But you look like a bit of wreckage yourself."

With the storm over and Miles safe, Sarah realized she was famished. She dug out Mama's basket of food. The bread was soggy, but the cheese and salted meat were still good. As the cousins sat on the floor of the tiny cabin and ate ravenously, Miles told what had happened during the night. One of the mainsails hung tattered and useless, but the *Red Queen* had hung tight in the storm and none of the cargo had to be dumped.

"But a man was lost," she said slowly. "His poor family." She remembered Master Tyndale bringing bread to the mother in Antwerp with three youngsters hanging on her skirts, waiting for their papa to come home from sea.

"What about the New Testament?" Miles asked. "Is it safe?"

The Testament! Sarah pulled up her skirts until she found the pocket sewn in her petticoat. She pulled out Tyndale's New Testament, slightly damp but otherwise all right. "Oh," she said weakly. "I better wrap it in some oilcloth to keep it dry from now on."

"Just in case you fall overboard, right?" Miles grinned.

The sun was warm and the wind brisk all that day, and the *Red Queen* made good time in spite of the useless sail. They were only five hours behind schedule as they sailed into the mouth of the Thames River that afternoon. Sarah's clothes had dried out, and she had tidied up as best she could. Now she stood on deck watching all the other ships, like a forest of tall masts. As they neared London, she could see the spires of St. Paul's Cathedral thrusting into the sky.

The *Red Queen* finally nosed into the dock near London Bridge in the heart of the city, and for a while there was a flurry of activity as ropes were thrown and dock hands tied her down. Then amid all the hubbub, a shout boomed out.

"Ahoy, Red Queen!"

Sarah saw several soldiers looking up from the dock and shouting.

"No one is to leave the ship! Stand by to be boarded!"

"Uh, oh," muttered Miles in her ear. "King's men. They're going to search for smuggled goods!"

Chapter 9

The Search

SARAH'S MOUTH WENT DRY. She was suddenly very aware of the weight of the small book sewn into her petticoat. What would happen if they found the New Testament she was smuggling into England?

The searchers came aboard, herded both crew and passengers onto the deck and posted a guard while several others went below.

"What is the meaning of this?" demanded the ship's captain. "We are a licensed English merchant ship."

"Who is the owner?" barked one of the soldiers who stayed on deck. He seemed to be in charge.

"Thomas Poyntz, Antwerp, Belgium," Miles spoke up. "I am Miles Walsh, his assistant."

The soldier smirked. "A bit young, aren't you? And who is this?" He jerked a thumb at Sarah.

"This is Miss Sarah Poyntz, daughter of Mr. Poyntz."

"Hmmm." The man looked at Sarah and Miles for a long moment.

"I repeat, what is the meaning of this?" the captain said.

The soldier turned to the captain impatiently. "We have heard on good authority that this ship is smuggling heretical books."

"Preposterous!" said the captain. "I demand—"

"You'll demand nothing! We will see for ourselves whether your 'cargo' matches your shipping list."

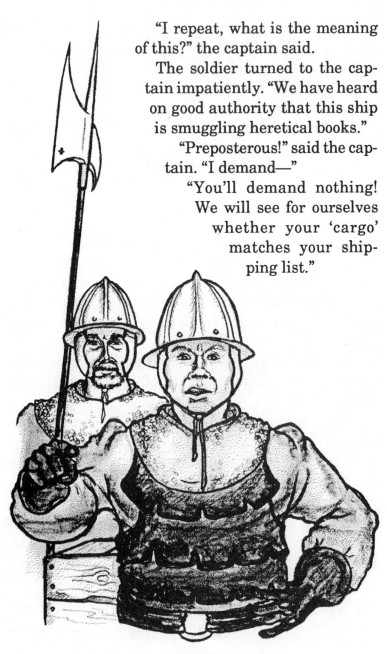

Sarah and Miles exchanged glances. On good authority? Did Henry Phillips also betray her father?

Just then the other searchers came back up on deck. "Didn't find a thing," said one.

"Then get this ship unloaded! We'll check the cargo on the dock."

Sarah saw Miles about to speak. The plan had been to hire a carriage and take her to the palace, then return to supervise the unloading of the *Red Queen*'s cargo. But instead Miles said, "Of course. Whatever we can do to assist. You will soon see this is all a mistake."

The searcher ignored him. "You, Captain, take Master Walsh and the young lady here off the ship and wait on the dock. Guard, don't let them out of your sight."

"But what about Miss Sarah's luggage, sir?" the captain protested. "It's still in her cabin."

"No one goes below! We'll see to the bags."

The captain, Miles, and Sarah stood on the dock and watched as the cargo was unloaded. The searchers selected certain crates, barrels, and bundles at random to be opened and the contents searched for smuggled books.

"This is going to take all night," Miles muttered.

Sarah watched the search, a feeling of dread growing in her stomach. If they didn't find the books in the cargo, would she be searched?

Just then the soldier in charge brought her bags. She could tell the contents had been dumped out and then stuffed back in. She blinked back the tears that sprang to her eyes.

"Sir!" said Miles suddenly. "I must beg your leave. Miss Poyntz is on her way to Whitehall Palace at the request of Queen Anne. The queen will be upset if this unnecessary search delays her arrival."

The man hesitated. "A likely story," he growled.

Miles drew Anne Boleyn's letter from his pouch. "Here."

Sarah held her breath while the soldier scowled at the letter in the fading light; dusk was settling over the waterfront. Abruptly he shoved the letter back at Miles.

"She may go."

"I must beg your leave to go with her," said Miles.

"No! Oh . . . all right. But you must return immediately. The *Red Queen*'s cargo is impounded until we clear it."

"Of course," murmured Miles, grabbing Sarah's bags and hustling Sarah off the dock toward the hired cabs.

Not until they were in a carriage heading for Whitehall Palace did Sarah finally relax. And then she began to laugh. "Oh, Miles, you were wonderful!"

"Should have thought of that in the first place," he said.

"I must look a sight!" Sarah groaned. "And all my things are a mess."

The carriage horse clipped along at a good pace, twisting and turning through the narrow streets which followed the Thames River toward the west end of London. Darkness had fallen over the city when the cabby finally reined in his lively horses and called out, "Whitehall Palace."

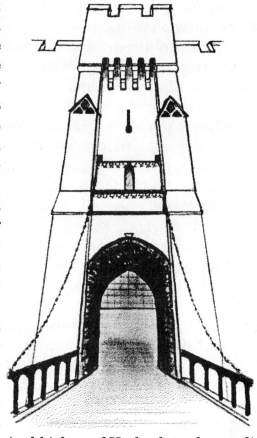

Miles asked the cab driver to wait, and approached the guards at the walled gate. Sarah craned her neck, staring in fascination at the magnificent house which had once belonged to the Archbishop of York, then the cardinal. The cardinal had fallen out of favor with the king, and the king had taken over the palace for his own use.

"Sarah? Come on!"

With a start Sarah realized the guard had opened the gate and was leading them toward the immense carved doors. They had to show the letter to the guards at two sets of doors before Sarah and Miles were standing in the outer court and a servant was sent to inform the queen.

After about fifteen minutes, the servant returned and motioned Sarah and Miles to follow him. Two more sets of doormen and they were in the inner court. After another wait, a stout gentlewoman swept grandly into the room. "I am Mrs. Stoner, the chaperone for the unmarried maids-in-waiting," the lady said. "The queen is expecting you, Sarah. We thank you, Master Walsh, for escorting your cousin."

Miles looked uneasy.

"I'll be all right, Miles," Sarah said, smiling at him with more confidence than she felt. She laid a hand on his arm. "God be with you."

"And with you," Miles said; his voice sounded strained. He bowed to Mrs. Stoner and turned to go. Then he turned back and drew Sarah aside. "Sarah," he said, "after I get things taken care of at the docks, I am going to visit my parents at Little Sodbury Manor. If you need to contact me in the next few weeks, just send a message. I'll try to see you before I return to Antwerp." He then followed the servant, and the immense doors closed behind them.

"Come now, Sarah," Mrs. Stoner said briskly. "Queen Anne is waiting for you."

Mrs. Stoner led the way up a curving stairway, through several passages and up another stairway. A servant carrying her bags followed. Rich drapes hung at every window; the floors were inlaid marble in wonderful designs. After the first few twists and turns, Sarah realized she could never find her way back the way they'd come. She had never imagined such a big house.

And then Mrs. Stoner stopped before a vaulted door and knocked. A woman servant opened it, and Mrs. Stoner and Sarah entered. Anne Boleyn was sitting on a lounge in a white dressing gown; her long dark hair hanging loose about her shoulders was being brushed by a young woman.

"Sarah! Dear Sarah!" Anne cried, jumping up and coming toward the young girl with her arms outstretched.

Suddenly Sarah felt very strange. The room was very warm; her head felt light. There were bright candles everywhere, yet everything was getting dim. The walls seemed to tip; the floor rushed up at her. Then everything went dark.

Chapter 10

The Maid-in-Waiting

SARAH OPENED HER EYES. Anxious faces stared down at her. Where was she? What happened?

Then she heard a familiar voice. "Sarah? Are you all right? Are you sick?"

Sarah sat up and shook her head, trying to clear the fogginess. Now she remembered. She had come to Whitehall Palace and . . . Oh, no. She must have fainted.

Several pairs of hands helped her up and led her to a lounge chair. Sarah smiled weakly. "I'm really all right. Please forgive me. I—I haven't eaten for several hours and it's been a long journey."

Suddenly she realized with horror that she was in the presence of the Queen of England—and she hadn't even curtsied! She was about to jump up when Queen Anne laid a firm hand on her shoulder. "It's all right, Sarah," the queen said with an amused smile. "You're the first person who's ever fallen at my feet!" And then she laughed that charming laugh Sarah remembered from years before. Mrs. Stoner chuckled, and even the servants smiled.

Anne Boleyn personally escorted Sarah to a small chamber down the passageway from her own rooms. "We can talk tomorrow," she said with her arm around Sarah's waist. "But right now, you need a good night's sleep!" A warm supper was brought; Sarah's clothes were shaken out and hung in the lovely tall wardrobe. A servant brought warm water so she could wash and then she crawled into the big soft bed with curtains draped from the big canopy. As she closed her eyes, Sarah realized that her journey was over . . . but the real adventure had just begun.

The next morning Queen Anne sent for Sarah and they went walking in the private garden behind the palace. Several ladies-in-waiting walked behind at a discreet distance. Sarah told Anne about the storm at sea, her fear that Cousin Miles had been swept overboard, and the searchers ransacking the ship at the London docks looking for "heretical" books.

"But why?" Queen Anne frowned. Sarah hesitated. She knew Anne was a friend, but she didn't know whether she dared say that her father had been smuggling Tyndale's English New Testament into England—at least not yet. But Anne didn't seem to be expecting an answer. "Well! I can see why a young lady might faint dead away after a harrowing night on the sea and soldiers searching through all your luggage. I'm so sorry, Sarah Poyntz! I had no idea—"

They were interrupted by a group of ladies-in-waiting and servants, one of whom was carrying a young child of about two years. Upon seeing Anne, the child held out her arms and crowed, "Mummy!" Queen Anne swooped up the child and said, "Sarah, meet Princess Elizabeth!"

Sarah had almost forgotten that Queen Anne and King Henry had a child! In a moment the princess wiggled out of Anne's arms saying, "Walk!" Elizabeth grasped one of Sarah's fingers as she toddled in the garden path, her nannies and the ladies-in-waiting hovering just behind. Sarah laughed; she had often wished for a little brother or sister.

"I hope you are not too tired," Anne said as they walked with Princess Elizabeth, "because we are having a masquerade tonight! King Henry is quite fond of parties and balls—and especially masks and disguises. Everyone in the palace attends, and many guests. Don't worry, we'll find something for you to wear."

The nannies soon whisked the princess away, and the rest of the day was spent preparing for the masked ball that evening in the Great Hall.

A gown of red and gold appeared in Anne's chamber, along with a Spanish tiara and veil. A servant helped her dress. "You look just like a grand Spanish lady!" the servant said approvingly. "But you need a mask; no one is supposed to know who you are."

The mask appeared mysteriously as well— a glittering red mask which just covered the top half of her face, sweeping out like wings on either side. Sarah joined the other ladies and maids in the Inner Court before going to the Great Hall. There was a "jester" with bells all over her gown, floppy cap, and shoes; an oriental "geisha" with powdered white face; even an "archbishop" in regal robes and towering hat. The other costumes seemed to be a chance to show off elegant gowns, topped with a mask on a stick so it could be held in front of the face.

Sarah gasped in admiration when Queen Anne appeared dressed as a Spanish bride in white gown, white mask and veil. Then it was time to go into the Great Hall. There were a great many lords and ladies, all disguised in strange and wonderful costumes. Sarah was nervous, but felt comforted by Mrs. Stoner's bulky presence at her side.

Musicians were playing but no one was dancing; everyone seemed to be waiting for something. Then there was a commotion by one of the great doors leading into the hall. A hunting horn sounded and a tall, broad man strode into the room followed by several other men. The big man wore green tights, a dark green tunic, a brown jerkin, and a black eye mask, with a pheasant feather in his cap. A quiver of arrows was strapped on his back and he carried a long bow. Several of the other men were dressed in similar fashion, except for one who was dressed as a monk.

A titter ran around the room, then clapping. "Robin Hood and his merry men!" shouted someone, and there was general shouting and laughter. "Hooray for the king!"

The king! Sarah stood on tip-toe trying to see. What a magnificent man. His legs were slender, but his shoulders were so broad he seemed to be two men standing together. He was throwing his head back and laughing with great guffaws, slapping some of the lords on the back and shouting, "Music! Let's dance!"

And then the hall was a swirl of noise and motion as the men and women danced. Sarah wanted to look everywhere at once. The king danced with Queen Anne—"Robin Hood" and the "Spanish bride"—and then they each danced with a dozen others. Two different young men bowed to Mrs. Stoner and requested a dance with Sarah, but the older woman just shook her head and stood protectively at Sarah's side. Sarah felt relieved; she was content tonight to just watch.

The masquerade was still going in full force when Mrs. Stoner escorted Sarah and several of the other young maids-in-waiting back to the private rooms.

Sarah was excited and not sure she could sleep. But a little worry nagged at the back of her mind: Would she ever get any time alone with Anne to give her the New Testament? Would Anne show it to the king?

One week went by, then two. Sarah was kept busy learning the ins and outs of court life. She had music lessons on the lute in the morning, reading lessons in French and Latin in the afternoon, prayers in the chapel, walks in the garden, visits with Princess Elizabeth, dinner parties lasting two or three hours. In between, Sarah was fitted for several new gowns to add to her wardrobe. However, except for the night of the masquerade, she did not see the king.

Sarah was getting anxious. Master Tyndale was sitting in prison; her family was counting on her getting Anne Boleyn's help. Every day she wore the petticoat with the special pocket and the little book. But there were always people around Queen Anne, helping her dress, attending her as she moved about the palace and grounds, serving her at meals. Several times a week the queen met with various lords and ladies and common folks, listening to their requests and pleas. Everyone wanted something from the queen.

Because Sarah could read and write, Anne began to dictate letters for her to write out, which were then sealed with the queen's seal and sent by messenger. At the end of one such writing session, Sarah grew bold. "Your Majesty, could I have a private word with you?"

Anne Boleyn lifted her eyebrows. "Why, yes, Sarah. How about this afternoon when we walk in the garden?"

Before going on her walk, Sarah took the New Testament out of her petticoat pocket and tucked it into the wide sleeve of her gown. And true to her word, Queen Anne asked her ladies-in-waiting and servants to withdraw and she sat with Sarah on a stone bench in the garden. "Did you wish to speak to me, Sarah?"

Sarah took a deep breath. "Do you remember the book that John Frith gave to you at Little Sodbury, the one written by William Tyndale?"

"Yes, of course. *Obedience of a Christian Man*. An excellent book."

"Did . . . did you show it to the king?"

Queen Anne laughed a little. "Oh, yes. He loved Tyndale's attack on the clergy who abuse their privileges. Especially when Tyndale wrote that the king should answer only to God for his actions, not to the pope."

Sarah's heart beat faster. "Then he approves of Tyndale's work?"

Queen Anne shook her head. "Well, not exactly. The king sent for Tyndale to come back to England and be his spokesman, but Tyndale refused. It seems Master Tyndale doesn't want to speak for the king, only for God. But this hurt the king's pride."

Voices could be heard coming toward them in the garden. Sarah didn't have much time. "Your Majesty, Master Tyndale has been put in prison—for printing the Scriptures in English!" She slipped the small book out of her sleeve. "I brought you a gift, a copy of the New Testament that Master Tyndale translated. I—I thought you might show it to the king. If the king likes it, then the charges against Master Tyndale might be dismissed."

Queen Anne looked at the New Testament, then at Sarah, eyes wide. "Tyndale's in prison for printing English Bibles . . . soldiers searched your father's ship, looking for illegal books . . . By God's heaven,

Sarah—don't you know you were risking your life to bring me this book?"

It was Sarah's turn to be startled. She hadn't really thought of it as risking her *life*; she had just been afraid the book would be found and taken away. But she had saved the New Testament from Henry Phillips' men; she had survived the storm and made it past the searchers. She couldn't stop now.

"Will you?" she asked again. "Will you read it and see for yourself that Tyndale has done nothing wrong? You're the only one who might influence the king!"

The nannies came into view with Princess Elizabeth. Queen Anne stood up, her face thoughtful. "Put it away, Sarah. But later this evening, bring it to me."

Chapter 11

The King's Gout

SARAH BROUGHT THE NEW TESTAMENT to Queen Anne's private rooms that evening. As she laid it in the queen's hands, she felt a sudden pang of sadness at letting it go. Memories danced in her mind: Master Tyndale helping her read Jesus' words from the Gospels . . . the mad flight ahead of the soldiers in Antwerp to snatch up the Testament from Tyndale's room . . . the weight of the book in her petticoat.

"Thank you, Sarah," Queen Anne said gently, seeing the tears in her eyes. "This is truly a gift."

As she lay in bed that night, Sarah was glad she had memorized several passages from the Testament, "hiding God's Word in your heart," as Master Tyndale had said.

"Our Father," she whispered into the darkness, "Who art in heaven, hallowed be Thy name . . ."

The very next day Anne sent for Sarah. The queen waved her servants out impatiently. When they were alone she exclaimed, "Sarah! I got very little sleep last night for reading your book! How precious to read the Word of God for myself. . . ."

Sarah watched as Queen Anne paced up and down her sitting room, brow furrowed. "To think that Master Tyndale rots in prison for opening up the Scriptures in our own language. . . . You are right, Sarah. The king must see this! It is the greatest gift he could give his people." Anne stopped by a window and stood quietly, thinking.

"But," she finally turned to Sarah, "it will not be easy. King Henry has many moods, and one never knows whether he will be generous and kind, or cranky and unreasonable. Sometimes it depends on whether his gout is causing his foot to pain him!" The queen sighed. "We have been married only two and a half years, and he is not entirely happy with me. You see, he wanted a son, an heir to the throne. . . ."

Unsure whether to respond, Sarah just listened as the queen continued to pace and think out loud. "He gets back from hunting today. . . . He is often tired but satisfied after a hunt. I will arrange a small dinner party for him as a welcome home. It's almost impossible to speak to him alone—all those grooms and gentlemen about. But, we'll just have to try."

Sarah did not see Queen Anne the rest of the day. But Mrs. Stoner brought word that Sarah was to eat with the queen that evening. Sarah's heart seemed to skip a beat. Did that mean eat with the king, too?

Mrs. Stoner brought one of the new gowns which had been made for Sarah—rosy velvet with long flowing sleeves—and helped her dress. She made Sarah practice her curtsy and fussed about royal manners: don't touch the king, don't speak unless spoken to, watch one of the ladies-in-waiting and do as she does. Sarah's hair was brushed back and bound to her head; then a gable headdress was placed carefully over her hair, framing her face.

Mrs. Stoner brought Sarah to Anne's private rooms, then the queen, Sarah, and three other ladies were escorted through a series of wide passageways and down a curving stairway to the king's rooms. The little company paused at a vaulted doorway.

King Henry was sprawled in a large chair, one foot resting on a stool. He was sipping a goblet of wine as several

99

gentlemen stood about.

Queen Anne swept toward her husband and curtsied. "My lord, I am glad to see that you are safely returned."

"Humph," growled the king. But he took one of Anne's hands and pressed it to his lips. "You are bewitching, as usual, dear wife—and your ladies are charming." He seemed to rise like a tidal wave from the chair, wincing slightly. "Come, come," he said impatiently. "Let's eat."

The king sat at the head of the table with the queen on his right; the ladies and maids-in-waiting were seated to the queen's right, the gentlemen to the king's left.

Sarah suddenly felt homesick. What was she doing here? How she would love to be sitting down to supper with her mother and father and Cousin Miles!

As steaming dishes appeared, Sarah felt overwhelmed by all the food. She ate tiny bites, not knowing how many courses would be served. She lost track after twelve.

The talk bantered about the hunt. Henry had bagged a small boar—not much bigger than a piglet—but the stags had been too swift. "The beasts live free on my own land," he grumbled half in jest. "They should have the decency to stand still long enough for my arrows to find their targets!"

The gentlemen laughed. "Ah, but Your Majesty," said one, "if a beast did not flee, you would probably say it was too lazy to be worth eating."

King Henry chuckled. "No doubt, no doubt." He drained his goblet of wine and shouted, "Cupbearer! More wine! Carver! Another slice of that boar!"

After supper, the king stood and belched. "Ladies, some music. Anything, anything." A servant appeared with several lutes and a flute. Sarah felt alarmed. *Play for the king?* She'd only had two weeks of lessons. But she took one of the stringed instruments and sat with the other ladies and maids-in-waiting around the music stand. Good, the piece was not too hard. One of the ladies began the melody on the flute; the lutes added harmony.

Over the music stand Sarah saw King Henry lean against the tall windows looking out into the twilight, holding his goblet and once again resting one foot on a footstool. Queen Anne went over and sat on the windowsill. Sarah could not hear what the royal couple were saying, but she saw Anne pull the New Testament from a velvet bag, open it and begin reading. Sarah lost her place and frantically searched the music. When she found it again, she glanced up to see the king's face gathered in a deep scowl.

"Enough!" he shouted over the music. The ladies stopped, but he was not looking at them. "Who does this Tyndale think he is! Have I not said we have no need for an English Bible at present? Have I changed my mind?" He kicked over the footstool and stood with his hands on his hips. "Someday! Someday! But it should be done by proper persons—great, learned, Catholic persons! Not some fugitive who ignores my invitations!" He limped toward the door, then suddenly whirled back toward his wife. "And who is polluting my own house with this traitor's nonsense? Get rid of him! And get rid of that book! I'll hear no more!"

The king stormed out, followed by his gentlemen who bowed apologetically to the queen. Still holding the New Testament, Queen Anne gathered up her skirts and hastened up the staircase and through the passages to her own apartments. Sarah and the other ladies followed close behind.

Once in her private chamber, the queen said to the ladies-in-waiting, "Please leave me alone." But in a few moments a servant came to Sarah's room with Anne's request that she return.

Queen Anne came right to the point. "Sarah, it breaks my heart, but . . . you must leave, and as soon as possible. You heard what happened tonight. If King Henry discovers that you are responsible for bringing Tyndale's New Testament into his own palace, you and your family will be in danger. And . . . ," the queen took a deep breath, "there are unfriendly eyes and ears everywhere in this palace. Someone may have seen or overheard us talk about this book— someone who could tell the king."

Sarah was stunned. It was all happening so fast. Couldn't Anne talk to the king again? Was this the end of her hopes? What would happen to Master Tyndale now? She lowered her eyes from Anne's intense gaze and her shoulders sagged.

Then she felt Queen Anne's fingers lift her chin. "Sarah, don't despair," the queen said gently. "I will keep the book and look for another opportunity to plead with the king. But for now, you must go."

Throwing royal manners aside, Sarah threw her arms around Anne's neck. Then she ran from the room, the tears hot on her cheeks.

Chapter 12

The Execution

A MESSAGE WAS PROMPTLY SENT from the palace to Little Sodbury Manor in Gloucestershire county. Miles and his parents came as quickly as they could, but because of the distance it was still several days before the Walsh carriage arrived at Whitehall Palace. Miles asked no questions, but was visibly relieved to walk with Sarah out of the palace gates.

Miles stayed in London to arrange for new cargo to be loaded on the *Red Queen*; Sir John and Lady Anne Walsh took Sarah home with them to Little Sodbury until the ship was ready to sail. It was good to see her cousin Johnny again—almost a grown man and called John now. While waiting to hear from Miles, Sarah walked with John through the woods to the stream which flowed through the manor lands. The old fallen tree still lay across the stream banks. "Strange," she said to John. "This is where everything started."

The Walshes took Sarah to London when Miles sent word that the *Red Queen* was ready to sail. The voyage across the North Sea and down the Schelde

River to Antwerp was uneventful; the breeze was stiff with a tinge of autumn in the air. It had only been a little more than a month since she had left her parents standing on the docks waving goodbye; but so much had happened, it seemed like a year.

As Sarah and her mother unpacked her clothes and hung the new gowns in her wardrobe, Sarah felt older, too. Nothing had changed since she left, and yet . . . everything was different.

Her first evening home, Miles and her parents listened carefully as she told what had happened at Whitehall Palace. When she was done, Mr. Poyntz patted Sarah's hand, but just sat quietly, stroking his beard thoughtfully.

Mrs. Poyntz broke the silence. "Queen Anne did the right thing to send you home. There was nothing more you could do, my child."

"Never did like the idea in the first place," Miles stated. "I'm just glad you're back."

Sarah gave Miles a small smile. But why didn't her father say something? Was he disappointed in her? They had all agreed that taking the English Testament to the king was a good idea. Hadn't her father tried everything else to get Master Tyndale released? But now . . .

Hot tears stung Sarah's eyes. Maybe it had been a foolish idea. Maybe she had just wanted to see Anne Boleyn again, and be her maid-in-waiting. Court life had seemed so exciting. But now the king was even more angry—not just at Master Tyndale, but at Queen Anne, too. Was it her fault? Anne had sent her away. What was going to happen? She didn't know!

Sarah buried her face in her hands. The pent-up feelings of the last few months seemed to roll up from somewhere inside and big gasping sobs shook her body. Then she felt her father's arms around her.

"Sarah, Sarah," he soothed, stroking her hair. "It's all right . . . it's all right. You did what you could; that's all any of us can do. All is in God's hands now."

A year passed. Thomas Poyntz was gone for weeks at a time, still making every effort to get Tyndale released. He left more and more of the decisions regarding buying and selling of goods in Miles's hands, but the business suffered from Thomas's inattention.

With her father and Miles often away, Sarah resumed her weekly visits to old Mrs. Gilly, accompanied by her mother. Mrs. Poyntz seemed to burn with a new passion to visit the poor, lonely souls in the slums who had once been cheered and comforted by Master Tyndale's presence. Mother and daughter baked bread, made soups and jellies, and sewed clothes to give to the needy crowded together in misery down by the docks. The list of those they visited seemed to grow each week. "It is something we can do to carry on Tyndale's work," Mrs. Poyntz often said.

Sarah and her mother were returning home from the docks one day in early August, when they saw two familiar horses tethered outside the English Merchants boarding house. "Thomas!" Mrs. Poyntz cried, bursting into the parlor. "I didn't know you were coming home today!"

Thomas Poyntz hugged his wife and daughter, but Sarah thought he suddenly looked old and tired.

"Thomas?" said her mother. "What's wrong?"

Mr. Poyntz sat down and sighed. "It's Master Tyndale. He has finally had a trial—after fifteen months shivering in that damp dungeon! They have condemned him as a heretic."

"No!" cried Mrs. Poyntz.

Sarah just stared at her father. This wasn't supposed to happen! Queen Anne had said she would talk to King Henry again. As long as there had been no trial, as long as Tyndale was alive, they had hoped.

"When?" asked her mother.

Mr. Poyntz ran his hands through his hair. "I'm not sure, but we must find out. Miles and I will go to his execution—to be witnesses to his death. He must not die alone."

Sarah swallowed. "I will go, too, Papa."

"No, Sarah. It is not easy to see a man die."

"I know," she said, her voice barely a whisper. "But he is my friend! If he sees me, he will know I have not forgotten him."

"Yes," said Mrs. Poyntz, tears running down her face. "We must all be witnesses."

The day of the execution in early October dawned dull and gray. Already the southern gate outside the town of Vilvoorde was crowded with onlookers. Thomas Poyntz, his wife, Sarah, and Miles tried to get close to the circle of posts that acted as a fence in the middle of the clearing. In the center of the circle was a large pillar of wood.

Several lawyers and clergy entered the clearing and seated themselves. Then Sarah heard Miles gasp. "It's Master Tyndale."

The prisoner was led into the clearing. He was very thin, his clothes threadbare and dirty. But William Tyndale gazed steadily around the crowd of common people. His eyes seemed to light up as he recognized first one, then another. Then his eyes rested on the Poyntz family and Miles Walsh, and a smile flickered on his tired face.

"William Tyndale, we ask you one last time: will you recant your heresy?" boomed a loud voice from the direction of the seated men. Tyndale said nothing, but continued to gaze out over the crowd.

The prisoner's feet were then bound to the stake, and piles of brush and logs heaped around him. An iron chain was fastened around his neck, and a rope noose settled around his throat. "Praise God," Sarah heard her father murmur, "he will be strangled and not burned alive." Sarah squeezed her eyes shut, but they flew open when she heard Tyndale's clear, strong voice.

"Lord!" Master Tyndale cried. "Open the eyes of the King of England!"

Then the executioner came up behind the stake and pulled with all his strength on the noose. The crowd gasped as Tyndale's head fell limply to his chest. Sarah felt Miles's arm tighten around her waist, catching her as her knees buckled.

"Stand, Sarah," Miles whispered in her ear. "We must stand for his sake."

A lighted torch was touched to the brush and the flames leaped around Tyndale's lifeless body. Only when the chain was released and the charred form fell into the flames did Thomas Poyntz turn and lead his family out of the crowd.

In the carriage on the way back to Antwerp, Sarah's eyes burned with unshed tears. What had Master Tyndale prayed? *Open the eyes of the King of England!*

It was too late for that. William Tyndale was dead.

She, Sarah Poyntz, had failed.

Chapter 13

The Victory

SARAH AND MRS. POYNTZ did not tell Mrs. Gilly that Master Tyndale was dead. Each time they visited, the old woman gripped their hands and with great difficulty whispered his name. "Master T'dale?"

"He is in a better place," Sarah said, once again changing the old woman's bedding and combing her hair. "He regrets he cannot visit you."

Mrs. Gilly nodded and seemed satisfied.

But it seemed harder to visit the smelly rooms and sad families in the slums along the docks after Tyndale's death. ". . . as you have done it for the poorest of my brothers," Sarah kept muttering to herself as she hauled water or held a squalling infant for a sick mother, "you have done it for Me."

She would have quit if it weren't for her mother. Mrs. Poyntz was not a strong woman, but she somehow managed to keep the boarding house going, as well as prepare food and do sewing and mending for Mrs. Gilly and others. Sarah knew she had to keep going as long as her mother wasn't giving up.

Belgium's rainy winter set in a few months after William Tyndale's death. One day, during a downpour, Thomas Poyntz and Miles arrived home from a business trip to England. No sooner had they walked in the door than they dumped their wet cloaks on the floor of the entrance hall and herded Mrs. Poyntz and Sarah into the parlor, shutting the door behind them.

"Thomas! What is it?" cried Mrs. Poyntz.

Mr. Poyntz took a package from his pack and unwrapped it. "Here," he said, handing it to Sarah. It was a book with a leather cover.

Holding the book, Sarah read the engraved title: "The Holy Bible." She looked up. "What is it, Papa?"

"The complete Bible in English!" her father said, excitement in his voice. "Do you remember the manuscript you saved from Tyndale's room, Sarah? And how I took it away secretly, and wouldn't tell you what I had done with it? Well, I sent it to a notable scholar at Oxford who is sympathetic to Tyndale's work, a man named Coverdale. He used Tyndale's manuscripts and completed the translation."

Sarah opened the cover to the title page. She looked up in dismay. "But . . . it says, 'Translated by Miles Coverdale'! After all the work Master Tyndale did—all he suffered in prison!"

Miles nodded. "I know. I thought the same thing at first. But if Master Tyndale were here, he would say it is not his name that is important, only that the people can read the Scriptures for themselves."

"And besides," interrupted Mr. Poyntz, "if Tyndale's name were on this book, it would surely be rejected by the king. But as it is . . ." And Thomas Poyntz threw back his head and laughed.

"Thomas! What are you laughing about?" demanded his wife.

"Come, come," said Mr. Poyntz, drawing his wife and daughter to sit by the fire. Miles leaned against the mantle grinning.

"As you know, my dear, business has been poor lately, so we went to London trying to find new agents. But this time there were no searchers snooping around; we breezed right through customs. We didn't know what to make of it."

"Then Uncle Thomas decided to go to Oxford University to see this Coverdale," Miles interrupted. "To see if he had been able to do anything with Tyndale's manuscripts."

"But we were hardly prepared for what happened!" Mr. Poyntz said. "Coverdale received us warmly and placed this book—the whole Bible in English—into our hands. Then he told us that King Henry himself had been given a copy!"

"And King Henry said, . . ." Miles deepened his voice and held his head haughtily. "'Well, if there be no heresies in it, let it be spread abroad among all the people!'"

Sarah stared. "He said *what*?"

"He said, 'Let all the people read it!' You heard me, you goose."

"Thomas, I can hardly believe this," said Mrs. Poyntz. "King Henry has given his permission to publish the Scriptures in English?"

Sarah's thoughts were all in a jumble. What was it that Tyndale had prayed just before he died? *Lord, open the eyes of the King of England!*

"God answered Master Tyndale's prayer," she said in awe.

"That's right, Sarah," said her father gently. "Not only that, but who knows how God opened his eyes? Maybe the New Testament you gave to Queen Anne was part of what God used to break down the king's defenses."

"But then . . . why did God let Master Tyndale die? It was all for nothing!"

"I think not," said her father. "Don't you see? Tyndale has won! They could kill him, but they couldn't kill his dream. Now every man, woman, and child in England can read God's Word for themselves—from the common plowboy to the king himself!"

"Then . . . Tyndale's work still goes on."

"And you helped make it happen." Miles gave Sarah a playful shove.

Sarah opened the Bible and gently turned its pages. "I never realized that God uses us to do His will—just like it says in the Lord's Prayer." She turned a few more pages and read . . .

"Thy kingdom come; Thy will be done,
In earth, as it is in heaven."

More About
William Tyndale

WILLIAM TYNDALE WAS BORN in the early 1490s near the Welsh border of England. Around the age of twenty, he went as a student to Magdalen College at Oxford, then on to Cambridge University. "Lutheran ideas" abounded at Cambridge in the early 1520s, so it is probable that Tyndale formed many of his Protestant convictions at this time.

Leaving the university in 1521, he joined the household of Sir John Walsh at Little Sodbury Manor in Gloucestershire county, apparently as a tutor to his two young sons; he may also have served as a chaplain for the Walsh household or as a secretary to Sir John.

The Walshes were well known for their hospitality to both nobility and clergy, and Tyndale engaged in many theological discussions around their table. He was shocked at the ignorance of Scripture displayed by the clerics, and to one he challenged, "If God grant me life, ere many years pass I will see that the boy behind the plow knows more of the Scriptures than thou dost!"

At that time the only English translation available was the hand-copied Wycliffe Bible (1380). Tyndale's passion grew to translate the Scriptures into the common language and have them printed mechanically, so that peasants and nobles alike could read God's Word for themselves. He accused the clergy of keeping the masses ignorant of what Scripture said to cover their own corruption and greed. For instance, selling "indulgences" (i.e., paying a fine to atone for one's sins) was making many clerics rich, and many had illegitimate "wives" and children.

It was not only his desire to translate the Bible that got Tyndale in trouble. He both preached and wrote that we are saved by faith alone, not by following the traditions of the Church; that God alone forgives sin and grants mercy; and that commoner and king alike are accountable only to God, not to the pope. He, along with other reformers, had many other so-called "heretical" ideas, including the belief that the elements of the Lord's Supper were not the physical presence of Jesus Christ, but symbols of His body and blood.

It was illegal at that time to translate the Scriptures into English without ecclesiastical approval, so Tyndale left Little Sodbury to seek permission for his project. He contacted Cuthbert Tunstall, the moderate bishop of London, but received no encouragement. So with the financial backing of people like Sir

John and Lady Anne Walsh and a wealthy cloth merchant named Humphrey Monmouth, Tyndale left England in 1524 to do his translation work in Europe.

In Hamburg, Germany, he worked on the New Testament, translating directly from the Greek and Hebrew texts. A printer in Cologne agreed to do the printing. However, word leaked out and opponents of the Reformation raided the print shop. But Tyndale had been warned and fled just in time with the pages that had come off the press thus far. One copy of this incomplete edition (1525) survives today.

A year later in 1526, the first complete New Testament was printed in Worms, Germany, a more reform-minded city. As copies were smuggled into England, the bishops themselves bought up hundreds of the books and had them burned—not realizing that the money went directly back to Tyndale and financed printing even more copies!

By 1530 Tyndale completed translating the first five books of the Old Testament from the Hebrew, along with writing several treatises such as, *The Parable of the Wicked Mammon*, and *The Obedience of a Christian Man*. In *Parable* he argued that justification is by faith alone; in *Obedience* he stated that Christians should obey the king and other civil authorities, unless that obedience came in conflict with God's Word.

A copy of *Obedience* was given to Anne Boleyn, a French-educated lady-in-waiting who became Queen in 1533. She in turn showed it to King Henry VIII, who loved it and proclaimed, "This book is for me and all kings to read!" King Henry, who was at odds with the pope over Henry's efforts to divorce his first wife, Catherine of Aragon, thought Tyndale would be a good scholar to write the king's propaganda. He sent an invitation to Tyndale, by a man named Steven Vaughn, saying he would be given safe passage and a salary if he would come to court.

Tyndale firmly refused. In fact, in *The Practice of Prelates*, he asserted that divorce was against God's will and King Henry should stick with his wife! This set the king against Tyndale, much to the satisfaction of the bishops who continued to see the reform-minded scholar as a troublemaker. The king proceeded to "solve" his problem of how to divorce Catherine through the Act of Supremacy, declaring himself head of the Church of England, even above the pope.

Anne Boleyn also came into possession of a copy of the English New Testament translated by Tyndale, and showed it to the king. (According to the Newberry Library in Chicago, Illinois, the 1534 edition of the Tyndale New Testament, printed in Antwerp, Belgium, was 81mm x 128mm or about 3¼" x 5".) Henry, however, denounced it, saying there was no need for an English Bible "at present," and if and when it was done, should be done by respected scholars within the Church, not a renegade priest who had skipped the country.

The hunt for William Tyndale by English authorities intensified. But in 1534, Thomas Poyntz, an English merchant who was residing in Antwerp, Belgium, invited Tyndale into the protection of the English Merchants boarding house. (Poyntz, who was a relative of Lady Anne Walsh, eventually suffered much for befriending Tyndale; Humphrey Monmouth was also brought to trial and imprisoned for assisting "the heretic.")

In the spring of 1535, a university student named Henry Phillips made the acquaintance of the English merchants in Antwerp and eventually met William Tyndale himself. Tyndale was attracted to the young student's charming manner and seeming interest in reform ideas, though Thomas Poyntz was uneasy. His opinion was that Phillips "rings as false as a counterfeit coin."

Thomas Poyntz's distrust was justified. On May 21, 1535, Phillips showed up at the Poyntz home in Antwerp and invited Tyndale for lunch. As the two men walked through a narrow alleyway, soldiers captured Tyndale and hauled him off to Vilvoorde Prison. Poyntz's many efforts on Tyndale's behalf went unrewarded. In August 1536 Tyndale was tried and condemned as a heretic. In October of that same year, he was strangled and burnt at the stake.

Who used Henry Phillips, son of a notable English family who had fallen into disgrace for his gambling debts? It may have been Bishop Stokesley, the bishop of London after Cuthbert Tunstall and a fierce enemy of Protestantism. However, Phillips gained nothing from his betrayal of Tyndale; he himself had to flee from King Henry's agents and wrote letters home begging for his parents' help and forgiveness, bewailing his poverty and misery.

However, even while Tyndale sat in prison, a fellow Oxford scholar, Miles Coverdale, completed an English translation of the Bible, largely based on Tyndale's work. Only months after William Tyndale's death, King Henry put his stamp of approval on the Bible, and by 1539 every parish church was required to make copies available to its people.

For Further Reading

Christian History, Vol. VI, No. 4, Issue 16. This entire issue is devoted to William Tyndale. Available through Christianity Today Inc., 465 Gundersen Drive, Carol Stream, IL 60188.

Duffield, George, ed., *The Works of William Tyndale*, The Courtenay Library of Reformation Classics (Berkshire: The Sutton Courtenay Press, 1964).

Edwards, Brian H., *God's Outlaw* (Phillipsburg, N.J.: Evangelical Press, 1976, reprint, 1986).

"God's Outlaw: The Story of William Tyndale" (film/video), Gateway Films, Box 540, Worcester, PA 19490.

Walter, Henry, ed., *The Works of William Tyndale*, Parker Society Series (Cambridge: University Press, 1848-50; reprint London: Johnson Reprint Corp., 1968).

Series for Middle Graders* From BHP

ADVENTURES DOWN UNDER · by Robert Elmer
When Patrick McWaid's father is unjustly sent to Australia as a prisoner in 1867, the rest of the family follows, uncovering action-packed mystery along the way.

ADVENTURES OF THE NORTHWOODS · by Lois Walfrid Johnson
Kate O'Connell and her stepbrother Anders encounter mystery and adventure in northwest Wisconsin near the turn of the century.

AN AMERICAN ADVENTURE SERIES · by Lee Roddy
Hildy Corrigan and her family must overcome danger and hardship during the Great Depression as they search for a "forever home."

BLOODHOUNDS, INC. · by Bill Myers
Hilarious, hair-raising suspense follows brother-and-sister detectives Sean and Melissa Hunter in these madcap mysteries with a message.

GIRLS ONLY! · by Beverly Lewis
Four talented young athletes become fast friends as together they pursue their Olympic dreams.

JOURNEYS TO FAYRAH · by Bill Myers
Join Denise, Nathan, and Josh on amazing journeys as they discover the wonders and lessons of the mystical Kingdom of Fayrah.

MANDIE BOOKS · by Lois Gladys Leppard
With over four million sold, the turn-of-the-century adventures of Mandie and her many friends will keep readers eager for more.

THE RIVERBOAT ADVENTURES · by Lois Walfrid Johnson
Libby Norstad and her friend Caleb face the challenges and risks of working with the Underground Railroad during the mid–1800s.

TRAILBLAZER BOOKS · by Dave and Neta Jackson
Follow the exciting lives of real-life Christian heroes through the eyes of child characters as they share their faith with others around the world.

THE TWELVE CANDLES CLUB · by Elaine L. Schulte
When four twelve-year-old girls set up a business of odd jobs and baby-sitting, they uncover wacky adventures and hilarious surprises.

THE YOUNG UNDERGROUND · by Robert Elmer
Peter and Elise Andersen's plots to protect their friends and themselves from Nazi soldiers in World War II Denmark guarantee fast-paced action and suspenseful reads.

*(ages 8–13)

Kidnapped
—by—
River Rats

Trailblazer Books

Gladys Aylward • *Flight of the Fugitives*
Mary McLeod Bethune • *Defeat of the Ghost Riders*
William & Catherine Booth • *Kidnapped by River Rats*
Governor William Bradford • *The Mayflower Secret*
John Bunyan • *Traitor in the Tower*
Amy Carmichael • *The Hidden Jewel*
Peter Cartwright • *Abandoned on the Wild Frontier*
Elizabeth Fry • *The Thieves of Tyburn Square*
Jonathan & Rosalind Goforth • *Mask of the Wolf Boy*
Sheldon Jackson • *The Gold Miners' Rescue*
Adoniram & Ann Judson • *Imprisoned in the Golden City*
Festo Kivengere • *Assassins in the Cathedral*
David Livingstone • *Escape from the Slave Traders*
Martin Luther • *Spy for the Night Riders*
Dwight L. Moody • *Danger on the Flying Trapeze*
Samuel Morris • *Quest for the Lost Prince*
George Müller • *The Bandit of Ashley Downs*
John Newton • *The Runaway's Revenge*
Florence Nightingale • *The Drummer Boy's Battle*
Nate Saint • *The Fate of the Yellow Woodbee*
Menno Simons • *The Betrayer's Fortune*
Mary Slessor • *Trial by Poison*
Hudson Taylor • *Shanghaied to China*
Harriet Tubman • *Listen for the Whippoorwill*
William Tyndale • *The Queen's Smuggler*
John Wesley • *The Chimney Sweep's Ransom*
Marcus & Narcissa Whitman • *Attack in the Rye Grass*
David Zeisberger • *The Warrior's Challenge*

Also by Dave and Neta Jackson

*Hero Tales: A Family Treasury of True Stories
From the Lives of Christian Heroes* (Volumes I, II, & III)

Kidnapped
–by–
River Rats

Dave & Neta Jackson

Story illustrations by
Julian Jackson

BETHANY HOUSE PUBLISHERS
MINNEAPOLIS, MINNESOTA 55438

Kidnapped by River Rats
Copyright © 1991
Dave and Neta Jackson

Cover by Catherine Reishus McLaughlin
Story illustrations by Julian Jackson

All Scripture quotations are from the King James Version of the
Bible.

Published by Bethany House Publishers
A Ministry of Bethany Fellowship International
11400 Hampshire Avenue South
Minneapolis, Minnesota 55438
www.bethanyhouse.com

Printed in the United States of America by
Bethany Press International, Minneapolis, Minnesota 55438

Library of Congress Cataloging-in-Publication Data

Jackson, Dave.
    Kidnapped by river rats / Dave & Neta Jackson.
        p.   cm. — (Trailblazer books)
    Summary: Arriving in London in the 1860s, orphans Jack and
Amy find themselves the prey of the worst elements of society until
they receive aid from William and Catherine Booth and their
Salvation Army people.
    [1. Salvation Army—Fiction.   2. London (England)—Fiction.
3. Orphans—Fiction.   4. Booth, William, 1829–1912—Fiction.
5. Booth, Catherine Mumford, 1829–1890—Fiction.   6. Christian
life—Fiction.]   I. Jackson, Neta.   II. Title.   III. Series.
PZ7.J132418Ki   1991
[Fic]—dc20   91–23816
ISBN 1–55661–220–6   CIP
                                                                AC

William and Catherine Booth, Charlie Fry and his Hallelujah Band, and George Scott Railton and the seven Hallelujah Lasses commissioned to "invade" New York were real people. All other characters are fictional. However, the situations presented in this story accurately portray the conditions of many children in London in the 1880s as well as the life and ministry of the Salvation Army.

CONTENTS

DAVE AND NETA JACKSON are a husband/wife writing team who have authored or coauthored many books on marriage and family, the church, and relationships, including *On Fire for Christ: Stories from Martyrs Mirror*, the Pet Parables series, and the Caring Parent series.

They have two children: Julian, an art major and illustrator for the Trailblazer series, and Rachel, a high school student. They make their home in Evanston, Illinois, where they are active members of Reba Place Church.

Chapter 1

Attack on the Cathedral Steps

THE GREAT HOUND nosed its way through the dense, sour fog that swirled in the narrow alleys of London's east side. Somewhere ahead it smelled human, maybe still alive or maybe food in the gutter. It was hungry enough to eat anything.

A growl rumbled deep in its throat as it rounded the corner and surveyed the cobblestone street ahead. Its huge head hung low to the ground, a torn lip revealing a sharp fang.

Coarse, gray hair spiked along the ridge of its back. The lone gas light in front of Saint Paul's Cathedral cast a greenish glow through the mist. No one there.

Or was there? Deep in the shadows of the side door to the cathedral lay a black heap. The dog approached quietly, sniffing the heavy air. No death here . . . but maybe there would be something to eat just the same.

Jack Crumpton came awake slowly. Why was Mama pulling on his night shirt? Why was his bed so hard? Why was he so cold?

And then it all came back to him. He wasn't in bed . . . Mama was dead, and he and Amy were homeless on the streets of London.

He rolled over with a start. There, snarling and pulling on the sleeve of his coat, stood the biggest wolf-dog he'd ever seen. Jack grabbed for his stick. It was caught under Amy. He pulled it free and swung it at the beast's immense head. The creature ducked the blow without loosening his bite on the coat.

Just then Amy sat up and screamed, "Don't let him have it, Jack! The biscuits in your pocket are our last food."

With one hand Jack pulled with all his might on his coat. With the other he swung his stick toward the dog's nose. This time the stout stick landed with a sharp whack. The brute yelped and made one more desperate lunge backwards, its ugly fangs still embedded in the sleeve of Jack's old coat. The strength of the beast pulled Jack over and he rolled down the steps. But he wouldn't give up his coat.

And then with a sickening rip, the sleeve tore free, and the dog made off into the gloom with Jack's sleeve flapping around its head like a neck scarf in a winter blow.

Jack rose slowly to his knees on the grimy street and tried to inspect his coat by the dim glow of the nearby street light. Safely in its pocket there remained two small hunks of bread no bigger than his fists.

"You all right?" asked Amy as she came down to help him up.

"Yeah, but he got me sleeve. Guess I'll have one cold arm come winter."

"Don't worry, Jack. By then we'll find Uncle Sedgwick, and he'll surely take us in."

"I hope so," Jack said as he followed his older sister back up the steps to huddle in the skimpy shelter of the doorway to the great cathedral. Amy shared her shawl with him, wrapping the garment that their mother had knitted around the both of them. In the dim light its beautiful light and dark greens looked like gray and black, but it was still just as warm.

London had been strange and unfriendly to the two children. They had come to the city a few weeks earlier with their mother after their father had died in a coal mine accident. Mama hoped to find her brother Sedgwick Masters, a successful tailor. But in London in the fall of 1881, it wasn't so easy to track someone down if you weren't sure of his address. Mama's cough seemed worse after the damp, two-day journey to London, so they found lodging where the landlady charged two shillings per night for an unheated gable room at the back of a dreary house.

The next day, Mother was too ill to look for Uncle Sedgwick. She soon got so sick that the children didn't dare leave her side. They took turns going out to find a penny's worth of bread or some vegetables or broth and bringing it back to Mama. And each day Mrs. Witherspoon, the landlady, came pounding on the door demanding the rent until in one week's time almost all their money was gone.

"You can't stay here without paying your rent," the old landlady had said gruffly. Jack thought her face looked like a prune.

"We'll pay," promised Mother, and then fell into a great fit of coughing that brought up more blood. When she finally got her breath back, she said, "Just give me a chance to get well and find my brother, Sedgwick Masters, the tailor."

"I've never heard of any tailor by that name. Besides, you got consumption, woman. You ain't never gonna get well."

The old woman had been right. Four days later Mother Crumpton died in her sleep.

When Witherspoon came for the rent the next morning, she started shrieking twice as loud as the children had cried during the night. "I told you! I told you she'd never make it. Now what am I going to do? What am I going to do? You two young'uns get out of here. I should never have let this room out to you in the first place." She paced back and forth wringing her hands. "What am I ever going to do?" Then she looked at the children again: "Get out! Get out, I told you."

"But we can't go—that's our mama," protested Amy.

"Was . . . was. She *was* your mama. She ain't no more. This here's just a body that I'm going to have to pay to have taken away. And this room ain't yours any more, so get out!"

Fighting back the tears, Jack went over and struggled with the trunk that held all their belongings. He was strong for twelve years of age, and Amy, who was just two years older, could put in a full day's work. But they would have done well to get the trunk down the stairs, let alone carry it any distance through London's narrow, busy streets.

"You can just leave that right there," growled old lady Witherspoon. "I'll hold it as collateral 'til you pay up. You owe me five days rent plus whatever it costs to have this body taken away. Until you pay up, you can just leave that trunk right here. Now go find that rich uncle of yours, if you got one."

The two children, numb with grief, had wandered aimlessly around London's lower east side until they fell asleep in the doorway of the great cathedral. Now wide awake, their hearts beating loudly as they peered into the darkness, fearful that the beast would return, Amy resolved, "Tomorrow, Jack. Tomorrow we'll go find Uncle Sedgwick."

They arranged their coats over themselves as they cuddled together. Jack listened to the night as the distant wail of a baby's cry drifted through the dense fog.

Yes, tomorrow they had to find Uncle Sedgwick.

Chapter 2

Blood and Fire

WHEN JACK AWOKE in the morning, his sister was already sitting up watching the hustle and bustle of the street. Jack rubbed his eyes and turned over to see what drew her attention.

They had slept late. The sun had already burned off most of the fog, leaving a bright haze overhead. Jack looked up. There was a hazy circle around the sun; must mean rain.

The street was full of people. A fat woman waddled by carrying a large basket of laundry. She was so fat that she seemed to have to work very hard just to get where she was going. "Hold on ta me skirts," she barked at three apple-faced children coming on behind her, each one a smaller copy of the mother.

A man pulled a creaking two-wheeled cart piled high with lumps of coal. "I miss Pa," Jack said as tears came to his eyes. He pulled his cap lower. Straight brown hair poked out all around. His hair was the same color as his mother's had been. Amy, however, had her father's hair—red and curly, but not so red as to look orange and not so curly as to be frizzy. For a sister, she could look very pretty, Jack sometimes thought. Today, however, smears of dirt trailed across her forehead and down one cheek. Her hair was tousled, her clothes a mess. Mother would never have let Amy go out looking like that. But now she was gone, and they were alone, so alone.

"What you lookin' at?" Amy asked. "Give me one of those biscuits."

Jack dug in his pocket and took out the hunks of stale bread. He handed one to Amy and stuck the other in his teeth as he examined his coat with its missing sleeve. He ought to go search for it. There was a good chance the dog dropped it once it realized it held nothing to eat.

"You think that dog would have eaten us last night?" he asked Amy.

"I doubt it. Who ever heard of a dog eating a person? It's not like we were sheep and it was a wolf."

"Dogs go bad and kill sheep sometimes," said Jack. "Besides, that one last night looked half-wolf."

"That it did. I've never seen such an ugly thing. I did once hear of dogs eating dead people during a famine."

Just then Jack heard the most peculiar sound. It was the high pitched sound of a flute and the deep thump, thump, thump of a drum. He stuffed the rest of the biscuit in his mouth and looked down the street. Coming around the corner about one street away was a small parade. Each person was in a uniform; most carried some kind of a band instrument, and one held high a brightly colored flag, but it was not the familiar British Union Jack.

"You think they're bobbies?" asked Jack, ready to run.

"Policemen don't march around with a band," said Amy. "Otherwise how would they ever catch any crooks?"

The troop continued marching up the narrow street beside the cathedral. Small children, chickens, and cats scampered to the side to get out of the way. Then, right at the bottom of the steps, a tall, wiry-haired man with a bushy, gray beard and a black top hat shouted a command, and the troop stopped and turned like a machine toward Amy and Jack.

"They *are* bobbies," yelled Jack as he grabbed his sister's hand and tried to make a break for it.

"Hold on there, lad," said the man with the big beard as he easily reached out and caught Jack's arm. "Where are you off to so fast?"

"We ain't done nothin'," stammered Jack. "We just . . . I mean, sir, we are just looking for our uncle." Jack squirmed to get free.

"Listen, lad, we're not the police, and we're not after anything more than your soul. But I do want to talk to you. So will you hold still a minute?"

After my soul? thought Jack. *Who could be after my soul other than God or the devil?* Jack had only occasionally gone to church, but he wasn't about to let anyone get his soul. On the other hand, you can't

17

just grab a body's soul, or could you? Jack stood still, and the man's iron grip loosened on his arm.

The man took off his top hat and stooped down with his hands on his knees until he was on eye level with Jack. The man's nose was large and somewhat hooked. His gray eyes shone like polished steel, deep-set under two eyebrows that were not shaped the same. The right one arched high while the left one sloped giving him a skeptical expression.

"So, where do you two live?" he commanded. His wiry beard jutted out and bobbed with each word, carefully pronounced with military precision.

"We live . . . ," began Jack.

"We live with our Uncle Sedgwick," finished Amy with authority.

"I see." The man cocked his head and examined Amy. "But you don't know where he is . . . , and so you must 'look' for him. Is that it?" Both children nodded. "A likely story, indeed," said the man.

"General, come now," interrupted a woman who stepped forward. "Can't you see that these children are scared to death? I'm Catherine Booth, children," beamed the woman with a warm smile. She wore a dark blue bonnet tied under her chin by a broad red ribbon. "And this man, who would love to take you captive, is none other than my husband, General William Booth of the Salvation Army."

It was only then that Jack realized that the troop was made up almost equally by men and women. While the women wore long dresses, their uniform was very military looking. And as for the men, they did look like soldiers on dress parade with sharply cut, dark blue uniforms and small brimmed caps with shiny metal crests on the front. The general was dressed the same except for his top hat and slightly different insignia on his uniform. Then Jack noticed that on the collar of each person there was a highly polished, brass letter S.

While Mrs. Booth talked, the other members of the troop set up the flag and the drum and prepared to play right on the steps of Saint Paul's Cathedral. A chill ran through Jack's body as a slight breeze waved the flag. He didn't read too well, but he easily made out the words "Blood and Fire" inscribed above a cross, two crossed swords, and again the letter S. "Blood and Fire" . . . "Blood and Fire" . . . what could it mean?

Mrs. Booth concluded her introduction by inviting the children to stay and listen to the music. Her face was solemn but her eyes were smiling.

"I think we'd better be going," said Amy as she pulled Jack down the steps and away from this strange army. "Jack, she *said* that the general wants to take us captive," whispered Amy when Jack tried to squirm away.

The children spent all that morning walking the streets of East London looking for their uncle. Time and again they would race forward when they saw a sign indicating a tailor's shop. But when they got close, it always had someone else's name on it.

Once when they were getting a drink of water from a public fountain, Amy said, "Maybe we ought to be going inside and asking, even though his name's not on the sign. Maybe his shop is in someone else's name."

"That means we have to go back and check each one we've been to," moaned Jack.

"But it might speed up our search," said Amy. "One tailor ought to know the others. If they are in the same business, someone is bound to know him, and can direct us to the right shop."

In the third shop they entered, a skinny old man as crooked as a dried-out oak limb glanced up over the top of his spectacles and said, "Sedgwick Masters, eh? What'cha want him for?"

"He's our uncle, and we're trying to find him," said Amy.

"Well, I don't know where he is," said the old man, returning to his sewing, "and I don't care to know, either."

"Why not?" asked Jack.

"'Cause the last time I heard of him was when he stole two of my best customers."

The children stared as the man put a handful of pins in his mouth. Finally Amy said, "But you *have* seen him, then?"

"Didn't say I'd seen him," mumbled the tailor as he took one pin after another from his mouth as fast as a dog scratches fleas and stuck them in the garment he was sewing. "Actually, I never laid eyes on the man."

"But you gotta know where he is if your customers went to him," persisted Amy.

"Listen here, young lady, I don't gotta know nothin'. When one of my customers came back to me, I was grateful. I didn't pry into why he had left or why he came back."

Jack and Amy walked to the door in despair. Then suddenly Jack turned back. "Wait," he said. "Who were those people, the customers of yours who went to our Uncle Sedgwick? Where are they now? Maybe they know where our uncle is."

"Like I said, only one came back. He was that dandy, Filbert. Wanted me to make him three new suits so he could impress the ladies of Europe. Last I heard, he'd set sail for France. Was going to tour the Continent for 'his cultural enrichment,' he said. I haven't seen him since."

"Who was the other person," said Jack, "the one who didn't come back?"

"Well, now, I *do* know that she's still around. But she's never come back to me, so maybe she's still using Masters. Who knows?"

"But who was she?" persisted Jack.

"Oh, she's the wife of that general, or so-called general. Booth, Catherine Booth, was her name. They're the ones who started that Salvation Army. They march around here all the time." The tailor looked up at Jack and added, "Say, boy, you better get your jacket fixed. You're missing a sleeve there."

Chapter 3

Caught for a Thief

A MY AND JACK LEFT the tailor's shop in high spirits. Their uncle couldn't be far, and now they knew someone who could lead them to him.

"But, Amy," said Jack, "that woman said the general wanted to take us captive. What if he does?"

"We can't let him," said Amy. "We'll have to find them when they're not together and ask her then."

They headed back toward the cathedral. It was a long walk, and it was getting late in the afternoon. As they hiked along, Jack noticed a most wonderful smell. He looked up, and there in the window of a building that was built right out to the street sat two steaming pies. Jack stopped, and that caused Amy to stop and look up too. "They're chicken pies, just like Mom makes," said Amy.

Jack's stomach growled and suddenly ached. The children were getting very hungry, not having had anything to eat all day except one hard biscuit early that morning, but Jack's stomach hurt from more than hunger. "They're just like Mom *made. Made*, Amy, not *'makes.'* Mother can't make pies anymore.

Remember? It's just like old lady Witherspoon said, Mom's dead." He stomped off down the street, keeping his head turned away so Amy wouldn't see the tears that swam in his eyes.

"Jack, wait." Amy caught up to him. "I didn't mean anything. Those pies just made me think about Mom; that's all. I miss her too, you know."

"Yeah, I know," he mumbled. "It's just that I wish she hadn't left us. It ain't fair; now we're all alone, and I'm starving."

"Don't be angry, Jack. It wasn't her fault. We just gotta hang together and find Uncle Sedgwick. Then we can get something to eat."

"But what if we never find him?"

"We will; we will."

They rounded a corner and came to a street market. Jack's mouth watered when he looked at the bright red apples in a grocery stall. *Just one bite, just one bite would taste so good*, he thought. The grocer was looking the other way, helping a customer. Suddenly Jack grabbed two apples, one for himself and one for Amy, and tried to put them into his pockets. But the apples were so big that they wouldn't fit. While he was struggling, the grocer turned around and saw him.

"Hey, you little brat," he yelled. "Put them back."

In fright Jack turned and started to run. "Amy, come on."

For a moment Amy was confused, but when she saw the grocer lunge around the end of his table with his cane raised high, she started running after Jack fast enough.

"Stop, thief. Stop, thief," yelled the grocer as they dodged between the other stalls in the street market. Jack turned down an alley, an apple clutched in each hand, and Amy was right behind him. The cobble stones of the alley were rough, and garbage and puddles of sewage made it slick. Jack looked back to see the grocer hot on their heels.

Suddenly Amy screamed, and Jack heard a loud crash. When he looked back, a rain barrel had tipped over into the center of the alley and had broken open.

Water was flooding everywhere. Amy was on the ground in the middle of it. Just then the grocer skidded to a stop above her and grabbed her by her hair. He raised his cane.

"No," yelled Jack and raised his two apples high so the man could see them. "Don't hit my sister."

"You bring them apples back to me, then, you little tea-leaf."

Jack approached the grocer. The man's face was purple, and he was breathing hard, but he hadn't let go of Amy's hair. Jack put both apples in one hand— they were almost too big to hold that way—and came closer, holding them out to the man. Suddenly the cane whistled through the air and came crashing down on Jack's hand and wrist. One apple exploded; the other went flying across the alley. Jack felt more pain shoot up his arm than he had ever known in his life. "That'll teach you ta thieve from me, you little brats. Every day, robbing me blind. It's got so a man can't make a livin' any more." And with that the man turned and lumbered back up the alley.

Jack realized that he was crying. He didn't want to cry; he wanted to be brave for Amy. But he couldn't help it. A great red welt was growing across his wrist, and his hand felt like he'd never use it again. Then Jack noticed that Amy was crying too. Her clothes were wet, and she was holding her ankle. "What's wrong," said Jack through his sobs.

"I think I hurt my ankle," she said.

"Can you stand up?" Jack asked.

"I don't know. I think it's really hurt. But what about your hand?"

Jack held it out and tried to move his fingers. At least they did move, but the pain throbbed harder than ever. "I think it's okay," he said, not at all sure that was so.

"Here, help me up," said Amy.

Jack offered his other hand to help her. Amy stood up using Jack for balance, keeping her right foot off the ground. Slowly she put it down and tried one feeble step, but the moment she put weight on it, she gave a little cry and almost fell again. "I think it's really hurt, Jack."

"What're we gonna do?"

"I don't know. Maybe it's just twisted. Here, let me lean on you."

The two hobbled back down the alley as evening turned the shadows to blue, purple, then gray. "Wait a minute," said Jack. "Grab hold of the corner of the building." Then he ran back down the alley searching for something.

In a few minutes he returned. "Here," he said as he held out the badly bruised apple that had not been totally smashed by the grocer's cane. "I know it isn't ours, and I shouldn't have taken it. I'm sorry about that, 'specially because of your foot. But I guess the grocer didn't want it. At least he didn't take it back, and we need something to eat. Want a bite?" He rubbed it on his pants to wipe off the alley's grime.

Amy took a bite, then held onto Jack's shoulder as they limped off down the street sharing the apple.

Chapter 4

The Cave in the City

IT WAS NEARLY DARK. The lamplighter was lighting the lamps on each post.

"Jack, I don't know where we are. I don't know where the cathedral is any more."

"Neither do I," said Jack. "But there's something different up ahead. It looks like the street ends. But then there's nothing."

As they approached, they found that the street butted into another one that went along the side of a great river. On the river moved large barges, barely visible in the dark except that some had a lantern on deck. On the other side of the river down farther were three ships tied up. The tall masts and rigging of these sailing ships made a lacy silhouette against the last pale light in the sky.

"I don't think I can walk any more," said Amy. "My foot's hurtin' something fierce. I wish Mother were here. She would know what to do." The two made their way out of the street just as a coach and four horses raced past, the wheels and hooves clattering on the rough cobblestones. Amy leaned on the

29

wall for support. Jack gazed at the shiny black water below.

"There's something down there," Jack muttered almost to himself. "I'm climbing down."

"Wait," said Amy as she reached for her brother, but he was already scrambling over the wall, lowering himself to the river. Then she, too, noticed it. Right below them the water did not come all the way to the wall. There was a little sandy beach not much wider than what a person could walk on.

Jack walked along it toward a nearby bridge. At the base of the pillar supporting the end of the bridge the little stretch of sand was replaced by large rough rocks. Jack's fingers found small handholds in the cracks between the stones of the pillar, and he hung on as he carefully inched his way around the pillar, stepping from one slippery rock to the next. There, under the end of the bridge was a small cave. It actually extended ten or twelve feet back under the street above. The floor of the cave was sandy, and when one got away from the river a ways, it was pretty dry. A large limb of a tree and other pieces of driftwood had piled up along one side. There was even a packing box and a broken bucket.

Something scurried across the sand and into the pile of driftwood. Maybe it was a cat . . . or a rat. But if it was a rat, it was the biggest rat Jack had ever seen. Jack reached down and picked up a stone. "Show your head just one time," Jack threatened. When nothing moved, he cut loose with a wicked sling anyway and the stone cracked against the old

bucket. Still nothing came out. Jack picked up a second stone and moved toward the back of the cave, ever watchful of the pile of trash. But the back of the cave was so dark that he could only sense its general location. He didn't *think* there was anything else lurking back there, but he wasn't going back there by himself to find out.

"Jack! Jack! What are you doing?"

Jack could just hear his sister's voice. He climbed back around the pillar and looked up at her. The evening gloom made her face barely visible. "There's a cave down here!" Jack said.

"So?"

"This is great! Come on down."

"Jack, why would I want to climb down there to explore an old cave? We don't even have a place to sleep tonight."

"Why not in this cave? At least if it rained, we wouldn't get wet. There's some wood down here. We could even light a fire."

Amy groaned. "Jack, sometimes I don't know what to do with you. Don't you realize that my ankle is hurt? I could never climb down there."

"Yes you could. It's not far."

Amy stood there looking at him, then out across the river, then back across the street into the part of London where they'd spent the day looking without luck for their uncle. Finally she turned back to Jack. "Okay. But you've got to help me get down. My ankle is swelling up bigger and bigger."

In a few minutes both children were standing together on the narrow strip of sand at the river's edge. The night sounds of the big city were cut off from them, and all they could hear was the gentle ding, ding, ding of the bell from the river buoy up near where the ships were docked.

Jack held Amy's arm as she inched herself around the pillar. Once her foot slipped on the rough rocks below and she turned her ankle again. She cried out, then caught her breath. He could see pain etched on her face.

"Here we are," Jack said encouragingly.

Amy hobbled across the sand toward the back of the cave. "It's dry now. But what happens if it rains and the river level rises. We'd be flooded out. In fact, how would we even get out?"

Jack shrugged, then realized that it was too dark in the cave for Amy to see his gesture. "Here, let's make a fire," he said as he drew a few of the smaller sticks from the pile of driftwood and trash. He tried not to think of the animal that had so recently run into that pile.

"How are we going to light a fire, Jack? We don't have any matches. There's no way we can light a fire down here."

"Maybe we could go borrow some coals from someone's hearth," offered Jack.

"Sure, just walk up to one of those pubs along the riverfront and say, 'Could we please have some live coals. We ain't got no place to live and we're camping under the bridge.' If we did that, one of those drunken sailors would throw us in the river."

Jack continued breaking sticks and laying them for a fire. There had to be a way; there just had to be.

"Jack! I know. Take a little stick and climb up one of the street light poles. Stick it in there just like the lamplighter does. But instead of lighting the lamp, you can light your stick to bring back for some fire."

It was a great idea. Jack found a small, dry stick in the pile of trash and left the little cave. He climbed the wall and ran down the street to the nearest lamp. But climbing the pole wasn't as easy as it looked. It

took him three tries before he made it. Then clinging carefully to the pole, he put his stick into the little hole and touched the flame. It flared brightly, and he slid down the pole.

The stick was burning fast. Jack ran down the dark street and scrambled over the wall and dropped to the sand below. But the fall through the air blew out the flame. He stood there by the black river with only a glowing ember in his hand. Carefully he blew on it to get a weak flame to return. It glowed brightly for a moment, but then went out completely.

"Amy, get me another stick—a little longer, and make sure it's dry. This one went out."

In a few moments Amy handed another stick around the pillar so that neither child had to navigate the slippery rocks. Jack climbed back up the wall. He was getting to know where the good hand and foot holds were now, even in the dark.

This time when he returned with the burning stick he was careful not to shake his hand as he dropped the last few feet to the ground. The flame held.

Back in the cave he held it to the little pile of wood he had made. Some of the smallest splinters lit easily, but they also burned down quickly. As the little flames on the sticks grew smaller and smaller, both children huddled close and blew gently, adding one twig at a time. Finally, when they thought they were going to be plunged back into darkness, some new sticks caught and the fire began to grow.

They fed it with new wood and smiled as it crackled cheerily. At last they began to feel warm as they cuddled together on the sand at the back of the river cave.

Chapter 5

River Rats

IT WAS DRIZZLING when the children awoke in the morning. They sat up and looked out into the river. A riverboat was pulling slowly upstream; two men worked steadily on the oars to move it against the current. The open boat was piled high with potatoes and cabbages—going to market, no doubt.

"Wish I could have one of them," said Jack. "I'm starving."

In the distance they could see several other boats on the water—people starting their day to the sour smell of coal smoke in the London air.

"Oh, no. Our fire's gone out," moaned Amy as she pulled her shawl around her shoulders. "And the street lamps will have been put out by now. We can't even get another light until tonight."

"It's not my fault," said Jack. "You could have gotten up in the night and put on more wood yourself. There's plenty of it."

"I didn't say it was your fault. I just said we don't have a fire."

"It sounded like you were blaming me," complained Jack.

"Well, I wasn't. So what's the matter with you this morning?"

"I'm just hungry," said Jack. Tears came to his eyes. "And I want Mama. Why'd she have to die?"

Amy put her arms around him, and together the two children cried. Finally Amy sniffed and wiped her face with her shawl. "But we can't give up, Jack. We just can't."

"But what are we going to do?"

"This morning you have to go find that Salvation Army woman. What was her name?"

"You mean the one the tailor said was Uncle Sedgwick's customer? Booth something, wasn't it?"

"Yes. Booth, Catherine Booth. You have to go find her, Jack. Catherine Booth, don't forget that name."

"But why not you?"

In answer, Amy stuck out her foot and pointed to her ankle. "I really can't walk, Jack. There's no way I can wander around the city until I get better."

"What about the river?" said Jack. "What if this rain makes it rise and floods you out like you said?"

"It's not rising yet. Look at those rocks, the water's even lower." She nodded over to the piling around which they had to climb every time they came into the cave. "You know, unless there is a real big rain or spring floods, I think the only thing that changes the water level in this river is the tide."

Jack looked suspiciously at the pile of trash. "The tide? But that comes from the sea every day, twice a day. We've already been here one whole night, and there hasn't been any high tide."

"No. I'm talking about big tides, the kind that come once a month. Maybe they come up the river this far. I don't know."

"Yeah, maybe that's how all this junk got here. It floated here sometime when the river was high, high enough to come up into this very cave. And we don't know when that's going to happen."

"Well, it's not going to happen today," said Amy. "I'll tell you what, you go looking for Catherine Booth, and if it starts raining hard, you can come back here and help me out."

That seemed to satisfy Jack, and he got up to leave.

Part way out into the river there was another set of pillars holding up the huge bridge. Up near the top in the shadows of the beams Jack noticed movement. He looked closely and then realized what it was. A rat was crawling along the beam, possibly the very one that had hid in their pile of driftwood the night before. Jack stooped down and found three stones in the sand. Carefully he eased over to the side of the cave to get a better angle. The rat was in full view now, stopping every few moments and looking around.

Suddenly Jack let fly with a rough, oblong stone. It was a long throw, but Jack was a good shot. The stone whizzed just over the rat's head. The ugly creature bounded forward a few feet then stopped and looked around, its round rump high and its

beady eyes shining. Apparently the rat was uncertain what had happened or where its enemy was. That moment of hesitation was all Jack needed. He took aim and flung a second stone with all his might. It sailed through the air and found its mark, hitting with a thud that knocked the rat off the beam and into the river.

"You got him, Jack."

"Yeah." Jack stared at the place where the rat had splashed into the water. In a few moments something floated to the surface and drifted lifelessly down stream. "Yeah, I got him good." In his excitement, Jack flung his third rock out over the river in the general direction of where the rat had been. But because he hadn't aimed, the stone flew beyond the pillar and landed on the front of a boat that had just nosed out from behind the pillar.

"Hey, what's the big idea?" yelled a burly voice as a huge sailor stood up in the boat. His partner continued rowing. "What you brats trying to do? You want to kill someone? I've a mind to come in there and thrash the both of you."

"We didn't mean to," answered Amy.

"Hey, Rodney," said the one still at the oars. "It's a girl."

"Yeah, and just about the right age too. But we got to get back to the ship. We'll take care of this later." Then he yelled again at Amy and Jack, "You throw any more rocks at us, and I'll bust your heads."

"We won't," said Jack.

"You bet you won't, and we'll be back to see that you don't too." They laughed with a roar as the big man sat down clumsily and took up his oars. Soon they were far down the river.

"That was a close one," said Jack. "I almost got two river rats." And he laughed.

"Don't joke about it, Jack. Those were evil men."

"You don't think they will be back, do you Amy?"

"Who knows. They probably go back and forth from their ship every day when they are in port. We'll just have to attract no more attention. Now you go on, Jack. See if you can find that Booth lady."

"But I'm starving, Amy. When are we going to get something to eat?"

"I don't know. I'm hungry too. Maybe you can ask someone to give you some bread when you are out."

"Yeah, maybe so. I'll bring you back something," said Jack as he worked his way around the rocks at the bottom of the piling. "I promise that I'll get you something."

Chapter 6

Three Good Hits

BY THE TIME JACK HAD CLIMBED up to the street, the drizzle had stopped, for which he was very grateful. The streets were full of people, and no one seemed to pay any attention to the young boy climbing over the wall along the edge of the River Thames.

Jack looked all morning for the Salvation Army. He found the church where he and Amy had spent the night, but they weren't there. He asked people on the street where they were. "Oh, they're around; they're around here every day somewhere," a boy about Jack's age told him. "Why, you looking to throw a little mud?" the boy asked.

"No. Why would I throw mud?" Jack said.

"Beats selling papers," the boy shrugged as he ran off.

Jack didn't understand what he was talking about. Why would throwing mud beat selling papers?

The smell of baking bread caught Jack's attention. It was coming from a bakery with rolls and loaves of bread in every shape and size in the window. There was black bread, brown bread, and even white bread. His mouth watered as he looked through the window, and he remembered his promise to bring Amy something to eat.

An idea struck him, and he ran down the street to the next corner. He turned and ran on until he found a little alley that led him to the back of the bakery shop. He pounded on the door until a bald man with bushy black eyebrows opened the door.

"Yeah, what'cha want?"

"Sorry to bother you, sir. But I was wonderin' if I could earn a loaf of bread?"

"Away with you. We got too many beggars around here already."

"I ain't no beggar, sir. I was wantin' to work for it. Any old job will do."

"Ain't got any. Come back when you can pay a copper. Then I'll be glad to *sell* you a loaf of bread," and he slammed the door.

Jack turned away and kicked at a cat in the alley. The thing hissed at him and jumped to the top of a rain barrel. Jack had a mind to grab it, lift the lid, and give the ugly creature a good dunking. But he knew his problems weren't the cat's fault. Instead, he hissed back at it until the cat scampered up on a shed roof out of his reach.

Jack was so discouraged when he came out of the alley that he was tempted to return to the river and tell Amy it was no use. But just then his ears caught the deep thump, thump, thump he'd heard the other morning on the cathedral steps. It had to be the Salvation Army band, but where was it?

He turned right and ran down the street, but the sound didn't get louder. Between the close buildings, the sound echoed so much that it was hard to tell from which way it came. Jack decided that it must be on the next street. He turned the corner and ran up to the next street. The band wasn't there, but the sound was louder. Now he could hear the flute and the horns. It sounded as good as a circus. He ran faster, and when he came around the next corner he was rewarded. There, halfway down the street was the Salvation Army band playing a song so joyful that it made Jack want to dance.

The band was on a loading platform for a warehouse. The platform was about the height of Jack's head. This put them up so everyone could see and hear them. But getting close was a different matter. The narrow street was jammed with people. Some were singing, some just standing there. Some were yelling, but Jack couldn't make out what they were saying.

He worked his way through the crowd until he was directly across the street from the band. Behind him was the open door to a pub. From there he could see the band clearly. Unfortunately, the general and the lady he had seen on the cathedral steps weren't among them. But he decided to listen to the singing and the band. Maybe afterwards he could ask them where Catherine Booth was. The song boomed out:

We're bound for the land
    of the pure and the holy.
The home of the happy, the Kingdom of love;
Ye wanderers from God
    in the broad road of folly,
O say, will you go to the Eden above?

Jack wasn't sure what it all meant, but he liked the tune, and he sure would like to go to some land where there weren't so many troubles. The chorus asked, "Will you go? Will you go?" over and over again with such earnestness that Jack almost shouted, "Yes."

Just then something went flying through the air and landed right in the bell of one of the horns. It jammed the horn into the player's mouth so hard that his lips began to bleed. Jack could see that the thing thrown was a dead cat.

A tremendous roar went up from the crowd. Some were cheering. Some were yelling to leave the band alone. "They're doing no harm."

More things went flying through the air: rocks, bottles, and mud that splattered on the band players turning their uniforms into an ugly mess.

The throwing seemed to be coming from a group of boys just about Jack's age, and most of them were right around him. As the fray continued, one after another yelled, "There, I got a hit!" "Count one for me." "Bull's-eye; that's a halfpenny for me."

The riot calmed down when the Salvation Army people got down from the loading platform.

"Hey, boy. Come here."

Jack looked around and through the doorway into the dark interior of a pub. A man stood there behind the bar wiping the counter, a pint of beer in his hand. His hair was cut short, but he had a huge walrus mustache, the ends of which drooped nearly to the bottom of his strong, square jaw.

"Yeah, you," the man said nodding to Jack.

Jack stepped through the open door. It was an ordinary enough pub with a bar down one side and a big barrel on the end of the bar. It would hold beer. On the wall be-

46

hind were several smaller barrels on their sides with taps in the ends. They would hold whiskey, rum, and gin of the cheaper variety. Above them were bottles of the expensive stuff. Around the dark room were a few tables with chairs and a big old stove with a bucket full of coal beside it.

Jack approached slowly. The man just stood there, sipping from time to time from the pint in his hand. He wore the faded-red top of long-handled underwear frayed at the sleeves and around the neck. His black working pants were held up with wide braces, and his heavy boots were worn and scuffed. "You seen them Salvationists before?" he asked, pointing out the door.

"Yes, sir. I seen 'em once before," answered Jack.

"You live around here?"

"Sorta." Jack squirmed.

"Well, listen here. That Salvation Army intends to ruin my business. They want to shut down every gin house in London, and quite a few of my regulars have already converted. It's hittin' me where it hurts. You know what I mean? Right in my money pouch. But I'm a fair business man, and I'm willin' to pay for what I need. You seen them boys out there?"

"Yes, sir," Jack said, not exactly sure who the man meant but certain he'd find out soon enough.

"I pay each and every one of those boys a halfpenny every time they make a hit that counts. You know what I mean?"

Jack shook his head no. He actually did have an idea what the man was saying, but he could hardly believe his ears.

"What I'm sayin' is, when they throw somethin' and they make a good hit, I keep score and pay a halfpenny each hit. The way I figure it, pretty soon those Salvationists will give up and find better things to do than trouble a legitimate business man. I got a legal license to run this pub, you know."

"Yes, sir," Jack said, not quite sure what he was agreeing with but feeling he ought to say something.

"So, what do you say? I'll pay you the same?"

"I got no cause to bother those people," Jack protested.

"No cause," the man growled through clenched teeth. "I just told you the cause, you little brat." And he made as if to lunge after Jack.

Jack turned to run out the door when the man changed the tone of his voice. "Wait. I didn't mean nothin' against you, boy. Look here. Come on back in here. You look like you could use a job. Am I right?"

"Yes, sir," said Jack. "Me and Amy, well, we need some . . ." Jack stopped, thinking it best to keep his troubles private.

"Okay, then. You need some money; I got a job for you to do. That's cause enough, wouldn't you say?"

Jack thought about it a moment. The hunger pains in his stomach were getting unbearable, and he'd promised to bring Amy something to eat. He could find that Mrs. Booth tomorrow. If they didn't get something to eat soon, neither of them would be strong enough to search the city for their uncle.

"All right. How do I get paid?"

"I'll be watching. You come back here after it's all over."

When Jack left the pub he expected that the Salvation Army would have packed up and left for some place safer. But instead one of the men was standing up on the platform speaking:

A lot of you don't have jobs, some of you lack a place to live, and maybe you are even hungry. When Jesus saw people just like you, He cared. He cared enough to do something. There were five thousand men plus women and children in that crowd. That's a lot more than there are of you gathered here today on East Tenter Street.

But Jesus asked a small boy to share what he had, and Jesus multiplied it. The Bible says that He "took the five loaves, and the two fishes, and looking up to heaven, he blessed, and brake, and gave the loaves to his disciples, and the disciples to the multitude. And they did all eat, and were filled: and they took up of the fragments that remained twelve baskets full."

Jesus said, "Come unto me, all ye that labour and are heavy laden, and I will give you rest." But so many of you try to find your rest in gin and beer. You think you can drink your troubles away, but the Bible says, "There is a way which seemeth right unto a man, but the end thereof are the ways of death."

Just then a howl went up from several people in the crowd, and a very ripe tomato landed right at the feet of the speaker splattering red juice all over his legs. Another tomato just missed the flag that flew above them.

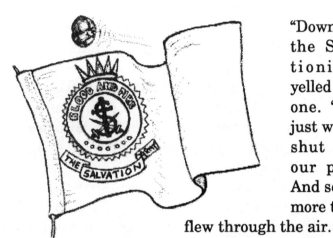

"Down with the Salvationists," yelled someone. "They just want to shut down our pubs." And several more things flew through the air.

Jack looked around and saw that some of the boys he had noticed before were again throwing things, so he, too, reached down and picked up a small pebble and gave it a gentle toss toward the speaker. He really didn't want to hurt anyone. The pebble flew through the air in a high arch and bounced harmlessly off the speaker's cap.

Jack glanced toward the pub. The owner was leaning casually in his doorway, his muscled arms crossed on his chest. He looked at Jack, scowled, and shook his head. Jack got the message: no halfpennies for little pebbles, even if he did score a bull's-eye. With a raised eyebrow the pub owner pointed to the street not far from Jack's feet. His hand barely moved as his finger made a sharp jab toward the spot on the ground and then another jab toward the speaker. Then the man looked away, ignoring Jack.

Jack looked down. There was a pile of fresh horse droppings. The man wanted him to throw those round, green "balls." Jack hesitated to pick them up. How could he? On the other hand, they wouldn't hurt anyone, and he was so hungry.

Tentatively Jack picked one up and gave it a toss. It went wide of its mark. Jack looked over to the pub owner. He shrugged slightly and looked away. Just then someone else's old shoe hit the speaker as he was repeating the verse about there being a way that *seems* right but leads to death. The crowd roared. Earlier—during the music—many people had seemed with the Salvation Army, even singing along. Now they had turned against them. They had become an ugly mob, enjoying being mean to the speaker.

Jack reached down and got another handful. This time he let fly. His aim was true, and the pub owner gave a slight nod. Jack threw again and again. Each time it was easier, almost like sport. He cheered when he got a second good hit and then a third.

Suddenly whistles began blowing and several police came down the street yelling, "Break it up! Break it up! That's enough now. Everyone go on home."

Jack ducked back into the pub. The owner was already behind the bar wiping glasses as though nothing had happened. When he saw Jack, he said, "Get out of here. I don't want those cops finding one of you boys in here."

"But my money," protested Jack. "You saw me get three good hits. You owe me a penny and a half."

The man flipped Jack the money, and then snarled, "Now beat it."

Chapter 7

Bread and Water

JACK RAN BACK TO THE RIVER with a loaf of bread under one arm and a half-penny still in his pocket. He hadn't found Mrs. Booth, but he was able to keep his promise to get something for Amy and him to eat.

He'd gone back to the same bakery where the man had turned him away when he'd asked for a job. At first he thought that he'd never give that man his business. But the more he thought about it, it made him feel good to imagine slapping down his penny on the counter and demanding the biggest loaf of that good-looking white bread that he could see. He'd show that bakerman that he wasn't a beggar.

But when he got to the bakery, the man wasn't anywhere around. There was only a girl just a little older than Amy minding the shop. He bought the loaf and soon forgot about the ornery baker as he ran to the river.

He scrambled over the wall and dropped to the narrow strip of sand below. "Amy, Amy. Look here," he called as he worked his way over the rocks and around the pillar.

"Jack," Amy said as she got up from the sand and came toward him. "Where have you been? You've been away 'most all day. What you been up to?" Then she saw the loaf he was holding out. "Jack, where did you get that bread? You didn't steal it, did you?"

"No. I didn't steal it, and I didn't beg for it either. I earned some money, and I *bought* it. What's more, I still got a half-penny left, right here in my pocket." Jack pulled out the little copper and held it in the palm of his hand for Amy to inspect.

"Oh, Jack. I'm so hungry. I'm glad you got something to eat." She broke off a hunk of bread and began eating it. Jack grinned and did the same.

Then Jack realized that in spite of how hungry he had been, he had come all the way back home to share the bread with Amy before taking any himself. *It wouldn't have been right to eat it by myself*, he thought. *Whatever we've got is for sharing*. What was even stranger, he was thinking of this damp cave as "home." He looked around as he chewed. The place really was terrible.

"Did you find Mrs. Booth, Jack?"

"No. But I'll look some more tomorrow. She's bound to turn up soon." He didn't want to tell Amy that even though he hadn't found Catherine Booth, he had found the Salvation Army. Then she'd want to know why he hadn't asked the Army where Mrs. Booth was. That might lead to telling her how he'd earned the money, and he knew she'd be angry. But she sure was enjoying the bread, and so was he.

"Look, Jack," Amy said after taking a few bites, "I appreciate the bread, but finding Mrs. Booth is more important than wasting time earning money."

"Well, I tried to find her."

"Trying's not good enough. We've *got* to find her."

"Well, we gotta eat, too, don't we?" Jack said angrily.

"But we can't keep staying in this old cave. We *have* to find Uncle Sedgwick. And Mrs. Booth is our only hope."

Amy fell silent, and Jack didn't try to answer her. What could he say without giving himself away? Besides, when Amy got silent like that, Jack knew she was angry. He decided to be silent, too, hoping that pretty soon the whole thing would blow over. Jack knew it wasn't the best way to work out problems, but he was a little bit mad at himself, and he didn't want to admit to what he had done.

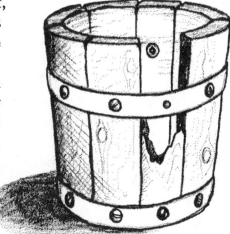

Sure enough, in a few moments Amy grabbed the old bucket and said, "I've been working on this broken bucket. I got the slats fitted back together, and I scrubbed it out with sand. Then all day I've been soaking it so the wood will swell. I put some rocks in it and held it under water. Now it doesn't leak. At least it holds water all the way up to where this one slat is broken. You could take it up and get some fresh water from the fountain up the street. Then we'd have drinking water."

"That'd be awful heavy to carry," said Jack looking at the bucket. It wasn't such a big bucket, but it didn't have a handle. And with the broken slat, he'd have to carry it tipped part way over to carry enough water to make it worth his trip. That could be heavy and hard to carry.

"But Jack, I haven't had anything to drink since we came down here last night. I was afraid to drink the river water. It's so dirty, I'm sure it would give a person the fever."

Her idea made sense, but he answered, "Let me just sit here and rest awhile. I been running all over town."

"Jack, I really am very thirsty."

"All right, all right. Just let me finish my piece of bread."

When Jack finally got back with the water, Amy had another fire laid. It was getting near dusk, and the lamplighter would be along soon. "I found a couple more sticks to use as matches," she said. "You know, if you were up there when the lamplighter came along, he'd probably just give you a light."

He probably would, but Jack didn't want to ask him. It would look so dumb asking for a light. Why would a boy on the street need to light a little stick? What would he tell the man, Jack wondered. "I'll just climb up the pole after he's gone," said Jack irritably. "Besides, since I fetched this water, I need a drink."

He started to reach his hands into their water bucket to scoop up a drink when Amy shouted, "Don't put your dirty hands in our drinking water. Go wash 'em first."

"I thought you said the river was dirty."

"So it is, too dirty to drink. But it's cleaner than your hands. It looks like you been playing in mud pies. And they stink too. What'd you do today to earn that money?"

"All right, give me that stick," Jack said, not wanting to answer Amy about his earnings. "I'll go up and get the stupid light, and wash my hands when I get back."

When the fire was blazing and the children were sitting around it eating some more bread, Amy bent her hurt foot back and forth testing her ankle. "It's a bit better, but I still don't think I should walk around town tomorrow. Would you mind going out by yourself again, Jack, to look for Mrs. Booth? We've got to find her! She's our only hope. We can't stay down here much longer."

Jack grunted but didn't feel like talking. What if he found Mrs. Booth and one of the Salvationists recognized him and told her he was one of the boys throwing things at the band? Maybe he'd just go looking for Uncle Sedgwick himself.

Later, when Amy was curled
up sleeping by the fire with her green
shawl thrown over her, he sat staring into the little
flames. The song that the Salvationists were singing
kept playing in his mind: "We're bound for the land
of the pure and the holy," and then that haunting
chorus: "Will you go? Will you go?"

The music had sounded pretty . . . he especially
liked that horn. Thinking about it now made him
feel bad that he had thrown stuff at them. Back and
forth he argued with himself:

It wasn't that bad. I didn't really hurt anyone.

But, I must admit, they didn't do nothin' to deserve it. And even if they had, throwing horse manure is pretty mean.

But we needed the money.

Finally he drifted off into a fitful sleep filled with dreams of the Salvationists climbing on a train and singing. But every time Jack tried to get on the train with them, they would sadly shake their heads and say, "Sorry, we're bound for the land of the pure and the holy, and pure and holy you're certainly not."

Chapter 8

Rockets Away

T HE NEXT MORNING Jack split the remaining bread with Amy and climbed up to the street. It was later than he'd started out the day before, and the day was already sunny and warm. The air had the memory of summer to it, maybe one last time before the chill of autumn.

At home he had liked the autumn. The trees turned such beautiful colors, and the apples got shiny and juicy. Mama sure could make the best apple pies. But in the city there were no trees to fill one's eye with flaming reds and yellows. In the city it was just gray and chilly, not the kind of crispness that made you want to take a deep breath and run and play. Autumn in the city just reminded him that he had no mother to bake apple pies, and he had no home to keep warm in during the cold wet winter. And winter was surely coming.

But today *was* sunny, and Jack felt better than he had last night. Maybe those Salvationists wouldn't recognize him. Maybe finding Mrs. Booth was the best way to find Uncle Sedgwick. That was what

Amy expected him to do; his sister had made it very clear. "It's the most important thing," she'd said. "We can't stay down here in this cave." When Jack pointed out that he had brought her some bread, she'd said, "What's a hunk of bread, Jack? We don't have a home, and winter's coming. You've got to find Mrs. Booth. Don't be doin' anything else today." Now as Jack trudged along, he knew Amy was right, but he was feeling pretty hungry again.

But where should he look? Finally he ended up on the street with the pub where the man had paid him the day before. Maybe the owner would know where the Salvationists were, and . . . maybe he could use some more "help." Just once more; then he could get something to eat. *Then* he would talk to Mrs. Booth.

When he got there and peeked through the door, the owner said, "You, boy, come in here. Don't stand there in the doorway. I don't want people seeing you hangin' 'round here."

As Jack walked up to the bar, he noticed three little stools on the floor in front of it. "What are these stools for?" he asked.

"Them's for children, of course. Where you from, anyway? You ain't from around here, or you'd for sure know what a children's stool was. Beside, you got a country accent to your talk."

"So what if I ain't from around here? Why do children need stools in here?" Jack insisted.

"It's so the little ones can reach the bar so's they can get themselves something to drink. What else?"

"You mean you serve beer to little children?"

"Ha! Only if they can't afford something stronger. It's good for business to get your customers started young. They develop a bigger thirst that way." The man polished the bar with his dirty apron for a few moments then said, "So what you want? You thirsty or something?"

"No," Jack said. "I was just wonderin' if . . . well, if you needed any more help with those Salvationists."

"Ah. So you want to earn some more money, do you?"

Jack nodded.

"Well, you go over on Queen Victoria Street, 'bout five streets down. Can't miss it—big building with a sign calling it 'The Christian Mission.' You hang 'round there, but not too close, mind you. You'll see some of the other boys about. Sooner or later a bunch of them Salvationists will come marching out. You follow them at a distance until they set up for their show. Then let 'em have it. You got it? You were a pretty good shot yesterday. Just keep it up."

"But how will you know how many hits I get so's to pay me?"

"I got someone watchin'—name's Jed. He'll keep track and report to me. You come by later and I'll pay you. But don't you come straight back here. I don't want no trouble. Understand?"

Jack headed toward Queen Victoria Street, but it was well into the afternoon before he found the building. As he approached, he debated with himself whether to try and earn some more money or go up to the door and see if Mrs. Booth was there. *Maybe*, he thought, *they've already gone.*

But the question was decided for him when one of the other boys noticed him looking at the place and called him to come around the corner. "What you doin' getting so close, mate?"

"I thought they might've gone out already," said Jack.

"Not yet, but you're going to give us all away, dummy," hissed the boy. "If they

know we're waitin' for them, they might not come out at all."

"Forget him," said an older boy standing near. "He don't know nothin'. I'm Jed, Winslow's man. You heard of me, boy?"

Jack nodded.

Jed snorted. "Those Salvationists go out every day, rain or shine, whether we throw stuff at them or not. They believe it's their God-given duty to save the world."

"Save the world?" asked Jack. "But I thought they were just trying to ruin people's business."

"Oh, yeah. They got it in for people in the sin business," Jed smirked.

"What's a sin business?" asked Jack.

"Gin houses, white slavers, and the like," said Jed. "Tell ya the truth, I'd just as soon they shut down the gin houses. My old man's a drunk, and he beats me every night he comes home drunk, which is nearly every night. So I say good riddance."

"Then how come you workin' for Winslow?" piped up one of the younger boys.

"It's a way to get a few coins," Jed shrugged.

Jack persisted. "But what are white slavers?"

"Don't you know what white slavers are?" The younger boy leaned close to Jack's ear. "They steal young girls."

"Yeah," said Jed, "*kidnap*'s the word for it. Sometimes they even sell the girls to rich men over in France or Holland or Germany who want to buy a mistress."

A kind of dread made Jack's stomach tighten. "Isn't there some kind of a law against kidnapping girls? And how do they get them over to Europe anyway. Somebody would see 'em."

"Law? There ain't no law that sticks. That's one of the things the Salvation Army is always yellin' about—tryin' to get the government to stop the slavin'. As for gettin' the girls over to Europe, that's easy." Jed was clearly enjoying his role of dispensing worldly wisdom. He lowered his voice. "They drug 'em. When the girls are unconscious they nail 'em in coffins with air holes drilled in 'em and ship 'em over. Ain't nobody ever asks to see a dead body inside a coffin, so no one ever knows that it's a live girl inside. 'Cept . . . they ain't always alive."

The knot in Jack's stomach got tighter. "What do you mean?" he demanded.

"Sometimes they drug the girls too much and they die," Jed said matter-of-factly. "And *sometimes* they don't give 'em enough, and they wake up 'fore they get there." He paused for effect. "What would *you* do if you woke up and found yourself nailed inside a dark coffin? Why, some of them girls go screamin' crazy, and some just plain die trying to scratch their way out."

All the boys were silent as they considered such a horrible fate. Finally one of the younger boys said, "My cousin was kidnapped by a white slaver, and ain't no one ever heard from her since."

"Your cousin?" asked Jack. "How old was your cousin?"

"Thirteen, but she looked older."

"Thirteen, fourteen, it don't make no difference," snorted Jed. "Those slavers will take any girl about that age."

Just then they heard a familiar boom, boom, boom. The Salvation Army band was coming out.

The boys stayed hidden until the band went marching down the street, then they followed just out of sight. Along the way they gathered things to throw. Jed picked up some stinking old bones that the dogs hadn't eaten. The other boys found some rotten tomatoes in a pile of garbage, which they loaded into a rag, gathering up the four corners to make a bag in which to carry them.

Jack looked but didn't see Mrs. Booth with the band. Good. After he got his money from Winslow, he could go back to The Christian Mission and ask for Mrs. Booth. But Jack was thinking hard. If the Salvation Army was against those white slavers, wasn't it better to help them instead of fight them? But his growling stomach kept him following the band with the other boys.

This time the Army went down near the docks where the ships loaded and unloaded. The docks were wide and stuck out into the water like big fingers. Warehouses were built on some of the docks. Others were just flat platforms to receive goods from the ships that would tie up between them.

The boys stayed back while the Salvationists set up right at the beginning of one dock, with their backs to its warehouse. There was no ship tied up at that dock. The next dock was the flat type. On the other side of it was a huge, square-rigged merchant ship. Dozens of sailors and dock workers were preparing it to set sail. It was to these men—across the narrow slip of water between the docks—that the Salvationists planned to sing and preach. Of course, there were plenty of people going back and forth along the street at the foot of the docks who would hear them too. And that's where the boys stood behind several bales of cotton waiting for their chance to pelt the Salvationists.

When the group was ready, one of the Salvationists picked up a megaphone to speak. It was General Booth himself. Somehow, as the boys had followed along, Jack hadn't seen Booth in the group. But there he was. Quickly Jack looked to see if Mrs. Booth was also there, but he didn't see her. Then the general began speaking.

Many people wonder why we call ourselves the Salvation Army. We're an army because we fight. We fight for the souls of men and women and boys and girls. We fight to release them from the shackles of sin and bring them to Jesus. We fight to bring them to that land of the pure and the holy.

Listen to me all you brothers who sail the seven seas and work these docks. While women weep, as they do now, I'll fight; while little children go hungry, I'll fight; while men go to prison, in and out, in and out, as they do now—yes, I can see some of you know what I'm talking about—well, I'll fight. While there is a drunkard left, while there is a poor lost girl upon the streets, where there remains one dark soul without the light of God—I'll fight! I'll fight to the very end!

That's why we're called the Salvation Army. But before I tell you about Jesus Christ and how He can free you from sin, listen to this beautiful song, sung by our three Hallelujah Lasses and accompanied by Charlie Fry and his Hallelujah Band.

As the band was getting tuned up, Jack's attention was distracted by a couple of sailors on the dock across from the Salvationists. One was holding a small torch as the other tipped over a crate and then wrestled it around. The first one bent down and was doing something with the torch. Then he stood up, threw the torch into the water, and both men started running. It was then that Jack recognized one of the sailors as the "river rat" he'd almost hit in the boat on the river the morning before.

Suddenly from the crate on the dock there came a cloud of white smoke and a loud "hissst" as something rocketed out of the crate, across the water, and landed among the Salvationists. Before the Salvation Army people could jump back, several more rockets flew into their midst. They were signal flares, shooting right at the Hallelujah Lasses. As Jack watched, two of the women were hit directly by the flaming torpedoes while other Salvationists jumped around dodging the flares as they landed among them. Soon there was thick smoke everywhere. The last thing Jack saw was the two women who had been hit trying to put out their flaming clothes.

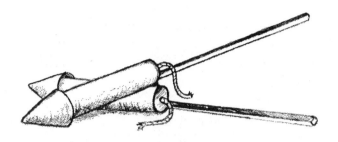

Everyone on the street began to run. Jack and the other boys were running with them. People scattered in every direction, and Jack found himself alone. When he had no more breath to run further, he slowed to a walk. He was heading back toward the river cave. Why would those sailors do such a thing? Yesterday Jack and the other boys had been throwing trash. It made a mess and might have left a few bruises, but those flares could have killed people. What was going on?

As Jack climbed over the rail beside the river, he felt dejected. The afternoon would soon be over and he still had not contacted Mrs. Booth. And today he had no money and couldn't bring back anything for Amy to eat. As he thought about it, Jack dreaded facing her. How could he tell her about what had happened?

He didn't call out to her when he climbed around the pillar, but even if he had, it would have done no good. She wasn't there. All that was left in the cave was her green shawl and a strange deep gouge in the sand by the river.

Chapter 9

Kidnapped

A MY! AMY!" JACK CALLED. She must be nearby some-where. But there was no answer. He kicked around amongst the trash at the back of the cave. He didn't know what he was looking for . . . maybe she'd left a note.

Nothing.

Jack picked up Amy's shawl. What now? Maybe she'd gotten tired of staying in the cave and had climbed up to the street to walk around. Should he look for her or just wait? As he stood uncertainly at the cave opening, his eyes were drawn again to the deep gouge in the sand at the river's edge. He inspected it more carefully. It was about four feet long, coming right out of the river. In fact, at the water's edge, where the water was no more than an inch deep, Jack could see that the groove extended into the river. Something had been dragged up out of the river, something heavy like a boat.

Of course! That was it. Someone had beached a boat in the cave. As he looked more closely, Jack could see large boot prints in the sand. Then, right next to the water, where the sand was damp and firm, Jack saw Amy's footprint on top of one of the boot prints.

The clues were clear: A boat had stopped, and Amy had gone away in it. But who could have been in the boat, and where could Amy have gone? Jack looked out over the river in the late afternoon sun. There were several boats on the river, but none small enough to be beached in the cave.

"Amy! Amy!" Jack yelled with all his might out over the water. His voice echoed in the hollow confines of the cave and off the stone bridge above. But there was no answer from his sister.

"Amy, Amy, Amy," muttered Jack as he stumbled around inside the cave, kicking the sand with his feet. "Don't leave me, Amy. Papa's dead, and Mama's gone . . ." He still didn't like saying the words out loud that admitted his mother was dead. Jack kicked angrily at the charred sticks in the fire pit. "And now you've run off! How will we ever find Uncle Sedgwick?"

That's when Jack noticed the water bucket. It had been tipped over. He felt the sand around it. Wet. *Strange,* thought Jack. *Amy wouldn't dump out our water.* But someone had, and not very long ago, either, because the sand was more than damp. It was wet, very wet, like someone had just poured out the water ten or fifteen minutes ago. One of Amy's footprints was planted squarely in this wet sand too. But it was also pulled off to the side as though her foot had been dragged away.

A terrible realization began to sweep over Jack. Amy hadn't gone off on some errand, and she hadn't gone off willingly with someone in a boat. She had fought. She had struggled, and then she had been taken away against her will.

Amy had been kidnapped.

That's why the water bucket was tipped over; that's why her shawl had been left behind, and that's what all the tracks in the sand indicated. Someone had grabbed her and pulled her into that boat. She had been kidnapped. There was no getting around it.

As soon as Jack realized what had happened, he felt certain he knew who had done it. It had to be those two men who had fired the flares at the Salvationists, the ones Jack almost hit when he was throwing rocks at the river rat. Yeah, those river rats were the only people who knew anyone was staying in this cave. And they would have had time. If they had come on the river instead of running all around through the streets of London as Jack had done, they could easily have been here and gone before Jack arrived. But why? Why would they have wanted to kidnap Amy?

Somewhere in the back of Jack's mind there was a clue. They had been angry at Jack for throwing rocks and had threatened him if he ever did it again. But there was something else, something they had said—not to him, but—about . . . about what? And then Jack remembered. It was what they'd said about Amy. The one rowing had said something like, "Hey, Rodney, it's a girl." And the other one, the big burly

72

one who had been standing up yelling at Jack, had said, "Yeah, and just about the right age too."

"The right age for what?" wondered Jack aloud, and the moment he said it a cold chill ran down his spine. Those men where white slavers. And they'd taken Amy.

Jack fought back the wave of panic that swept over him. He had to find his sister. He had to get her back.

Out of the cave Jack ran, almost slipping on the rocks as he scrambled around the pillar. In a moment he had scampered up the wall and was on the street. Where would he go? Whom could he ask? How could he find her? He ran along the river's edge looking at all the boats going peacefully back and forth below. Amy had to be in one of them. But what if he were going the wrong direction? While he ran himself breathless going up the river, what if the kidnappers were rowing as fast as they could down the river with Amy tied up under an old blanket in the bottom of the boat so no one could see her? Jack's mind ran wild as he tried to imagine what could be happening to her. Would she be nailed in a coffin and thrown down into the dark, damp hold of a ship? Would she die from too much of the drug? Or would she wake up and go crazy trying to scratch her way out? Would she be sold to someone who would beat her? And then he sucked in his breath with a start— whether the person who bought her beat her or not, she wouldn't be free. He might not ever see her again.

Jack ran all the faster. He dodged through day merchants pushing their carts back from the market. He pushed aside groups of other children in his way. He tripped over the bucket of a fisherman who stood with a pole and line at the wall by the river's edge.

But he never saw Amy. In fact, he didn't see even one boat that looked like the one the sailors had been in.

Finally, Jack fell to the cobblestone street exhausted and crying in great sobs as he tried to catch his breath. It was useless. He could never find his sister this way. He could run up and down the Thames River and all over London for days without ever seeing her. By then she might be shipped off to face some horrible life. . . . He didn't want to think about it.

Slowly he picked himself up and walked back toward the cave. Maybe he was wrong. Maybe he was imagining all this. Yeah, that had to be it. Amy wasn't really kidnapped. She had just gone out to get some fresh air and would be back in their cave by the time he got there. He should just settle down and quit imagining the worst.

He took a deep breath and thought about the Salvationists. If there was a God like they said there was, He certainly wouldn't let such a terrible thing happen to his sister. After all, she had never done anything so bad. She hadn't even thrown stuff at the Salvationists.

And then another thought crossed Jack's mind. What if God was punishing her because of the bad things he had done? "Oh, God," he found himself saying, "please don't. Don't let her be kidnapped. I won't throw any more stuff at that Salvation Army, and I won't steal any more apples or anything."

But when he got to the cave, it was just as he had left it. Amy was not there.

Chapter 10

The Devil's Mile

WHEN JACK GOT BACK up to the street, the lamplighter was coming along, but Jack didn't care.
Unless he could find Amy, he wouldn't need a fire
tonight.

What was he going to do? Somehow he had to get
help. He thought of trying to find a bobby, but then
he remembered what Jed had said: there were no
laws the policemen could enforce to stop the slave
trade. The Salvation Army was fighting to get such
laws passed, but so far there was very little the
police could do. Besides, why would a bobby believe a
wild story like his?

No, the police weren't likely to search the city for
his sister on the mere word of a boy, who had no
home and no parents to back up his story. But if he
could just find out where they were holding Amy . . .
then maybe someone would believe him and help.

Slowly an idea began to form in Jack's mind.
Maybe Winslow, the pub owner, would know about
the slave trade. At least he was dead set against the
Salvation Army and their attempts to change things,

76

and he wasn't against doing some shady deals on the side.

It wasn't much of an idea, but it was the only one he had. Jack set off through the darkening streets at a jog.

When Jack got to the pub, Winslow was busy with customers. In fact, the popular bar was full of loud-talking workmen who probably should have been home with their families. A woman played a piano as several men around her sang songs. The bright flames in the fireplace reflected off the bright copper pots hanging from pegs on the wall. Candles sat in the windows and elsewhere to light the room.

Jack stepped up to the bar and tried to get Winslow's attention. When the pub owner saw Jack, he scowled and kept on filling pints with beer. When he finally came Jack's way, he was obviously irritated. "Whatcha want? Don't go tellin' me I owe ya some ha'pennies. I heard what happened down at the dock today, and I don't pay boys who run off."

"I didn't come to collect," Jack said anxiously. "I just wanna ask if you know a big sailor named Rodney?"

"Maybe I do, and maybe I don't. Rodney's a mighty common name. What's it to you?"

"He kidnapped my sister, and I got to find her," Jack pleaded.

Winslow's scowl deepened. "Listen, boy. I don't have nothin' to do with kidnappin' girls. Never have, never will. I just run a legal pub."

"Yeah, but both you and Rodney don't like the Salvation Army."

"How do you know that?"

"'Cause it was Rodney and another guy with him that fired those flare rockets at the Salvation Army this afternoon. I saw 'em do it," said Jack.

"So what?" said Winslow. "Rodney's got his reasons for not liking the Army, and I got mine. That doesn't mean we work together."

"But you do know him, then?"

"I know who he is, nothin' more," said the pub owner as he walked back down the bar to serve a new customer.

When he returned, Jack persisted. "All I want to know is where he took my sister. Do you know where Rodney might be?"

"I don't know nothin'. Understand? I don't want anyone thinkin' that I'm tied in with Rodney and his kind. It's a dirty business they're into." Winslow turned away to draw a pint of beer for a customer. In a few minutes he came back over to Jack. "You say he took your sister? Hmmm. Come to think of it, I have seen Rodney hanging out with Mary Jaffries. She runs at least a dozen bawdyhouses. There's four of 'em over on Church Street in Chelsea, and another just over on Gray's Inn Road. But there's one I've heard tell where Rodney hangs out. Up on Devil's Mile. You might try there for your sister."

"Where's the Devil's Mile?" said Jack.

"Ain't the real name. That's just what they call it. Uh . . . what's the name of that street? Hey, Peter,"

Winslow called to a customer across the room. "What's the name of that street they call the Devil's Mile?"

"You mean Islington?"

"Yeah, that's it, Islington High Street. But it ain't a mile long; it's just a little short street."

"But where is it?" asked Jack.

"Stubborn boy, ain't you! Drivin' me crazy." He stared at Jack for a few moments. Then he said, "All right. Here's what you do. Go up Aldersgate. It turns into Goswell. Soon's you cross Pentonville Road, you're right there. 'Bout a mile and a half from here. Can't miss it. Now beat it. Go on; get out of here."

Jack discovered that you *could* miss the street and rather easily, too, especially at night. But once he found it, he knew it was the "Devil's Mile." Every other door seemed to be a pub that was open and noisy, even this late in the evening. Many people were out on the street, some well-dressed and businesslike and others dirty and drunk. Jack even had to walk around three men sleeping on the sidewalk, or maybe they were passed out drunk.

But how was he going to find Amy? She wasn't likely to be in one of the pubs, or she could have just walked out. Winslow had mentioned a "house" operated by some woman. But how would he know which one? There were several houses along this street . . . at least between the pubs. Jack wandered along the street, looking in the door of every pub and studying every house hoping to find some clue.

Then from across the street Jack heard a familiar voice. A huge man came out of a pub and yelled back to someone inside: "You don't need to worry. I always deliver my merchandise." It was Rodney, and he was coming across the street right toward Jack! If Rodney hadn't seen him yet, he soon would. There was nowhere to hide. Suddenly a horse and carriage came clattering down the street at a fast trot. It was a fancy four-wheeler with two little lanterns twinkling brightly.

Yelling at the driver, Rodney jumped back out of the street to avoid being run over. The driver swerved toward Jack and tried to slow down as he cursed back at Rodney. "Look before you stagger across the street, you fat lout, or you'll end up greasing my wheels."

It was Jack's chance. As the carriage swung past, he jumped on the back step where a coachmen sometimes stood. He held on with all his might and crouched down in the shadows as the carriage whisked him down the street away from Rodney. When he looked back, Rodney had crossed the street and was entering the house right by where Jack had been standing.

That must be where he's hiding Amy, thought Jack.

He dropped off the carriage and ran back up the street, weaving between the night revelers and jumping over the drunks until he got to the house into which Rodney had disappeared.

But how could he find out whether his sister was inside? Lights glowed dimly in the windows behind heavy red drapes, and piano music tinkled softly through the night air. From time to time, Jack could hear laughter within the house.

Finally, Jack could wait no longer. He had to do something, so he dashed up the steps and pounded on the door. Immediately the door opened, and a pinched-faced little doorman leaned out. "What do you want?"

"I'm looking for my sister, Amy," Jack said. "Is she here?"

The man sneered. "I don't know you, so how could I know who your sister is. Now be gone with ya," and he started to close the door.

"Wait," said Jack. "Maybe you've seen her. She's a little taller than me, and she has dark red hair. It's curly, and she's very pretty. Have you seen her? She's been kidnapped by a man named Rodney. He just came in . . ."

At the mention of Rodney's name, the man slammed the door before Jack could say more.

Jack stood on the steps wondering what to do until he saw another horse-drawn cab approaching. The cab stopped, and a finely dressed man opened the door, stepped out and approached the house. Jack was feeling desperate. "Excuse me, sir," he said, "my sister has been kidnapped, and I think she's being held inside this house by some very bad people."

The man reacted as if he had seen a ghost. He stared wide-eyed at Jack for a moment then raised his cane in a threatening manner. "You haven't seen me here," he commanded. Then he turned and ran after the cab that was just starting to pull away. He caught the driver's attention and got him to stop. Then the man rode off without looking back.

Jack realized that if he was going to free his sister he wasn't likely to get any help from anyone on the street. He would have to find some other way to get Amy.

Most of the buildings and houses on Devil's Mile were built side by side with no space between them. But three houses down, Jack found a little passage between two buildings that allowed him to walk back to the alley behind the house. The passageway was even too narrow to drive a cart through. Jack turned and walked up the alley, counting three houses to the building he thought Amy was in. Maybe, he thought, he could find a way inside through a back entrance.

The only light was from a half moon that shown through a hazy sky. Laundry hung like dancing ghosts from clotheslines strung across the alley. When Jack was sure he had located the correct building, he was disappointed to find the back door securely locked. The door actually led into a low lean-to shed that was built onto the back of the house. Above the shed were two windows leading directly into the house. They were both shuttered. But through the cracks in the shutters on one of the windows, Jack made out the dim shine of a light. *Could Amy be in there?* Jack wondered.

A little further down the alley, he found some old boxes. He brought them back to the shed and piled one on top of the other. Then he climbed up. It gave him just enough height that he was able to pull himself up onto the roof of the shed. From there he crept toward the window with the light. He tapped on the shutter softly, but there was no response. He tapped again harder and called out, "Amy! Amy! Are you in there?"

In the quiet evening, he was certain that everyone in the neighborhood could hear him. But still there was no answer.

Jack waited a moment adjusting his weight so as not to slip down the shed's roof. Finally, he decided he had to try for all he was worth. What difference would it make if he was careful not to get caught but never found Amy? So he beat on the shutter with his fists and yelled with all his might.

The shutters flung open, knocking him down the roof where he fell to the ground just as a man leaned out and bellowed, "What do you want out here, anyway? Get out of here or I'll beat the daylights out of you!" Then the shutters closed.

Jack picked himself up and started to run when he heard another voice. It was a girl's voice coming from behind the dark window, the one with the shutters still locked. "Jack! Jack! Is that you?"

It was Amy!

"Amy!" Jack called back in relief. "I came to get you. Let's get out of here."

"I can't. I'm locked in this little room."

"Are you okay? Have they hurt you?"

"No. No one's hurt me yet." And then Jack could hear her start to cry. "But Jack," Amy sobbed, "you gotta get me out of here. I'm scared. This is an awful place, and I think they are going to take me away tomorrow."

Just then someone came running out of the little passage between the buildings and into the alley. In the dim light Jack could see that he was big, and he was headed right for Jack.

Chapter 11

Midnight Raid

JACK HAD ONLY A GLIMPSE of the man running down the alley toward him, but he was sure it was Rodney. He took off the other way not knowing if he could get out of the alley in that direction. He stumbled over trash and fell two or three times, but finally he came out into another street where the glow of a distant street lamp gave him some hope. He ran faster, and after he had crossed a couple other streets, he was convinced he was no longer being chased.

He slowed to a walk, keeping to the shadows where he couldn't be seen, but his heart went on racing for quite some time.

He had found Amy; that was good. But finding her confirmed all his worst fears. If he couldn't get her out of that place, she would soon be shipped away, and he might never see her again.

He had to get some help! But who could help him? Who would believe him? Who would even care? And what could one or even two people do. What he

needed was an army to raid that place and rescue his
sister . . . .

Jack stopped in his tracks. That was *it*—an army!
What was it General Booth had said down by the
docks? "While there is a poor lost girl upon the
streets . . . I'll fight! I'll fight to the very end!" Jack
needed the *Salvation Army*. Maybe they would help
him save his sister.

It was nearly midnight when
Jack found the Salvation Army
headquarters again on Queen
Victoria Street, not far from
the river. Everything looked
so different at night that he
almost didn't recognize it.
Inside all the lights were
out. But Jack was deter-
mined. He pounded on the
door until a young man in
his nightshirt and looking
very tired answered. A
candle flickered weakly in
the room behind him.

"I have to speak to
General Booth," Jack said
urgently.

"He's not available right
now," the man said. "He's trying to sleep. Look, son. If you
need something to eat, come

back tomorrow morning. We'll serve you breakfast."

"That's not it! I have to talk to the general."

"I'm sorry. He can't be disturbed. He's very tired."

Jack was close to tears. "But he said he would fight! And I need him to fight for my sister right now. Tomorrow may be too late!"

The young man opened the door a little wider. "What do you mean, 'fight for your sister'?"

"She's been kidnapped," said Jack, fighting back the tears. "Rodney took her—that, that sailor down at the docks, the one who fired those flare rockets at you today! Now she's locked up in a house on the Devil's Mile. They're going to ship her out tomorrow!"

The young man reached out and pulled Jack through the doorway. "I see. That's different. Come on in, son." He led Jack through a long hall to a huge kitchen where he lit a lamp and put it on a small table. "Wait here," he said. "Oh, if you want something to eat, help yourself to those bran muffins on the counter."

Jack thought that muffins had never tasted so good. In his fear for Amy he had forgotten he hadn't eaten anything all day. He was licking his fingers when the general himself came into the kitchen, his steely gray hair sticking almost straight up and his shirt buttoned crooked.

"What's this about your sister being kidnapped?" he boomed. His eyes looked like a storm about to strike.

So Jack told him, and the general kept asking questions, his voice getting more gentle as he talked. Soon the whole story came out . . . including Jack throwing stuff at the Salvation Army to earn some money for bread and the fact that he and Amy had been living in a cave under a bridge since their mother died.

"This is terrible," thundered the general. He stalked back and forth in the kitchen tugging on his beard. Then he asked Jack to describe again very carefully where Amy was being held. When he had asked a few more questions about the shed on which Jack had climbed, the general mused, "Hmmm. If they haven't moved her to a different room, there's a chance we could climb up there with a bar and pry open those shutters. We just might be able to have her out of there before they even notice. But son, I need to know whether you are telling me the whole truth, and that you're not leaving anything out. Because if we make a mistake, we could be in very big trouble for breaking into some citizen's home. Now are you completely sure your sister is being held there against her will?"

"Yes, sir!" said Jack. "She talked to me through the shutters. She said, 'I got to get out of here,' and I know it was Amy."

"All right," said the general. "Philip," he turned to the young man in the nightshirt, "get a couple of the other officers, and let's go see what we can do."

When Jack and the four Salvation Army men got back to the Devil's Mile, a cab was just pulling away from the front of the house. "Is that the house?" asked General Booth in a low voice.

"That's it," said Jack. "And the way to get around back is through that little passage between those two buildings up there. Come on; I'll show you."

"Not yet," said the general. "First we ask God's help."

They all stood in a little circle in the shadows across the street a little way down from their objective, and the general's gentle voice spoke quietly. "Lord, You know of the great sins that plague this city and the terrible suffering it brings to so many people. Now we ask Your help and protection as we try to free one of your little ones. Give us success, and protect her from any harm. Amen." The general straightened.

"All right, son. Lead the way."

When Jack and the men got to the shed behind the house, the boxes he had piled up were still there. It gave him hope that Rodney and his gang had not done too much to secure Amy.

The boxes, however, weren't strong enough to hold the bigger men, so they gave a boost to young Philip. From the top of the shed, Philip pulled one of the other men up.

"Now you listen to me, Jack," whispered the general. "If we get your sister out, but someone discovers us in the process, grab her and take off running back to headquarters. We'll try to delay them to give you some time. Think you can find headquarters again?"

"I think so," said Jack. He was trying not to shiver in the cold night air.

Just then Jack looked up to see the two Salvation Army officers getting ready to pry open the shutters over one of the windows with the iron bar they had brought with them. "No!" said Jack in a desperate whisper. "Not that window. The other one." He'd almost been too late.

The men moved like cats across the shed roof to the other window. In the near black night, they looked at Jack. "Yeah, that one," he whispered.

The men put their bar between the two shutters and gave a pull. There was a creak, but nothing happened. Again they pulled. This time there was a loud snap and a splintering sound as the shutters swung open. Both men hung on to the swinging shutters so as not to lose their balance on the steep roof.

From inside the room there came a scream.

"Amy!" Jack called. "Amy, open the window."

Amy's scream had come only from the fright of waking up in the middle of the night to see a couple dark shapes outside her window. Now Jack could just barely see Amy standing inside the window working frantically to get the window open. But just as the latch came free, and Amy was raising the window, a light appeared in the room behind her.

"Hey, what are you doing there?" came a woman's angry voice. "You get back in here. You can't leave."

Amy was climbing out the window just as the woman caught her and tried to drag her back inside.

"Help her!" screamed Jack to the two men on the shed roof.

They grabbed on to Amy's arms while the woman inside held fast to one of her legs, but it wasn't much of a tug-of-war. In just moments the men had pulled her free, and Amy was standing on the roof holding tightly to her rescuers.

The woman inside was screaming for help as the two men on the roof lowered Amy to the general and the other man in the alley below. As soon as Amy was safe on the ground, the general said to Jack,

"Don't wait for us. Get her out of here. We'll see you later."

Jack and Amy ran for all they were worth. They were three streets away before Jack even dared to look back. No one seemed to be following. "Let's slow down," he gasped. "We've got a long way to go." But Amy kept running, her arms swinging like windmills, and her hair flying back.

When Jack caught up to her side again, he noticed in the dim light of a street lamp that tears were streaming across her cheeks. "Amy, what's the matter? Come on; slow down." He reached out and put his hand on her shoulder. She jerked away, but she did slow down. As soon as she was walking, great sobs began to shake her body, and she buried her face in her hands.

"Hey, Amy, what's the matter? Are you hurt?" Jack awkwardly patted her shoulder, while he tried to catch his breath.

She shook her head wildly. "No," she sobbed. "I'm just so glad we're back together." She stopped and threw her arms around her brother. Jack looked around, but there was no one on the street to notice. He wrapped his arms around his sister and hugged her close. In a few moments they continued on toward the Salvation Army headquarters.

Within an hour, the strange little group was all together again, being served hot tea in headquarter's kitchen by none other than Mrs. Catherine Booth. As the men told their story with big gestures and Mrs. Booth murmured sympathetically, Jack and Amy looked at each other. Finally, they could ask the lady with the smiling eyes about their Uncle Sedgwick, the tailor.

Chapter 12

Escape to America

WHEN THE STORY was told and second cups of tea had been poured, Amy spoke up. "Mrs. Booth," she said, "one day when we were looking for our uncle, we asked another tailor about him. He said you did business with our uncle for a while. Do you remember him?"

Mrs. Booth knit her forehead.

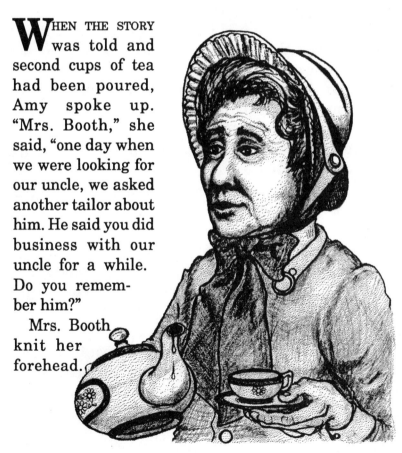

"Well, it's been almost two years since I've used any tailor. We sew all our uniforms ourselves these days. It helps teach the new recruits a useful trade."

"But when you did use a tailor," said Jack, "you used to go to one over on . . . oh, I can't remember the name of the street. Anyway, he was an old man, and he said you had been his regular customer until you switched to our uncle, Sedgwick Masters. Don't you remember?"

"Why yes, Sedgwick Masters the tailor. Now I remember. I used him for only a few months. Actually, he was the one who suggested that we sew our own uniforms."

"But where is he now?" asked Amy. "You see, he's our only living relative. We don't have any other family. We've got to find him so we can have some place to live. Mother said he had some money, so he could take us in."

The lines on Mrs. Booth's forehead deepened. "I don't know where he is anymore. But I don't think he's in London. At least the other day I noticed that his old shop was empty. Come to think of it, he used to talk a lot about the great opportunities overseas—in India, Canada, even Australia. Maybe he finally packed up and left. I just don't know."

Both children sat in stunned silence. Their last hope for finding their uncle had evaporated. Amy blinked away the hot tears that sprang to her eyes. It was a terrible lost feeling not to have any home. The cave wasn't comfortable, but they'd made the best of it—even pretended it was an adventure—because there had always been hope, the hope that they would soon find their uncle and have a home and family again. Now that hope was gone. She had been rescued, but now what were they going to do?

Jack looked down at the floor, hoping that the hair that fell over his eyes would hide the fact that he was crying. But looking down made him feel all the more hopeless. The sole of his right shoe was tearing loose from the uppers, and they had no money to buy new ones, or even to get it fixed. And they couldn't go back to the cave—it was too dangerous. What would they do?

Mrs. Booth stepped between the children and put a hand on each of their shoulders. "There, there," she said, "remember what our Lord Jesus said: 'Are not two sparrows sold for a farthing? and one of them shall not fall on the ground without your Father knowing.' So, 'Fear ye not therefore, ye are of more value than many sparrows.' God will not forget you, my young friends. Besides, for now you can stay here with us. And now it's very, very late. Let's get to bed."

The cots were plain, but they were the first warm beds that Jack and Amy had slept in for many nights. A feather bed in a palace couldn't have felt better.

Three days later the children were enjoying their life at the Salvation Army headquarters. They had received a bath, clean clothes, and were eating three good meals a day. Jack even had a different pair of shoes. They weren't new, but at least they weren't falling apart. The children had also been given chores to do, but Jack and Amy didn't mind; it made them feel useful. Philip Barker, the young man who had met Jack at the door the night he came for help, and his wife, Martha, had taken special responsibility for the children. They assigned chores for the children to do and found clothes for them.

One day the Barkers took Jack and Amy to Mrs. Witherspoon's. There they paid the debt for the rent that the children had been unable to pay when their mother had been so sick. "I ought to charge interest, it's gone unpaid for so long," grumbled Mrs. Witherspoon.

"Well, it's only been a few days. That hardly seems appropriate . . ." began Philip.

"We'd be glad to add whatever you think's fair," broke in Martha, "provided you tell us where their mother was buried. I'm sure the children would want to visit her grave. And, of course, you will be returning their trunk now, won't you?"

"You can have that old trunk, but you'll have to go up stairs and get it yourself. I'm not going to carry the thing down for you."

"And where was Mrs. Crumpton buried?"

"How should I know? I'm not the mortician."

"But you would have a receipt. It's the law," said Philip, holding a small coin out toward Mrs. Witherspoon.

"Oh, all right. It's probably around here somewhere."

The Barkers took the children that very afternoon to the cemetery and found the pauper's grave where their mother was registered as having been buried. They stood there a long time and cried as they thought about her and the ways their life had changed in the last few days.

That evening they cried again as they went through their belongings from the old trunk. Jack and Amy had never prayed much before, but every evening before bedtime, the Barkers asked them to come to their room for family prayers. There Philip read a few verses from the Bible, and both he and Martha prayed. This evening the prayers were for the children's loss of their mother and that God would comfort them. "Would either of you like to pray too?" Martha asked. Jack liked the way she smiled at them—but he wasn't sure about praying, not even at a time like this. But Amy prayed, and afterward, Jack wished he had too.

The Barkers prayed like Jesus was a friend sitting right there in the room with them. It made Jack feel like the Barkers really cared about them and that God cared about them too. It was almost like being part of the family.

But the children were afraid that this good arrangement couldn't last. And sure enough, one afternoon about a week later, General Booth called them into his office. When they entered the small room, the general was sitting behind his large desk and Catherine Booth was sitting in a large straight-backed chair to his side. Standing with their backs to the tall bookcase were also Philip and Martha Barker.

Oh no. This is it, thought Jack. *They're going to tell us we have to go. Or maybe the general remembers what I told him about throwing stuff at the Salvation Army, and he's going to punish us.*

After the general cleared his throat, he spoke as though he were addressing a crowd of people on the streets. "Miss Amy Crumpton and Master Jack Crumpton," he began, "you may not realize it, but Officers Philip and Martha Barker, here, have been commissioned for a very important mission.

"You see, a year and a half ago we dispatched Commissioner George Scott Railton and seven hallelujah lasses to establish a beachhead for the Gospel of our Lord Jesus Christ in New York City in the United States of America. They have been very successful in the fight and are now asking for reinforcements. The Barkers have volunteered as brave soldiers of the Cross, along with another family. Soon they will be leaving and will no longer be able to care for you here."

Just as I thought, worried Jack. *It's all over.*

"However," continued the general, "we'd like to give you a choice. If you choose, you can stay here working in the headquarters, doing the kinds of jobs you have been doing for the last few days. Maybe in time you'll be able to track down your uncle, but I can't make any promises in that regard. Actually, Philip has been doing some investigation around town, and there doesn't seem to be a trace of Sedgwick Masters anywhere. He seems to have disappeared. We're very sorry about that; I'm sure it brings you great sorrow to be without family. But you are welcome to stay here if you choose."

Jack looked at Amy. The relief that showed on her face was exactly what he felt. At least they would have a place to stay. Jack already knew what his choice would be. He wasn't about to go back to that cave under the bridge with no food and no bed except the cold hard sand.

But the general was continuing: "But there is another choice. As you know, the Barkers here have no children of their own—as much as they have wanted them. And they would like to invite you to be their adopted children and go with them to America. This is your other option. We don't want to put any pressure on you, so you choose freely to go or to stay."

Both Amy and Jack turned in astonishment to the Barkers. The Barkers were smiling. "We would like to have you," said Martha gently. "We've already come to care about you very much."

Jack just stared. Go to America? Be adopted? He opened his mouth but no words came out. To his relief he heard Amy stutter beside him, "Th-thank you, Ma'am. Thank you, General, sir. We . . . uh . . . Jack? Do you want to go?"

Jack nodded dumbly. Then a big grin spread over his face. They were going to America!

❖ ❖ ❖ ❖

Just two weeks later Jack and Amy stood on the deck of a great ship. "There's our trunk," said Jack, as they watched the last of the crates and luggage being loaded into the hold. The morning fog was lifting and London's towers were coming into view. Jack looked over the ship's side. The dockmen had loosened the great ropes that held the ship and the sailors were hauling them on board.

"Jack, look!" Amy said, tugging on his sleeve. Jack looked up. A couple of the smaller sails had been loosened and were slowly filling with air. The ship edged away from the docks into the River Thames on its way to the sea.

The children looked around for Philip and Martha. The Barkers were standing near a pile of their belongings talking to another man and woman. A small child clung to the other woman's skirts. An older boy—maybe fifteen—and a girl about Jack's age completed the group.

"That must be the other Salvation Army family who's also going to America," Amy whispered.

"At least there's some other children on this ship. I wonder if they'll be friendly—us being adopted and all."

The word felt funny to Jack. *Adopted.* They had gone with the Barkers to the magistrate, who had asked them a lot of questions about their parents, their Uncle Sedgwick, where they had lived before and what they were doing in London. Then Philip had talked a long time with the magistrate, and Jack overheard words like, "highly irregular," and "you do-gooding Salvationists."

Then, abruptly, the magistrate motioned to Jack and Amy once more. "Do you children desire to be adopted by Philip and Martha Barker, and do you choose to go to America of your own free will?" Both children nodded firmly.

"So be it, then," the magistrate had growled, scrawled his signature on some papers and pushed them forward for the Barkers to sign.

Now as they stood on the deck of the ship, their new father interrupted Jack's thoughts. "Come on, then," Philip motioned to Jack and Amy. "Let's take our satchels to the cabin and get settled for the voyage. Martha needs some help."

The ship had moved out into the Straits of Dover by the time the new little family had made up their bunks and unpacked their things in the cramped cabin. They hadn't talked to the children from the other family yet, but the boy had nodded friendly-like at Jack and stood back so Jack could go down the narrow steps to the lower deck with his bundles.

Now he and Amy were back up on deck as the sea breeze tugged at the large white sails above them causing the rigging to creak. In the distance the White Cliffs of Dover seemed to wink and wave in the sunshine. Martha Barker stood beside them humming a tune that Jack recognized, but he couldn't remember the words. Finally, he said, "Ma'am, excuse me for interrupting, but what's that song you're humming?"

"Oh that?" she said, and she began to sing:

We're bound for the land
*   of the pure and the holy.*
The home of the happy, the Kingdom of love.

"Is that where we're headed, Mrs. Barker?" asked Jack.

Martha smiled. "It sure is, but not on this ship. That song speaks of God's Kingdom. It is Jesus, alone, who can take us there. But we're on our way, sure enough. And just like you and Amy chose to be adopted into our earthly family, you can choose to be adopted into Jesus' family too. Then we'll be bound for that other Kingdom together."

Mrs. Barker rested her hand lightly on Jack's shoulder. He let it stay there as he looked out over the choppy blue waters. Amy caught his eye and smiled. They were heading for a new life, and, yes, he wanted to know more about that Kingdom of love.

More About
William and Catherine Booth

BORN IN NOTTINGHAM, ENGLAND, on April 10, 1829, William Booth grew up learning the trade of a pawnbroker. His father died when William was just fourteen, and life got harder for the poor family. But the next year William became a Christian and soon committed his life to telling others the Gospel. William was especially influenced by the methods of the great evangelist, Charles G. Finney.

Catherine Mumford was also born in 1829, on January 17, in the English town of Derbyshire. Her parents were Methodists and took great care to give Catherine a good education. Catherine was a good student and is said to have read through the Bible by the age of twelve. She gave her life to the Lord at home at the age of seventeen.

As young people, both William and Catherine were very concerned about how much damage drinking could do to people and families. In fact they first met each other at a friend's house when William quoted a poem about the evils of alcohol. Their relationship grew over four years until they married on June 16, 1855, in South London.

Together they forged a great partnership in a traveling evangelistic ministry. Most remarkable was the fact that Catherine, in addition to William, became a powerful preacher, something women didn't do in that day.

They became particularly concerned for the poor people of England. To minister to them, they opened the East London Christian Mission in 1865. In a short time, William Booth began calling the mission the "Salvation Army." This name reflected his and Catherine's sense that in order to save people from evil and bring them to Christ, Christians needed to organize and behave like an army, the Lord's army, going into spiritual battle. Their newspaper was called *The War Cry,* leaders in their mission were "officers," converts were called "captives," and people began calling William, "General." Outreaches of their mission into new cities (and later other countries) became known as "invasions."

In 1881 the Salvation Army moved its headquarters to a former billiards club at 101 Queen Victoria Street, just a block away from Saint Paul's Cathedral.

The enthusiasm of this movement not only brought the Gospel to people, it gave poor people something new to live for. Even though the characters of Jack and Amy in this book are fictional, their situation was very real. The slums of East London were said to have a "gin shop" every fifth house with special steps to help even the tiniest children reach the counter. By five years of age many children were severe alcoholics, and some even died.

But the street corner preaching of the Salvation Army was so effective in converting people and influencing them to stop drinking and gambling that business began to drop off at the pubs and gin shops. In response, the owners encouraged ruffians to attack the Salvationists. In the town of Sheffield in 1882, an organized street gang—a thousand strong and known as the "Blades"—attacked a Salvation Army procession. Later that day, General Booth reviewed his "troops" all covered with blood, mud, and eggs, with their brass band instruments bent and battered and said, "Now is the time to have your photographs taken!" It showed how hard they were fighting for the Gospel. There were many such mob attacks. The incident referred to in this story about sailors firing rockets at point-blank range into a group of singing Hallelujah Lasses happened at Gravesend, on the River Thames. In 1882 alone, 669 Salvationists were assaulted and sixty of the Army's buildings were wrecked by mobs. Over the years, in many outposts around the world, Salvation Army members were actually killed by violent attacks.

As this story shows, prostitution was also a severe problem in London. The city was said to have 80,000 prostitutes in the early 1880s. Over a third of these girls had been forced by white slavers into prostitution when they were between thirteen to sixteen years old. Kidnapping and shipping the youngest, most innocent girls to Europe was very common.

The Salvation Army confronted this problem head on. They staged "rescues" (as in the case of Amy). They set up shelter homes for the girls coming out of prostitution. One home, operated by a Salvation Army sergeant, Mrs. Elizabeth Cottrill, redeemed 800 girls in three years. Finally, seeing that a main problem was that there were no laws protecting young girls, General Booth staged seventeen days of nonstop protest meetings in London and gathered 393,000 signatures on a petition that measured two-and-a-half miles long. The Salvation Army soldiers grimly marched to Parliament and demanded that the government pass and enforce new laws. This the government did on August 14, 1885.

Hunger was an equally severe problem in the slums of London. Because of the poor health conditions, orphans were everywhere. By 1872, the Salvation Army had opened five lunch rooms where—night or day—the poor could buy a cup of soup for a quarter of a penny or a complete meal for six cents. Thousands of meals were given away free.

In time, Booth realized that what the poor needed was training in new job skills and relocation out of the city. This the Salvation Army attempted in the 1890s. Urban workshops (initially safety-match factories) were set up to get homeless and jobless people employed and off the street. The next stage was to move them to colonies in the country where they could learn farming skills. Finally, they were given the opportunity to move to new settlements overseas where they could get a new start on life. While this grand plan did not last past 1906, the Salvation Army still provides effective urban workshops to help homeless and jobless people. Today the Salvation Army helps 2.5 million families around the world each year. Also, their program to help people stop drinking is the largest in the world.

William Booth used to say that he liked his religion the same way he liked his tea—"H-O-T!" By this he meant that he did not like the dull and boring kind of services that took place in most churches. The Army's banner that announces "Blood and Fire" refers to the saving blood of Jesus Christ and the fiery power of the Holy Spirit. This "hot" Gospel was one key to the Salvation Army's effectiveness. Not only did the Salvationists employ a kind of street evangelism that was more like a modern-day protest march, but Booth used music to attract people. It wasn't the somber kind heard in most cathedrals; it was lively music that stirred people up. He encouraged his musicians to write Christian words to the popular tunes of the day. And it worked. People soon began singing along, and the message got through. Even today, Salvation Army bands play on street corners at Christmas time, inviting people to contribute money for the poor.

The Booths had eight children of their own and adopted a ninth. Seven of the Booth's children became well-known preachers and leaders—two as generals of the Salvation Army. But on October 4, 1890,

Catherine Booth, who had never been strong physically, died of cancer at the age of sixty-one.

William Booth continued in the ministry, traveling world-wide and preaching 60,000 sermons before he finally died on August 20, 1912, at the age of eighty-three.

Joining the Salvation Army with its challenge to take the world for Christ provided excitement and direction that attracted many of the otherwise purposeless and hopeless youth a century ago. And the Army's dramatic social work truly transformed several aspects of bleak urban life. But the heart of the Gospel as preached by the Booths called people first to repent of their sins and then surrender to Jesus Christ as Lord and Savior.

And that solid foundation has lasted. Today the Salvation Army's three million members minister in ninety-one countries of the world.

For Further Reading:

Bramwell-Booth, Catherine. *Catherine Booth*. London: Hodder and Stoughton, 1970.

Collier, Richard. *The General Next to God*. New York: E.P. Dutton & Co., Inc., 1965.

Ervine, S. J. *God's Soldier: General William Booth*, 2 vols. London: Heineman, 1934.

Gariepy, Henry. *Christianity in Action*. Wheaton, Illinois: Victor Books, 1990.

Ludwig, Charles. *Mother of an Army*. Minneapolis, Minnesota: Bethany House Publishers, 1987.

"William and Catherine Booth" in *Christian History*, Issue 26 (Vol. IX, No. 2), 1990. (The whole issue of this periodical is devoted to the Booths and the Salvation Army.)

www.trailblazerbooks.com

"TRAILBLAZER BOOKS are fantastic—facts, fiction, excitement, and the Christian faith all in one totally awesome set of books!"

— Kristy, OH

Here is a sneak peak at another
TRAILBLAZER BOOK you don't want to miss!

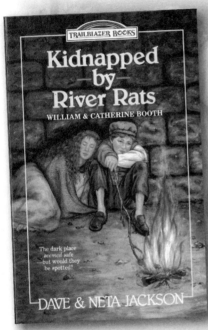

Kidnapped by River Rats

Jack and Amy have come to London searching for their uncle. On their own without money, food, or shelter, they have nowhere else to turn.

But what if they can't find him? They don't even know where he lives!

But life on the streets is filled with terrible dangers: wild dogs, thieves, rats, and kidnappers. Where can they find safety?

When those strange Salvation Army people approach them on the street, should Jack and Amy run away? Can the General and Catherine Booth be trusted?

Will they help Jack and Amy when ruthless men come after them?

For a complete listing of TRAILBLAZER BOOKS, see page 2!

◆ ◆

Available now for $5.99 each from your local Christian bookstore or from Bethany House Publishers.
Mail orders, please add $3.00.

The Leader in Christian Fiction!

BETHANY HOUSE PUBLISHERS
11400 Hampshire Avenue South
Minneapolis, Minnesota 55438
www.bethanyhouse.com

Escape
–from the–
Slave Traders

Trailblazer Books

Gladys Aylward • *Flight of the Fugitives*
Mary McLeod Bethune • *Defeat of the Ghost Riders*
William & Catherine Booth • *Kidnapped by River Rats*
Governor William Bradford • *The Mayflower Secret*
John Bunyan • *Traitor in the Tower*
Amy Carmichael • *The Hidden Jewel*
Peter Cartwright • *Abandoned on the Wild Frontier*
Elizabeth Fry • *The Thieves of Tyburn Square*
Jonathan & Rosalind Goforth • *Mask of the Wolf Boy*
Sheldon Jackson • *The Gold Miners' Rescue*
Adoniram & Ann Judson • *Imprisoned in the Golden City*
Festo Kivengere • *Assassins in the Cathedral*
David Livingstone • *Escape from the Slave Traders*
Martin Luther • *Spy for the Night Riders*
Dwight L. Moody • *Danger on the Flying Trapeze*
Samuel Morris • *Quest for the Lost Prince*
George Müller • *The Bandit of Ashley Downs*
John Newton • *The Runaway's Revenge*
Florence Nightingale • *The Drummer Boy's Battle*
Nate Saint • *The Fate of the Yellow Woodbee*
Menno Simons • *The Betrayer's Fortune*
Mary Slessor • *Trial by Poison*
Hudson Taylor • *Shanghaied to China*
Harriet Tubman • *Listen for the Whippoorwill*
William Tyndale • *The Queen's Smuggler*
John Wesley • *The Chimney Sweep's Ransom*
Marcus & Narcissa Whitman • *Attack in the Rye Grass*
David Zeisberger • *The Warrior's Challenge*

Also by Dave and Neta Jackson

Hero Tales: A Family Treasury of True Stories
From the Lives of Christian Heroes (Volumes I, II, & III)

Escape
–from the–
Slave Traders

Dave & Neta Jackson

Story illustrations by
Julian Jackson

BETHANY HOUSE PUBLISHERS
MINNEAPOLIS, MINNESOTA 55438

Published by Bethany House Publishers
A Ministry of Bethany Fellowship International
11400 Hampshire Avenue South
Minneapolis, Minnesota 55438
www.bethanyhouse.com

Printed in the United States of America by
Bethany Press International, Minneapolis, Minnesota 55438

Library of Congress Cataloging-in-Publication Data

Jackson, Dave
  Escape from the slave traders / Dave & Neta Jackson
    p.   cm. — (Trailblazer books)
  Summary: In the 1860's two African boys are taken captive and
mistakenly left in the care of David Livingstone, whom they
accompany on his quest to find a way to stop the slave trade and to
open the interior of Africa to missionaries.
  [1. Africa—History—19th century—Fiction. 2. Slave trade—
Fiction. 3. Livingstone, David, 1813–1873—Fiction.]
I. Jackson, Neta. II. Title. III. Series.
PZ7.J132418Es   1992
[Fic]—dc20   92–11170
ISBN 1–55661–263–X
                                                           CIP
                                                            AC

All the named characters in this book are real. Though greatly simplified, the story draws from events in David Livingstone's second trip to Africa, the Zambezi expedition, and concludes by incorporating elements from his third expedition. Further details on how history has been condensed and simplified may be found in the "More About David Livingstone" section at the back of the book.

DAVE AND NETA JACKSON are a husband/wife writing team who have authored or coauthored many books on marriage and family, the church, and relationships, including *On Fire for Christ: Stories from Martyrs Mirror*, the Pet Parables series, and the Caring Parent series.

They have two children: Julian, an art major and illustrator for the Trailblazer series, and Rachel, a high school student. They make their home in Evanston, Illinois, where they are active members of Reba Place Church.

CONTENTS

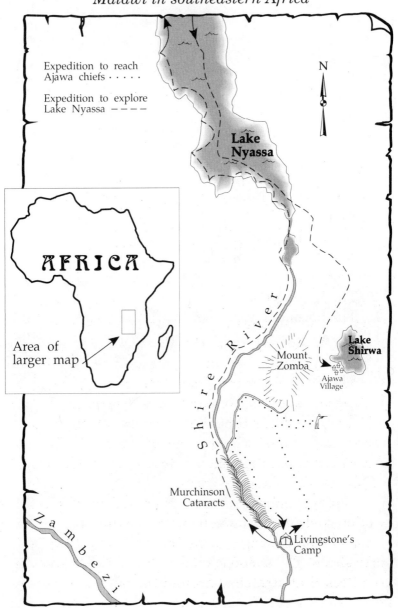

1861 in the area now known as Malawi in southeastern Africa

Expedition to reach
Ajawa chiefs · · · · ·

Expedition to explore
Lake Nyassa — — —

N

**Lake
Nyassa**

AFRICA

Area of
larger map

S h i r e   R i v e r

Mount
Zomba

**Lake
Shirwa**

Ajawa
Village

Murchinson
Cataracts

Livingstone's
Camp

Z a m b e z i

Chapter 1

Red Caps in the Mist

"CHUMA! CHUMA!"

The urgent call cut through the morning mists that floated along the shore of Lake Shirwa. *Why is Wikatani yelling at me again?* wondered Chuma. He thought the older boy bossed him around too much, especially so early in the morning. What was the hurry this time? They would get the village sheep to the pasture soon enough, well before the African sun rose high enough to drink the dew drops off the tender blades of grass.

"Chuma, help. . . !" And then Wikatani's voice was choked off as though he were gagging on a ball of wool. Chuma swung his staff at the heels of the last lazy sheep. The sheep leaped ahead to catch up with the flock that stretched around the bend of the lake shore and disappeared into the mist. *Wikatani is always in a hurry,* Chuma thought. *What difference does it make whether the sheep eat along the trail or in the pasture?* Still, he couldn't remember Wikatani's voice ever sounding so urgent.

Instead of trying to push his way through the flock of sheep, Chuma ran out into the shallows of the lake to get around the woolly animals. The cool water splashed high over his body with each step until he hit a hole and suddenly sunk in water up to his neck. Chuma was a good swimmer, and there was no danger, but he grabbed quickly at the folds of his clothes to make sure the yam he had hidden there for lunch was still safe. He also checked to see that his drinking gourd still hung from the cord around his neck.

He swam strongly until his feet touched bottom again, and he waded to shore. With a brief scramble that dislodged sand and gravel, he made it to the top of the bank and plowed through the tall grass to a point where he could again meet the trail. He paused to scan the trail and listen for Wikatani. Straight ahead of him, through the fog he thought he could make out his friend, but who were the strange men, and what was wrong?

Wikatani looked as if he were fighting for his life! One man held him securely from behind while another man tried to bind the boy's feet with cords. Frightened, Chuma barely held back a scream. What should he do? Should he rush to the attackers and try to free his friend or hold back until he figured out

what was happening? Just then Wikatani must have
bitten the hand of the man who held him because the
man yelped, and Wikatani began yelling again:
"Chuma! Chuma! Run for help!" Quickly the man
clamped his hand back over Wikatani's mouth and
looked at Chuma.

Chuma stared in disbelief and shock as the
stranger's fierce eyes locked on him, but only for a
moment. Chuma spun around to run back down the
lake shore to their village—but he was not fast
enough. A third man who had hidden in the tall
grass jumped out and faced him with a spear pointed

right at his heart. Chuma froze in his tracks before he noticed that the man's spear had no point and looked more like a sawed-off canoe paddle with the handle pointed toward him.

Chuma thought of diving into the lake; not many people could outswim him. But before he could move, the man poked him hard in the chest with the pointless spear. It did not cut, but pain shot through his bones. Chuma decided not to make a run for it. Then the man began speaking to him in a strange language and motioning with his pointless spear. Chuma understood that he was being ordered to join Wikatani and the two strangers, so he turned and slowly walked through the deep grass to the trail.

When Wikatani saw that Chuma had been captured, the older boy's shoulders sagged. One of the men quickly tied Chuma's feet and then left both boys sitting helplessly on the ground by the trail while the men spoke to each other in their strange language.

Swallowing his fear, Chuma studied the features of the unusual looking men. He had never seen anyone who wore bright red caps or pants or vests. He knew they weren't from his tribe, the Ajawa. And they didn't look like Manganja tribesmen either. Even though the Ajawa tribe had sometimes feuded with the Manganja, they were the only two tribes in the area. The Ajawa villages were primarily situated around Lake Shirwa, while most of the Manganja villages were to the west, near Mount Zomba. So who were they?

One of the men near Wikatani stood up and raised his pointless spear to his shoulder. He pointed it toward one of the sheep that was grazing along the trail. Suddenly the pointless spear made a terrible boom, and white smoke shot out of the end. Both boys cried out with the thunder, then opened their eyes. There lay one of their sheep—dead!—while the others ran off. That was bad. The village elders would be angry at the boys for having lost a sheep, but what if the strangers stole or killed the whole herd? Fear gripped Chuma's stomach.

And what about the stranger's awesome weapon? To Chuma, it looked like the pointless spear had killed the sheep without the stranger having thrown it. "Very powerful magic," Chuma whispered to Wikatani.

"They are guns. I have heard of them," said Wikatani. "They can kill from far away."

"Of course . . . guns," said Chuma. He did not like to admit it when Wikatani knew something he did not know, even though Wikatani was thirteen and he was only twelve years old.

Then Chuma was surprised to notice the man pick up a regular spear. He could see by its tribal markings that it was a Manganja spear. The man walked over to the dead sheep and wiped some of the sheep's blood on the spear. He broke the spear over his knee and brought the pieces back and threw them on the ground near Chuma and Wikatani. Then he ordered one of the other men to pick up the dead sheep and carry it over, too.

Seeing the other man obey his order convinced Chuma that this man was the leader of the group, maybe even a chief, though they were all dressed the same.

When the other man brought the sheep back, he let some of the blood drip on the sand and grass around the area where the boys were bound. Chuma did not understand these strange actions, but it was getting scarier by the moment. Were they performing some kind of magic?

Next, the leader grabbed the drinking gourd that hung by a thong from Chuma's neck. With one jerk he broke the thong and then smashed the gourd on the ground. Chuma stuck his chin out at the man defiantly. He could make another drinking gourd. He only carried the gourd with its fresh water because it was convenient when he was watching the sheep on the hills around Lake Shirwa.

But the man also ripped the family bracelets from Wikatani's arms and threw them to the ground not far from the broken gourd. He gave more orders. One man tied Chuma's hands behind his back while the other tied Wikatani's behind his back, and then they cut the cords on their legs.

Finally, the leader of the Red Caps started up the trail while the other two men prodded Chuma and Wikatani to follow. *Now what's happening?* thought Chuma with alarm. *They are not stealing our sheep; they are taking us!*

One of the men carried the dead sheep over his shoulder. It was still dripping blood on the trail as they walked. In a short distance, they turned off the main trail along the lake shore and marched west, away from the lake. The path was barely visible as it wound uphill through the thick grass toward the jungle.

Chuma looked back anxiously. The mist was lifting from the lake, and before they entered the jungle he could see its peaceful surface shining in the morning sun. Far back along the shore were wisps of smoke rising from their village. That was home, and

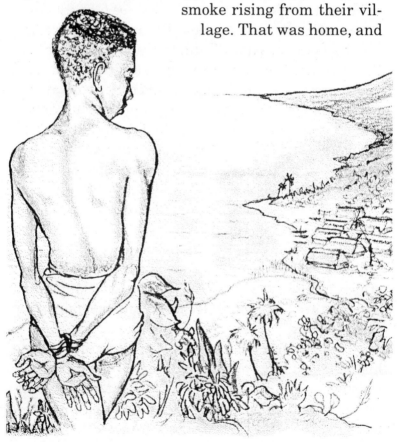

they were being taken away. *No one will know where we are!* worried Chuma. *They won't even miss us until tonight when we don't return with the sheep. By then we'll be so far away that they will never find us!* Below, their sheep were wandering away from the trail along the lake front. Suddenly a hopeful thought came to him: *Maybe some sheep will wander home. Someone will certainly notice and know something is wrong and come looking for us. Or else,* and his spirits fell, *or else they'll just think we've been careless.*

As they entered the jungle, Chuma could no longer see the lake. The dew that had clung to the grass of the open fields now dripped like rain from the trees and vines overhead. Monkeys screeched and swung from limb to limb as the boys and their captors passed beneath. As the Red Caps hurried the boys along under the dark trees, Wikatani said in a hushed voice, "They had a Manganja spear. Do you think they are from the Manganja tribe?"

"I don't think so," answered Chuma. "Why would the Manganja take us away?"

"They're our tribe's old enemies."

"Yes," said Chuma, "but it is a disgrace to send others to fight your battles. These aren't Manganja, and we are only boys. What could be gained by capturing us?"

"Well, I am a chief's son," said Wikatani, lifting his head proudly. "Much trouble will come from attacking *me*. We are headed west into Manganja country. The Manganja must be behind this, and they will pay!"

"But the Manganja have no reason to attack us," said Chuma again.

At that point a Red Cap slapped Chuma on the back of the head so hard that he stumbled and fell. With his hands tied behind his back, he was unable to catch himself, and his face plowed into the dirt. Fortunately the ground was soft, and Chuma was not hurt. He quickly got up spitting bits of leaves and dirt from his mouth.

"No talking! Just march," shouted the Red Cap angrily, gesturing, and raising his hand as though to strike again. Chuma was as surprised that this man could speak their language as having been hit on the back of the head. *What'd I do? What's so wrong with talking?* Chuma wondered.

Wikatani said, "Don't hit him. He didn't do anything."

"I said, 'No talking,'" yelled the Red Cap again, this time at Wikatani. He spoke the boys' language well enough for them to understand him, but his accent was very thick. Then the Red Cap swung his gun at Wikatani like a club. Wikatani dodged out of the man's reach and hurried on up the trail. Chuma followed as quickly as he could.

By noon Chuma was feeling hungry and thirsty. Safely tucked in the folds of his loincloth was the small, cooked yam that his mother had set aside for him to eat while he herded sheep. He longed to take it out and eat it, but his hands were tied. Besides, he was afraid that the Red Caps would throw it away as they had his drinking gourd.

17

Plodding along the jungle trail, Chuma's thoughts kept returning to the house with its sturdy mud walls and thatched roof where he lived with his father and mother and three little sisters. He wanted to be brave, to face this difficulty like a man, like his father . . . but he kept thinking of his mother. *Who'll fix my food?* he wondered, even though he knew that wasn't his worst problem at the moment.

Chapter 2

War Drums

As the sun dropped lower, its warm rays pierced the jungle roof only occasionally. But when they did, the golden beams sliced through the forest to turn various ferns a bright green or the trunk of a tree a rich, brick red.

Chuma no longer knew where they were. The country was turning hilly, and Chuma felt certain they were headed toward Mount Zomba, but he had never been this far west. Would they soon arrive at a Manganja village? He had no way of knowing, but he almost wished that they would. He was so tired he thought he would drop, and he was hungry.

Then suddenly, without any warning, they stepped out into a small clearing and the Red Caps stopped. It seemed to be their camp. There were two simple shelters made of palm branches under which supplies were piled high. And there were two other Red Caps already there, sitting near a smoldering fire while they smoked rolled leaves of tobacco.

The man carrying the sheep dropped it on the ground by the fire, and the leader gave more orders in the strange language. Soon the men by the fire butchered the sheep and put it on a spit over the fire to cook it.

The man who had slapped Chuma herded the boys over to the edge of the clearing and tied a rope tightly to each boy's ankle. The rope was also tied securely to a tree. He cut the cords that bound their wrists together, then left to join the others near the fire. Chuma and Wikatani tried to make themselves comfortable on the ground between the great roots of the tree and waited to see what would happen.

Nighttime in the jungle can be very dark; very little starlight makes its way through the dense roof of leaves. Even at the edge of the clearing it was dismally dark. Chuma and Wikatani sat dejectedly watching the five Red Caps around their small fire feasting on the roasted sheep and passing a jug of some sort of liquor. *Those men have no right to be eating our sheep!* Chuma thought angrily. Hunger kept him hoping that the Red Caps would bring them some of the mutton, but soon the men were so drunk they fell asleep.

With the pain mounting in his stomach, Chuma finally dug into the folds of his loincloth and pulled out the cold yam. He took a bite. It was *so* good . . . or maybe it was just that he was *so* hungry. He took another bite, then nudged Wikatani: "Want some yam?"

"What?"

"You want a bite of my yam?" whispered Chuma.

"Where'd you get that?" said Wikatani, groping in the dark until he found the yam.

"My mother. It was wrapped in my clothes."

"I never knew a yam could be so good," Wikatani sighed, handing the remainder back to Chuma. "Do you think we can get these ropes off our ankles?"

"I don't know," said Chuma, taking another bite and then putting the rest of the yam back into his clothes. He went to work trying to wiggle his foot out to the loop that held it firmly. But the harder he pulled, the tighter the rope seemed to hold him. "I can't get it off."

There was a quiet moan from Wikatani. "I made it."

"Then help me."

Wikatani pulled and tugged. He used his teeth to

try and tease the knot loose, but it was no use. The rope held Chuma fast to the tree.

"See if you can find something sharp to cut the rope," said Chuma.

Wikatani slipped off into the dark, and suddenly Chuma felt terribly alone. He waited a long time. *Wikatani ought to be back by now,* the boy thought, his heart beating fast. *Maybe he got lost. What if he never comes back?*

And then, as if he had never been away, Wikatani was at his side. "I can't find anything sharp. Only a few stones around here, and they're all smooth. I can't see a thing in this darkness."

"What about a knife from the Red Caps?" asked Chuma.

"Are you crazy? What if they woke up?"

They sat in silence for a while. Finally, Chuma said, "Maybe you should go for help."

"In the dark? I'd get lost for sure and the hyenas would find me."

It had been a bold suggestion, and Chuma shivered. The short time that Wikatani had been away had been enough to let him know how much worse it was to be a captive alone. But it seemed the only way. "How about just before it gets light? You could hide in the jungle until you can see and then find your way home."

"I guess so," admitted Wikatani. "But for now, let's get some sleep."

The constant chatter of jungle birds and monkeys woke Chuma. He had been dreaming about his three sisters playing at the edge of the lake. *Home. Home is so good,* he thought, and a heavy sadness spread through his heart when he remembered where he was.

A faint light tinged the sky above the clearing. They had slept longer than they should have! He shook Wikatani, and they both sat up. But in addition to the jungle noises, they could hear something else: the thump, thump, thumpity-thump of distant drums.

"Chuma, listen—Ajawa drums."

"You're right." Chuma imagined some of the head men of his village beating the hollow logs that sent their messages for miles through the jungle. Their rhythms could announce many things, but this beat meant . . . . "War. It's war against the Manganja," concluded Chuma in a hoarse whisper.

"Because we're missing?" his friend asked.

"Maybe." Chuma thought for a moment. "That broken Manganja spear and the sheep's blood did make it *look* like the Manganja had captured us."

"And now Ajawa warriors will attack them."

"Yes. I think the Red Caps set it up that way. But why?" wondered Chuma out loud.

"Right now, who cares? I've got to get out of here."

"Take care," said Chuma, putting his hand on his friend's shoulder. "And come back soon. I don't like being a prisoner."

As Wikatani slipped away, Chuma could barely

see him moving through the dense jungle as he tried to get around the campsite and find the trail by which they had entered the small clearing. Then suddenly a terrible howling erupted. Wikatani must have come upon some baboons that were trying to raid the Red Caps' camp. The baboons screeched and yelled as they scampered up the vines to reach the safety of the trees.

Chuma held his breath and wished he could silence the baboons, but it was no use. Two of the Red Caps sat up and spotted Wikatani running down the trail. They grabbed their guns and tore down the trail after him.

"Run, Wikatani, run," urged Chuma under his breath, his fists clinched in fear. If Wikatani did not escape, they might not be rescued. And if they were not rescued, there might be a war, and many Ajawa would die.

Chuma wanted to pray to the spirits, but he knew the spirits didn't care. Their help could only be ob-

24

tained by a sacrifice, and he had nothing to give. Then he remembered the small scrap of yam left from the night before. He dug it out. *It's my only food*, he thought. *If I throw it to the spirits, I might die. But if I don't, Wikatani might not escape.*

Before he could decide, a gun boomed in the distance. Chuma's heart sank. *Had the Red Caps killed Wikatani?* He waited but heard no more booms, just the sounds of the jungle coming alive in the morning—birds singing, insects buzzing, and still in the distance the talking drums.

When he felt he could wait no longer, he heard footsteps coming up the trail. The sight of Wikatani staggering back into camp was a tremendous relief. At least he was alive! One of the two Red Caps who followed him had cut a stiff vine and was using it to whip Wikatani every few steps if the boy did not move fast enough. The boy's arms were tied behind him. When they arrived at the tree where Chuma was tied up, the Red Caps gave Wikatani a shove that knocked him to the ground. The man was yelling at the boys in his strange language as he retied the rope around Wikatani's ankle, leaving some extra rope to tie around his other ankle, too. Then he gave Chuma's rope a big yank to see that it remained tight. Chuma's ankle throbbed with pain, the rope was so tight.

"What happened?" Chuma asked as the Red Cap went back to his camp. Then he realized what bad shape his friend was in. He was smeared with mud, and he had scratches and scrapes up and down both

25

legs. There was a cut across his forehead that was oozing blood and beginning to swell. "What happened to you?" asked Chuma again anxiously.

"They caught me," pouted Wikatani, tears welling up in the corners of his eyes.

"I can see that," said Chuma. "But how?"

"I don't know," Wikatani said, looking away into the jungle. "I ran and ran. I knew they were behind me. I ran down a little hill and crossed a stream. I was climbing the other side when they shot at me with a gun. I did not want to die, so I stopped. When they caught me, they beat me."

Chuma asked no more questions.

By noon the Red Caps still hadn't given the boys anything to eat or drink. Chuma began to worry. He'd been thirsty before, but this was serious. His mouth was completely dry, and his tongue had swelled up so that he talked funny. His head felt light, as if he might fall over if he stood up. And Wikatani looked worse as the hours passed.

Finally, he decided they must do something, even if the Red Caps got angry. So he began to yell. "Give us food! We need water!" He knew that at least one of the men understood the Ajawa language. But when the Red Caps looked over at him, they just pointed and laughed. Still, Chuma kept yelling. Maybe their captors would get tired of the noise and give them what they needed.

One Red Cap grabbed a leg bone from the sheep they had feasted on the night before. Chuma eagerly saw that there were still some shreds of meat on it.

The Red Cap walked toward the boys, and Chuma sat quietly in expectation. The Red Cap stopped a short distance away and gave Chuma a wicked grin. Then he dropped the bone to the ground, kicked dirt on it, and said, "Hungry?" When he made a gesture for Chuma to come get it, Chuma lunged, but the bone was out of reach. He pulled hard on the rope that bound him to the tree, got down on the ground and stretched out on his belly reaching as far as he could, but the bone was still beyond his reach.

The Red Cap broke into a great laugh, and the others joined in. The more Chuma stretched and groaned, the more the Red Caps roared until they were bored with their game.

But Chuma refused to give up in defeat. He crawled back to the tree and began looking around until he found a small stick. Then, attracting as little attention as possible, he scooted back toward the bone and reached out with the stick.

It just reached, and he began rolling the bone toward him. He got it rolled half way over, then it rolled back. He tried again, but just when it was about to come a full turn, he slipped and bumped it back—even farther away! After that, he could not reach it at all.

"Chuma, Chuma," Wikatani whispered. "Try this." It was a longer stick with a little branch on the end.

Using it like a hook, Chuma was able to roll the bone back and finally retrieve it.

Back at the tree, the boys eagerly pulled the

remaining meat from the bone. It may have been too dirty even for the dogs back in the village, but they were so weak from hunger, they didn't even care. They ate it anyway, and it tasted good.

As Chuma was gnawing the last bit of gristle from the bone, Wikatani said, "Where did they go?"

In their excitement over having something to eat, the boys had not noticed that the Red Caps had left camp. "Ah, they're around here somewhere," Chuma said.

"I don't think so," said Wikatani. "I think they've left. Look. The supplies under that far shelter are missing. They've gone somewhere."

"Now's our chance!" said Chuma. "We've got to get free and get out of here!"

Chapter 3

In Camp With the "Enemy"

TRY AS THEY WOULD, the boys couldn't make the knotted ropes give. And soon the boys' hunger and thirst became a nightmare that overshadowed their desire to escape. Wikatani hurt everywhere from his beating, and his cuts were already infected. Chuma hated the thought of dying tied to a tree. He and Wikatani lay on the ground, weak with hunger, dehydration, and exhaustion. What seemed like an eternal day of torment finally blended into the night and the boys drifted off into a fitful sleep.

In the middle of the night, something woke Chuma. At first he was confused. *What was happening?* Then he yelled, though the sound came out more like a squeak. "Rain! Wikatani! It's raining!"

Cupping their hands, the two boys caught the

sweet water, satisfying their thirst again and again. The shower did not last long, and soon they were both asleep again.

The next morning the clearing was still deserted. "Are the Red Caps going to leave us here to die?" asked Chuma.

"No, they will come again," Wikatani assured Chuma. "Some of their supplies are still here."

The water had renewed their strength, but the hunger grew worse. As the day wore on, Chuma had a thought. He reached over and picked at the bark of the tree they were tied to. Then he began ripping off the bark as fast as he could. Termites! And grubs! *Why hadn't they thought of it sooner?* Wikatani helped him, and the boys popped the insects and little white grubs into their mouths as fast as they could. It took a lot of termites, but the terrible pain in their stomachs finally settled into a dull ache. Both boys hoped their meal stayed down, but it was not their last meal from the tree.

Two days went by before the Red Caps returned to camp with dozens of new captives. Men, women, and children were tied together with stout ropes. Many of the children were younger than Chuma and Wikatani. The Red Caps frequently hit the men with the butts of their guns and slapped the women and children. The younger children were wailing with fear.

The Red Caps cracked real whips this time, not just vines like they'd used on Wikatani. The whips whined through the air and cracked on bare skin,

raising huge welts and sometimes cutting the skin
open as the people were pushed into the center of the
clearing.

Chuma and Wikatani stared open-mouthed.
"Look!" Chuma whispered as he noticed the tribal
markings tattooed on the bodies of the captives.

"They're all Manganja."

"You're right. And some of the men are wounded."

"Not gun wounds . . . spear."

The boys watched as two of the Red Caps set to work attaching Y-shaped poles to the necks of the men. Each pole was about six feet long and branched into a Y at the end. The Red Caps put a Y around a man's neck and fastened it by driving a long metal spike through the tips of the open ends of the Y. This left the man with a huge pole sticking out in front, or to his side or back. It made any fast movements impossible because the poles had a tendency to catch on things, giving the wearer a sharp and painful jolt in the neck.

"They're making slaves of them!" Wikatani said in shock. "Those poles keep slaves from running away. No one can run through the jungle with one of those things around his neck." Just then one of the captured men spit on his captors after they'd put the Y on his neck and began kicking wildly. A Red Cap grabbed the pole and flung the man to the ground without getting close enough to be kicked or hit.

Chuma stared in awe. He, too, had heard of this practice for controlling slaves. In fact, once he had seen a thief treated this way as a punishment.

When the Red Caps had attached Y-sticks to all the men, they set to work retying the frightened women together with strong ropes from one woman's neck to another's, creating a human chain.

Chuma counted a total of eighty-three captives. Several of the children couldn't be more than five years of age, and there were a few who were still in their mothers' arms. Some of the Manganja carried personal belongings—cooking pots, water gourds, and bags probably containing cornmeal or cassava root flour.

Many of the women were crying with grief and fear, their tears mingling with their children's who clung to them. But as evening approached some of the people began trying to make the best of their situation, arranging a family space to sit down and huddling everyone together. At first this activity created a great deal of confusion because of the women who were tied together. One wanted to go one way, and the next woman wanted to go another. Finally, things got sorted out so that they weren't continually pulling at one another's throats.

The children began gathering wood for fires while the men stumbled around in their neck yokes putting water and cornmeal in the cooking pots and setting them over the small fires to make the familiar porridge *nsima*.

With the situation under control, the Red Caps stayed back and allowed the captives to prepare their food without yelling and using their whips, except when one of the men got too near the edge of the clearing where he might try to run away into the jungle.

Wikatani and Chuma tried several times to talk to the new captives. The Ajawa language was similar enough to the Manganja language so that the boys could understand them speaking to one another. But the only response they received was angry glares; one woman close by spat on Wikatani.

"I know our tribes are enemies," Wikatani pouted, wiping off the spittle, "but *we* can't hurt them. Why are they so nasty to us?"

"I don't know," Chuma said, watching a Manganja girl in the glow of the light from the many small fires. She was about their age. "We are all captives of the Red Caps; we should help each other."

"Yes. We both have the same enemy now. The Red Caps don't belong here; they are outsiders." Wikatani was watching the same girl. She was pretty and not tied up like the older women.

When the girl looked their way, Chuma motioned to her to come over to them. She looked around to see

if any Red Caps were watching, but she did not come. A few minutes later she looked at them again. Wikatani smiled, and she smiled back. He, too, motioned, but she shook her head.

Then she casually walked away from her people and began gathering wood near the edge of the clearing. Slowly she made her way around to the tree where Chuma and Wikatani were tied. "What do you want?" she asked when she was within hearing range.

"Water," they both said. "And food," added Chuma.

She walked on, picking up sticks until she got back to her family's fire.

In a few minutes the girl returned with a small gourd of water. "Have they not fed you?" she asked.

"Just a bone," said Wikatani.

"If this tree didn't have termites in it and a few grubs, we would have starved."

The girl looked closely at the boys. "You're not Manganja," she said in surprise.

"No. We're Ajawa," said Chuma. "The Red Caps captured us three days ago when we were taking our village sheep to pasture."

"The Ajawa are hyenas," the girl snapped. "They attack when one's back is turned." And she grabbed the water gourd and started to walk away.

"Wait!" said Wikatani. "Why do you say that?"

The girl turned slightly and gave them a hate-filled stare. She spoke in a tone of deep anger: "The Manganja and the Ajawa were supposed to be at peace. We kept the peace, but your people attacked us! In the dark I did not see that you are Ajawa, or I would never have brought you water."

Chuma thought fast. Their people had attacked the Manganja? He began to understand what had happened.

"But it was a mistake!" Chuma pleaded as the girl

started to walk away again. "Our people thought *you* had captured us. That's why they went to war with you. They knew nothing about these Red Caps."

The girl hesitated.

Wikatani continued. "That's right. If our people had known that the Red Caps had captured us, they would have come here to rescue us."

The girl faced them again, still angry. "Why did the Ajawa think it was us?" she demanded.

"Who else?" said Wikatani.

"No; there's more to it than that," said Chuma. "The Red Caps broke a Manganja spear and left it on the trail where they caught us."

"And they spread blood all around to make it look as if we had been killed or badly hurt," added Wikatani.

"But why would the Red Caps do all that?" asked the girl skeptically.

"We think they *wanted* the Ajawa to attack the Manganja, so they made it look as if your tribe had captured us."

"But we don't know why," Wikatani admitted. "Why start a war between our two tribes?"

"If what you say is true," said the girl, "their reason is clear. They wanted to buy slaves. There are only five of them. So this was the only way to get many unarmed slaves."

"What do you mean?" asked Wikatani.

"We were captured by your people and taken to an Ajawa village. The Red Caps came the very next morning and bought all of us and brought us here."

"Bought you? With what?" asked Chuma.

"Rolls of bright colored cloth, pieces of copper wire, new cooking pots—white men's things," spat the girl.

Neither boy had ever seen a white man, but they had heard plenty of stories about them. Far down the Shire River, where it joined a larger river—the Zambezi—white men traveled on the water in their gigantic smoking canoes. Rumor said they had a village named *Tete* many miles up the Zambezi.

"Slave traders," breathed Wikatani. The only source of the brightly colored cloth, wire, and iron pots was white men. Often they traded those things for slaves.

A new fear shone in Wikatani's eyes. "Will we be sent away to the white man's land?"

"*We* won't," said the girl proudly. "Manganja warriors will soon rescue us."

"Yes. I'm sure they will try," said Chuma slowly, pondering the situation. "But they don't know where you are. They will attack Ajawa villages and take more captives in revenge—"

"And probably sell them to the Red Caps, too," added Wikatani.

The girl stared at the two boys in dismay. "Then . . . we might never get home!"

Chapter 4

The Trail of Tears

HOOT—HOOT—HOOT!
Chuma woke up with a start to the terrible racket. When he sat up, he saw one of the Red Caps walking among the captives blowing loud blasts on a bright tin horn.

Wiss-crack! Wiss-crack!

Another Red Cap followed the first one cracking a whip over the heads of the people. "Get up! Get up! Today we march," he yelled in the Manganja language, kicking those who weren't quick enough to rise.

The Red Caps then took the men to the shelter and loaded them with the remaining supplies stored there: more rolls of cloth, copper wire, iron cooking pots, heavy boxes, and bags of grain.

"Let's go! Let's go!" yelled the Red Cap, cracking his whip and letting it land on any captive who was not moving fast enough to suit him. The other Red Caps were going among the women making sure that the ropes that linked them together were still securely tied.

With the Manganja men loaded down by the Red Caps' supplies, the women had to shoulder all their own supplies. Several women had a huge bundle balanced on their head, a child in one arm, and a cooking pot or some other item in the other.

Hooting on his tin horn again, the leader of the Red Caps started off down the trail while the other Red Caps whipped the rest of the people into line to follow.

Chuma and Wikatani remained silent under their tree. "Maybe they will leave us," whispered Chuma. "Then we could escape."

"How?" answered Wikatani. "We haven't managed to get free yet. We'll starve tied up here if we don't have anything more to eat than these termites."

"We'll figure out something. I just hope they don't take us and sell us to the white men."

But the last Red Cap in the caravan stepped over to their tree and cut their bonds. "Hurry up. Catch up with the rest of them," he barked in his strange accent.

The boys started off down the trail at the back of the caravan. Children were crying, the Red Caps' whips were cracking—sometimes causing a captive to yell out in pain. And through it all, the women were trilling their grief: a high-pitched cry made by moving the tongue back and forth rapidly, creating a mournful wail. Chuma remembered his grandfather's funeral, and the feeling stuck in his throat.

The men were having a terrible time managing the Y-yokes. The poles seemed to catch on every bush, and when the caravan climbed a little hill, the poles constantly jabbed into the ground in front of the men almost knocking them over backwards.

The progress of the caravan that morning was very slow, and the constant whipping of the captives' backs made it all the worse. Shortly after noon, the strange company worked its way down a hill like a long centipede to a lush, green valley. There, tall sugar cane plants lined both sides of the trail, and the Red Caps were obviously worried that one of their captives would dart from the trail and disappear into the cane. They kept running back and forth along the line making sure every one remained right in the center of the path.

But one man did make a break for it. In spite of the cumbersome yoke attached to his neck, he spotted a small game trail going off into the cane and tried to run into the tunnel before the Red Caps saw him.

A Red Cap near Chuma and Wikatani saw the man. He laughed loudly and yelled, "You cannot escape us. Go ahead and try, and you will all see that no one can run from us." Just then the Y-pole on the man's neck caught in the cane and threw him back onto the path. He choked and coughed as he struggled to his feet trying to untangle the pole and swing it around behind him while he desperately pushed into the cane. Then the Red Cap lifted his pointless spear to his shoulder and—just as it happened to the sheep—there was a loud boom, a lot of smoke, and the runaway crumpled to the ground, bleeding from his back.

He gasped once and died.

Many of the captives screamed, and a woman who must have been the man's wife tried to run to his side, pulling other women with her by the rope between their necks. But the Red Caps beat her back with their whips. "Move on! Move on, or you will die with him," they shouted to the terrified string of captives.

Chuma and Wikatani stared in horror at the man who had been shot as they silently walked past his body. The Y-pole remained stuck in the cane, holding his head up off the ground in a half-way sitting position. His eyes were still open, and they stared, unseeing, into the sky.

"Get moving," snarled the closest Red Cap.

The column of stunned people marched on in silence except for quiet sobbing by some of the women. No longer were they trilling the traditional grief songs. Their spirits were broken.

In the afternoon black clouds piled high in the sky, and thunder signalled a heavy downpour. The rain made walking on the muddy trail difficult, but still the downpour was welcomed by many of the captives. They had been traveling since the Red Caps woke them so roughly at dawn, and many had not had time to get anything to eat or drink. The heavy rain at least provided a little water. The storm did not last long, however, and soon the sun broke through the clouds to warm the travelers from the chill of the rain.

As the clouds drifted away, the march continued without relief until the sun slipped behind the hills. With night falling on the strange caravan, the Red Caps chose a small meadow with a stream flowing through the middle to set up camp. The stream was a welcome place to soak sore, tired feet that had been scratched by thorns or cut by sharp stones during the day's long march.

However, the meadow had one disadvantage. It contained very little wood for fires. The few fires that were started had to be fed with bunches of twisted grass. But the recent rain had dampened the grass so much that it made a heavy smoke and gave off very little heat for cooking—when it burned at all. The Red Caps would not allow the children to venture into the forest to gather wood. This meant that most people could not cook their food and had to make do with raw cornmeal or other tidbits they had with them.

The Red Caps did not supply any of their own provisions for their captives, so the only food for the slaves was what they had managed to bring with them. Chuma and Wikatani had none, and with the Manganja blaming them for their captivity (because they were Ajawa), no one offered to share.

Chuma closed his eyes against the sharp pain in his stomach. He felt weak all over and knew he could not walk again tomorrow without food. He sat for a long time, trying not to think, then was startled when he heard someone call his name.

His eyes flew open. It was almost dark and at first he saw no one. Then he saw the girl. She had brought each of the boys a leaf with a scoop of cold cornmeal mush on it. Both Chuma and Wikatani ate eagerly. Not having been cooked, one could not say it was real *nsima*, but it did ease the gnawing pains in their stomachs.

"How did you know my name?" he asked the girl.

She nodded at Wikatani. "I heard him call you. And you call him Wikatani."

"What is your name?"

"Dauma." The girl sat on the ground near the boys. "Do you know where they are taking us?"

"We've been traveling southwest most of the day," said Wikatani. "We should be deep into Manganja country by now. I thought you would know where we are."

"My people do not know this land," the girl answered. "They fear we are being taken to the white men at Tete on the Zambezi River. We will never see our homes again!"

The next day the captives made sure that they

43

got up before dawn so that they could prepare something to eat, gather their belongings, and be ready to move out before the Red Caps started cracking their whips.

Several of the Manganja men invented a smart way to ease the pain on their necks caused by the Y-shaped poles. With twine woven from meadow grass, pairs of men tied their poles together. The man in front arranged his pole to extend straight out behind him, and the man following swung his pole around to stick straight out to the front. Then, with the ends of each pole overlapping, a third person wrapped twine around the poles, tying them together. This bound each pair of men together as though there were just one pole between them

with a Y on each end. The invention kept the ends of the poles from flopping around and getting caught on things. Apparently the Red Caps did not think it made escape any easier, because they did not object.

That day and the next several people got sick and could hardly walk, but the Red Caps had no mercy on them. The whip fell just as harshly on their backs as on the backs of those who were still healthy.

In the afternoon of the third day on the trail, one of the men stumbled and fell. His bag of corn—belonging to the Red Caps—broke open when it hit a log. Chuma saw the corn come spilling out and dove for a handful. The corn had not been ground, but he stuffed his mouth with the hard kernels anyway and grabbed for more. By then more people were reaching for the food. Some of the women pulled others to the ground with them because of the ropes connecting their necks. Pretty soon a huge pile of people were scrambling to get a bite to eat.

As Chuma tried to wiggle his way out from under the pile, he could hear a Red Cap yelling at the people. The whip whistled through the air and landed with a crack on someone's back. It whistled again, and this time the stiff rawhide cut into Chuma's leg. He yelled, spewing the corn from his mouth, and pulled himself from the pile of people. Quickly, he ran down the trail before he caught another lash from the whip.

He squeezed his eyes hard to keep the tears from coming; a few trickled out, which he wiped on the back of his arm. Then he realized that he still had

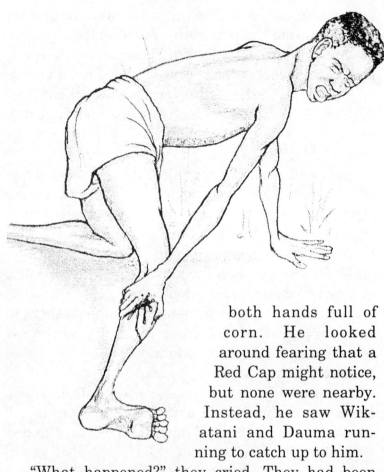

both hands full of corn. He looked around fearing that a Red Cap might notice, but none were nearby. Instead, he saw Wikatani and Dauma running to catch up to him.

"What happened?" they cried. They had been farther back in the line and had not seen what had taken place.

Chuma told them about the bag of corn ripping open. "And look what I got," he said, holding out his clenched fists. Chuma poured a little corn in the eager hands of his friends, and then put some of the kernels in his mouth.

"Aiee! Your leg is bleeding!" cried Dauma. "What happened?"

Chuma looked down. "The whip got me," he said.

Funny . . . before Dauma had mentioned it, Chuma had not noticed the torn skin on the back of his leg, but now the pain seemed to increase to the point where there was no stopping the tears. And the throbbing got worse before the caravan stopped for the night.

All night the burning ache stole Chuma's sleep. The next morning, he could not stand on that leg.

"Here," said Wikatani, "let me help you. We don't want to attract another taste of the whip."

When it was time for the caravan to get going, the two boys hobbled off down the trail near the front of the column, staying away from the Red Caps.

They had not traveled more than an hour when they came around the top of a hill and saw below them a valley with a river winding through it. A strange village lay by the river's edge. It was strange because it was not made up of the usual mud houses with grass roofs. This village had canvas tents, something the boys had never seen before, but something that filled them with dread.

The Red Caps gestured excitedly to one another, and the leader of the Red Caps got out his tin horn and began blowing on it, announcing their arrival to the camp below.

The boys saw people stop what they were doing and look up the hill to see who was coming; others came out of the tents. Suddenly, among the people coming out of the tents, Chuma and Wikatani saw their first white man.

Chapter 5

Deliverance

SEVERAL MEN FROM THE CAMP came running up the trail to meet the slave caravan. Following them came a white man.

The leader of the Red Caps was tooting his horn and waving and shouting his greetings. The Red Caps seemed very proud of all the slaves they were leading down the trail. The captives now numbered eighty-four—eighty-two Manganja (after the man who had tried to escape was shot) and the two Ajawa boys. But several slaves, like Chuma, were either injured or seriously sick and barely able to travel. If the trip continued much longer, several would die.

But to the boys' surprise, as soon as the first men from the camp met the leader of the Red Caps, they grabbed him and took away his gun. Two strong men held his arms while several other men ran on up the trail and tried to catch the other Red Caps. But seeing what had happened to their leader, the other Red Caps disappeared into the forest.

"Wha—what's happening?" asked Chuma, bewildered.

By then Dauma had caught up with the boys. She stood behind Wikatani, looking around him like a child hiding behind her mother.

"I think the white man is stealing us from the Red Caps . . . and without paying for us, either," said Wikatani. "He has double-crossed them!"

Chuma was glad to see the Red Caps run off. But if the white man was stealing the slaves, it didn't help them any; a slave was a slave whether someone paid for you or not. The white man might even be crueler. "I hope we don't have to travel anymore until my leg gets better," he grumbled. He hopped around on his good leg, keeping his balance by holding on to Wikatani's shoulder.

The black men who held the leader of the Red Caps were yelling at him, demanding to know where he had gotten the slaves, from what tribe they came, and for whom he worked.

"Quiet!" ordered Wikatani as Dauma started to say something. "This might be our chance to escape." The older boy began guiding his friends back through the crowd that was gathering around the Red Cap and the new strangers who held him.

"Wait," said Dauma, pulling away from Wikatani.

The white man had arrived at the top of the hill

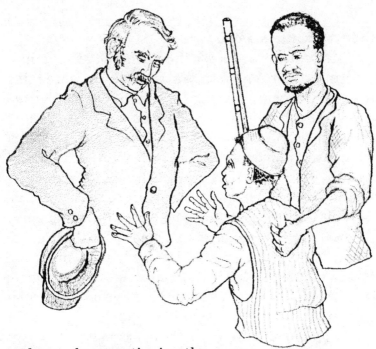

and was also questioning the
Red Cap. Chuma thought Dauma was only interested in seeing a white man for the first time. He was
curious, too, but Wikatani interrupted his observa-
tion. "We can't wait," the older boy said. "This may be
our only chance to get away."

"No," insisted Dauma. "Listen! The white man is
not stealing us." The stranger was speaking
Manganja; she could understand him better than
the boys and was listening closely, trying to figure
out what the white man was doing. "He's telling the
Red Cap that taking slaves is wrong. . . . He says his
God is against slavery. . . . He is talking about letting
us go free!"

"It's a trick," said Wikatani. "We have all heard that the white men buy slaves."

"Then just look what's happening," said Dauma.

Some of the men from the tent village were tying the Red Cap's arms behind his back. Others started going among the slaves, cutting the ropes that bound the women together by their necks. As the truth of what was happening began to dawn on the weary travelers, shouts of joy spread through the column, and the people began to run forward to be released. In their eagerness, many who were still fastened by the neck rope got tangled up. Some fell to the ground, others were choking or calling for help. Dauma ran to her mother and tried to help her get untangled; then the girl guided her mother to one of the strangers with a knife.

A cloud of dust soon concealed the eager slaves.

"I don't like it," said Wikatani. "I don't trust the white man. He is evil!" He pushed Chuma away from the trail toward the forest. "Let's get out of here before he can do whatever he's up to. Look—he's got the Red Cap's gun!"

Chuma's leg hurt fiercely as the bushes at the edge of the forest tore at it. "I don't think I can keep going," he told Wikatani. "Can't we just hide here for a little until we see if the white man is lying?"

"That won't do much good if they start looking for us."

"But why would they look for us?" Chuma sat down and rubbed his leg gently. "Look. Even if the white man is planning to take us for slaves, he doesn't know how many captives there are, and since we're not Manganja, no one else will miss us, either."

Still not convinced, Wikatani sat down beside Chuma. "Well . . . most of the Manganja think this whole thing is our fault anyway, so, if we're gone, maybe that will just make them *sure* we were involved." Wikatani remained quiet for a few minutes. Then he said, "But I don't want Dauma to think that."

"What do you mean?"

"She trusts us. I don't want her to think we lied to her."

Chuma moved some branches aside with his hands so he could look out. "I don't think you need to worry about that," he said. "They really are letting the captives go. Look, they're cutting the yokes off the men."

Wikatani peered through the bushes. Several of the strangers were gathered around as the white man used a saw to cut the yoke that held one man's neck. Suddenly it gave way, and the yoke was pried off the man's neck. A great cheer went up among the men as the freed slave jumped to his feet and began dancing around. Other slaves were calling, "Me! Me next!" The white man gave the saw to one of his men who proceeded to free the rest.

As the boys watched from the shadows of the forest, several of the newly freed women and the children began gathering wood for fires and setting up the heavy metal pots to cook food . . . right there along the trail. Then the boys noticed that the white man was walking among the people giving instructions. They could hear his booming voice as he spoke in the Manganja language: "Set up another pot over here. Sure, go ahead and use the Red Caps' corn. Use any of their supplies! You need food, and they were making you carry it. So eat up. Have a feast."

A little farther up the trail the man knelt down beside a woman who was sitting in the dust with a sick child in her lap. With kind hands, the man felt the child's forehead and then pressed gently at different points on the child's stomach. He talked quietly to the women for a few minutes, then opened a large pouch that hung from his shoulder and poured a thick brown liquid from a bottle into a small cup, which he held to the child's lips.

The child coughed as he drank it and then made a sour face. The white man laughed and stood to his feet.

Chuma struggled to get to his feet. "He's not going to make slaves of us," he said. "I'm not staying here in the bushes anymore."

"Wait," protested Wikatani. "Maybe he poisoned the child. You saw how he laughed. It's better to stay hidden a little longer until we are sure."

"Maybe for you," said Chuma, "but my leg hurts, and he's a medicine man." He hobbled out onto the trail. "Doctor! Doctor!" he called out to the white man. "Would you fix my leg?"

Chuma followed the white man as he attended to other people who were sick. Finally the doctor noticed the boy behind him and turned. "What's the

matter, son? I've never seen slavers take cripples before."

"I'm not a cripple. My leg's been hurt," said Chuma, turning so the strange man could see the back of his calf. He tried to stop his leg from trembling, but it hurt too much.

"My! What happened to you?" the man exclaimed as he stooped down to get a closer look.

"It was a whip," said Chuma.

"Mmmm, yes. But it's also infected. It looks very nasty." He withdrew a small silver tube from his bag and squeezed something from it that looked to Chuma like white grease and smeared it on the wound. Then he wrapped the boy's leg with a clean strip of cloth. "There," he said as he stood up. "Now run over there and get yourself something to eat."

But Chuma didn't move. Standing next to the tall white man he took a long look. The man wore a blue suit and blue hat, like nothing Chuma had ever seen before. His face was rough, and his sharp eyes were set deep below bushy eyebrows. *Very strange*, Chuma thought. "Doctor," Chuma said, working up courage to speak, "the Red Caps tied us up and starved us, but you cut the ropes and tell us to eat. What sort of a man are you? We thought all white men took slaves. Where do you come from?"

"Sadly, you are right, young man. Many white men buy slaves, and the Red Caps have been helping them. But I was sent to Africa by God, the great God who created everyone and wants you to be free."

"Your God does not like slavery?" asked Chuma. By then Wikatani was standing beside him.

"He hates it," said the man as he stroked a large mustache that completely covered his upper lip. "If you want, I will tell you more about God later. But now I must see to the others."

As the boys gathered with some of the other freed captives around one of the pots bubbling over a hastily built fire, they were distracted by a commotion down the trail. Chuma turned just in time to see the Red Cap leader running at top speed into the jungle. Two of the men from the tent village ran after him but the white doctor called out in his loud voice, "Let him go. He'll never bother these people again."

Chapter 6

"Livingstone's Children"

WHEN ALL THE MEN WERE FREE and everyone had eaten, the people gathered up their belongings with the remains of the Red Caps' possessions and headed down to the valley. The white doctor had invited them to set up a temporary camp along the river until they were ready to return to their home villages.

When the newcomers got to the valley, they discovered that the doctor was not the only white man in the area. From snatches of conversations he overheard, Chuma figured out that the tent village was really a temporary camp, and there were several more whites traveling with the doctor, along with the black men who were working as his porters.

As the boys dropped the bundles of supplies they'd

carried down the hill, three new white men came into the little camp from the other direction. They had been up the river, bathing. The doctor went to them quickly, and the white men stood together talking seriously in low voices.

"I don't like it," said Wikatani. "They fooled us into coming to their camp, and now they will keep us as slaves. Don't forget that so far no one has tried to leave. These white men have guns and so do many of their porters. We have no chance to escape."

"You're too afraid," said Chuma. "The doctor is a *good* medicine man. My leg feels better already. I believe him."

"Well, if your leg feels better, I think we should leave tonight and go home."

"Home? That's a four-day trip! I said my leg felt better. I didn't say it was completely healed. Besides, how would we find our way?"

Just then the white men ended their discussion and the little group broke apart. They came toward the former slaves. "Gather around, please gather around," called the doctor. Then he climbed up on the stump of an old tree and started speaking.

"My name is David Livingstone, and this is Bishop Mackenzie," he said, pointing to one of the other white men. "The bishop and his assistants have come to the Shire Valley to build a mission station to tell you about the great and good God who loves all people.

"We were happy to set you free you today, and we are ready to help you return to your villages as soon as you wish. However, you are also welcome to stay here and be the first members of Bishop Mackenzie's mission station. You would be able to learn about God the Father and His Son Jesus. The bishop would teach you. You could build a village right here on the banks of the Shire River. The land is good, and we would teach you how to grow new crops, crops that you could trade for many goods. You could have a good life and help in the great work of the bishop.

"The bishop will also build a school and teach you to read and write," the doctor continued. The Manganja people nudged one another and spoke in loud undertones, shrugging their shoulders. Chuma was confused too: what did "read and write" mean? The doctor stopped, realizing that the people did not know what it meant to read. He tried to explain: "When you hear the drums, you understand the message. Right?" The people murmured their agreement. "And when you follow a trail in the jungle, you read the signs and know which animals have passed that way—a footprint here, a broken reed there, fresh droppings. In the same way, the bishop will teach you how to read little marks on paper to get the messages put there long ago by other people."

"Why would we want to learn to read such old and small signs?" someone in the crowd asked.

"They will give you much wisdom," the doctor said. "They will tell you about things and people far away; they will teach you about the one true God. God has spoken, and His words are written in a book for you to understand. Reading is very useful." He looked around the crowd. "Take time to think carefully about this offer to be part of the new mission and give us your answer in a few days."

He then got down from the tree stump, and he and the bishop strolled among the people, greeting them.

The white men and their helpers gave the former slaves machetes to cut palm branches, and the people quickly set about making temporary shelters. Chuma and Wikatani offered to help Dauma's family, but her mother said coldly, "We don't need any Ajawa help to build a hut. You have already done enough damage. Now get away from here!" And then she turned on Dauma and yelled, "I thought I told you to stay away from those Ajawa brats. If I ever see you talking to them again, I'll beat the—"

But by then Chuma and Wikatani were running down the trail away from the Manganja camp.

"She still thinks it's our fault they were captured as slaves!" Wikatani grumbled.

"It's probably hard for her to believe anything else. After all, our Ajawa warriors did attack their village and take them captive and sell them into slavery."

"But the Red Caps set it all up!" argued Wikatani.

"We know that, but how can she?" asked Chuma.

"We told Dauma, and she believes us."

"Yes, but it's not always so easy to convince adults. That tribe truly hates us."

At the edge of the clearing the boys made themselves a small lean-to. It wasn't much, but it was enough to keep off the rain.

When they finished, they went exploring. Down
by the river they both gasped when they discovered
the white man's smoking canoe. No smoke was coming out of the top of it, but it was so big that at first
the boys thought it was a strange island in the river.
There was a bridge that went from the bank to the
boat, but they did not risk going up the ramp. The
boat was so big that if it floated away with them,
they knew that they could not paddle it back. Instead, they waded into the river and touched the side
of the great boat. It was hard and cold, and when

they tapped on it with a stick it sounded like a strange drum.

"It is made of iron," said Wikatani. "But that is strange; everyone knows that iron cannot float."

"It must be filled with wood," offered Chuma. "Wood floats."

"Yes. Maybe so. Maybe so."

Just then the boys heard someone coming. They quietly slipped away from the boat and swam downriver for a short distance, then climbed out to dry on a warm rock.

Three days later, when the friendly white men came to visit the camp of the former captives, they discovered that most of the Manganja men were missing. Chuma and Wikatani knew where they had gone. The men had returned to their home land to join in the fight against the Ajawa. "We could follow behind them until we got close to home, then we could slip away," Wikatani had suggested the evening the men had departed.

"Sure," Chuma had countered, "but if they noticed us, we'd be dead." Still, Chuma felt deeply homesick as the men had walked single-file out of the camp.

But now the Manganja who remained—mostly women and children—were ready to give their answer to the bishop's invitation: they would stay and become part of the mission.

The bishop could not yet speak an African language that the people could understand, but when he understood the people's decision, he began talking excitedly to Doctor Livingstone. The doctor interpreted to the people: "Bishop Mackenzie is very happy with your decision. He says that you will not be sorry you have chosen this way. You will have a fine village here, and God will bless you."

Blessings or not, Chuma and Wikatani were not happy. "How will we ever get home?" said Wikatani as the boys walked away from the gathering of people.

"I don't know," admitted Chuma. "I guess we could walk by ourselves. My leg really is a lot better now. But how would we find our way? And what if there are still slave traders about?"

"Or what if we got caught in the middle of the war?" added Wikatani. "The Manganja will not think twice about killing us."

"But I don't think we can stay here in the new village," said Chuma. "I am afraid of these Manganja. Some night they might cut our throats."

"You're right, but what can we do?"

The boys had wandered away from the gathering and without intending to, came to the white men's camp. Some of the porters were working around the camp, cooking or cleaning various things. Others lounged under trees or in their own huts, which were set up alongside the white men's tents.

"What if we moved over here?" said Chuma. "Then we'd be safe."

"They'd send us back," said Wikatani.

"But why? If we talked to the doctor, maybe we could help him. Then they wouldn't send us away."

It was an idea worth trying, and the boys stayed near the edge of camp so as not to attract any attention until the doctor came back into camp. The bishop was not with him. Wikatani hung back, but Chuma ran right up to him. "Doctor, Doctor," Chuma said, "can we help you?"

"Well, if it isn't my boy with the sore leg. How's it doing? Let me have a look." The doctor stooped down and removed the well-used bandage from Chuma's leg. At this, Wikatani came closer to watch. "That looks a lot better. Does it hurt anymore?" the doctor asked.

"I hardly notice it," said Chuma, grinning.

"Good. You don't need this bandage anymore, but try to keep the wound clean. Now you run along, and get to work on that mission station for the bishop."

"But Doctor, we want to help *you*."

"No, no, no. I don't need any more porters. Besides, you boys are a little small to carry heavy loads on the trail."

"But we could run errands for you," said Chuma eagerly.

"And we could clean things for you," offered Wikatani, "and build your fire in the morning, and—"

"And," interrupted Chuma, "we're good sheepherders."

"Sheepherders?" said Doctor Livingstone, raising one of his bushy eyebrows skeptically. "I didn't think the Manganja kept sheep."

"Oh, they don't," said Wikatani. "But we do. We're Ajawa."

"You're from the Ajawa tribe?"

"Yes. See?" Chuma said, pointing out his tribal tattoos.

"Yes, I see," said Livingstone. "Hmm. Come over here, and tell me about your village." The doctor walked over to his tent and sat on a chair. The boys had never seen a wooden chair before and inspected it carefully to see how the sticks held the man up without tipping over.

Livingstone interrupted their exploration. "Tell me where you live. How did you end up being with the Manganja?" he asked, pulling at the corners of his large mustache.

Carefully, the boys told the doctor how they were caught by the Red Caps as they were herding sheep near Lake Shirwa. They also explained how the Red Caps made it look like they had been captured by Manganja. "That started a war between our people and the Manganja," said Chuma.

"Why would that start a war?" asked the doctor.

"Because Wikatani is a chief's son," explained Chuma.

Wikatani looked distressed with the idea that the war had started because of him, and hastened to say, "But the Manganja and the Ajawa are old enemies. In almost every generation war breaks out."

"But this time it started when the slave traders made it look like the Manganja had captured you?" asked Livingstone.

"Yes," Chuma said, "and when our warriors attacked and took many captives, the Red Caps came the next day and bought them for slaves. Dauma told us so."

"Who's Dauma?"

"She's a Manganja girl," explained Wikatani.

"She's the only one who gives us any food," said Chuma. "Everyone else thinks we are the enemy."

"That's why we can't stay in the Manganja camp," explained Wikatani. "Someone will kill us—just because we are Ajawa."

The doctor didn't respond. Instead, he leaned forward with his elbows on his knees and his head in his hands. He sat that way so long the boys thought he might have gone to sleep. When he finally raised his head, there were tears in his eyes. "I'm very sorry," he said. "I'm so sorry."

"That's all right. You don't need to cry," said Chuma, unable to understand why the good doctor was so upset about their situation. "We'll be fine if you will allow us to live in your camp and help you. We won't be any trouble."

"Of course, you can stay here for now," Livingstone said, sighing heavily. "But my heart is very sad at what you have told me. I feel partially responsible for this terrible situation." The white man stood up and looked to the north, frowning. "I have come to Africa from my country to find new tribes—like the Manganja and the Ajawa—so that missionaries like Bishop Mackenzie can establish missions and schools, to tell people the good news about the great God in heaven, and His Son Jesus, who loves them. I have only recently made contact with some of your people, the Ajawa. Before my visit, the Ajawa would not allow *any* outsiders to come into their area. But as soon as I gained their trust and opened the door, other outsiders like the Red Caps have followed me and brought death and slavery with them."

Chuma and Wikatani didn't know what to say. They weren't sure that it was the doctor's fault, but they could see it was very upsetting to him.

That night in the white men's camp the boys had a good meal and slept soundly for the first time in many days.

However, the next day some of Livingstone's men intercepted another slave caravan coming through the area. This time they captured and held the Red Cap in charge and brought him to be questioned by Livingstone. It turned out that this Red Cap was the head servant for the Portuguese commander in that part of Africa.

"Does the commander know that you are buying and selling slaves?" Livingstone yelled at him.

"No, no. He does not know anything about this. He thinks I have gone to visit my relatives."

Livingstone looked at him a long time and then said, "I do not believe you. I think the Portuguese are fully aware of this terrible slave trade." Turning away, the doctor snapped, "Get him out of my sight."

"What shall we do with him?" asked one of Livingstone's men.

"I don't care."

"Shall we release him, Doctor?"

"Yes, yes. Just get him out of here."

Wikatani and Chuma followed Livingstone as he doctored and talked with the newly freed slaves, but the news they heard was very disturbing.

All the villages to the northeast were at war. Many of them—both Manganja and Ajawa—had been completely destroyed. Most of the people were either dead or had been taken captive and sold as slaves.

"The Red Caps move freely through all the area," said one old man. "They call themselves 'Livingstone's children.' But I do not know who this Livingstone is."

Livingstone winced as if he had been struck. "*I am David Livingstone*," he said as he cleaned a wound in the man's forehead. His voice hardened into a snarl. "But it is a lie. The Red Caps have no right claiming they are connected with me."

Chapter 7

A Desperate Plan

O H, GOD," MOANED THE DOCTOR as he walked back to his camp. The two boys following along behind were the only people to hear the pain in his voice. "Why, God? Why have you let my work lead to such tragedy for these people?"

The white man stumbled on a tree root, but hardly seemed to notice. Chuma and Wikatani weren't sure who this God was he was speaking to. "I came to Africa to bring the good news of your love. I have risked my life and worked hard to get these tribes to allow me to enter their territory. But wherever I go, the evil slave traders follow. And now they have the brashness to use my good name to gain access into tribes that were once safe from all outsiders!" He raised his voice until he was almost shouting. "My

God! It's not fair! What should I do?"

The boys had never heard anyone talk to a god like this, but they knew this God must be different than the gods of their tribe.

The tall man walked along in silence for a few moments, then suddenly turned to the boys as though he had been talking to them all along. "You boys live near Lake Shirwa, don't you?"

"Yes, Doctor," answered Chuma. "Our village is right on the shore of the lake."

"My father is chief of our village," added Wikatani proudly. "Often he has taken me in his canoe on Lake Shirwa."

"That's right . . . you said you were a chief's son," said Livingstone with interest. "Then I must speak to him." He turned and strode resolutely back to camp.

The boys looked at each other, startled, then hurried to catch up with the doctor. "Are you going to our village? You will take us with you?" they asked breathlessly.

The man did not answer but busied himself looking through his maps and books on the table outside his tent.

"Doctor," Chuma tried again, "can we come with you?"

Finally, the doctor stopped his rummaging and turned to the boys: "I don't see how you can. This will be a very fast trip—and dangerous, too, if all these reports of war are correct. We will be heading right into the middle of the conflict. And—"

"But this may be our only chance to return to our village!" Chuma interrupted.

The doctor gave the boys a kindly smile. "I know how you must feel—you are far away from your home and family. But I will be taking only my best porters and moving fast. However, I promise that if I see your families, I'll tell them that you are here and that you're safe. Maybe they can come get you."

The boys were deeply disappointed, and their faces showed it. Certainly their families would send for them . . . if Livingstone found them. But they did not want to wait. They wanted to go home—now! Chuma started to beg the good doctor to take them, but Wikatani put his hand out and cautioned him to be quiet while Livingstone continued to study his maps.

When the doctor looked up again, he seemed surprised to see the boys still there. "What are you standing around here for? Run along and find something useful to do." They did not move. He stared at them a few more moments, then he said, "I'd like to take you home, but . . . Say, have you boys ever seen my steamboat?" He grinned at the boys as he changed the subject. "Tell you what. I'll give you a tour of the *Pioneer*. I'll bet you've never been on board a steamboat before. I've got to go down there anyway, so come on. Maybe I can find something useful for you to do."

The boys followed the doctor reluctantly. They knew he was trying to distract them from their determination to return home with him. His smoking canoe might interest them at some other time, but if he thought they would forget their longing to return home, he was mistaken.

When they were on board, the boat seemed even bigger than before. It didn't even move when all three walked up the ramp and stepped on deck. "See how big it is," said the doctor. Chuma noted the size of the deck, but all he could think about was his home: *A whole herd of sheep could fit in back and there'd still be room for all the boys in our village to play a game up front.*

"In the rainy season, when the water is high, I can travel up the river in much less time than if I were trying to go over land through the swampy lowlands. And of course, it would take hundreds of porters to transport what the boat can carry," explained the doctor. "On the other hand," he laughed, "if the water in the river is too low, the boat gets stuck on sand bars, and it takes forever to make the trip."

A house was built in the middle of the boat while a canvas awning sheltered the front and back decks. On each side of the boat were huge wheels with paddles on them. "The engine makes these wheels go around and they push the boat along," explained Livingstone. *Just like paddling a canoe on Lake Shirwa*, thought Chuma.

"This is a very wonderful boat," said Wikatani politely, trying to sound grateful for the doctor's attention.

"The fact is," said Livingstone, "this old tub is nearly ready to sink. We've patched it up so many times, you can't tell what's the boat and what's a patch. I've ordered a completely new riverboat built in England—spent every last penny I own to do it, too. It will be taken apart, and the pieces will be loaded on a great seagoing ship and brought to Africa by the end of the year. Then we'll put it back together and have something worth traveling in. Maybe I'll take you boys on a trip in it. Would you like that?"

What we'd like is to go home, now, with you, thought Chuma, but he didn't say it. Instead he politely asked, "Where is the smoke for this smoking canoe?"

"'Smoking canoe,' is it?" laughed the doctor. "Well, there's got to be some fire before we get any smoke. Come with me." Taking the boys into the engine room, he showed them the big boilers that made the steam to drive the boat. The boys had never seen so much metal, all of it shiny like silver and gold.

"How would you boys like to polish the brass on this engine?" offered Livingstone. "It'll give you something to do."

The boys just stared at him sadly.

The doctor let out a long sigh and ran his fingers through his unruly hair. "Listen, you boys must understand one thing: my most important objective is to get this war stopped." He pointed a bony finger at Wikatani. "The fact that your father is a village chief may be of some help—if I can find him. . . ." The doctor stopped and stared at the boys for a long minute. Then he broke into a big smile and clapped his hands together as he said, "Why didn't I think of that before? Of course, of course. You boys are the key. You are the ones who can prove that the Manganja did not steal you—that there is no cause for this war. And with you along to tell your story, I can stop these rumors that the Red Caps work for me. Of course you can come!"

"Thank you, Doctor! Thank you!" both boys said gleefully.

"We leave in the morning—overland," the doctor said abruptly as he headed out the engine room door and stomped off the boat.

The boys followed him, playfully punching each other on the shoulder. "I didn't see any wood to keep this thing afloat," whispered Wikatani as they ran up the ramp.

"Well, the doctor said it is about ready to sink. That's probably why," noted Chuma.

The boys were up before the sun rose the next morning. "I'm going down to the river to bathe," announced Chuma. "It seems like a good thing to bathe before such an important journey."

"You go ahead. I'm going to see Dauma," said Wikatani in a secretive whisper.

"But what about her mother?" asked Chuma.

"She won't catch me."

"You want me to come?," asked Chuma.

"No. You go on down to the river. I'll be there as soon as I tell Dauma goodbye."

"Then tell her goodbye for me, too," said Chuma, and the boys went off in different directions.

"Today we leave for home. Today we leave for home," Chuma chanted quietly to himself as he walked down to the river.

The eastern sky was a bright pink, casting an eerie glow everywhere, silhouetting the doctor's boat like a great mountain against the sky. Somehow the strange light made everything look unfamiliar, or maybe it was because today he was going home, and that made the whole world look different. But there was also an odd smell in the air, like sour smoke— not the smoke that rose in thin wisps from last night's campfires.

The boy slid down the bank to the river's edge.

The tied-up steamboat sheltered the water near the bank from the river's fast current and only small waves played along the muddy bank. Chuma jumped in the water and glided toward the side of the steamer. Two ducks scurried around the back end of the boat, trying to get away without having to take to the air.

Then Chuma noticed two strange objects bobbing in the water under the boat's huge paddle wheel. Whatever they were, they were caught there by the river's current. They were round, dark, and smooth, floating just at the surface of the water. *Probably just pieces of driftwood,* he thought. He'd seen driftwood worn smooth and shiny by bumping along the river rapids mile after mile. He swam toward the paddle wheel, thinking he would remove the logs so they wouldn't jam when the big wheel turned.

He touched one of the objects and it rolled over.

"Aieee!" he screamed at the top of his lungs and swam for the shore. He kept on screaming as he scrambled up the bank and ran for the camp.

Instantly everyone in camp was awake and coming out of their tents. Some of the men had picked up their guns.

"What's the matter, Chuma?" boomed David Livingstone when he saw the boy running toward him.

Chuma pointed back toward the river. His mouth hung open, his eyes wide. Finally he said in a hoarse whisper, "A body . . . two of them—in the river."

The men ran down to the shore. As they pulled

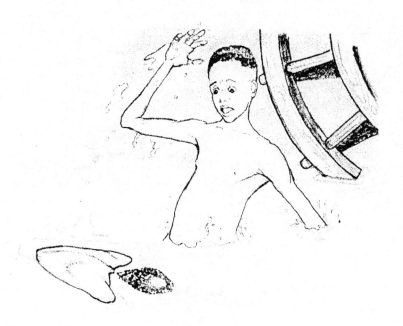

the bodies from between the paddles of the riverboat, Wikatani noticed the tribal markings and whispered, "Ajawa."

The doctor sighed. "Probably war victims. Call the bishop; we must bury them. Then we'd better get on our way. Things aren't getting any better between the Ajawa and the Manganja."

Chuma and Wikatani looked at each other in horror. For the first time, Chuma realized his own family might be in serious danger.

Chapter 8

Ambush!

THE SUN HAD ALREADY begun to slide toward the horizon when Chuma noticed the same sour, smoky smell he had whiffed that morning. The little party had been traveling at a good pace all day. The group included Doctor Livingstone, six porters—each carrying a load of supplies and trade goods—and the two Ajawa boys.

"I don't remember any of this country. Do you?" asked Wikatani.

"No. It must be a different route than the Red Caps took."

"I hope the doctor knows where he's going."

"He's got maps," assured Chuma.

They worked their way down a steep, wooded hill to a small river. On the other side, several canoes were grounded on a small beach beneath a steep cliff.

"There's a Manganja village up there that I visited when I came through here two years ago," said Livingstone as they waded across the shallows. "The canoes are still here, but where are the children? Why aren't they coming out to meet us?"

Climbing the trail to the top of the cliff, Chuma worried whether the Manganja would welcome them when they realized the boys were Ajawa. But the village was empty; every house had been burned. Chuma then realized that the strange smell came from burning huts. On the still night air, the smoke had drifted throughout that part of the Shire River Valley.

"Where are the people?" asked Wikatani.

"Dead . . . or fleeing the war," said one of the porters grimly.

In the ruins of one of the houses they found the body of an adult woman—possibly someone too sick or old to flee. They buried the body and then sat under a tree near the edge of the village while Livingstone studied his map. After a time he looked up at the boys and said in a very tired voice, "I think if we are going to find your village, we'd better turn east here and go around the bottom of Mount Zomba and approach Lake Shirwa from the south.

"We had a good march today," he announced to everyone. "My guess is that the Manganja who lived here are either captured or still on the run and too afraid to return. And since the Ajawa know this village has already been defeated, I doubt that they will return. So, let's stay here for the night."

But the porters let out a loud protest. The idea of sleeping where people had been killed and homes burned terrified them. So the party hiked east until darkness forced them to stop and make camp.

That night, however, they built no fires, not wanting to attract any attention. They also posted two guards all night. Chuma and Wikatani took their turns on guard, though not at the same time.

"What was it like? Did you fall asleep?" asked Chuma when Wikatani woke him for his turn in the middle of the night.

"Are you kidding?" said Wikatani. "I was too scared that someone would sneak up on our camp."

The next morning as they hiked east they began meeting Manganja fleeing the war. At first there were just one or two at a time, but soon they passed whole families. Some people had wounds that Doctor Livingstone tried to treat as quickly as he could. But his greatest urgency was to get to the front and make contact with the leaders of those who were fighting in the hope of achieving peace.

Around midday they came to another deserted, burned village. No dead were found, but corn was dumped out of the storehouses and spilled all over the ground. A few scraggly chickens pecked at it but flew away, squawking when anyone came near.

In the afternoon the little party saw the smoke of other burning villages. In the distance they could hear shouts of victory mixed with the cries of women mourning over their dead. They had traveled a few miles out onto an open plain with high grass, huge boulders, and occasional trees when one of the porters pointed out a line of Ajawa warriors coming down a distant trail with Manganja captives.

"This is our chance," said Livingstone. "Maybe I can reason with them and arrange a meeting with the chiefs."

But when the two groups met, one of the Manganja captives recognized Livingstone and started yelling, "Our general has come! The white man will free us! The white man will free us!" Other Manganja joined in, and for a few moments there was great confusion. The Ajawa warriors panicked and fled, yelling, "War! War!" Then the Manganja also ran off in the opposite direction, toward the distant hills, leaving Livingstone and his party standing alone in the open country, unable to talk peace with anyone.

"Why did he start yelling that I was their general and liberator?" said Livingstone, taking his blue cap off and slapping it on his leg in frustration. "Where did he get that idea?"

"Excuse me, Doctor," Wikatani offered, "but I think I recognized the man. He was one of the slaves of the Red Caps. We traveled together before you freed us."

"Of all the . . . I should have known," said the doctor in disgust as he sat down on a rock. "He was one of those men who did not stay to help build the mission. They probably told the story to every

Manganja they met. And he thought I was going to free him again. Now we'll never make contact with the Ajawa."

But he was wrong.

The white man and his companions had traveled only a short distance when a much larger number of Ajawa warriors appeared, closing in on the little group from both sides. "Down!" yelled Livingstone. Chuma and Wikatani dropped to the ground and crawled behind an enormous ant hill; Livingstone and the porters took cover in the tall grass and behind the few rocks at hand. As the Ajawa came closer, Chuma caught glimpses of movement as the warriors darted skillfully through the tall grass from rock to bush to tree. When they were within a hundred yards, they began shooting their arrows at Livingstone and his men.

Their accuracy was amazing and would have been deadly if the travelers had not taken cover so quickly. The porters had their guns ready and would have shot back, but Livingstone kept saying, "Hold your fire! We don't want bloodshed." Then he called out in a loud voice, "Ajawa warriors! We have not come to fight, but to talk peace!" But the number of arrows flying toward them seemed only to increase.

Finally, in desperation, Wikatani scrambled onto the ant hill, stood up, and yelled in the native Ajawa language, "Don't shoot! Don't shoot! I am Ajawa!" Chuma was ready to join him when Wikatani let out a yell and fell back down to the ground with an arrow through his left arm.

"We've got to get out of here," said Livingstone,
moving quickly to Wikatani's side. He pulled the
arrow from the boy's arm and pressed hard to stop

the flow of blood. "They're not going to listen to reason."

Chuma raised his head and saw the Ajawa warriors advancing on their position more quickly, doing a wild war dance as they came to within fifty yards. One of the porters shouted, "Doctor, they are surrounding us! The trail is cut off!"

Livingstone was tying his handkerchief tightly around Wikatani's arm. "Then we'll have to fight our way out," he said grimly. It was exactly what the frightened porters had been waiting for. They opened fire with their guns and soon the Ajawa warriors pulled back.

"I hit two!" one of the men cheered. "I got one!" said another. In all, the porters claimed to have shot six Ajawa, but when the doctor climbed to the top of the ant hill and surveyed the area, no dead or wounded could be seen.

"Let's go before they return," he ordered, and the group moved warily back up the trail toward the protection of the forest.

As they reached the safety of the jungle trail, Livingstone walked between the two boys with a hand on each of their shoulders. "I'm very, very sorry," he said. "I did not want to shoot at your people."

Chuma felt uncomfortable. He had been afraid and was glad when the fighting stopped. But he had also felt angry when the porters began shooting their guns at Ajawa warriors—his own people. But seeing how discouraged the doctor looked, he finally said,

"You couldn't help it."

"Maybe not," Livingstone said. "But I have been in Africa for twenty years; I have been face-to-face with some of the fiercest chiefs in the whole land; I have been within an inch of losing my life . . . but I have never before had to shoot at an African. I have always found another way." The doctor walked in silence for a few minutes, then said, "It feels like the end of my work here. Word will spread; how will the people ever trust me?"

Chuma looked at Wikatani; pain etched the other boy's face from the wound in his arm. But both boys seemed to realize that their friend the doctor was also struggling with pain.

Toward evening the travelers came upon a group of Manganja refugees fleeing for their lives. Livingstone invited them to share their fire, hopeful that the increased numbers would be sufficient protection from attack.

"What do you know of the fighting around Lake Shirwa?" the white man asked their guests, gently cleaning Wikatani's wound in the firelight and putting medicine on it from the shiny tube.

"There is no fighting there," said the head man.

"Is it possible to get there from here?"

"No. Terrible fighting is between here and there; there is no way through."

"How do you know that there is no fighting around Lake Shirwa?" asked Wikatani, wincing as Livingstone bandaged his arm.

"Because Manganja hold all of Lake Shirwa now,"

the man said proudly. "We have taken it from those treacherous hyenas, the Ajawa." The man snarled out the last words, staring directly at the boys. Both Chuma and Wikatani shivered. Did he know they were Ajawa?

The doctor frowned. "What happened to the villages around the lake?"

When the man answered, he did not turn to the doctor but continued staring at the boys. "All—Ajawa—villages—have—been—burned." He spat out each word distinctly. "The only Ajawa near Lake Shirwa are dead ones whose bones are being picked clean by buzzards. Soon that will be the fate of all Ajawa."

Chapter 9

The Raging River

I KNOW BOTH OF YOU want to return to your families," Livingstone spoke to the boys the next morning as they prepared to leave the camp of the Manganja refugees, "but I cannot risk repeating what happened yesterday. If what the Manganja say is true, the villages around Lake Shirwa have been destroyed, and the likelihood of finding your families there is not good. . . . And even if we did," he said, seeing the fear in their eyes, "it wouldn't be safe for you to remain in this part of the country right now."

"But . . . what will we do?" Chuma asked, disappointment sticking in his throat.

"Come back to the mission station with me. If I had been able to avoid bloodshed, we might have arranged safe passage through the war zone to reach the chiefs. They are the only real hope for bringing peace to this senseless war. But now . . ." Livingstone shook his head. ". . . we are likely to be targets for their arrows whenever we encounter Ajawa."

It was a dejected and weary band that cautiously set out down the trail. No longer did they march along with confidence. Livingstone decided that the only safe way to travel was by stealth if they did not want to have to use their guns again. So he sent out a man to scout the trail ahead, and only when it was clear would the rest of the party silently follow.

Once, when the scout discovered a party of Ajawa warriors resting beside a stream, Livingstone decided they should leave the trail and cut through the dense jungle to circle far around the warriors. It was an exhausting detour. At times they found themselves in the middle of brambles with seemingly no way out. The thorns caught and would not let go. If each one was not carefully unhooked, it would tear skin or clothes. Worse, the bramble vines were so tough that they required several hacks from a machete before they would give way.

"Quiet! Quiet!" Livingstone would whisper when someone would yelp or curse with the difficulty. "We must not announce our presence."

Finally, they came upon the trail of a herd of elephants and followed along with more ease where the beasts had beaten down the jungle in their passing.

The second night of their return trip was spent without any shelter or fire while a hard, chilling rain fell. "But Doctor," protested some of the porters, "no warriors will be moving about in weather like this."

"Good warriors will endure anything. Good peace-makers must do the same. No fires here!"

It rained most of the next day and only let up in the evening as the tired party trudged into the burned-out village on the cliff above the river.

"I still think this village is safe," said Livingstone. "If you can find dry wood that makes no smoke, I think we could have a small fire tonight. But try to shield it from view."

The porters did not want to spend the night in the burned-out village, but the prospect of sleeping in the cold, wet jungle again drove them to brave it. They found a couple huts with their roofs still in place.

Later, Livingstone spread his map by the fire and said, "I think this little river dumps into the Shire River just a few miles above the mission station. If those abandoned canoes are still down there on the beach, we could use them. It would be farther—two legs of a triangle, to the west and then south rather than cutting directly cross-country—but it would be safer than traveling through the jungle."

"Yes, but Doctor," said one of the porters, "the great rapids and waterfalls begin just above the mission station. They go on for many miles. Once we hit the Shire River, we'd be in the worst of them."

"Indeed, the Murchison cataracts are too rough to take my steamboat up, but don't you think canoes could come down quite safely?"

"Doctor, they are terrible. Many people have lost their lives in them."

"Well," said Livingstone, folding up his map, "if it gets too bad, we'll just put ashore and walk."

Travel on the small river the next morning was a pleasant change from hacking through the jungle. After assuring Doctor Livingstone that they were skilled in handling a canoe, having used one often on Lake Shirwa, Chuma and Wikatani were allowed to share a small canoe of their own. Three other canoes made up the remainder of their flotilla. Livingstone and two porters were in one, while the other two canoes carried two porters each plus most of their supplies.

"We still must travel in silence," warned the doctor, and it was good advice. An hour later they were gliding through an area where the jungle hung far out over the river from each bank, almost touching the water. Suddenly there was yelling from both sides of the river just behind them, and a shower of arrows sailed after them. One arrow landed harmlessly in the bottom of the last canoe as the whole party paddled hard to get out of range.

"That was too close," murmured Wikatani as they sprinted around a bend in the river.

"If they had heard us coming and been ready, we would have been like big fish in a little pool. No one could have missed," said Chuma.

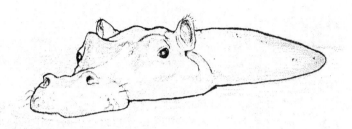

Where the small river joined the Shire River, a herd of hippopotami were swimming in the shallows. The paddlers steered well out of their way, knowing that the round, gentle-looking animals are some of the most dangerous animals in Africa. They do not like to be disturbed and can easily crush a canoe with a single bite of their powerful jaws.

But by watching the hippopotami, the travelers were taken by surprise when the four canoes suddenly swept out onto the angry Shire River. Instantly, they were shot downstream with a force that the paddlers couldn't resist. At that point there were no rapids, so the surface was deceptively smooth, but the speed with which the water moved was far beyond anything the boys had ever encountered. They could feel the powerful water drawing them this way and that with a will of its own.

Within less than a mile, they came to the rapids. They were so steep and turbulent that as their canoe came upon them, it looked like they were ready to slide down a white mountain. "Look out!" yelled Chuma, who was sitting in the back. But there was nothing Wikatani could do as a huge wave of water came over the bow of the canoe and landed in his lap with the weight of a bag of corn being dropped from a tree. The gallons of water in the bottom of the canoe made it heavy and even more difficult to handle.

"Straighten us out," screamed Wikatani over his shoulder as the current swept the canoe sideways toward a huge rock sticking out of the river. Chuma paddled hard, knowing that if the canoe hit the rock broadside, it would break in half like dried reed. But the current was too powerful; he could do nothing to straighten the canoe. And then, at the last moment, the bulge of water rising up before the rock swung their canoe around, and they shot past down into the trough beyond like an eagle swooping down on its prey. But then they faced a mountain of water. The little craft rose on the curling wave and seemed to hang in mid air for a moment and then came down, dumping both boys into the raging river.

The water around Chuma churned white with bubbles, and the strong current sucked him deeper into the darkness below. He kicked hard as he fought for the surface, but there was no resisting the cold monster that clutched him in its grasp. Down, down he went until all was blackness, and he had no idea which way was up. Suddenly something raked the length of his back like the claws of a lion, and his head crashed into stone. He tumbled helplessly over and over along the bottom of the vengeful torrent. The river was intent on knocking every bit of breath out of him.

It began to get lighter, and Chuma noticed

bubbles swirling around him. Were they his air, knocked from his lungs, or was he rising to the foaming surface? And then the river spat him out, and he flew into the air, face up with legs and arms outstretched toward the dazzling blue sky. For an instant he looked back over his shoulder and saw what must have happened. Above him was a roaring waterfall. Somehow he had plunged over it and been driven to the bottom of the pool below, then was coughed up by the river.

He landed back on the water with a stinging splat and righted himself quickly. *Where is Wikatani? Where is the canoe?* He looked around desperately. Twenty yards downstream he caught a glimpse of Wikatani, clinging to the bottom of their overturned canoe as it bobbed on down the river. Chuma took a big breath and then struck out, swimming toward his friend. *At least he is alive,* Chuma thought.

Something rose to the surface to his right. It was someone's clothes—dark blue, like the doctor's. *I should get them for him,* the boy thought. But he was too exhausted and had swallowed too much water. *I better just save myself, otherwise I might not make it.* And then Chuma realized that it was more than the doctor's blue jacket. It was the doctor himself, floating face down in the swirling water!

"Help!" Chuma yelled to anyone who might hear. He altered his course and swam for the blue patch, hoping it would not be sucked under before he got there. But the river was playing more tricks on him and kept moving the doctor away.

"Oh, God," gasped Chuma, "if you are the black man's God, too, as the doctor says, don't let him die. Help me . . . help me reach him in time." Finally, in one last sprint, Chuma reached out and grasped the back of the blue jacket. He rolled it over and pulled the doctor's face above water. There was a wound over one eye, and the older man didn't seem to be breathing. Chuma got a big handful of the white man's lank hair and tried swimming toward the western shore.

But the river bank was too far away; he would never make it. Every time he tried to take a fresh breath, a wave slapped him in the face, leaving him coughing and gasping. He seemed to take in more water than he spat out. Then, when he was about to give up, a rock island appeared right in front of him. He maneuvered to get his feet around in front of himself to catch his weight so they wouldn't crash into the rock too hard. When

he hit, he got a footing on the upstream side, then reached for a handhold to pull himself up onto the slab of rock. He really needed two hands, but he was holding on to the doctor with the other. Grunting and straining, he pulled and pulled on the handhold and finally rolled to safety just as the current caught the doctor's body and swung him around downstream. Chuma almost lost his handhold. With all his might he wrestled the doctor out of the grip of the terrible current, then dragged the doctor up onto the smooth stone beside him.

The boy lay panting for a moment, but knew he couldn't wait if the doctor had any chance of living. He rolled the soaking man over onto his stomach; the doctor's legs still hung in the river, buffeted by the rushing water. Chuma sat on top of the man and pressed all his weight into the middle of the man's back. Chuma raised himself then pressed back down. Again and again he did the same. Suddenly a great stream of water gushed out of the doctor's mouth and he began coughing and choking. Chuma rolled off and collapsed on the rock beside him.

Then everything went black.

Chapter 10

The Second Journey

C HUMA AWOKE IN THE SHADE of a spreading acacia tree, its flowers giving a sweet smell to the warm air. Faces etched with concern were staring down at him. He looked from one to the other: the doctor—his clothes still dripping wet; Wikatani; and all six porters. Everyone had survived.

"How did I get here?"

"All our canoes were lost—except one, thank God," said the doctor. "With it some of the men were able to come over and take us off that island."

Chuma sat up, but quickly wished he hadn't moved. His back burned like fire.

"I want to thank you. You saved my life . . . at a great risk to yourself. But," the doctor said as he turned Chuma to look at his back, "I'm afraid I lost all my medicine and have nothing to put on those scratches on your back. Looks like you tangled with a lion," he chuckled.

"I think it was just a river—but it almost won," said Chuma.

"Well, I think you'll be all right until we get something for it. But we'd better get going, if you feel well enough to walk. It's going to take another full day or maybe even longer to get back to the mission station."

In the days and weeks that followed at the mission station, Chuma and Wikatani often worried about what the Manganja warriors had said about their village. "What if our families are all dead as that Manganja said?" said Wikatani one day. Both boys had been afraid to put their worst fears into words.

Chuma thought for a long time. When he broke the silence, there were tears in his eyes. "If they are, I will stay with the doctor and be a Christian. But we do not know that. We cannot give up hope."

"Besides," said Wikatani. "The Manganja like to boast. He was just trying to scare us. But . . . we must go back and let our families know we are alive."

It was only a couple of days later that Livingstone called the boys to him while he was sitting outside his tent studying his maps.

"I have heard reports of another lake to the north

of your homeland. It is said to be a very great body of water. Do you know of it?" he said, looking up at the boys standing beside his table.

Chuma shrugged, but Wikatani said, "I have heard of it. It is called *Nyassa*."

"Yes, Lake Nyassa," mused the doctor, pulling at the corners of his mustache. "Have you ever seen it?"

"No, Doctor, but my father has."

"He has? Did he tell you anything about it?"

"Only that it is very, very long. One old man told him that if you started as a boy, you'd be an old man before you finished walking around it."

"Really?"

"He said it, but everyone else laughed and said it would take two months to walk around it—but it can't be done."

"Why not?"

"I don't know."

"That's still pretty big. I must explore this Lake Nyassa. It may be the key to stopping the slave traders."

The boys did not understand.

"You see," the doctor continued, punching a point on the map with his finger, "if we could get a steamboat onto Lake Nyassa, we could bring in the supplies and people to set up a mission station there. I could claim that part of the country for England, and it would be out from under the control of the Portuguese slavers. *Then* we could be much more effective in stopping this terrible slave trade."

"But Doctor," said Chuma, "how would you get

your steamboat beyond the rapids?"

David Livingstone shrugged. "That's why I must explore the lake. If it is as big as you say, then it has to have another outlet besides the Shire River." Livingstone got up and started pacing around his camp, slamming his right fist into the palm of his left hand with each step. He whirled and pointed at Wikatani. "Did your father say anything about a river running out of the lake to the east all the way to the sea?"

"No."

"Well, there must be one, and I will find it. The whole geography of the region demands one."

As the boys left the doctor's camp, Wikatani turned to Chuma and said excitedly, "Did you look at the doctor's map?"

"Yes. What about it?"

"We could not get home from the south because of the terrible fighting between us and Lake Shirwa. But what if we approached Lake Shirwa from the north?"

"There might not be so much fighting up there."

"Right," said Wikatani eagerly. "If we could go on this expedition with Doctor Livingstone, we could travel up the Shire River, around all the fighting to Lake Nyassa to the north—"

"From there," interrupted Chuma eagerly as he saw the plan, "we could come down to our homeland."

The boys had to do some fast talking, but three days later they were again part of the doctor's expedition. They did not, however, tell him their real hopes for wanting to go along.

The Murchison cataracts that began just above the mission station on the Shire River did not allow for any boat travel. So four porters carried a four-oared rowboat as they headed north along the west bank of the river. Two more men went ahead and cleared the way with machetes. Livingstone preceded them, trying to scout out the easiest path—which was never very easy as they were always going steeply uphill. Chuma and Wikatani followed, loaded down with the heavy oars, the sail, and an awning. "When we get on that lake, we'll be glad for this sail," the doctor had said. "And the awning will protect us from the sun day after day."

When the men were exhausted, they put the boat down and everyone got a rest—if you could call it that—while all but two (left as guards) hiked back to pick up their supplies. Then everyone hoisted boxes and bundles onto their backs and carried them up to the point where they had left the boat. Then they did it all again.

On a good day, this routine was repeated three or four times.

Along the way, the boys marveled that they had ever tried to come down the river in canoes. Often they would hike for miles along the top edge of a deep gorge with the raging river at the bottom and no shore at the water's edge where they could have

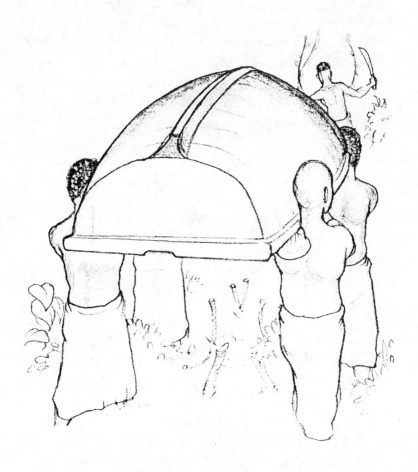

sought safety or taken a rest.

Once Livingstone showed the boys the map. "The Murchison cataracts on the Shire River are forty miles long. I think the Lord God was protecting us by getting us out of that river as quickly as He did," the doctor admitted.

Soon they passed the point where their canoes

had come out of the small river onto the Shire. But it took a total of three weeks of torturous work portaging the rowboat overland before the party arrived at a point where they could safely put it in the river.

Having finally arrived at calm water, they took a day to rest, hunt for fresh meat, and prepare for the next leg of their journey.

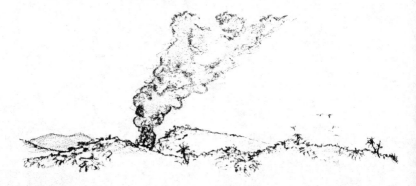

Travel on the river the next day was a pleasant relief from the constant toil of carrying their heavy loads uphill. The water was relatively smooth, and their rowing—while hard work—made good progress.

Along the rapids they had not seen any signs of the tribal war. But that day, in the rolling hills to the east, a great pillar of black smoke rose high into the silvery sky. Since the area was mostly green jungle, it did not seem likely that the fire was accidental but probably a village that had been put to the torch.

That night they camped at the base of a cliff in a damp, marshy area. "No fires tonight," said Livingstone. "We don't want to attract any attention."

Later, as everyone slapped at the mosquitoes that would not let them eat in peace, Chuma decided it was time to bring up their plan.

"Doctor Livingstone, when we get to Lake Nyassa, won't we be almost straight north of Lake Shirwa?"

"Almost, Chuma. Why do you ask?"

"Wikatani and I were thinking that it might be safe to travel to Lake Shirwa if we came down from the north since the battles we ran into were south of the lake."

The doctor sat silently for a few moments, a deep frown creasing his forehead as he pulled at his mustache. "It might be possible," he finally agreed. "But here we are almost straight west of Lake Shirwa and we saw that burning village today. So the fighting is not only in the south. But why do you ask?"

"We were wondering," jumped in Wikatani, "whether, when you got that far north, you might decide to go south to meet the Ajawa chiefs."

"And you could take us with you to find our families," added Chuma.

Livingstone got up and walked down to the water's edge. The boys did not know whether he was angry or not. Finally, he strode back to the rest of them. "I *had* hoped to bring a quick end to this fighting by trying to reach the Ajawa chiefs," he explained. "But we failed. Since then, I've come to feel that God has a larger purpose for me: I believe we *must* establish a mission base in the interior. It's the only way to break the back of this wicked slave trade—"

"But you wanted to stop the war. Remember?" said Chuma.

"Yes, and I would still give my life to accomplish that. But I must not be shortsighted. I do not know how much longer the Portuguese will allow me to remain in this part of Africa. We must establish a permanent base farther north—around Lake Nyassa—and the only hope is to find a waterway from it to the sea. Then I can get a steamboat with supplies into the interior."

All the porters were quiet and listening intently.

"You see, as terrible as this tribal war is," Livingstone went on, "there is a more serious mission. The bishop and others like him want to bring the Gospel—the story about God's Son, Jesus—to all these tribes. Jesus showed people a new way to live with one another. He forgave His enemies; He showed that everyone—old and young, men, women, and children, black and white—is important to God. Most important, Jesus died to take the punishment for our sins, so that all of us can live with God in heaven forever."

No one spoke. This was something to think about.

"You see, the only real way to stop the slavers and the fighting is to change people's hearts. If the people hear the Gospel, maybe they will obey God's commandments and stop warring with one another and selling people into slavery."

Livingstone looked kindly at Chuma and Wikatani. "I'm sorry, my young friends. I must try for the greater purpose first. We must go on to Lake

Nyassa and find the river to the sea. Then maybe we can make another attempt to reach the Ajawa chiefs."

Chapter 11

Lake Nyassa

I<small>N THE AFTERNOON</small> of the next day a breeze arose along the river; Livingstone put up the sail, and they moved along even faster than the men could row. What a welcomed rest! Chuma and Wikatani had never seen a sailing vessel, let alone ridden in one. "We are like kings with invisible slaves rowing us along," Chuma grinned.

Three days more they traveled with much the same routine, rowing in the morning and sailing in the afternoon, until—four weeks after leaving the mission station—the river mouth widened and they came out onto Lake Nyassa. It was so big, the water seemed to run right into the sky. Doctor Livingstone was even more excited than the boys; he wrote the date in a little book and read it to the boys: "We found Lake Nyassa on September second, 1861."

Beaching the boat on a gentle bank, the travelers were met by hundreds of Africans who had never seen a white man before. Even the men were very curious, wanting to touch Livingstone's skin and feel his strange, limp hair.

The people were friendly and eagerly provided plenty of food for the newcomers, including fish from the lake. However, they did not speak a language that any of the travelers could understand, so communication was very difficult. But Chuma and Wikatani were impressed with the doctor's skill in learning a new language. Before the evening was over he had mastered dozens of words and could put together a few simple sentences to the great amusement of the local people.

Each day the little boat of explorers traveled farther north on the great lake and spent the evening in a new village on the shore. As soon as Livingstone was able to communicate with the people, he began telling them about Jesus, how He was the Son of the only true God, and that He had come to earth to tell everyone of God's love and forgiveness of sin. The people listened attentively, but few responded. "That's all right," said the doctor. "I planted a seed."

At every stop Livingstone also asked if there was a river that flowed east out of the lake. But every person he questioned gave a different answer. One man declared positively that they could sail right out of the lake on such a river; but the next man said, no, they would need to hike overland fifty or even a hundred miles before reaching a river of any size.

"We're going to have to see for ourselves," Livingstone said stubbornly.

But as they made their way along the shore of the great lake, trouble began to develop. One night robbers crept into their camp while they slept and stole nearly all their supplies. The most serious loss was their food and trade goods. The trade goods were important in making friends with new tribes and in paying tolls to the chiefs for permission to pass through their territory.

The next night no one met them when they beached their boat. Pushing into the surrounding jungle, the travelers found a village burned to the ground and strewn with rotting bodies. "More tribal warfare," Livingston muttered, poking through the ruins. "I'll bet the slavers are behind this, too."

Once again the porters insisted that they leave the place of death; they rowed by moonlight until they saw a deserted beach and pulled toward shore.

But no sooner had they landed than a large group of warriors ran out of the jungle, painted for war and waving their spears fiercely. "Mazitu!" one of the porters cried fearfully. As the warriors advanced, the porters immediately raised their guns. With nothing to trade, Chuma was sure they would have to resort to their guns again to avoid being killed.

"Wait!" Livingstone ordered. At the last minute he rolled up his sleeves and opened his shirt, exposing the whiteness of skin that had not been tanned by the sun. In the moonlight his skin shone pale and

ghostly. The warriors stopped in their tracks. Cautiously, one moved forward, his spear extended. He brought the tip to Livingstone's chest and drew it down slowly across the skin. The tiny trickle of blood that followed the sharp point looked black, rather than red, in the strange, pale light.

Suddenly the warriors let out a frightened cry, turned, and fled back into the jungle.

Startled, the little group stood staring at the dark edge of the jungle that had swallowed up the fierce warriors.

One of the porters finally broke the silence. "We must not continue!" he declared. "We have no food and nothing to trade for more. The next war party may not be so scared by your trick. It is time to go back."

"Yes. Yes. We must go back," the others insisted.

But Livingstone protested and there was a big argument. Finally he convinced the men to go on one more day in hopes of moving out of the war-torn area.

They posted guards that night as had become their custom wherever trouble threatened, and it was Chuma's lot to draw guard duty with Doctor Livingstone. Because they had set up camp on the open beach, no one could approach the camp without being seen. The guards did not have to patrol so much as watch over the camp in the moonlight. Chuma and the doctor chose the top of a small dune near their sleeping companions and sat down.

When all was quiet, Chuma said, "Doctor, I would like to become a Christian like you, and follow your God."

"That's good, Chuma. But tell me, why do you want to do this?"

"Well, you could have ordered those warriors shot tonight, but God gave you great courage to do a good thing."

"Yes, He did, Chuma. But what if I had not had that courage?"

Chuma thought for a while. "I still think you would have *wanted* the good thing. I think you really love the African people."

"But *why* do you think I love Africans?"

"Because you love God, and God loves all people.

That's why God sent His Son, Jesus, to die for us." Chuma grinned, remembering what he had heard the bishop and the doctor say.

"That's right, Chuma. And you must remember that. Even if I completely fail to do what's right, Jesus did not fail. Put your trust in Him, not in how well other people behave."

They listened in quietness to the waves gently lapping at the beach, then Chuma asked, "But, how do I become a Christian?"

"Well, you know that we're all sinners. And that's more than occasionally doing an evil thing like lying or stealing—those, of course, are sins. Even when we try hard to do good—like I'm trying to find a way to stop the slave trade—it doesn't always work out. And sometimes we make things worse, and people get hurt. Then we realize how badly we need someone to save us."

"I know that, and that's what I want. I want Jesus to save me. But how?"

"The Bible says, 'As many as received him, to them gave he power to become the sons of God, even to them that believe on his name.' Do you believe that, Chuma? Do you want to give your life to Jesus?"

"Yes."

They talked some more, and then Chuma prayed. The next morning before setting out, Doctor Livingstone baptized Chuma in the lake as a new Christian while the others watched.

That night, when the explorers stopped, they were met by local people who laughed at them and thought they were fleeing from the Mazitu. For some reason—Chuma never found out why—a shoving match started between the porters and the villagers that soon broke into a fight with sticks. Livingstone did his best to stop it, and the local people finally withdrew sullenly. The travelers made camp, but decided not to sleep by the fire. Instead, they made beds filled with grass to look like sleeping people and crawled away into the nearby tall grass to sleep. Once again they posted guards to watch over the camp.

In the middle of the night, warriors snuck into the camp and stabbed their spears into the fake sleepers. When they realized they had been fooled, they ran away, thinking that the trick was an ambush.

The continual obstacles and constant threat of harm from tribal warriors was too much for the porters. "We must go home," cried all the porters in the morning. "If we do not, we will all die!"

Reluctantly, Livingstone agreed. They had traveled nearly two hundred miles up the lake shore, but still the water to the north seemed to run on into the sky. They had not yet discovered a river flowing east to the ocean . . . on the other hand, they had not proved that a river didn't exist, either.

As they sailed back down the lake, Chuma noticed that the doctor said very little. Clearly he was discouraged by their failure. It made Chuma sad, too. They had come so far—for nothing! The more the doctor had talked about finding a river going to the ocean so he could start a mission, the more the boy had wanted to help make it happen. Like Livingstone, Chuma had been happy when they had a good day traveling or made friends with the local tribespeople, and he was sad when things went wrong.

Chuma thought about this as the boat creaked under the sail. Just last summer he was a sheepherder. Now he was traveling with the white doctor who wanted to stop the evil slavers. He didn't understand everything the doctor said, but he did know that Livingstone wanted all the tribes to live peacefully with one another. He was a good man. Chuma was only a boy . . . but he wanted to help Livingstone, too.

As they journeyed southward on the lake, the explorers avoided the areas where they had encountered problems before. But they faced a new problem: the weather. One morning Wikatani said, "The big winds are coming; we must not go out on the lake today."

Everyone looked up at the sky and wondered what he saw. While there was some haze in the sky, the sun was bright, and the day seemed like any other. If anything, the breeze was a little lighter than usual. "What do you mean?" laughed Livingstone. "It's a beautiful day." He proceeded to get ready to shove off.

Chuma knew that Wikatani had gone out frequently on Lake Shirwa with his father, and was probably more familiar with the weather in the area than anyone in the group. But even Chuma thought his friend was mistaken.

"The windy season is starting," Wikatani insisted. "It will blow today, and it will blow so hard that we could sink." The boy was truly frightened and at first refused to get in the boat, even after everyone else had climbed in and actually pushed off from shore.

From a few yards off shore Doctor Livingstone called back, "Come on, Wikatani. We don't want to leave you, but we *are* sailing this morning. So get in the boat."

With fearful eyes the boy waded out to the waiting craft and reluctantly climbed in. He actually shook with fright as he sat down in the bottom of the boat and looked up at the sky.

They traveled almost two hours under a good breeze and sunny skies when suddenly the wind shifted. Within minutes it turned into a gale. The waves in the shallow lake grew enormously, driving the little boat toward an angry surf crashing on a rocky shore. Livingstone and the boys immediately lowered the sail, and the men began to row with all their might. But still the wind drove them directly toward the rocks. Finally, Livingstone ordered, "Drop anchor! It's the only way to keep us out of those breakers."

But with the anchor out, the waves broke over the side and filled the boat, threatening to sink it. Everyone bailed out the water as fast as possible. Chuma

and Wikatani had nothing to scoop water, so they used their hands. Hour after hour the little band struggled to keep the boat afloat. Many times Chuma clung terrified to the side of the boat, sure it was going to tip over or sink, and they would all drown.

But six hours later the wind finally slackened; exhausted, the men rowed slowly away from the rocks and beached on a sandy shore.

From then on, Doctor Livingstone listened to Wikatani's advice when he said a wind was coming up. As a result, they spent many miserable days on shore waiting for the waves to go down. But in Chuma's mind, it was a lot better than bailing water.

On October 26, they arrived again at the south end of the lake. That night as they all sat dejectedly around the fire, Wikatani said, "Doctor, now can we try going south to Lake Shirwa?"

A hush fell over the whole group as everyone's eyes turned toward the doctor. Finally, he said, "All right. In the morning we'll find a place to hide the boat and set out on foot."

But in the morning, the doctor and the boys awoke to a terrible shock. During the night all the porters had run away.

Chapter 12

Home and Beyond

W HAT WILL WE DO NOW?" asked Chuma.

"Well, we can always sail the boat by ourselves," said the doctor. "Even one man can sail it."

"But you said we'd go to Lake Shirwa," said Wikatani.

Livingstone laughed wryly. "It would be foolish without any porters. They took the guns. What if we were attacked?"

"But Doctor, you said you didn't want to use guns, anyway," protested Chuma.

"I don't, but it's never good to appear weak in the face of danger."

"Won't God protect us if we are doing His work?" asked Chuma sincerely.

The doctor turned away from the boys and looked

north across the lake shimmering in its morning light. When he turned back, he sighed deeply. "I'm not sure I know what God's work for me is anymore," he confessed, pulling the ends of his moustache. "I was so sure, but . . . everything I try seems to fail."

He got up and set to building a fire. When it was crackling its comfort into the chill air, he turned to the boys again. "I guess there is still one thing I know to do." He looked into the fire and tossed a twig at it. "I should take you boys home. You've risked your lives for me, and even though I may not be able to save all of Africa from this evil slave trade, I can pay my debt to you. Let's go."

The boys were elated. But first they rowed the boat up a small stream flowing into the lake until they came to a marsh where they concealed the boat among tall reeds.

"There," said Livingstone. "Unless someone knows right where it is or comes on it accidentally, it'll never be found. I may not come back this way to explore Lake Nyassa again. But if I do, I'll have a boat." And his craggy face broke into a grin.

Then the doctor and the two boys waded out of the marsh and headed south.

It was near sunset three days later when they came over a hill and saw in the distance the shining mirror of Lake Shirwa. This country was more open—rolling hills, groves of forest, and open grassland.

The three travelers were hungry and bone-tired. Along the way, they had avoided other people and all villages. They did not want to announce their presence. But that also meant that they had no way of getting more food except for what they could gather along the trail.

And the land to the north of Lake Shirwa had not been free from warfare, either. From a distance they had seen burned villages, and on the trails they frequently came across a warning sign: a skull atop a spear that had been driven into the ground.

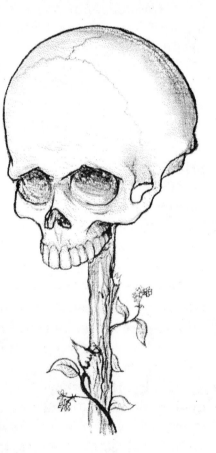

But as they looked at their lake in the distance, Chuma asked, "Can we keep on going so we can get home tonight?"

Livingstone surveyed the lake glistening in the distance and then looked at how close the sun was to the horizon. "The lake is still several miles away. Where's your village?"

"Around the lake,

on the west shore," offered Wikatani.

"It's a pretty big lake; it could take quite a while to get there. I think we ought to wait until morning."

Though the boys were greatly disappointed, they did not complain. They knew the doctor was very tired and had already taken great risks in bringing them this far. But when they made camp, the boys could hardly sleep.

"I wonder if our sheep all wandered back to the village?" whispered Chuma as they stared up at the bright stars.

"Our sheep? They are too dumb. If someone didn't go out and round them up, they'd wander right off the earth."

"You think our families think we are dead?"

"Probably," said Wikatani. "Won't they be surprised when we come marching in?"

"I'm going to have my mother make a big feast for Doctor Livingstone." Chuma could hear the man already snoring softly near them.

"Maybe my father will assign some men to be new porters for him," said Wikatani.

In their excitement, the boys left unspoken any fears they had about the Manganja boast that all the villages around Lake Shirwa had been burned out. After all it was just a boast; the Manganja had been trying to frighten them.

Finally, they dropped off to sleep. But they were up early in the morning, and, with the doctor in tow, they covered the distance to the lake shore while the air was still cool.

"Look," shouted Wikatani. "That's our village across the lake. See the white strip of beach and the little trail of smoke rising in the air. My mother is probably baking bread for breakfast."

Several times the doctor had to urge the boys to slow down as they traveled around the edge of the lake. After they had gone about five miles, Chuma pointed out that they were now on the trail that they often used when they took the sheep to pasture.

In another quarter hour, he said to the doctor, "Right down there, that is where the Red Caps got us."

"They tied me up," said Wikatani, "and broke a Manganja spear and shot one of our sheep."

"And I came running through the shallows to help him," said Chuma. "But an-other Red Cap was waiting for me, and he had a gun."

A few min-utes later, when the boys came in sight of their village, they began to race each other for home. Chuma was two strides behind Wikatani when Wikatani suddenly

121

stopped short. Chuma ran ahead in glee, looking back over his shoulder as he shot past his friend. But Wikatani was staring strangely ahead. Chuma also slowed down as he looked down the hill toward the village.

Something was wrong. There were no canoes on the beach. Some of the houses had been knocked down, some burned. Chuma pushed the panic away and forced himself to walk. There were no joyful sounds of children shouting and playing. No dogs came out to bark at them. But the village was not deserted. A few people could still be seen moving from hut to hut.

Again he began to run. He tore past the old sheep pen. There were no sheep in it. *Of course, someone else is out herding them*, he reassured himself. He turned right after the first house. Its thatched roof was caving in. In the doorway of the next house sat a strange woman. *Who's she? I know all my neighbors. I know everyone in the village*, he thought. *Maybe she's a visitor*. His own house was next, but as Chuma rounded the corner of his neighbor's house, he faced a burned-out pile of rubble. Half of one mud wall was still standing, and a few roof beams lay haphazardly against it like a blackened logjam on a river after a spring flood.

He turned to the right and left. The only building belonging to Chuma's family that still stood was their corn crib. He ran over to it and around to the door, thinking his family might be taking shelter within, but that whole side was knocked out. Not one single ear of corn remained.

"Mother! Father!" Chuma yelled. "Mother, where is everyone?" He ran to the next house—just a hut, really—but it was completely empty. He ran on from house to house. All had been badly damaged; many had been burned to the ground.

Panic completely engulfed him. He ran up behind an old grandmother—finally, someone he knew! He grabbed her, and spun her around. "Where is my mother?" he demanded. But the old woman didn't say a word. She just stared at him as if he were a ghost.

He ran to the other side of the village to Wikatani's house. As he approached, he saw with relief that it was standing and that people were home. Wikatani was standing outside, talking to someone standing in the dark doorway.

"Where's my family?" he insisted as he skidded to a stop.

Wikatani turned to him with horror on his face. "They're dead. Almost everyone is dead!" His voice came out in a high-pitched whisper.

"No. It can't be! Who are these people?" Chuma pushed past the woman standing in the doorway of Wikatani's house. He looked around. There were several others in the dark interior, but he recognized no one. "Who are these people?" he demanded as he came back out into the blinding sun.

"They say they are my cousins," said Wikatani. "They're from another village . . . over the hills." He pointed back toward the north.

"But what has happened?"

The boys looked at each other in silence. Finally, the woman standing in the doorway spoke up. "The Ajawa had many great victories, but then the battle turned and the Manganja overran this village. Many warriors from our village in the hills came down to help, but we were too late."

Wikatani sat down in the dust and began to rock back and forth, moaning quietly. Chuma just stood there. He knew that war killed people, but he had refused to believe that his family might die, not even when the Manganja man had said that the villages around Lake Shirwa had been defeated.

"But all are not dead," said the woman as she came out and put her hand on Wikatani's shoulder. "Your little brother is still alive."

At first it seemed that Wikatani had not heard. Then he looked up slowly and said, "What?"

"I said, your little brother is alive."

"Where?"

"He is with your uncle, down at the lake."

Wikatani jumped up and ran toward the water. Chuma turned and followed along slowly, walking as though he were in a dream. Suddenly Doctor Livingstone was walking beside him. The white man put his arm around the boy's shoulder and pulled him close.

At the lake front, Chuma and the doctor stood at a distance while Wikatani and his little brother hugged each other and cried. They stood there in silence a very long time. Finally, the doctor said,

"You know, Chuma, you *could* come with me."

That night the two boys went for a walk along the lake shore. They followed the path they had taken with the sheep that fateful day and stopped again at the point where they had been ambushed. They sat on the sand thinking about all that had happened in the last months.

"Chuma, when you get back to the mission, try to talk to Dauma again. Tell her that I'll never forget her kindness to us."

"Without her, we might have died," agreed Chuma.

Soon a new moon rose. It was nothing more than a golden fingernail of light, but it laid down a shimmering path across the placid, black waters.

"The doctor saved our lives, too," added Wikatani.

"Yes," said Chuma. "He's been like a father to us."

"You know, I think he knew what we might find here . . . and he didn't have to bring us back."

"But I'm glad he did. I had to know."

"Me, too."

Somewhere in the distance a hyena howled its hideous laugh. In a few minutes Wikatani continued. "You once said that if our families were dead, you would become a Christian and stay with the doctor. Is that why you are going with him?"

Chuma thought before answering. "No. I became a Christian when I still thought our families were safe . . . and I would still be a Christian even if the doctor hadn't offered for me to go with him."

"Yes. I think you would. And I believe in Jesus, too. Do you think he would baptize me before you go?"

Chuma grinned at his friend. "Of course! Ask him—first thing in the morning!"

"But I wish I could help the doctor, too," said Wikatani wistfully. "He *is* doing a great work, even if he can't see the benefits."

"That's true," agreed Chuma. "How else would we have heard about Jesus? Someone had to come tell us."

A slight breeze turned the path of moonlight on the lake into a field of glittering diamonds. Again, Wikatani broke the silence. "I just wish I could go with you."

"Me, too. But you need to take care of your brother, and we don't want our village to die out."

"No. I guess not." After a moment Wikatani turned to Chuma. "You wouldn't desert the doctor like those porters did, would you? Promise me!"

Chuma grasped Wikatani's wrist, as his friend's hand clasped his own wrist in a sign of friendship.

"As long as God gives me the strength and courage, I will remain with Doctor Livingstone and help him in his work," Chuma vowed. "You can count on that, my friend."

Chapter 13

Epilogue

C HUMA REMAINED at Doctor Livingstone's side for seven more years of missionary exploration in Africa's interior. When the good doctor died from exhaustion and fever, Chuma and others carefully preserved his body and then carried it across half of Africa to the coast where it could be sent by ship back to England for burial.

Chuma was also invited to England to help tell the story of Livingstone's life to all those who had admired and supported his great work.

Though Livingstone never had the privilege of seeing the fruit of his efforts, he opened the way for hundreds of missionaries to enter central Africa and establish mission stations there. One of the most important was located on Lake Nyassa and named

Livingstonia. And within fifteen years of his death, through the influence of the Gospel, as well as other factors, the slave trade was brought to an end in central Africa.

More About David Livingstone

DAVID LIVINGSTONE WAS BORN on March 19, 1813, on an island off the coast of Scotland. He grew up in a Christian home where his father was a tea merchant.

After receiving a degree in medicine from Glasgow University in 1840, Livingstone became connected with the London Missionary Society. With the Society's support he went to South Africa in 1841. He ventured north by lumbering ox-wagon on a ten-week trip. But what he saw troubled him. The mission stations he visited seemed more interested in creating comfortable British outposts than pressing on to reach the unreached peoples of the interior. He also discovered that some of the missionaries were racist about the very people they were trying to reach with the Gospel. They did not think the Africans were suited for much more than servants or field hands.

Livingstone's complaints to the mission headquarters earned him the disapproval of some, and he was not granted permission for an extended missionary journey for several years. So he spent his time learning everything he could about Africa and its people. He became convinced that when English missionaries founded a mission station, they should set about training African converts to take it over as soon as possible. He quickly mastered several African languages and learned the customs of the people.

On one shorter foray into the bush, Livingstone was attacked and severely mauled by a lion. It took months for him to recover, and the injuries to his shoulder bothered him the rest of his life. However, while he was recovering, he got to know Mary Moffat, the daughter of Dr. Robert Moffat, Bible translator and mission director.

Shortly after they were married in 1844, the Livingstones set out to establish a new mission station on the frontier. From there it was Livingstone's intention to make journeys deep into Africa to reach people who had never heard the Gospel before.

This he did in three dramatic expeditions.

The first expedition extended north across the eastern edge of the Kilahari Desert to the River Zouga and then west; he become the first white man to see Lake Nagami in 1849. He then went on to reach the Zambezi River in 1851.

Before long he came to realize that he wasn't an evangelist but had been called by God to explore and open up new areas for other missionaries to follow. Between 1853 and 1856 he made a most remarkable Trans-Africa journey, first out to the west coast, then back across Africa, down the Zambezi River to sight the Victoria Falls, and then on to the east coast.

It was on this first journey that he became aware of the devastation of the slave trade in Africa. When he returned to England in 1856, he was honored by the Royal Geographic Society as a major explorer and commissioned by the government to return to Africa as a British Consul.

He went back to Africa on his second expedition and started up the Zambezi River by river boat. There he intended to establish Christian mission stations in the hope of spreading the Gospel and stopping the slave trade. That situation provides the setting for this story.

Though greatly simplified, this story follows the events of the Zambezi expedition with the following exceptions: (1) It is only conjecture that Chuma and Wikatani were the spark the Red Caps used to ignite the tribal war. (2) While at least two freed slaves accompanied Livingstone in his attempt to contact the Ajawa chiefs on his Nyassa exploration, they are not named. (3) Livingstone's rescue from the Shire River is fiction, though he had an equally close call with death earlier when coming down the Zambezi River. (4) Chuma and Wikatani did not return to their homeland for another five years. For the sake of this story, the time frame was condensed. What actually happened in the meantime was that Livingstone's second expedition came to a tragic end.

Livingstone's wife as well as the wife of Bishop Mackenzie and some other women came to join the men at the mission station. However, when Livingstone was away exploring Lake Nyassa, the bishop made a canoe trip on which he foolishly carried most of the mission's medicines. The canoe capsized and all the medicines were lost. By the time Livingstone got back, everyone was so sick with malaria that the bishop and all the women died—including Mary Moffat Livingstone.

Shortly after that, even in the middle of his great grief, Livingstone came across an official dispatch that conclusively proved that the Portuguese were involved in the slave trade. He sent off this proof to England, thinking the government would put international pressure on Portugal to stop the trade. However, it was more important to England to maintain good relations with Portugal at that time than to embarrass their ally by exposing Portugal's violation of the treaty. To avoid any further "incidents," England ordered Livingstone out of Africa.

Heartbroken and discouraged, Livingstone withdrew, vowing to return at his own expense as soon as he could. Rather than allow his riverboat (it was his third one by this time) to fall into the hands of the slave traders, he sailed it across the open sea to India. Chuma and Wikatani—as well as some other African and white sailors—volunteered to accompany him on this wild and dangerous voyage in which all nearly lost their lives. In India, Livingstone enrolled Chuma and Wikatani in a mission school and sold his boat before returning home to England.

Several years later Dauma was reported to be a fine teacher in a mission school in South Africa. She had been among some of women and children Livingstone brought down the river to safety on his boat before he sailed to India. He arranged for them to be cared for at the mission station on the island of Zanzibar.

Three years after leaving Chuma and Wikatani in India, Livingstone returned to take them back to Africa for his third expedition. They faithfully accompanied him until they arrived in their homeland. There Wikatani stayed—probably to get married—but Chuma continued on with Livingstone.

Livingstone went deep into the interior of Africa and lost all contact with the outside world. Many thought him dead until the *New York Herald* sent newspaper reporter Henry Stanley on an expedition to find him or bring back conclusive news of his death. In March 1871, Stanley started his search from Zanzibar. In the fall he finally located Livingstone. The doctor was sick and out of supplies, but in good spirits. Their meeting is remembered by Stanley's famous words: "Doctor Livingstone, I presume?"

Though grateful for the visit and the fresh medicines and supplies, Livingstone would not come out of Africa. So Stanley returned to world-wide fame for having found the great missionary/explorer.

When Livingstone died on April 30, 1873, Chuma and some other faithful companions carefully wrapped and embalmed his body and carried it to the coast. There, Chuma went with the body to England where Livingstone was buried with great honor. Chuma met with the Queen and toured the country telling others about the expeditions of Livingstone.

Spy for
—the—
Night Riders

Trailblazer Books

Also by Dave and Neta Jackson

Spy for
–the–
Night Riders

Dave & Neta Jackson

Story illustrations by
Julian Jackson

BETHANY HOUSE PUBLISHERS
MINNEAPOLIS, MINNESOTA 55438

Published by Bethany House Publishers
A Ministry of Bethany Fellowship International
11400 Hampshire Avenue South, Minneapolis, Minnesota 55438
www.bethanyhouse.com

Printed in the United States of America by
Bethany Press International, Minneapolis, Minnesota 55438

Library of Congress Cataloging-in-Publication Data

Jackson, Dave.
     Spy for the night riders / Dave and Neta Jackson
          p. cm. — (Trailblazer Books)
     Summary: After coming to Wittenberg to seen kan education,
Karl Schumacher becomes a student of Dr. Martin Luther and,
when the latter is declared a heretic, Karl accompanies him when
he travels to Worms to defend his views.

     [1. Reformation—Fiction. 2. Luther, Martin, 1483–1546—
Fiction. 3. Christian life—Fiction.
I. Jackson, Neta. II. Title. III. Series.
PZ7.J132418Sp   1992
[Fic]—dc20   91–44063
ISBN 1–55661–237–0   CIP
                                                           AC

All the adult characters in this book were real people, and the major events involving them are true with the exception of the escape down the Werra River.

In addition, Martin Luther *did* have two companions with him on his return from Worms. One was Brother John Petzensteiner. The other is unnamed in the historical records. Who knows? Maybe he was a young boy like our fictitious Karl Schumacher. In any case, it was this unnamed traveler who worked with the captain of the Wartburg Castle to arrange for Luther's abduction/rescue.

DAVE AND NETA JACKSON are a husband/wife writing team who have authored or coauthored many books on marriage and family, the church, and relationships, including *On Fire for Christ: Stories from Martyrs Mirror*, the Pet Parables series, and the Caring Parent series.

They have two children: Julian, an art major and illustrator for the Trailblazer series, and Rachel, a high school student. They make their home in Evanston, Illinois, where they are active members of Reba Place Church.

CONTENTS

The Road to Worms

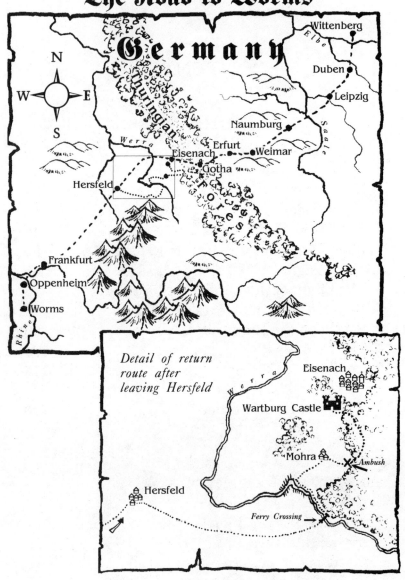

Germany

Wittenberg

Elbe

Duben

Leipzig

Saale

Naumburg

Weimar

Erfurt

Werra

Eisenach

Gotha

Thuringian Forest

Hersfeld

Frankfurt

Oppenheim

Worms

Rhine

Detail of return route after leaving Hersfeld

Werra

Eisenach

Wartburg Castle

Mohra

Ambush

Hersfeld

Ferry Crossing

Chapter 1

The Wanted Poster

WHEN I WAS TEN YEARS OLD, I saw a burning. Forgive me, but I need to tell you about it so you will understand why I got so scared when I saw my master's name on a wanted poster tacked to the door of the Wittenberg church.

That burning was the first time I had ever seen a person die. They said he was a *heretic*—that he did not believe the truth about God and the church. But I found it hard to believe.

It happened early on a cloudy Tuesday morning. My papa is a shoemaker. (That's why I'm called Karl Schumacher—you know, son of the village shoemaker.) He had sent me to deliver the mayor's boots. Papa had repaired them, and they were black and shiny. They looked great, as Papa's work always does. But when I knocked on the mayor's door, he was very upset. He grabbed me by the ear and said, "Get in here, boy, and help me get the boots on. I haven't got all day. I can't be late for the burning."

I'd heard that there was going to be a burning, and I also knew that Mama wouldn't want me going near it. But I was curious, and I figured this was my chance to see one without her knowing. So I helped the mayor with his boots and then followed him to the town square in the center our little village of Duben, Germany. There the constable had everything prepared, and a crowd had gathered. I tried to fade in among the other people hoping no one would notice me and tell Mama. As it turned out, everyone was so captivated by the burning that they probably wouldn't have noticed me even if I had stepped on their toes.

As soon as the mayor arrived, the constable struck a spark to the tinder of a huge woodpile and lit the fire. Then the two of them disappeared into the courthouse. They stayed there so long that I almost gave up and went home—Papa would be wondering why I was delayed. Even the fire would have burned down if several of the village people hadn't thrown more sticks on it. Someone in the growing crowd called, "Bring him out! We haven't got all day, ya know." Soon others picked up the cry until everyone was chanting, "Bring him out! Bring him out! Bring him out!" I was saying it too, but that was before I knew what a burning was like.

Some older boys, about fifteen (my age now), were standing nearby talking about burnings. "It's just like singeing the hair off hogs. 'Cept with a heretic, it ain't hair that gets burned away, it's heresy." They all laughed and pushed each other, pretending to throw one another into the fire.

Finally the mayor, the constable, and two helpers came out and ordered everyone to clear a path between the courthouse steps and the fire. At first nobody moved; everyone wanted a front row spot, I suppose. The constable had to poke them with the blunt end of his spear before they would move. Then the churchmen came out dressed in their fine red robes. I didn't know any of them. They were not from our town and had come as judges to conduct the heretic's trial. Finally the constable went back in and came out leading the heretic, whose hands were tied behind his back. Following them was our village priest, who looked in worse shape than the heretic— head hanging down, hair all mussed. He looked like a wild man.

I recognized the heretic as the man I'd seen preaching in the marketplace once or twice. He was also from out of town. People said he only came to our village to make converts.

He was tall and thin, with a long scraggly beard that grew mostly from his chin and very little on his cheeks. He didn't look nearly as old as Papa, but he was half bald. As he came down the steps and through the crowd, he gazed very calmly at all the people, and at one point he stared right at me and smiled. I can still see his eyes—deep-set and very light blue, almost chalk colored. I think . . . I hope I smiled back.

I had heard about people being "burned at the stake." But there was no stake for this burning. Instead the heretic was made to lie down with his back on an old ladder. There he was tied securely. The fire was again built up with fresh bundles of brush until it was roaring high.

All this time our village priest knelt beside the heretic. I was close enough to hear him pleading with the heretic to repent and save his life. When I looked, tears were pouring down our priest's face as he fumbled with the cross around his neck. It's hard to watch a grown-up cry. But the heretic just smiled and said, "I'm sorry, Father. I cannot unless I am shown by God's Word to be wrong." What he was supposed to be wrong about, I had no idea. To disagree with the church on anything was enough.

Then the constable and his men tipped the ladder up and balanced it on one end. The heretic was tied to the other end with his back toward the fire. It was shocking how he looked like Jesus Christ Himself as he hung there above the crowd. Then one of the judges asked if he had any final things to say and warned him that he could still save his life if he would change his mind.

The heretic looked around, and then shouted so loudly everyone could hear, "I have only this to say." And then he began to sing in as clear and beautiful a tenor voice as I've ever heard.

In thee, O Lord, do I put my trust.
Let me never be brought to confusion.

Deliver me in thy righteousness,
And forgive those who plot my ruin.

They allowed him to sing it twice, then let the ladder fall back so that the heretic landed squarely in the fire. Sparks flew up everywhere, and some of the burning sticks flipped out toward the crowd causing some people to jump back out of the way. But there in the flames, instead of screaming in pain, the heretic continued to sing until he had no more breath. And then, as the fire burned through the cords that bound his arms, he miraculously raised one hand toward heaven. It stayed there until it looked like a charred branch from an old tree.

I can tell you that the smell of burning flesh was something awful. I'll never forget it. In fact, I get sick just remembering it.

I learned from his execution that more than just bad people could be condemned here in Germany, or anywhere in the Holy Roman Empire for that matter. Anyone who could praise God while he burned and not curse those who had put him into the flames must have had the Spirit of Christ within him. And I think others felt the same. From the moment he began singing until we all drifted away to our homes, there was not one word spoken, not even by those older boys who thought they knew so much.

Ever since then, whenever anyone mentions the burning that happened in Duben, it's with the respect you'd expect for a saint—no mocking, no laughing. And our village priest? The next day he wandered off muttering to himself and has never been heard from since.

So now maybe you can understand why I got so worried when I saw my master's name on that wanted poster on the church door. In big, bold letters the poster called him *heretic*! But even though my master, Doctor Martin Luther, is one of the most famous teachers in the empire, that wouldn't keep him from burning if he were tried and convicted for heresy.

I don't live in my home town of Duben anymore. As the youngest son, there was no room for me in my father's shoe business, and I wanted an education rather than a trade, anyway. To get my education I came here to the German city of Wittenberg and asked Doctor Luther to take me on as his servant. I run his errands, keep his clothes and quarters clean, and serve as his stable boy when he travels. In return he lets me sit in on his lectures at the university, and he even tutors me in the evenings if he isn't too tired. It's the perfect situation for me. And maybe someday I'll even become a regular student.

But this particular day as I was coming down the street after returning a horse and a cart we had borrowed to visit some nearby villages, I noticed a new poster tacked to the church door. The poster wasn't a single sheet of paper. Actually, it was more like a booklet, what people call a *bull*. In Wittenberg that door is the city's most reliable source for news. All the official notices get put up there for everyone to read. That's the door where Doctor Luther posted his famous ninety-five theses three years ago; they were his arguments against the church's false doctrines and practices. The paper was his way of protesting the evil practices in the church and was saying they had to change. Of course, the church officials didn't like it.

But what caught my eye this time was my master's name. I read quickly. It was dated June 15, 1520—five months ago—and was from the pope, the top official of the Roman Catholic Church. It seemed to say that Doctor Luther would be kicked out of the church unless he went to Rome and repented of his *heretical* writings and ideas.

Go to Rome? Repent? That was just a nice way of saying that the church had already condemned him! I read on. The notice forbade anyone from defending Luther's writings or helping him in any way. My heart began beating faster. This was a formal Bull of Excommunication! He was being kicked out of the church, and anyone who helped him would be condemned too.

I tried to think through what this meant. Doctor Luther might be famous, and he might be a very good teacher, but unless he changed his mind about the importance of God's Word—and I knew he wouldn't—he wasn't safe.

I scanned the street to see if anyone was watching. People were going about their own business, not paying any attention to me . . . except for a girl about my age standing by a fruit stall in the street. I'd never seen her before. She was dressed better than a common peasant girl, but she carried a basket, so she had probably come to market. She had unusually long black hair that hung freely and waved in the breeze. Most girls her age covered their heads. *Enough of that*, I told myself. This was no time to gawk at a pretty girl. When she turned away, I tore the poster from the door and quickly rolled it up. Then I stuffed it inside my tunic as I raced toward the university.

My master was in danger. But in helping him, so was I.

Chapter 2

Risky Business

I FOUND DOCTOR LUTHER in the university square talking to some of his students about his afternoon lecture. As politely as I could, I interrupted them. "Please excuse me, sir. But I must have a word with you!"

He probably thought I'd had some problem returning the horse and cart and answered, "Don't worry about it, Karl. We'll talk about it tonight and get it all straightened out then. Now you go along and prepare something nice for my birthday." Then he smiled good-naturedly.

Oh, no. I'd completely forgotten! It was November 11, and—I figured quickly—Doctor Luther was thirty-seven years old. I was about to press my news, but he had already turned back to his students. So I left the square and hurried to the market, where I purchased some new candles, fresh bread, wine, cheese, and a small honey cake.

When I finally returned to our quarters, Doctor Luther was already there. I dumped my parcels on the table and quickly pulled out the bull. "I found this on the church door," I said.

Luther flattened out the booklet and began paging through it. "So John Eck has finally gone public, has he? It doesn't matter that the bull was already delivered to me privately."

"Then you've already seen it?" I asked.

"Yes, yes. It was presented to the headmaster of the university, and he showed it to me some time ago. But I should have known. Eck wouldn't miss the chance to stick it to me publicly."

John Eck is my master's chief enemy. I'd seen him once at the University of Leipzig, where he had opposed Luther in a public debate. Eck was a very determined and cunning man.

"So you think he did it?" I asked.

"Who else?" Luther tossed the papers onto the little pile on the floor beside his desk.

"Aren't you going to do anything about it?" I asked.

"What's there to do? Write another pamphlet telling why this is unfair?"

"Well, maybe. But . . . don't you have to go to Rome to defend yourself?"

"There's no defending myself against a charge like this in Rome. The pope issued the bull, though John Eck probably dictated the whole thing word-for-word. But when you're called to Rome, you either go and repent fully, making yourself look like a fool, or you . . ."

"Or you do what?"

"I don't know. But I'll think of something."

I stood looking at the paper on the floor, but Doctor Luther was rummaging in my parcels. So I tried to forget the threatening paper and what could come of it, turning my attention to my master's birthday celebration. Doctor Luther was quite merry and made a big show of cutting the honey cake.

After we'd eaten, I asked, "Doctor Luther, when you were a boy, what did you want to be when you grew up?"

"What did I want to be—what?—when I was your age?"

"Yeah. In my family, my parents always asked us on our birthdays: 'What do you want to be when you grow up?' So on their birthdays we'd ask them what they had wanted to be when they were our age—sort of a joke, I guess."

"Hmmm. I don't know." Doctor Luther scratched his chin. "I didn't want to be a miner like my father. His was a terrible life, breathing dust all day and coughing it up all night. I wanted to be something different. Maybe that's why I took a liking to you, Karl. I know what it's like to not follow in your father's footsteps. I admire you for wanting to do something different."

"But did you always want to be a teacher?"

"No, no." He laughed a little as he dipped his sweetcake in his cup of cider. "I guess as a boy I wanted to be a knight fighting for a powerful lord, defeating all the evil that threatened the land! In fact, there was an old folk hero named Knight George who freed his people from a cruel foreign king and won the land back for the rightful and true king. Did you ever hear that tale?"

I nodded. I'd heard it a time or two.

"Well, I wanted to be Knight George," grinned Doctor Luther. "What do you think of that?"

"I don't know," I smiled, trying to imagine the scholarly professor riding a charger and swinging a sword. But that night lying in my cot before I fell asleep, I couldn't help but think that Doctor Luther had become a kind of knight "fighting for the right." The church of Rome had become very corrupt. Many of the leaders didn't seem to care about helping people know God. All they wanted was to get people's money. And they did it any way they could—like selling *indulgences,* which were sheets of paper that said a person's sins were forgiven. This had made Doctor Luther very angry. He preached that forgiveness can't be bought and sold—it's a gift from God, received by faith when a person truly turns from their sin and asks God's forgiveness.

That's how John Eck became Luther's enemy. Eck defended these evil practices; Luther opposed them. I knew a real battle was brewing—not just between those two men but all across the church and throughout the empire. But because the Roman Catholic Church and the Holy Roman Empire stood together, people like Luther who were calling for the church to change its practices were said to be traitors.

But weeks passed and Doctor Luther did nothing about going to Rome as ordered by the pope. Then one day I overheard him talking with some of the other university professors. "I have appealed to the emperor," he said. He meant Charles the Fifth, the ruler of the entire Holy Roman Empire.

"You did *what?*" Brother Nicholas exclaimed. "Don't you think that's rather risky, Luther? If the emperor condemns you, it could mean the death sentence!" Nicholas von Amsdorf was a fellow monk and teacher who shared many of Luther's views—at least in private.

"That may be true," Luther said calmly, "and I have no faith in the emperor himself. We all know he's young and so weak in character that he's controlled by others, mostly the pope's men. But at least in that court I will get a fair hearing. Our German protector, John Frederick, sits on the council as duke of the state of Saxony. He, among others, will see to a fair trial."

Listening to my master, I still felt uneasy. I wasn't sure the Duke of Saxony liked Doctor Luther. Some said he did; some said he didn't. But . . . I'd also heard that he worked hard to protect all his citizens, and he was a very powerful lord. He would never allow one of his most popular professors to be condemned as a heretic without a fair trial. So maybe what Luther did was smart.

But early on the morning of December 10, as I walked to the university, I noticed a large crowd gathered around the university bulletin board. As I wedged my way close to the board, one of the students was reading aloud.

Let all who follow the true Gospel be present at nine o'clock outside the town walls, where books of ungodly papal decrees and false religious teachings will be burned just like the Apostle Paul burned the books of witchcraft in the city of Ephesus. For today the enemies of the Gospel have grown so bold as to daily burn the evangelical books of Luther. So come, pious and zealous youth, to this religious spectacle, for possibly now is the time when the Antichrist must be revealed!

Had Luther put up the notice or had someone else? "Or maybe," said one student, "an enemy has posted this challenge to get Doctor Luther in trouble."

"He can't get into any more trouble than he already is," said another. "Haven't you heard that he has been ordered to answer charges of heresy?"

We all crowded into Luther's classroom, and shifted impatiently as Doctor Luther proceeded with his lecture. But at the end of the morning lecture, Luther cleared up the mystery:

"My dear students. You know that my writings have been condemned by the pope. And, in some southern cities, the corrupt church leaders have taken the chill out of the fall air by burning my writings. Well, it's nearly winter here in the north. So if you have nothing better to do after class, I invite you to accompany me outside the town gate where we will have a little hand-warming party of our own. I intend to burn all these false writings and decrees from the pope." And he held up a pile of manuscripts and books.

A great cheer went up from the students. They were eager to put action to the teachings they had been hearing during the previous weeks. Like a school of minnows startled in a pool, they all broke and darted for the door. "Karl," said Doctor Luther, "help me gather up these writings."

Outside Wittenberg's Elster Gate, Luther encouraged the students to build a fire. Doctor Luther's classes were often attended by over three hundred students, but this afternoon the crowd was even larger. Others must have joined the crowd as we marched through the streets. Several other univer-

sity professors accompanied us.

When the fire was well lit, Luther picked up the writings one by one, announced what each one was, and then tossed it onto the fire. Then, lifting high the bull calling him to come to Rome and renounce his writings and beliefs, Luther said, "Some of you have heard that I have been served with a Bull of Excommunication. If I do not recant of my beliefs and writings, I am to be thrown out of the Roman church. However, because the pope has brought down the truth of God, I also throw down this bull into the fire today. Amen!" The crowd cheered.

After that Luther and the other faculty members walked solemnly back to the university. But the students remained, and in a few minutes they were singing and dancing around the bonfire. Soon a kind of wildness took over the crowd . . . but it reminded me of the other burning I had witnessed as a young boy, so I just watched.

To my surprise, at the edge of the crowd, I noticed the same girl I'd seen near the church door the day I'd torn down the bull. This time her long dark hair was tied back at the nape of her neck, but it was still uncovered. And though her clothes were rather plain, her face had a beauty so serene that I doubted whether a thunderstorm could disturb it. She stood quietly as though she was . . . as though she was a "watcher." I can't think of a better word for it. It seemed that was her job—watching. And in response, I couldn't help but watch her. However, when our eyes met, she looked quickly away. Why look away when nothing else bothered her? And why wasn't she joining in the merriment? Did the fire remind her of something unpleasant, like it did me, or did she hold back for some other reason?

"Let's collect all the false writings in the whole town," shouted one student. As if on cue, the crowd swarmed back through the city gates. Soon someone produced an old cart that several mounted while others pulled it. Another student had a trumpet and began blasting off-key notes as the procession went through the streets. As the mob got rowdier, they began banging on people's doors demanding: "Do you have any of the pope's poison papers here? We intend to purge the town."

I had followed them down three streets and returned once to the bonfire to burn some more papers when I noticed the girl with the long dark hair leave the others. I probably wouldn't have paid any attention, but she looked all around as if checking to see if anyone noticed; then she ducked down a dingy alley. When I got to the same alley and glanced down it, she was running and had nearly reached the other end. Not very thrilled with the mood of the mob, I decided to follow her. After all, she was very pretty, and mysterious . . . why not find out where she lived?

I barely managed to keep her in sight. But after several turns she entered Raven's Tavern. Raven's Tavern? Why would she go in there? That's not where a family would live. Only strangers rented rooms there.

I stood outside trying to work up courage to go in

and explore when the door suddenly swung open and two men came out talking excitedly to each other. I recognized one: John Eck, Doctor Luther's enemy!

I started to turn around and walk away, but then I realized that Eck would not recognize me. So I just leaned against the tavern, crossed my arms and looked down the street like I was waiting for someone. But what I heard was startling.

"If Luther burned the pope's bull, then I must return to Rome at once," said Eck.

"Brother John, you know that wasn't the pope's bull," laughed the other man. "We wrote every word of it ourselves. The pope just signed it."

"That makes it the *pope's* bull. Now go to the stable and get us horses. I'll be along shortly," Eck said as he turned and walked down the street.

I couldn't believe it. That girl, the watcher, must have been a spy for Eck! The first time I had seen her was the day the bull was posted on the church door. Now she'd gone straight to the tavern, and in just a few minutes Eck knew what Doctor Luther had done and was preparing to leave for Rome!

I returned immediately to the university and

reported to Master Luther. He listened soberly, but all he said was, "There's no way to stop Eck from doing the Devil's bidding. The matter is clearly in God's hands. But it's those rampaging students that bother me! What did you say they were doing?"

As I told him again about the raid on the town, I could see Luther's displeasure. The next day in class, he lectured his students soundly: "Do you know what you're doing? You had no business accosting the townspeople. This fight against false religion isn't for fun and games! The mood in the land is very dark and dangerous; it could end in death for each of us."

A chill ran down my spine. I hoped Doctor Luther was wrong.

Chapter 3

No Time for Quitters

TWICE IN THE NEXT FEW WEEKS I was surprised to see "The Watcher," as I had come to call her. I thought she would have gone with John Eck back to Rome. Had Eck left her behind to spy on Doctor Luther? On the other hand, if that was what she was doing, why didn't I see her more often?

The first time I spotted her was on Christmas Day and quite by accident. Doctor Luther was preaching in the Castle Church, and she was right there in the congregation. I could hardly believe my eyes. A black lace veil partially covered her face, but it was her—no doubt about it.

After that I made it a practice to watch for her. At various times I would step quickly to our window and survey all the people in the commons down below. But she was never there. All I saw were the regular students and professors or special visitors to the university. I tried this evening and morning and midday. Always the same. If she was watching our quarters, I never saw her.

Whenever I was out with Doctor Luther, I would

glance behind us to catch her if she was following us. This created something of a problem as I kept bumping into things or into my master if he stopped or turned for some reason. The funny thing is, that's when I saw her again.

We were going to the printer's to pick up some fresh copies of Luther's popular little pamphlet, *The Freedom of a Christian*. Occasionally I would turn around and walk backwards for a few steps. Well, we were just passing Raven's Tavern when the door flew open, and I nearly smashed into The Watcher. I stumbled and nearly fell down. Then I felt so foolish

that I couldn't think of anything to say, but when Doctor Luther spoke for me and said, "Please excuse us," the girl turned and ran off as fast as possible. It seemed like she didn't want us to take any more notice of her than we already had.

"That's the girl," I said to my master as soon as she was out of earshot. "That's The Watcher."

"The who?"

"The girl who's spying on you for John Eck—the one I told you about on the day you burned the bull. She's the one who told Eck just before he left for Rome."

"You're sure *she* told him?" Luther said.

"Well . . . I saw her come directly here to Raven's Tavern, and that's when Eck found out. You saw her come out of there just now. And did you notice, she didn't want us to pay any attention to her?"

"Maybe. Or maybe she just felt awkward having crashed into a young man her age." My master chuckled. "By the way, how come you don't look where you're going—or else go where you're looking? You seem to be stumbling into things all the time these days."

I didn't see the girl for quite some time after that, but I didn't give up. One day I was on my way to Raven's Tavern to see if I could catch sight of her again when a finely dressed man came riding up the street on a great white, prancing horse. He carried an imperial banner, which could only mean that he was on royal business.

Just after passing me, he pulled up and addressed

all the people along the street who had stopped to stare at him. "I am Casper Sturm, imperial herald of His Majesty, Charles the Fifth, Sovereign of the Holy Roman Empire!" he announced haughtily as he surveyed the people. He looked down on us not only because he sat on a high horse, but as though he considered us commoners beneath his dignity. "Can one of you loyal citizens direct me to a certain Doctor Martin Luther?"

I hardly knew what to say. The emperor had a message for my master, a message so important that he had sent his herald to deliver it! While I stood there considering whether this was a great honor or a dangerous threat, two or three people stepped forward and tried to give the herald directions to the university. Finally I gathered my wits and said, "I'll take you there, your majesty. I work for Doctor Luther."

He turned in his saddle and said, "I am not 'his majesty,' young man. But if you can take me to Luther, I'll excuse your ignorance. Lead on. I've had a long ride and am eager to be off this beast."

My master was still giving his afternoon lecture—one on the evils of indulgences that I'd heard three times before (which is why I'd skipped the class). The herald didn't wait for him to conclude but marched right in. "Are you Martin Luther?" he interrupted. The students stared.

"I am."

"I am Casper Sturm, imperial herald of His Majesty, Charles the Fifth, Sovereign of the Holy Roman

Empire. You are to appear before the Imperial Council within twenty-one days. The Imperial Council is already in session in the city of Worms."

"And for what reason am I requested to appear?" asked Luther calmly.

"You are not *requested* to appear," the imperial herald said, looking at Doctor Luther out of the corner of his eyes. "You are *required* to appear to be tried on the charge of heresy. John Frederick, Duke of Saxony, has arranged for you to be guaranteed safe passage. That means I have the sorry task of accompanying you to Worms. We leave in the morning."

"I can't possibly leave tomorrow," Doctor Luther protested. "I have far too much to do to get ready. Besides, if I have twenty-one days, it doesn't take that long to get to Worms. How about next . . ."

Luther stroked his clean-shaven chin. "How about next Tuesday?" Tuesday was four days away.

"*You* may have twenty-one days to arrive at Worms," said the imperial herald, "but I don't. You're coming with me. We leave in the morning."

With that the herald turned on the heels of his fine riding boots and marched out of the classroom. I had to jump out of the doorway or I think he would have walked right over me.

The students sat in stunned silence. I thought Doctor Luther would rush to get ready, but instead he said, "Let's see, where was I? Oh, yes. . . ." And he continued his lecture. I closed the door and walked in a daze back to our quarters, not even noticing the swirling snowflakes that began to sting my cheeks.

The more I thought about it, the more it looked like the end of my education. My master was leaving Wittenberg. And even if he prevailed at his trial and didn't get condemned to death (which was the most likely outcome), the trial could last for months. Even with the best outcome, there almost certainly would be a prison sentence—for years, probably. Maybe if I served him in prison, he could continue instructing me. . . .

I shook my head to clear it. What was I thinking of? Doctor Luther's *life* was at stake, and I was trying to figure out a way to get a little more education. How could I be so selfish? No, it would be best if I returned to my village and took up the family trade of shoemaking. That's where I belonged. Maybe, though—maybe I could travel with Doctor Luther for a day or so. Most likely he'd be going right through my little village of Duben.

Just as I was about to turn into the little stairway that led up to our rooms, I looked back over my shoulder—out of habit, I guess. And there she was. The Watcher was just coming around the corner, the same way I had come. When I stopped, she jumped back out of sight. Even through the swirling snow, I was sure it was her.

When Luther got home, his first words were, "Well, Karl, have you got my things packed?"

"No. But I'll get right to it."

"No need to rush," said Luther. "I talked to Sturm again and convinced him to wait a few days before we leave."

I let out a sigh of relief. I had a few more days before having to say good-bye. "How'd you do that?"

"I told him we have no way to travel. Unless he wants to pile the three of us on that big horse of his, he'll have to wait until we can arrange some kind of conveyance."

"The three of us?" I asked.

"Yes. Brother Nicholas has agreed to come with us. And his support will be such a comfort. Not that I don't value you, Karl, but Nicholas, being a fellow monk, will lend a degree of . . . oh, I don't know. I'll be glad for you both."

"Both? You want me to come, too?"

"Of course! You aren't thinking of quitting on me just when I need you most, are you?"

Chapter 4

Night Rider

Almost a week passed before all the arrangements were made. And it was the good people of Wittenberg who finally made possible our transport. An old wagon and three horses were donated along with a considerable collection of funds to help pay for our lodging along the way.

Early on Tuesday morning, April 2, our party rambled out the city gate and pulled onto the ferry to cross the Elbe River. What a sight we must have been. Astride his powerful horse rode Casper Sturm, dressed in his imperial finery. His horse pranced impatiently as its great hooves thudded on the ferry deck.

Down the bank creaked our wagon, drawn by two horses and trailing the spare. Doctor Luther was in his professor's robe. Nicholas von Amsdorf was in his brown monk's habit. I was driving the wagon, wearing a beautiful green wool cape, a far better garment than I had ever owned. It had been donated for our trip by a town merchant. The three of us were perched atop our wagon, hanging on tight lest we be pitched off by every rock or rut.

Quite a crowd turned out to see us off, and who knows how far they would have followed along if it hadn't been for the river. Some students tried to negotiate a free passage from the ferryman: "But we're not going anywhere. We just want to see Doctor Luther off. We'll ride back on your return trip, so there's no need for us to pay."

"Goin' across and comin' straight back don't make it any easier to pull this ferry across," the ferryman grumbled. "Fact is, our load is too heavy all ready. I wouldn't take you even if you paid double toll."

The ferry was pulled across the river by means of a rope stretched from one bank to the other. The rope ran through guides on the raft as well as through one end of a wooden lever, about three feet long, called a "come-along." When the ferryman pulled on the lever, it bound the rope, giving him a good grip. By this means he pulled the raft as far as he could walk along its deck. Then he would loosen the come-along and slide it back up the rope for another bite.

We had just moved away from the shore when the ferryman turned and pointed at me. "You there, boy. Get down off that wagon and block your wheels. And keep those nags steady. I don't want them moving side to side, or we'll all take a drink."

And he was right, too. Halfway across, the spare horse started switching its tail and stamping one of its rear feet to shake off a horsefly. Each time it stamped its hoof, it moved over a few inches to a new position. Soon it was standing sideways to the wagon, and the upstream side of the ferry dipped down so that water began washing up over the deck. Just then an eddy in the river's current caught us and pushed that side lower still as the water washed higher.

"Quick, get that horse back to the center," yelled the ferryman as he pulled with all his might on his come-along to move us out of the fast current.

I splashed down the side of the ferry, already three or four inches under water and gave the horse a big shove. That nag must have realized she was on unsteady footing, because she didn't even push back but stepped right over.

Slowly the low side of the ferry rose, the flood retreated over the edge, and we were stable once more, or at least as stable as we could be.

The moment we touched the ground on the other side, Casper Sturm spurred his horse up the steep bank. But with the load on the front end suddenly reduced, the ferry bobbed up and freed itself from the muddy bank. The ferryman hadn't yet secured his rope, so the current started swinging us around. He cut loose with a string of swear words that would rot your teeth. "Get over here, kid, and give me a hand with this rope," he yelled, as though it had been my fault. I felt awful until I noticed him tossing angry looks in Sturm's direction. The ferryman didn't say anything to Sturm—the herald represented the emperor, after all—but it made me feel better to realize he wasn't really blaming me.

When we finally had the wagon up the bank, we

stopped a moment and looked back toward Wittenberg. It seemed so far away . . . like we'd been gone a week already.

As the day wore on, Brother Nicholas took a turn driving the wagon while I crawled back on top of our luggage. Doctor Luther had brought his lute, and

played and sang to us from time to time. I sat staring at the passing forest and small farms.

Casper Sturm rode ahead, supposedly to ensure our safe passage. There were robbers in the forest, but since they were outlaws anyway, I couldn't see what good one man could do if a band of them attacked. The imperial herald carried a small sword, but it wasn't like he was a knight or something. "It's not robbers he's protecting us from," explained Luther. "We don't have anything worth stealing anyway. He's protecting us from those in the Roman church who would like to do me in."

"You mean John Eck?" I asked, as I took off my cape. The day was starting to warm up.

"Well, I'm not sure he'd stoop to murder on his own. But there are others, even others he might hire."

"But why would your enemies want to attack you when they have already succeeded in bringing you to trial?" Then without thinking I said, "They're likely to get you anyway."

Luther leaned back and laughed. "You sure don't have much faith, do you, Karl? That's all right. That's all right. That could well be the outcome. I have faced it squarely. But to answer your question. There are many who *don't* want me to testify in Worms. No matter what happens to me, my trial could be the most important sermon I will ever preach. Never again am I likely to have an audience like this one."

"What do you mean?" I asked, trying to find a more comfortable position among our few bags and supplies.

"This Imperial Council is shaping up to be the most important conference ever held in Europe. Charles the Fifth is finally bringing more states together in the Holy Roman Empire than ever before. The Roman church, of course, is fighting to maintain control. But my booklet, *Address to the Christian Nobility*, has caused the princes from all the states to ask whether they really want to be under that much control by the Roman church. And the people are sick of the priests' greed and cruel use of church law."

The wagon creaked loudly as Luther continued. "All winter the roads were full of travelers going to Worms. You've seen some of them yourself coming through Wittenberg. I heard that William, duke of Bavaria, took five-hundred horsemen with him; Philip, the prince of Baden, had six-hundred. All the great bishops will be there as well as the knights, lesser nobility, representatives of cities, and many lawyers from the universities. Already the ambassadors from England, France, Venice, Poland, and Hungary have arrived."

"How will everyone fit in the council?" I asked, realizing as soon as I said it that it was a foolish question.

"Only designated delegates will be in the meetings, and only the meetings to which they have been invited. The more important question is," Luther winked at me, "where will they all stay in the little city of Worms? We may find ourselves sleeping under a tree outside town!"

"But why would so many people come if they can't be part of the meetings?"

"To be where the action is. The printers will be the ones getting rich on this council. Every day papers will be published on what has happened. They will be posted everywhere. People will get the news of the events that are shaping our world almost as soon as it happens from these . . . these newspapers."

We rode in silence for a while. Then Luther said, "Whether I am condemned or freed, the whole world will hear the truth. That's why I want to be there. But it is for that very reason that some of my enemies don't want me to testify."

I looked up at Casper Sturm, riding ahead to protect us from Luther's enemies. He was asleep in the saddle, his head hanging down and bobbing along with the plodding steps of his horse. Luther must have guessed what I was thinking—that Sturm didn't look very fierce at the moment. "No, Karl. His defense of us does not come from his ability to fight but from his position. He's the *imperial* herald. If he or anyone in his charge were harmed, the imperial army would be after them."

At midday we stopped by a small stream to water our horses and eat some bread and cheese. We weren't that far from my village. I knew this valley, and Duben was only over the next ridge.

When we got underway again, I asked if I could take the spare horse and ride on ahead. Doctor Luther said that would be fine. As I jumped on the horse and trotted off, Casper Sturm called after me: "Hey, boy, reserve me the best room in the best tavern in town."

"Yes, sir," I called back, knowing my assignment was easy. There is only one tavern in Duben, and it has only two rooms—both the same, as far as I knew.

That old nag gave me one of the roughest rides I've ever had. Trotting down the hill into Duben an hour later was like sliding down a steep mountain stream over rocks, sitting down.

I hadn't been home since last summer, and

Mother was wild with joy when I surprised her and Father by walking right into the house. She kept trying to hug and kiss me like I was still a little boy. I don't know, sometimes the way a mother can act makes a fellow feel like the only safe way to meet her is on opposite sides of a creek too deep to wade.

But as soon as Mother found out that Doctor Luther, Brother Nicholas, and the imperial herald were following behind, all my troubles with her fussing over me ended. She immediately began bustling about fixing a fine meal to feed us all. I tried to tell her that Casper Sturm would be going to the tavern, but she said, "He can't eat there. The food is terrible. Besides, it's probably been ages since he had a home-cooked meal." Then Mother assigned everyone jobs: I was to go reserve the room for Casper Sturm. Father was sent out to kill a couple of chickens and pluck them. (Mother doesn't usually order Father around, but this was a special situation, and he went off in good humor.) My sister, one year older and still living at home, fixed a place for Doctor Luther and Brother Nicholas to sleep. I thought that they'd probably stay with our church priest, but Mother wouldn't hear of it.

That evening after our meal—which Casper Sturm gladly accepted, to my surprise—Father started asking about the purpose of our trip. The more Luther said, the quieter Father got. I could see he didn't approve, so I jumped right in to defend the good work that Doctor Luther was doing. I was carrying on like a defense lawyer when Father interrupted. "Karl, I fully support the views of Doctor Luther. And," he continued, turning to Luther, "I have read every book of yours that I can find. My concern is with Karl's safety. This trip could be very dangerous, couldn't it?"

"I don't think it will be dangerous for Karl," said Brother Nicholas. "After all, he is not responsible for Martin Luther's ideas or writings. On this trip he's merely a stable boy."

"That's not entirely right," said Luther, holding up his hands as though to stop Brother Nicholas. "There could be danger. That I'll admit. The pope's bull warned of severe consequences to anyone who supports me. If the emperor and the imperial council rule against me and take a nasty turn, they could strike out against all who help me."

"Could that include Karl?" asked my mother. "He's only a boy."

"When the name 'heretic' starts getting thrown about, it can stick to anyone," Luther said.

"Then I don't want Karl going along," said Mother. "Two grown men ought to be capable of caring for their own horses and driving a wagon. You don't need a boy along."

"You are quite correct," said Luther. "And we wouldn't want to take him along against your wishes."

"But Mother, I want to go!" I protested. "No one is forcing me to go. I want to continue my education. And just today Doctor Luther was telling me about what an important council this will be. I may be able

to see many of the most important people in the whole world. Besides," I carried on, revealing my little plan, "even if Doctor Luther is sent to prison, I could still serve him—he will need someone to run his errands and bring supplies—and he could tutor me there. I'd learn even more."

When I finally shut up, I felt heat rising up my neck and knew I was turning red. There I'd gone and let everyone know how much more I was thinking of my own welfare than of Doctor Luther's. But for the moment, no one else seemed to notice.

"But our good doctor *could* be sentenced to death," said my father solemnly. "Still . . . I think it should be Karl's decision if Doctor Luther is inviting him."

"Oh, I am," assured Luther. "I would welcome his company and service. I think we will have good use for him. And I'll do my best to make sure that he remains safe. But the truth is, in this situation, I can make no guarantees."

"Well, then," concluded my father, "sleep on it tonight, Karl. But don't forget your mother's wisdom and feelings."

That settled it for me. There wasn't anything to think about; come morning, I'd be off down the road in that creaky old wagon.

Doctor Luther and Brother Nicholas were to sleep inside near the hearth, and that left little room for me. So I decided to curl up in the hay in our barn. The hayloft had often been a favorite place to be by myself when I was a small boy. But when I went out to get my green cape from the wagon—it would provide welcome warmth against the April night chill—someone on horseback took off galloping down the street.

Whoever it was had stopped by our wagon! I ran out to see if anything was missing. As I gazed into the gloom of the moonlit night, trying to make out the rider on the retreating horse, I thought I saw long flowing hair streaming out behind the rider's head.

Chapter 5

The Triumphal Entry

WAS IT THE GIRL, The Watcher? I tore off down the street as fast as I could go. I'd heard a fast runner can sometimes beat a horse. But that's only when the person and the horse have an equal start and the distance is very short.

Our village is small, and soon I pulled up winded at the edge of town. I was just able to hear the faint thumpity-thump of the horse's hooves disappearing on down the road—the road to Leipzig that we'd be taking the next morning.

I turned and walked slowly home. Was it The Watcher? How could it be? What would a young girl be doing riding alone, let alone galloping through the night? It just didn't make sense. If it was the girl, there didn't seem to be any reason for her to follow us. Eck, who was probably already in Worms, certainly had learned by other means that we were coming. Many people would travel faster than our slow wagon. They could tell him that we were on our way.

And if, as Luther had hinted, Eck wanted to

arrange for a band of robbers to attack us on the highway and prevent Luther from making it to Worms, what good could a girl do? She couldn't swing a sword in combat.

Then it came to me. Eck needed a special messenger. That's why she was hurrying on ahead. Eck couldn't wait for casual travelers to bring him news that we were on the way. He needed to know early so that he *could* arrange a trap.

I picked up my pace, intent on getting back home to warn Luther. But then I paused. Who would believe me? I hadn't actually seen the rider. I didn't know for sure it was the girl. And even if my story was believed, my parents might just use it and the new danger it represented to say I couldn't go. No. I'd wait. Tomorrow, once we were on the road, would be plenty of time to tell Luther.

In the morning I said good-bye to my folks, and I tried to reassure my mother that everything would be all right. She gave me a hug that I thought wouldn't quit, but finally she let me go and wiped a tear from her eye. "You be good, Karl, and I'll pray for you." Then we were off.

But by the light of morning, my story about the night rider seemed even more unbelievable. "When I came out to get my cape from the wagon last night," I said as the wagon rolled out of town, "there was a rider." I paused, but no one responded. "The rider was stopped right by our wagon . . . looking in." Still no one seemed interested enough to ask who the rider was.

"I think it was a spy," I said.

Brother Nicholas, who was driving again, turned and looked at me quizzically. But then he shook his head and turned back to staring at the road, or rather the rear end of Casper Sturm's fine horse.

"As soon as I came out, the rider took off and galloped all the way out of town."

Finally, Doctor Luther responded. "Now I know this is a small town, Karl, but it's not so small that you can see all the way from one end to the other. How do you know the rider galloped all the way out of town?" Luther asked just like the lawyer trying to teach one of his students to think more logically. "Maybe the person lives on the other side of town and turned in at home." He thought he had me.

"I know she left town because I followed her."

"Her?" challenged Brother Nicholas. "What's a woman doing riding around in the middle of the night? You must have been dreaming."

"I wasn't dreaming," I said. "It was The Watcher. And you know what I think she was doing . . ." Then I stopped. Doctor Luther's eyes narrowed as though he found my story quite ridiculous. I too began to see that my theory was pretty farfetched. Bad things *do* seem so much tamer by the light of day. So instead of telling them about the ambush I had imagined the night before, I just said, "Well, I think it was that girl. It kind of looked like her."

No one asked what I thought she was doing, so I didn't say any more. But I decided to keep a sharp eye out during the rest of the trip, and if I saw her again or if I saw anything suspicious, then I would tell everyone my theory.

That afternoon we arrived in Leipzig. It had been at the University of Leipzig that Martin Luther and John Eck had held their fiery public debates. The university and the city had mostly supported Eck, so we were wary and hoped to enter the city unnoticed—at least as unnoticed as one could with an imperial herald riding in front of your wagon.

But we had no such luck. It seemed everyone in town knew we were coming and had turned out to meet us. Most were friendly, though. And the city council officially welcomed Doctor Luther by giving him the traditional cup of wine when we reached the

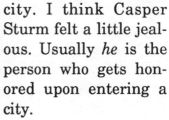

city. I think Casper Sturm felt a little jealous. Usually *he* is the person who gets honored upon entering a city.

We spent the night in rooms provided at the university. But when I was trying to fall asleep, I started thinking: How had everybody known that we were coming . . . and just when we would be arriving?

There had been other travelers on the road, and one or two had passed us. But I couldn't remember that they had recognized us. So how had the City of

Leipzig—Eck's old stomping grounds—known when we would arrive? It made me suspicious. Maybe that girl had announced us. And why had Luther's "enemy" city welcomed us so warmly? It felt like a set-up.

When the next day came, however, I still didn't say anything about my theories.

Leipzig was as far to the south as I had ever been, so the countryside was all new to me in the days that followed. I loved it—beautiful hills, rich forests, and snug farms and villages nestled in the ends of the green valleys. From Leipzig our road led southwest to Naumburg, picturesquely clustered about its great cathedral in the valley of the Saale River. Then we went over the hills to Weimar and on west to spend the night of April 6 in Erfurt.

"There could be danger awaiting us in Erfurt," warned Luther when we took our lunch break. "I went to the university there. However, from what I've heard, the leaders are firmly aligned with the Roman church, so they may be particularly displeased with me. They may feel I have embarrassed them and hurt the reputation of their school. If any problem appears," he said, turning to Casper Sturm, "let's ride right on through. We can camp a night in the woods if need be."

"No one would dare threaten the charge of the imperial herald," said Sturm in disgust.

"No one you could charge or identify," agreed Luther. "But crowds have a mind of their own and can easily turn into an angry mob. I have written to my friend, Lang, in Eisenach. If there is any trouble, he is prepared to come to our rescue and take us secretly on our way."

Sturm snorted his disregard for such arrangements, tossed the chicken bone he had been gnawing on into the brush and stood up. "If there's a chance that we will have to travel beyond Erfurt tonight, let's get going or we'll be traveling in the dark."

But long before our little party reached the gates of Erfurt, we were met by a crowd of joyful students declaring their support for Luther. They escorted us into the city and through the narrow streets right to the university. Far from being an embarrassment, Doctor Luther was considered a hero.

The following morning, Sunday, Luther preached in the university chapel. So many people wanted to hear him that the foundation of the porch cracked from the weight of people waiting to crowd into the church.

In the afternoon we traveled on to Gotha just a few miles down the road. There Luther again preached. It was Palm Sunday, and the crowds had been wild with enthusiasm and support for Luther. I could see that the spirit of the people as well as what Doctor Luther was saying was having an influence on Casper Sturm. The imperial herald always stood at the back with his arms crossed. At first he had been very somber whenever Luther was speaking of the Gospel and the problems in the church, but more and more I noticed Sturm smiling and nodding in agreement.

I, too, was being affected by the eager way people welcomed Luther, and my theories about his receptions being false and set up by Eck and The Watcher drifted from my mind like the memory of a bad dream from the night before.

"Isn't it great how the people support you?" I said excitedly to Doctor Luther that evening when we were in our quarters.

"I'm not so sure," he said. "A Palm Sunday reception can turn into a crucifixion mob in a very short time, if you'll remember what happened to Jesus."

52

Luther stood by the window, hands clasped behind his back, and looked out into Gotha's streets. "This is actually making me more wary than the possibility of highway robbers or the legal tricks that Eck might try to pull before the council."

But as the days passed, Luther did not shrink from the crowds that seemed to be larger in every town through which we passed. And, when at each evening's stop the people begged him to preach, he would go to the church and give them a sermon of an hour or more. But the pace exhausted him, and before we made it over the hills to Eisenach, he came down with a fever. Still the crowds met us in the towns and villages, but Luther could no longer preach in their churches.

The days passed and my master pretty much recovered by the time we arrived at Frankfurt. The next day we crossed the Rhine River and traveled up its broad valley to the town of Oppenheim, from where we could almost see the cathedral towers in Worms. Our journey was almost over.

"Let's get an early start tomorrow," said Luther that evening as we sat around the table in the local inn.

"Suits me," said Sturm. "It's been several weeks since I've seen my family."

"I didn't know you had a family," said Brother Nicholas.

"You never asked," said Sturm. It was true. We knew very little about the imperial herald, probably because we'd never bothered to ask. The whole trip had focused on Doctor Luther, his ideas, his dangers, and the people's response to him.

"I'm sorry," said Luther, looking pained. "I would have made a greater effort to leave Wittenberg sooner had I known. How many children do you have?"

"Three girls and two boys, and I'll be as glad to see them as my wife."

The image of the imperial herald riding into Wittenberg and looking down on the crowd by Raven's Tavern came into my mind. I could hardly imagine little children running to greet him—even his own.

Just as we finished eating we were joined by a stranger, a former monk who introduced himself as Martin Bucer. "I bring a message," he said, "from the great knight, Franz von Sickingen. He admires your fight against Rome. And he is willing to defend you militarily if you wish to take refuge with him."

I immediately realized that such a move on Luther's part—when he had been summoned to court—could be considered treasonous. There were rumors of war among the peasants and even with powerful warlords like Sickingen. But the empire was also held together by religious connections. If Luther sided with Sickingen, it could double their power.

Luther looked over at Casper Sturm. Sturm said, "Excuse me, gentlemen, but I think I'll be turning in. An early start tomorrow?" And with that he left the table, not staying to hear Luther's response one way or the other.

"That," said Luther to Martin Bucer, "is the imperial herald. We all could have been arrested for treason."

Bucer's face turned gray. "I had no idea. I never imagined that the herald would be eating with you. Usually . . ."

"Yes, I know," said Luther. "Usually the nobility do not socialize with the accused. But we have become . . . almost friends."

Suddenly, I saw Casper Sturm in a whole new light. He may have been the imperial herald, but his heart had been touched by Doctor Luther's message and person. He had left the table to protect Luther and to give him the freedom to accept the offer if he wanted to.

"Thank Sickingen for me," said Luther. "Maybe some other time I will need his hospitality. But right now I must go to Worms."

The next morning we were loading the wagon before the sun peeked over the hills on the east side of the Rhine. Still, there were a dozen townspeople who accompanied us out of town and promised that they would be praying for Doctor Luther.

Several miles outside Worms I pulled the wagon to a stop on the top of a hill high enough to see over the valley; at some distance we could see a cloud of dust rising through the trees. Casper Sturm straightened in his saddle and called back to us, "If there's any problem, let me handle it."

When we had driven down off the hill and were traveling among the trees, we discovered the source of dust. It was a crowd of people on horseback and on foot; among them Luther recognized some members of Duke Frederick's court. When the multitude recognized who we were, they ran toward us cheering and clapping.

As I clucked to the nervous horses, I noticed that there were several nobles, a number of other university professors, and at least a hundred horsemen—some of them heavily armed—who had ridden out to welcome us.

"I don't like this," Luther said as we approached the gates of the city.

"Why not?" I asked. I thought it was great.

"It's too much like Christ's triumphal entry into Jerusalem. No good can come of this."

More people joined us as we traveled through the city streets, until at about ten in the morning we came to the house of the Knights of Saint John. There we were informed that Duke Frederick had arranged rooms for us at his own expense.

We were safely at our destination, and a good thing, too. I don't think we could have pushed our way any farther through the streets packed with people.

Doctor Luther stood in the wagon, waving to the people, then climbed down and went with Brother Nicholas into the house. I busied myself carrying in our things.

Finally, when I came out for the last load, the crowd had thinned. But across the street among some other men I saw John Eck. I just stood there looking at him for a couple minutes, then grabbed the last bag and went in.

It was a sober reminder that more than friends were waiting for us in the City of Worms.

Chapter 6

Bound and Gagged

THE VERY NEXT AFTERNOON a marshal knocked at
our lodgings and summoned Doctor Luther to
the bishop's palace where Emperor Charles had
taken up temporary residence. We left immediately
with the marshal. I was surprised to see that Casper
Sturm accompanied us, as did several other of
Luther's supporters.

A crowd packed the street in front of our lodging.
More people were on the roofs of the adjoining buildings looking down at us. We tried to make our way
through the mass, but it was impossible, so we retreated and went out the back way and down the
side streets and alleys.

At the bishop's palace we were taken to a small
hall which was packed with spectators. The emperor
sat at one end, surrounded by the Imperial Council. I
stood gawking at all the splendid nobles, almost
forgetting why we were there. Me! In the same room
with the emperor! If only my mother could see me
now.

Then suddenly the crowd quieted as John Eck

stood up and said, "Most Honorable Doctor Luther, we are so grateful that you could be with us. We trust your journey was pleasant." Right away I was suspicious. His words did not seem sincere. Then he went on and we got the real bite of his attitude: "You are here to answer charges of heresy, and we do not want this hearing to turn into a debate. Therefore, you are instructed to answer only the questions put to you and make no other statements. Is that understood?"

Brother Nicholas and I and some others who openly supported Luther gathered close around Luther. He seemed at ease, smiling and looking around at the crowd that was made up of both his friends and enemies. He wore the clothes of an Augustinian monk, a leather belt over his dark, coarsely spun robe. And in the style of monks, he had freshly shaved the top of his head, leaving a ring of hair above his ears and around the back as though he were naturally bald. Doctor Luther was not yet forty years old, but his stocky body was strong for one who spent most of his time in a classroom.

The tall John Eck was quite a contrast to the short Martin Luther as he stood behind the bench waiting for Luther's commitment to not engage in debate. Finally my master said, "I will answer only as God bids me."

Eck was not pleased. He looked toward the emperor, but the emperor did not respond one way or the other. Finally, Eck proceeded, referring to the pile of books on the bench in front of him. "Martin Luther, His Imperial Majesty has summoned you for two reasons: to know whether you acknowledge having written these books; and having written them, whether you are willing to renounce them. What do you say?"

Then a secretary read the names of the books piled on the bench.

Luther said, "Yes, I wrote those books, if they are indeed the titles mentioned. As to whether I can renounce their content, that would take some discussion, and you do not want any debate."

"Why must there be discussion?" challenged Eck.

"First of all, no one in this room would argue against the majority of their content. To deny that material would in itself be heresy since we all can agree that it is from the Holy Scriptures. As for the other content, the material which you and the church of Rome might object to, I cannot deny anything unless it is shown to me to be in conflict with the Scriptures. After all, it was Jesus himself who said, 'Whoever denies me before men, him will I deny before my Father in heaven.' I would at least like time to consider these matters."

It was a fine opening, I thought. But although Luther had spoken boldly, he seemed to be very nervous. Of course we all had reason to be nervous, standing there in the presence of the emperor and the other nobles. For the first time I began to wish I had taken my mother's advice and stayed in Duben, because Eck came back just as strongly on the attack.

"What do you mean, you need time? Have you not had time enough ever since you were summoned to  this court? Maybe, instead of violating the pope's bull and preaching in every village as you traveled here, you should have been preparing to answer His Imperial Majesty. Do you not respect this court and the *emperor's* valuable time?"

"Of course I respect the emperor and this court. It's just that these are weighty matters, and I would not want to do harm to God's Word or my own soul by denying something that is, in fact, true."

After that, things started to go badly. Others stood and protested that Luther should not be given any further time to prepare his case. The evening wore on and lights in the hall were lit. Soon food and drink were brought for the emperor and other nobles behind the bench, but no provision was made for Doctor Luther or the rest of us. I began to worry that in his weakened condition after his recent illness,

Doctor Luther could be in great need of nourishment. I knew I was getting hungry.

Finally, I slipped out of the crowded room thinking that I would get something for us to eat and drink. It was dark outside in the open portal that ran up the side of the hall, and I stood there thinking of where I could go to get some provisions. Suddenly, a figure stepped up beside me. As my eyes adjusted to the darkness, I realized it was The Watcher.

I jumped as though she were death itself when the girl reached out and touched me. "Come with me," she said, allowing the long scarf she held over her nose and mouth to fall away from her hauntingly beautiful face. Her blue eyes flashed as she said, "We must talk!"

The mystery of the girl almost caused me to follow, but I had more sense than that. "Who are you, anyway? And why are you always following us?" I asked. She looked around as though hoping no one heard, but I continued just as loudly, "I know why you follow us. It's Doctor Luther, isn't it?"

"Yes," she hissed. "Now you must come with me."

"Not on my life. I will never betray him."

Just then a group of people came out of the hall and turned our way. The Watcher quickly adjusted the scarf over her face again, turned, and hurried away.

That was a close one. But now I had my proof. She *had* been following us all the way to Worms, and her interest was Luther. She had said so herself. This time when I told the others, they would have to believe me. I started to go back into the court but realized there was no way I could say anything about her during the hearing. My report would have to wait until we were alone later that night. So I went on out to the street to find some food and drink, all the while keeping a sharp eye out for The Watcher.

I had not walked far from the bishop's palace when two figures jumped out from a narrow passageway between two buildings and grabbed me. Before I knew what was happening they pulled me into the passageway and tied a rag around my mouth to gag me. But then I began fighting as hard as I could. I stomped on one's foot and tried to knee the other. With all my strength I twisted and turned to free my arms, but there were two of them, and soon they overcame me and had my arms bound behind my back.

"Just calm down," said a man's voice. "We intend

you no harm. We just need to talk to you."

Right. I'd already heard that one tonight. But this time there didn't seem to be much I could do without getting myself hurt, so I decided to go along, looking every moment for some means of escape. I hoped they would take me out into the street where we might meet other people. Then I'd make a run for it, trusting that they wouldn't risk hitting me over the head or something worse right in front of others.

But my hopes were in vain. They kept to the dark passageways and corridors of the old city. Then they pushed me through a door and—nearly carrying me by each shoulder—marched me down two flights of steps to a damp and dark dungeon. It was lit by a single flickering candle, and the bulk of a third stranger was seated behind a small table. The huge door clanged closed behind me.

I looked around at my surroundings. If this wasn't a prison that I'd landed in, it was the next thing to it.

Chapter 7

The Assignment

THE ROOM WAS DAMP AND COLD, and the single candle cast flickering shadows on the stone walls. There were no windows in the cell.

"What's your name, lad?" asked the large man behind the small table. He nodded at my captors and they removed the gag.

"Karl."

"Well, Master Karl, do you have a last name?"

"Schumacher. My name is Karl Schumacher. But why did you bring me here? Why are my hands tied? Let me go."

"Please forgive us," said the man behind the table. He was large and rugged looking but not unkind in his appearance. "I hope these men did not hurt you, but it seems you would not join us by simple invitation. We needed to talk to you immediately. We could not risk missing our opportunity."

"So you jumped me in a dark alley, tied me up, and dragged me down here to this dungeon. Why? I haven't done anything wrong." I hoped they could not hear the wild thumping of my heart.

"Of course not." He looked at the two men who were standing on each side of me. "Gentlemen, let's untie Karl. I'm sure he no longer needs to be restrained."

The man on my right untied the thong around my wrists. I rubbed them to get the feeling back into my hands. "Thank you," I managed. "Now why did you bring me here? I want to go."

"We need your help with Doctor Luther."

My mind was spinning. I had once heard that if you are ever captured, the best time to make your escape is immediately. Well, it seemed that I was already too late for that. They had me in a stone cell behind a closed door. But maybe I could talk my way out of this prison. I'd have to be careful, though—not give away anything that would betray Doctor Luther.

"I'll not answer any questions as long as you have me locked in this prison."

"Prison?" said the large man, and the other two chuckled. "Karl, you're not in prison. We just needed somewhere to talk in private."

"Then how come that big door is bolted behind me?"

"It's not bolted. Franz, show Karl that he's not locked in here. Leave the door open a little bit if that makes him more comfortable."

Franz, the man on my right, opened the door a few inches.

"Does that mean I can walk out of here?" I turned and started for the door, wanting to seize my first opportunity, thinking it might be my last.

"Wait a minute," said Franz, putting his hand on my shoulder as he stepped between me and the door.

Just as I thought, it wasn't going to be that easy.

"Give us a minute," said the large man.

"It looks like I have no choice," I said.

"We just want to talk to you about Doctor Luther. We need your help. Look, Karl," continued the large man, "we represent a very important person. You might be able to guess who he is, but we cannot say his name." (Yes, well, I *did* have my ideas who was behind this—probably Eck.) "Our master wishes to make sure Luther is treated fairly, and that's why we need your help."

"I will never betray Doctor Luther no matter how long you keep me in this dungeon."

"Good," said the large man. "We need loyalty. But we have no intention of keeping you down here. If

67

the trial for Luther goes badly, we may need to arrange his escape. But to do so, we'll need an insider. And that's where you come in. We want you to tell us about his every move before he makes it so that he can be rescued if need be."

Suddenly I began to feel very confused. Here these fellows had jumped me and thrown me in prison—or at least it seemed like a prison to me. But they claimed it was not a prison, that I was free to go. On the other hand, they insisted on talking to me first. Worse still, it sounded like they wanted me to spy on Doctor Luther. But then they were talking about rescuing him, arranging his "escape." What was going on? What did it all mean?

"Karl, if John Eck has his way, your master will be condemned as a heretic. If that happens, it is very hard to predict what the emperor will do. If it strikes his fancy, he might dismiss the whole thing. On the other hand, he could as easily condemn Luther to be burned at the stake. We have no way of knowing."

"Therefore," Franz spoke up, "if we are to save Luther we must be ready to move at a moment's notice. So we need your help."

Who were these people? I had at first been sure they were Eck's representatives. But possibly they were Duke Frederick's men. How could I be sure?

"Who are you?" I demanded.

"Who we are—personally—doesn't make any difference, Karl. Will you help us? Will you help Luther?"

"But if you won't tell me who you are, at least tell me who you work for."

"As I said earlier, we can't say our master's name. You can probably guess, but if you were ever questioned, it would be in everyone's best interest if you could honestly answer that his name was never mentioned. Do you understand?"

Well, I did, in a way. And then again I didn't! I needed time to think, time to figure out whether these men were setting a trap or planning to help Luther. "What do you want from me?" I asked, hoping that a little more information would help me figure things out.

"You'll be our inside man. It will be your duty to know where Luther is going and when—every minute of the day or night. Things could go badly for him at any point. We can't take time to chase him down if he's taken it into his mind to go speak in some chapel. If he is condemned, we may have no more than a couple of hours to get him out of town. We will remain in regular contact with you so that you can tell us where he will be."

"Is that all?" I asked, thinking it was far too much if these were enemies. But the plan did sound reasonable—the kind of plan friends would make.

"Yes, that's all—be our insider and keep us informed, and help out when the time comes."

"When what time comes?"

"If we need to rescue him."

"Can I think about it?" I asked.

The large man glanced at the two men at my side. "Tomorrow. We need your answer by tomorrow at the latest. If you won't help, we'll have to get someone else. But you are the ideal insider. You have been with him from Wittenberg. As a boy, as his servant, you can come and go without anyone noticing. We need you. Your master, Doctor Luther needs you. Don't let him down!"

"Can I go now?"

"Yes. Our contact will approach you tomorrow while you are at court. There will be a password. The contact will say, 'I rode through Duben.' Give your answer to that person only. Speak to no one else about this. Now go."

I turned and left, stumbling up the stone steps in the dark. "I rode through Duben." What a strange password. A lot of people ride through Duben. That's my home town, and I had ridden through just a few days before. Did he know where I came from? It seemed very eerie to have someone know more about me than I knew about him.

The next day other court business delayed Doctor Luther's hearing until late in the afternoon. For me it was very hard to wait, but Luther used the time peacefully, preparing what he was going to say.

An old friend of Luther's, a monk named Brother John Petzensteiner, joined us for lunch. "I have come to join you," he said to Luther. "Whatever your lot may be, that will be my lot."

"That's a rather bold claim," laughed Luther. "Maybe your name should be Brother Peter—your claim sounds something like Peter's boast to Christ our Master."

Brother John was obviously hurt, though I don't think Doctor Luther had any intention of scolding him. Soon, however, the tension eased, and they were discussing old times together. Luther insisted that Brother John stay with us in our rooms, small as they were.

When we were finally called for the hearing, it was to a much larger hall in the bishop's palace, but it was just as crowded. In fact, even the emperor had a hard time getting through the mass of people to his place.

When the hearing got underway, John Eck started right in by demanding that Luther answer the second question of the day before: was he ready to renounce the content of his writings?

Doctor Luther spoke boldly, his preparation of the day and the help of the Lord giving him extra strength. Luther used many verses from the Bible to prove the rightness of his claims and objections to the corruption in the Roman church.

When he finished, Eck said tersely, "Heresy. All of it is heresy!"

Martin Luther turned to the emperor and said, "Your Majesty, unless I am shown from the Scriptures that I have made mistakes, I am neither able nor willing to revoke even one word of what I have written. Here I stand; God help me, I cannot do otherwise."

I thought it was a wonderful conclusion as did

most of his other German friends who were standing with us. The hearing was then dismissed, and we were all congratulating each other as we pushed our way out through the crowd. When we got outside, some of the crowd was cheering . . . but then swelling louder and louder rose another sound, a large number of people chanting: "To the flames! To the flames!

To the flames!"

Fear tightened my throat. In my mind I saw the ladder with the "heretic" tipping over into the flames five years ago. A chill went through me. The emperor had not yet made his judgment, and it could be death.

Then, as I strained against the crowd to see ahead through the night, I heard a female voice next to me saying, "I rode through Duben. I rode through Duben."

I whipped around, and there was The Watcher tugging on my sleeve.

Chapter 8

The Flight of the Condemned

COME ON. COME ON. I need to talk to you," The Watcher said as she pulled me to the edge of the crowd.

"You? You're my contact?" I blurted.

"Quiet," she said, but the mob was so noisy that only those closest to us could have heard either of us. She kept pulling on my arm, and soon we turned in through a gate to the secluded plaza of a fine villa.

"So that was you who rode through Duben the other night. What were you doing snooping in our wagon?"

"Nothing. I just wanted to make sure it was yours—that you were staying there."

"Why did you want to know that? Why were you following us?"

"There's no time to explain all that now. Have you made up your mind to help us . . . or not?"

"How should I know? I don't even know who you people are."

"What difference does it make? We're friends of Luther, and he may need our help. Didn't you hear what the crowd was chanting just now? There are many who want him burned at the stake."

I tried to swallow, but my throat still felt tight and dry. I could still hear the chants in the street. "I know that. And you and those men who ambushed me last night might be part of them." I stared at her, getting a good look at her face for the first time. "At least tell me your name."

"My name is Arlene . . ."

Just then a group of people came through the gate. They must have lived in the villa because they immediately started yelling at us: "You there. This is a private courtyard. How did you get in here? Get out! Get out, now!"

The Watcher ducked her head and in a moment we were back on the street, which was still filled with people. "Make up your mind—soon! Remember your assignment," she hissed. Then The Watcher slipped into the crowd and was gone.

I made my way back to our quarters, thinking all the way about what I should do. Finally I decided I needed to talk to Doctor Luther and tell him that I had met The Watcher, that her name was Arlene, but Arlene . . . what?

However, when I got back to our rooms there was a celebration going on. Along with Brother Nicholas and Brother John, many strangers were there congratulating Luther on his brilliant defense or advising him on what next steps he should take. Luther greeted everyone by raising both fists above his head and declaring, "I've come through; I've come through." He felt certain that tomorrow he would receive a favorable ruling.

But early the next morning when two guards arrived at our door, I wasn't so sure. Had they come to take Doctor Luther to prison? No. I soon discovered that they had been sent merely to escort him through the crowd back to the palace hall.

Our mood was very confident.

When the council was gathered once more, Emperor Charles rose to speak. This in itself was quite a surprise. No one expected him to respond to Luther directly. He was young and weak-hearted and let his advisers establish policy—at least that's what we had been told. But there he was reading his judgment.

". . . in view of the State's long tradition of supporting the church, I, too, will support the church. I cannot accept that one man's opinion is correct if all the church leaders and theologians speak against him.

"I should have moved against this Martin Luther's heretical ideas much earlier. I intend to send him safely back to Wittenberg, but only because I keep my promises of safe conduct. But no more preaching. No more teaching. If he wants continued safety he must remain silent. All of his books and writings are to be burned. Anyone caught reading, printing, or distributing them should be condemned.

"Once he has arrived home, my promise of safe conduct will have ended, and I will proceed against him as a notorious heretic."

I was stunned. I couldn't believe what I was

hearing. But Charles wasn't through.

Turning to the rest of the council members, he said, "I call upon each one of you to prove your loyalty to the empire by doing your duty and keeping your promise to me. I agreed to hear this man fairly. And you," he said as he looked directly at Duke Frederick, "agreed to uphold the Imperial ruling."

The whole court erupted with shouts—some in support of the emperor, some in protest. And then in the middle of the hubbub I noticed Duke Frederick rise from his seat and slip out.

I guess no one had expected such a strong statement from the emperor. And no one with any real authority rose to defend Doctor Luther. There was just a lot of grumbling and shouting. Soon Luther and the rest of our party were ushered out of the hall as the Imperial Council moved on to discuss other matters of state.

That evening some other friends came to our room to discuss Doctor Luther's plight with him and Brothers Nicholas and John. There was no certainty that Luther would be sentenced to death, but the possibility was greater than ever. Some of the Council members who favored Luther were trying to arrange further hearings on Luther's behalf. Maybe, they hoped, the emperor's declaration could be softened.

Days passed as negotiations continued. Sometimes Luther was summoned to testify before various committees, but no real improvement happened. At least once a day I saw The Watcher—or Arlene, as

I now knew her. I would be walking to one of the meetings with Doctor Luther, or coming back from shopping at the market, or delivering a message, and there she'd be standing in a doorway or by a fountain or reading the daily news posters on the bulletin boards. Each time I would just shake my head. I had pretty much decided to trust her and the men behind her, but there was still some doubt, and I didn't want to commit myself. Besides, there was no news to report.

Then one day Casper Sturm, the imperial herald, came to our quarters. "There are only twenty-two days remaining on your guarantee of safe conduct," he said very solemnly to Doctor Luther. "I think it might be wise if you did not wait too long."

"But certainly it does not take that long to get back to Wittenberg," said Brother Nicholas, who was trying to mend his sandal.

"No. It is quite easy to make the trip in a couple of weeks or less," Sturm agreed, "but it would also be possible for bad weather or illness to delay you so you would be on the road past your safe-conduct period. Then you could be in greater danger."

"I was sick on our trip down here," said Luther, "and it did not slow us much. And how could bad weather do anything worse than make our traveling unpleasant?"

"I have seen heavy thunderstorms flood streams and rivers so that they were impassible for two or three days at a time in the spring," said the herald. "But to be frank with you, Doctor Luther, the greatest danger is from your enemies who might *arrange* delays—a broken wagon wheel, lame horses, bandits—many things can go wrong on the highway. You must realize, Doctor Luther, now that you have been condemned by the emperor, your life could be easily taken by others. Your remaining time of safe conduct may protect you from official harm, but others . . . they could attack you without fear of prosecution. You are a condemned man."

"Hmmm, yes. I see what you mean," said Luther.

Brother John spoke up. "You know, Doctor Luther, I don't think there's much value in remaining in Worms any longer. I've gone to a couple of those meetings with you, and I don't think anything is being accomplished."

"I suppose you're right," said Luther. "I might as well get back to my students at the university."

"There'll be no imperial escort for you on this trip," said the herald, "but I wish you well. I've come to respect your fight, Doctor Luther."

"Thank you," said Luther. The two men clasped hands briefly.

"Let's leave tomorrow," said Luther as soon as the herald had taken his leave. "If we have no imperial escort, maybe we can slip out of the city unnoticed. A quiet trip home could be the safest."

"I agree," said Brother Nicholas. "But your departure will be known within the day. People are always coming by and asking to see you."

"That's true." Luther looked out the window, rubbing his chin. "What we need is for one of you brothers to stay behind for a few days. If you could simply tell people that I am not available, my absence wouldn't be so apparent."

"I'll be glad to do that," offered Brother Nicholas. "Since I arrived with you, most people will assume we would leave together."

"Good. Brother John, can you come with us?"

"I told you I was with you all the way."

"Then why don't you two brothers begin packing. I'm going out into the streets and talk to people so that many get a good chance to see me. That should hold them for a while."

"Don't go preaching, now," said Brother Nicholas. "You must not tempt the emperor to enforce his ban on your public speaking."

"I'll be careful. And Karl, why don't you go purchase supplies and get our wagon and horses prepared. No one will take much notice of you. Let's plan to leave as quietly as possible tomorrow."

All the rest of that afternoon I made trips to the market. I bought bread and cheese and apples and jugs of wine, each time trying not to carry so much as to attract attention. Then in the evening I made similar trips to the stable to load things into the wagon, waiting half an hour or an hour between each one so as not to attract attention.

It was late when I made my last trip to the stable—without a lantern—but I decided to give the horses extra feed in preparation for the journey. I scooped oats into the feed bins of the first two horses, then groped in the dark of the last stall. As I felt my

way along the horse's flank, I
stumbled over something in the
straw on the floor. As I fell,
I suddenly found myself
tangled with an-
other body.
And then
someone
screamed.

"What's going on out there," called the stable man
from his shack in front of the barn.

Before I could answer, someone clamped a strong
hand over my mouth. "It's me, Arlene," said The
Watcher's hushed voice. "I didn't mean to scream,
but you stepped on me." And then the hand was
removed from my mouth.

"What . . ?" I started to protest.

"Shhh. Just answer the man."

"Nothing," I called. "I just tripped over something."

A door slammed.

"What are you doing here?" I asked.

"You're getting ready to leave, aren't you?" said Arlene.

"What makes you think so?"

"I've been watching you all day—going to market, packing the wagon. I figured you'd check your horses, but I fell asleep waiting. Now, when are you leaving?"

Before I realized what I was doing, I told Arlene our whole plan. I hadn't really decided to trust her, but there—I'd gone ahead and done it.

"I think it's wise," she said. "I just hope you can get out of town without being noticed." And then in the dark she laid her hand on my arm. "Thank you, Karl, for trusting me. You did the right thing."

"How'd you know my name?"

"It's only fair. I told you mine, didn't I?"

"Yes, but I *didn't* tell you mine."

"Well, someone else did. Goodnight, Karl." And then she was gone into the dark.

When I got back to our rooms I was tired and went right to bed, but Arlene filled my dreams, riding off into a moonlit night with her long dark hair flowing behind her.

We'd hoped to leave early the next morning, but Doctor Luther was summoned to a meeting that did not finish until after ten o'clock, so it was nearly lunch before I pulled the wagon around and Doctor Luther and Brother John climbed in.

We rattled down the street as though we were in no particular hurry and turned toward the city gate. All seemed well. No one seemed to be noticing our departure.

But as soon as we passed through the gate, we were greeted by a small troop of horsemen. There must have been at least twenty of them, many of them armed.

"We're your escort," announced a man with a pointed gray beard and a brass helmet.

How had they known?

Chapter 9

Escape Down the Werra

THE HORSEMEN RODE IN FRONT, alongside, and behind us. I barely had to drive our horses; they just plodded along as part of the herd. Had it been Arlene who had arranged the escort, I wondered, holding the reins idly. There was no slipping out of the city unnoticed now. Soon everyone would know. Why had I trusted her? It had been foolish of me to let down my guard.

But Doctor Luther and Brother John didn't seem concerned about our company and traveled along in high spirits until we reached the town of Oppenheim late that afternoon. Frequently Luther would get out his lute and lead everyone in a country folk song. Sometimes he would put new, Christian words to it. We took a break in the marketplace, where the people greeted Luther. Suddenly, we were startled by a horseman who came riding at full gallop and reined hard to a stop among the people in the marketplace.

When the cloud of dust settled, we saw it was Casper Sturm, the imperial herald!

"I thought you couldn't accompany us!" said Luther.

"And I'm not here," laughed Sturm as he swung down from his lathered horse. "At least I'm not here *officially*—not as the imperial herald, that is. But no one else need know that. Actually, the emperor gave me a holiday from my service, so I decided to tag along for a couple of days."

I was glad to see him. He'd become a friend we could depend on in situations where I trusted very few.

Before setting up camp for the night we crossed the Rhine River, and most of our escort turned back instead of paying the toll. Maybe they considered the imperial herald's presence sufficient security; maybe they had to get back to families and other business; or maybe—I speculated—maybe some of them were not along to protect us after all. Maybe they intended some harm that was blocked by Sturm's arrival. Whatever the case, from there on we were accompanied by a small escort of only four other men plus Casper Sturm.

Our journey was uneventful for the next three days except for Luther's insistence on preaching in every town where he was invited. We warned him against this, reminding him that preaching was in direct defiance of the emperor's orders, but Luther persisted.

Then one day after a rather strong protest from the imperial herald, Luther said, "I have not accepted the emperor's condemnation any more than I accepted the pope's bull against me. God is my judge! Why should I obey man rather than God?"

"But my Dear Doctor," protested Casper Sturm, "if you will not take care for your own safety, consider the rest of us. Can you not see how your preaching compromises my presence with you? I do no wrong in merely accompanying you. I am on holiday, and you are still under the emperor's safe passage. But to expect me to stand by while you defy the emperor . . . well, it makes me equally guilty."

"I am truly sorry," said Luther, softening in his way of speaking. "However, the Scriptures say: 'Preach the word; be instant in season, out of season; reprove, rebuke, exhort with all longsuffering and doctrine.' The emperor may have declared my preaching 'out of season,' but that does not release me from the obligation to declare God's Word anyway."

We stood about in awkward silence as the disagreement between Luther and Sturm came to a deadlock.

Finally Sturm bowed his head and then looked up at Luther. "Maybe I should turn back. I only have a day or two left, anyway, before I would have to return to court. You don't seem to be encountering any danger. You have friends in each town who will be looking out for your safety."

"Maybe that would be best," said Luther. "I understand your situation. We greatly appreciate your service and . . ." slowly Luther extended his hand, ". . . your friendship." The imperial herald took the offered hand and clasped it warmly.

"Maybe it would be best if the rest of us left you at this point, too, Doctor Luther," said one of the armed men who had been accompanying us from Worms.

I was shocked. We had never expected an escort, but then our plan had been to travel unnoticed. Now we had been traveling four days with a large group. People all along our route knew we were coming, almost like it had been when we were going to Worms. Without Casper Sturm and the others in our escort, we would be completely vulnerable. I squinted my eyes and looked at the mountains which had been creeping closer, where the forests were thicker and the towns more remote. But what could we do?

That evening Doctor Luther preached in the town square in Hersfeld. The people were begging him to speak, but the local priest would not risk offering the chapel, though he kept claiming he greatly admired Doctor Luther. So everyone gathered in the square and lit the place with torches held high on poles.

I was standing in the shadows at the edge of the crowd when a voice said to me, "I see you have lost your escort." By now the voice was familiar. I turned and could just make out in the darkness the figure of The Watcher.

"Arlene! What are you doing here?"

"Shhh. I'm your contact; remember?"

"But I had no idea you would follow us from Worms."

"Well, I did."

Her beauty was magnified in the flickering light of the torches, but I could not erase all my suspicion. "You know you ruined our quiet departure from Worms, don't you? That was really stupid arranging for a troop of twenty horsemen to escort us."

"Me? We didn't arrange for an escort."

"Well, who else knew? I trusted you and told you we were leaving. Otherwise we planned to leave secretly. No one else knew."

"When you spend all day shopping and loading your wagon, several people might know—the stable man for one."

I had never thought of him. After leaving Worms I had assumed it was Arlene and the men behind her who had arranged the escort. Though it shook my trust in her, I had finally accepted the escort as a safety measure.

"We were actually worried about the escort ourselves," said Arlene, "especially when the imperial herald joined you. It looked like a trap."

"How'd you know Casper Sturm joined us? Have you been spying on us all the way?"

"It's my *job* to be your contact. So I have to stay close enough to make contact when need be."

"Well, you needn't worry about Casper Sturm. He's become a loyal friend, as loyal as they come. I'd trust him before I'd trust . . ." I was going to say "you," but as I looked into the deep blue of her eyes in the torchlight, it didn't seem like the right thing to say.

"I'll see you again at Eisenach," she said and started to leave.

"Wait!" I said. "We're not going on to Eisenach. Doctor Luther wants to turn east before we get there and head up into the Thuringer Mountains. He has some relatives there he wants to visit."

"Where, exactly?" Arlene asked.

"I don't know. He mentioned a village named 'Mohra,' or something."

"Thank you. We will meet again." And then she was gone.

The next morning we got a very early start and I found myself looking for Arlene at every crossroads and in every little village we passed through. I blamed my daydreams on the boredom of driving that old wagon mile after mile. Certainly *I* wouldn't be thinking about some girl if there'd been anything more interesting to do.

We turned east on a smaller road and soon began ascending the mountains. "It's actually a shortcut," said Luther. "Instead of going on north to Eisenach before we turn east, we're taking a cutoff and will catch the main road at Gotha. We'll miss Eisenach completely."

"Well, if it's a shortcut, why doesn't everyone take it?" I asked.

"You'll see," said Luther.

And in a short time I did. The road was so steep

that we were slowed down considerably. Again and again as we crept along my mind would drift to Arlene: bumping into her outside Raven's Tavern back in Wittenberg, Arlene racing through Duben in the middle of the night with her hair flying behind her, Arlene looking so beautiful in the soft torchlight the last time I'd seen her.

If I could really trust her, I thought, guiding the horses around a place where the heavy spring rains had washed out part of the road, she *was* the kind of girl a fellow could get interested in. There was no denying her haunting beauty. But there was more. What courage she must have to be out on the highway by herself! She had confidence, a self-assurance I didn't see much in other girls I knew. And if she really supported Luther's teachings . . . that spoke well of her faith in God.

On the other hand, I snorted to myself, she must not be from a very good family if her parents let her travel around the country alone like that. It just wasn't done!

In spite of the rough road, Doctor Luther was sitting in the back of the wagon, sometimes working on a sermon, sometimes playing on his lute and singing. Brother John was curled up among our bags . . . asleep again, as usual.

We reached the summit, and I guided our wagon down the steep road to the ferry that crossed the Werra River. The river at that point is calm, but as I came down the mountain I could see that just a little farther downstream the river became a wild and rushing torrent cutting through a steep gorge.

This was a better ferry than the one we rode on over the Elbe River outside Wittenberg, and there was no problem loading the wagon and our three horses. I blocked our wheels, paid the ferryman, and settled back to enjoy viewing the rich forest that clung to the sheer walls of the river's gorge. I noticed that these woods had dark evergreens among them, offsetting the light green growth of new spring leaves on the hardwood trees.

We were in the middle of the river when I saw a group of men waiting on the opposite bank. They were all mounted on strong horses that pawed the ferry landing impatiently. The men were heavily armed, some with the armor of knights, but they carried no flag or banner to announce what lord they rode for.

A chill ran through me, and I jumped down from the wagon. "Do you know who those men are?" I asked the ferryman as he pulled steadily on his come-along and drew us across the river.

He looked up without interrupting his slow pace and squinted across the water. "Can't say as I do. Are you expecting someone to meet you? There are too many of them to ride this ferry in one trip."

Expecting someone? No, we certainly weren't expecting anyone—at least not anyone we wanted to meet. But they might be waiting for us, nonetheless. I mulled over the possibilities. It would make an ideal trap. We couldn't outrun them. In fact, I wouldn't even be able to drive the wagon through the middle of them. And there'd be no hiding from them. We couldn't jump off and run through the brush. There was absolutely no escape.

And then I thought of one.

I scampered around to the back of our wagon and pulled out the old axe that we used to cut firewood when we camped. With one mighty swing I chopped in two the ferry rope that slid across the deck between the guides. It was the rope that was stretched across the whole river and prevented us from floating downstream. It was the same rope that the ferryman was pulling on with his come-along to bring us to the other side.

"Wha—! What have you done?" he screamed as the rope slid instantly through his come-along and splashed into the water at the side of the raft. We were already starting to float downstream.

His yell awoke Brother John and brought Doctor Luther to attention. "What's happening?" asked Luther.

"Those men," I answered, pointing to the river bank. At that very moment they were backing their horses off the landing and guiding them downstream and pointing toward us. "It's an ambush!" I said. "They were waiting for us, and there was no other way to escape."

The current pulled the rope out of the ferryman's hands, and we floated freely toward the narrowing gorge. The ferryman was yelling at me. "You foolish kid. You've lost my ferry, and maybe our lives. Even if we survive the rapids, it will take me weeks to build a new ferry. Are you out of your mind? What possessed you?"

But soon there was no more time for yelling. White water was coming up as we approached the rapids in the gorge. The ferryman ordered Brother John to help him with one oar and Doctor Luther and me to man the other oar. "Watch ahead! Watch ahead!" he yelled. "Just try to keep it off the rocks or it will break up."

We were already starting to bob as we went over the smaller rapids. But ahead I could see much larger ones. Soon he was shouting and pointing for us to guide the ferry back toward the side of the river we'd first started from. Then I could see why. We were headed directly for a waterfall. It was small but big enough to tip us off even if it didn't break up the ferry. Doctor Luther and I pulled for all we were worth on the oar, but it didn't seem like we were making any progress at guiding the ferry. And then slowly we caught a new current that began to spin us sideways but also toward the safer side of the river.

I was actually going backward down the river as we passed the falls. Most of the ferry rode the smooth water, but the end with the ferryman and Brother John went partially over the falls. That twisted the ferry so that it groaned and creaked and snapped loudly enough to be heard over the rush of the river. We all nearly lost our balance, and would probably have fallen to the deck if we hadn't been hanging on to the oars.

The two horses at the front of the wagon remained steady, but the one at the back panicked and began rearing up. On the second time it slipped and fell over the side of the ferry into the river. But it was still firmly tied to the back of the wagon. That halter and rope must have been one of the strongest made because they were pulling the wagon sideways toward the edge of the ferry at the same time they were pulling the horse's head under water.

"Cut him free," yelled Luther as I ran to help. "Cut him free, or we'll lose everything."

I grabbed the axe that was still lying on the deck and hacked the rope in two. The horse quickly swam away even as we floated on downstream, and as I watched, it gained solid ground and scrambled up the bank.

We, however, were still in danger. More white water loomed ahead. And as I glanced at the far shore, I could see the horsemen picking their way along the steep bank in an attempt to keep up with us.

The next stretch of white water included a series of waves higher than the ferry. The ferryman yelled for us to turn the ferry sideways. "We have to roll with these waves, or we'll break apart," he called. Again, we pulled and pulled on our oar and managed to get the ferry almost sideways just as we hit this new stretch of white water.

We bobbed and rolled, all right. Up and down, up and down, up and down. Both remaining horses were driven to their knees and then onto their sides by the rolling of the deck. Their eyes were rolled back and they were squealing like stuck pigs as they tried to regain their feet.

But then we were through and still afloat.

For the next half mile the water was smooth, and I looked back at our pursuers. They had been stopped by the sheer cliffs at the river's bank. There had been no trail by which they could follow us downstream.

We twisted and turned with the river through its narrow gorge and passed over two more stretches of white water—neither as bad as the one that had put the horses down. Then we came out into a small valley where the river ran calmly and were able to slowly guide the ferry to the bank where we managed to beach it on a sandy bar.

Chapter 10

Seized on the Highway

I GUESS THE FERRYMAN was as glad to be alive as we were because he didn't immediately begin yelling at me. Instead, he joined us in getting the wagon off the ferry and onto solid ground. And that wasn't so easy.

First we had to cut some driftwood logs to make a little ramp from the ferry deck down to the sand about two feet below. But then the sand was so soft that the wagon sank nearly to its axles and the horses churned up a mire.

With poles for levers and brush to get some footing on, we finally made it up into a beautiful meadow.

"Now where?" said Brother John.

"This is a fine time to ask that question," growled the ferryman. "You should have thought of that before your fool kid cut us loose. You will pay. You will pay for a new ferry," he said. Then turning to me: "Whatever possessed you to do that?"

"It was those men on the far bank," I said. "They were after us, and there was no other way to escape."

"After you? You're imagining things. What would

they want with an old wagon, a couple of monks, and a crazy kid?"

I looked at Doctor Luther for support, but he just gazed at the afternoon sky. I think he was enjoying the tongue-lashing I was getting.

"Well," I said defensively, "you did see them take off down the river trying to keep up with us, didn't you?"

"I didn't notice." His tone was sarcastic. "But did you ever think that maybe they were trying to help us? We were in considerable danger, in case *you* didn't notice."

"We do have reason to be cautious," said Luther, finally coming to my defense. "There are those who would be glad to see me dead. So we have been on the watch against an attack."

The ferryman looked my master up and down. "You look harmless enough. Why should you have enemies?"

Luther looked at Brother John and then at me. "Does the name Martin Luther mean anything to you?" he asked.

"Martin Luther? Are you Martin Luther? Of course I know about Martin Luther." The man grabbed his hat off his head. "My, oh my. Wait until I tell my wife. What a privilege to have carried you on my ferry."

Luther roared with laughter. "Even after we lost it for you?"

"Don't worry about that. I would have done anything to help you escape," said the ferryman,

twisting his
hat in his hands.
"And we'll be sure to
pay you for the loss of
your ferry," reassured Luther.

"Come to think of it, that was pretty smart, kid. What made you think of going down river?"

I shrugged. "There was no place else to go."

"But now the question is, how do we get out of this valley?" put in Brother John.

"Oh, that's no problem," the man said. "We're only about three miles down river from the crossing, and at the end of this valley is a farm. And if it hasn't been washed out with the rains, there's a road from that farm over the mountains to the village of Mohra."

"Mohra?" said Luther. "That's where we were headed. All my relatives live there. Ah-ha! Now I know where we are."

It took us the rest of the afternoon to drive through the dense forest to reach the village of Mohra. The area was very remote. We saw only one woodcutter and two farmers. By dusk we pulled into the little village of Mohra and stopped at a fine house.

"My grandmother lives here," said Luther grinning broadly, and indeed she did. In minutes we were surrounded by more aunts and uncles and cousins than I could count, let alone remember their names.

As though they had been expecting us, Luther's relatives had soon arranged a village potluck in the family garden, and everyone was begging the Doctor to give them a sermon. Of course, he had one ready—the one he had been working on that morning before all the excitement broke loose.

That night I slept well, maybe better than I had on the whole trip. Doctor Luther's grandmother put me up in a room all my own with a feather bed. What luxury!

The next morning we had a truly proper breakfast: fresh milk, fresh bread—so light and soft—with cheese and jam, and tea. Doctor Luther seemed in no hurry to go, either. In fact, every little while some other relative of his would arrive. Many were miners like his father, some were farmers, and others were woodsmen.

It was afternoon before we finally climbed into the wagon loaded with a huge food basket and headed off down the road toward Gotha. I still hadn't seen Arlene, but as I began to think about that incident on the Werra River, my doubts returned. Had she arranged for those men to be waiting for us? If it wasn't her, who had notified them of our approach? The average person would have assumed we would have gone on ahead to Eisenach.

My feelings and thoughts tugged back and forth, not knowing if this was a girl I could trust or not . . . but still *wanting* to trust her.

Finally, I shook my head as if to dismiss her, concluding that we would be in Wittenberg again within a few days. If she showed up there, maybe I could find out what had happened and how she fit into the picture.

Traveling through the dense forest was slower than we had expected. The road was rough and wove in and out of many trees. It was getting on toward sundown and we still had not sighted Gotha.

The road came out of the woods and went along the edge, with the forest on our left side and a beautiful meadow on our right. Across the meadow was a small peasant village. There were only four or five poor hovels in which people lived, but since dark was approaching, I asked, "Do you think we should spend the night over there? Or should we look for a place to camp on our own?"

Luther and Brother John studied the shacks, trying to decide if the people were too poor to take in three more hungry mouths. Over the tall grass we could see some children playing around the houses. A dog must have caught scent of us because it started barking up a storm.

Suddenly a group of highwaymen came thundering out of the woods and surrounded us. Though it was almost dark, they looked like the same group who had been waiting on the far side of the river the day before.

Brother John must have been the most alert among us. He jumped from the wagon and took off running through the grass toward the village, yelling "Help! Help!" at the top of his lungs.

As a couple of horsemen started, a rider with a fully drawn bow and arrow pointed it at Doctor Luther and said, "Are you Martin Luther?"

"I am," he quickly responded.

"Forget the one running away," called the bowman after the two riders. "We got Luther here."

Brother John, with the riders right behind him, had nearly reached the village before they turned back.

"Get down. Get down out of that wagon," the leader ordered us. And to the others he snapped, "Take them both."

It happened so fast, and it was so dark, that I couldn't have told you at the time whether there were six or eight riders. But they soon had ropes around us and were riding off into the forest with us in tow. Only then did I notice some feeble cries coming from the village across the field. I looked back to see Brother John and three or four peasant men running toward us waving pitchforks and scythes in the air. I groaned. They would be no help.

Once among the trees, it took my every effort to keep from tripping over roots or getting slapped in the face by low-hanging limbs. Unable to move my arms because of the ropes that bound me, I was soon completely out of breath from running. I was surprised that Doctor Luther didn't fall down dead.

Once he did trip and
fall, and I tried to run
to his aid only to have
my tow rope whip me back and slam me into a tree.

Finally, our captors stopped in a small clearing.
There two extra horses waited. "Mount up," said the
leader. The ropes that bound us were untied and we
were assisted into the saddles.

"Here, drink this." We were both offered a skin
bag with fresh, cool water in it. I hadn't realized how
thirsty I was and took a long drink.

"Don't take all day," said the leader after we both
drank. He grabbed the bag and set off again through
the forest.

Among the trees it was completely dark by this time, and only when we were on a clear path or road with the trees broken above us could I even see where we were going.

We rode as fast as our horses could carry us, sometimes cantering, sometimes trotting, occasionally galloping. I had no idea how far we had traveled, but our horses were winded.

We finally slowed down to a walk and turned on to a road with two wagon tracks. A hooded rider pulled up beside me, and a low, youthful voice said, "We would have picked you up yesterday if you hadn't made that fool trip down the river. That wasted a lot of time."

What? It sounded like Arlene, but before I could be sure, another horseman came between us, and soon our pace picked up again to a trot.

Chapter 11

The Dark Castle

W E CAME OUT OF THE HEAVY FOREST onto farm land. The moon rose, and I was finally able to make out our company. Our captors always kept two or three riders behind us while the others went on ahead. I counted . . . four, five, six other riders besides Doctor Luther and me.

Now that we could see slightly by the moonlight, I noticed that we slowed down to a walk whenever we came near a farmhouse. *Maybe that would be a way to escape,* I thought. When we were near a farm, I could break for the farmyard yelling for help. But in a while I gave up the idea. What could one sleepy farmer do against six armed men?

But . . . were they all *men*? Now that I could see a little bit, I looked for the hooded rider who had spoken to me. One of the riders near the front seemed to be wearing a hood. I tried to work my way closer.

As we reentered the forest, I could only get glimpses of those around me when moonlight filtered through the canopy of trees. I pressed my horse to move forward. "Is that you?" I asked another rider.

"Who else d'ya think I am?" answered a gruff voice.

Embarrassed, I dropped back, but later tried with another rider only to be told: "Depends on who you were expecting." It was a man's voice.

Finally, I pulled alongside a rider who I could see in the occasional moonlight wore a hooded cape. Only this time the hood was thrown back and long dark hair flowed from the rider's head.

"Arlene! What's happening?" I demanded angrily, but keeping my voice quiet. A quick glance showed me that Doctor Luther was several lengths behind us. "Why have you ambushed us?"

"It's not an ambush," she said calmly, the pungent smell of our hot horses rising around us. "It's a rescue."

"A *rescue*?" I asked. "How could this be a rescue? And what did you mean about our escape down the river? How'd you know about that unless you set up those bandits to attack us?" I was determined to get some answers, but Arlene spurred her powerful horse, and it lunged ahead.

My head was swimming with weariness and confusion. What was happening? She claimed it was a rescue. But I felt like a prisoner, and it seemed more and more like Arlene was a spy for these night riders!

Within a short while we came to a halt, and everyone dismounted, apparently to rest the horses. In an instant Doctor Luther was at my side. "Karl," he whispered, "when I give the word, let's make a break for it. You ride just ahead of me. If we get into some deep woods again, try to hang back to create a space between yourself and the next rider. Then if there's a fork in the trail . . . maybe we can take it. Keep alert." Then he drifted away and began asking our captors for some water.

When we mounted up again, I maneuvered so that Doctor Luther fell in line behind me. And as we rode along, I hung back a little. But soon one of the men behind us called out, "Keep it closed up there." It had been the wrong place. I needed to wait until the trail narrowed and it was too dark for anyone to see.

But then I began to wonder: what if Arlene was right? What if this *was* some kind of a rescue? That's what she and the men who had recruited me back in Worms had planned. They were going to plan a rescue, and I was the insider who was supposed to help it succeed by keeping them informed of where Doctor Luther was and what he planned to do at any time.

On the other hand, Arlene had scolded me for our trip down the river. How had she known about it unless the men who had been waiting for us and this group were one in the same? If this was a rescue, maybe the incident at the ferry had been planned as one too.

I wrestled the question back and forth: should I trust her? or should we try to make a break? And then we came to deep woods again, and the trail narrowed and became very winding.

"This could be it," said Doctor Luther in a low voice behind me.

I started dropping back until there was one horse length, then two, and finally three between me and the rider ahead. "Keep a watch," muttered Luther.

I was keeping a watch, but was still uncertain what to do. *Could I trust Arlene or not?* The circumstances were all confusing. If this was a rescue, why didn't these people just come out and tell us what was happening? Of course Doctor Luther wanted to escape, because he knew nothing about any rescue plans. But . . . what if I helped him escape from people who were trying to help him? I tried to think what the options were. A wild dash into the dark woods. If we made it, we might get home to Wittenberg . . . but we'd still face possible arrest—not very inviting. Our other option lay with these strange riders and a girl who asked me to trust her. And suddenly I knew what my answer had to be.

The horseman behind Doctor Luther had dropped back just out of sight when an escape opportunity presented itself. Our horses were moving at a fast walk, and just as we came around a blind bend to the right I noticed that if one turned even more sharply to the right and ducked under some low hanging limbs, there was the hint of another trail that went steeply down into a ravine. Doctor Luther was close behind me and saw it at nearly the same time.

"That's it," whispered Luther.

I jumped my horse into the opening, but then I reined her in so hard that she reared up, whinnied, and almost threw me off backwards. I had acted on my decision to trust Arlene. I completely blocked any avenue of escape. Doctor Luther couldn't get by me even if he had tried to flee alone.

Hearing the commotion, the horseman behind us rode up and said, "That's not the way! Get back up here on the trail, and keep it closed up with the rider ahead of you. We don't want you getting lost out here in this forest."

"What's the matter with you?" said Luther through clinched teeth. "We had a chance, and now look what you did."

I didn't answer. I had made a decision. Now I would have to live with it.

Shortly we returned to riding on an open road, and there were no more opportunities to make a break from our captors. The road rose sharply as we climbed a hill, and then suddenly out of the gloom I realized that we were facing the walls of a great castle.

We stopped and the horseman who seemed to be in charge rode back along the column giving the message: "Silence! Silence. Our arrival is not to be known."

Then he went back to the front and whistled twice. A small light appeared in a tower, and soon I heard the muted clinking of chain. The drawbridge was being lowered for us.

We rode our horses one at a time over the drawbridge to keep down the noise. Inside the castle we dismounted and were met by a very large soldier. The moonlight glinted from his helmet. "Welcome," he said in a hushed voice. "I am the captain of this castle. Would you please follow me."

That voice . . . I was sure I had heard it before but couldn't place it.

The captain led us through several dark passageways and up two flights of stairs. The labyrinth was only occasionally lit by torches hung on the stone walls. The captain went first; Luther followed. From time to time I tried to pass so that I could get a closer look at the captain's face when he was in the light, but the halls were too narrow. Then the captain stopped by one torch. Below it was a box from which he took another torch and lit it. On we went into a

dark tunnel until the captain stopped in front of a ladder that went up through a trapdoor in the ceiling.

"Up the ladder, if you please, Doctor Luther," he

said as he handed Luther the torch. Just before Luther disappeared with the light though the dark hole in the ceiling, I got a glimpse of the captain's face. His voice was definitely familiar, but I still couldn't see enough of his face to place him. "You next," he said to me.

Doctor Luther gave me his hand to help me up through the trapdoor. "These will be your rooms," came the captain's voice from the dark below. "We're sorry they couldn't be more spacious. Tomorrow we can talk." Then he pulled the ladder down. The trapdoor was attached to the end of it, and soon it settled snugly into the opening.

I looked at Doctor Luther in the torchlight. I didn't know what he was thinking. But I knew what I was thinking. Had we been rescued, or were we in prison? It was hard to say, but there was no handle on our side of the trapdoor.

Chapter 12

Confined to the Tower

I AWOKE THE NEXT MORNING to the joyful racket of birds singing. When I went to the window, I discovered below us a sea of trees that swept away to a vast valley with a town visible in the distance.

I realized that Doctor Luther had come to stand beside me. "Quite a view, isn't it?" he said.

"I would consider it a more pleasant view to be on the outside looking in," I answered.

"Yes. Indeed. The question is, why have they brought us here?"

"I'd just like to know *where* we are."

"Oh, I recognize where we are, now that it is day. The town you see over there is Eisenach, where we were headed before we took our ride down the river. So this must be Wartburg Castle. I've seen it from a distance, but I've never been here before. I've heard, however, that it's a very strong fortress, not one a person can get in or out of very easily."

Our quarters were high in the wall of the castle, and the castle was on the peak of such a steep hill that approaching the base of the walls would itself be a hard climb. We occupied two rooms separated by an arched door so low that I had to duck to step through. Our furnishings were sparse: two narrow bunks, a small table, a writing desk, two chairs, and a chamber pot.

"The strange thing is," said Luther, "we're in Saxony, and this castle belongs to Duke Frederick. I have always considered him my friend—at least as much as it was politically safe for him to be. So why would he go against the emperor's guarantee of safe passage and attack us openly on the highway?"

The duke's castle? I tried to swallow the lump that was rising in my throat. "Do you think . . . I mean, could the emperor have canceled your safe passage early and ordered your arrest?" I said slowly.

"The emperor can do anything," said Luther with a shrug. "But if Charles has ordered my arrest, and if Duke Frederick has been so quick to do the emperor's bidding against me, I may, indeed, be without friends in high places."

"Except in heaven," I said.

"Right you are, Karl. Right you are." Luther chuckled. "Where has my faith gone? A little trouble comes and already I am forgetting who is in control of the universe." He once again surveyed the landscape that fell away below us. "Karl, this may seem like an impenetrable castle, but consider what a mighty fortress is our God. On earth is not His equal."

Just then a thud came from the square in the floor, and slowly the trapdoor rose. The ladder was put in place, and out of the hole emerged the bulky captain who had received us the night before. Behind him, of all people, was Arlene. Together they had brought us breakfast, bottles of water, and a pot of steaming hot tea.

"Have something to eat," said the captain. And then, as I got a good look at him in the light, I realized where I'd seen him before. "You're the man in the dungeon in Worms who tried to get me to report on Doctor Luther," I blurted.

"Yes, my young insider—Karl Schumacher, wasn't it? You've done a fine job for us, too . . . except for that unexpectedly long ferry ride."

I caught my breath. Maybe . . . maybe there was hope that I had made the right decision in not trying to escape last night. There was no doubt that this captain was the same man who had recruited me in Worms. He said it was for a "rescue." Arlene kept speaking of wanting to help Doctor Luther. Maybe I had done the right thing. But if so, why were we being held in this castle? Had they deceived me? I still wasn't sure.

Luther took a hunk of bread and a cup of tea and sat on the edge of the writing desk. "Please be seated," he said, indicating the two chairs for the captain and Arlene. I sat on the edge of the bed. Then with a very quizzical look on his face, Luther said, "What does this mean, Karl? You seem to know this man. And he calls you his 'insider.'"

"Maybe I should explain," volunteered the captain. "Duke Frederick has been concerned for some time that you might not get out of Worms alive. That's why he worked so hard to get the emperor to guarantee you safe passage. But there's no predicting what this young Charles might do. He could cancel it any day.

"So the duke told me to arrange for your safety. He did not tell me what to do. In fact, he doesn't want to know because he expects to be questioned, and he wants to be able to honestly say that he doesn't know.

"I decided that the best thing would be to kidnap you. Common bandits or, more likely, men working for your enemies were a likely hazard on the highway. So we decided that the best kind of a rescue would be one that looked like an attack by highwaymen. Hopefully the emperor

can be convinced that some too-eager churchmen jumped the deadline of your safe conduct and that, in fact, you are already dead."

I looked at Arlene. Her lips betrayed a small smile.

"But," the captain went on, "we needed an insider, someone close to you who could keep us informed about your comings and goings. So Karl, here, has been helping us."

"Did you know about all this, Karl?" said Doctor Luther.

"Not really . . . well, I knew about some of it. I did agree to help rescue you. But I had no idea about the ambush until Arlene told me what should have happened at the river . . ."

"You've been betraying me, Karl?" broke in Doctor Luther. "You've been telling these people where we were going and what we were going to do? How could you?"

"Wait a minute; wait a minute," calmed the captain. "Try to understand, Doctor Luther, that we have brought you here for your own safety. Even if you had gotten safely back to Wittenberg, it would have been only a matter of days before your safe passage would have expired and you would have been arrested. That is certain! And after that, only a miracle could have kept you from burning at the stake."

"Well, possibly so," admitted Luther. "But, Karl, how did you communicate with them?"

I felt relieved that it was all going to come out.

"Remember when we came through Duben and I told you that someone had been looking in our wagon, someone who went galloping off into the night?"

"Hmmm, yes. You thought it was that girl you had seen in Wittenberg, the one you called The Watcher."

"Well it was, and this is the girl," I said, pointing to Arlene. "She met me in Worms and arranged for me to tell her when we'd be traveling and where we were going. But what I don't understand," I said, turning to Arlene, "is, why you? Why a young girl out on the road alone?"

Arlene laughed. "This is my father," she said, indicating the captain. "And he was never *that* far away."

"Your father?" I said. "But why weren't you here at the castle, dressed in the fine clothes of a noble lady, learning the manners of court?"

"I have. I mean, I do want to learn those things. It's just . . ."

"Maybe I can explain," offered the captain. "My wife—Arlene's mother—died eight years ago. I have no other children, and I value Arlene's companionship. So I have undertaken to teach her the things *I* know: how to ride, how to shoot a bow, how to be resourceful. And she's become very skilled and courageous, don't you think?"

"Well, yes. But girls just don't . . ."

"Karl," said Doctor Luther, "certainly you remember Joan of Arc, the young French girl who led her whole country to victory in battle. There's a place for everyone with courage."

I reddened. What could I say?

Doctor Luther then turned to the captain. "I appreciate your rescue—I think. How long do I need to stay here?"

The captain cleared his throat. "I suggest that you remain in these rooms, unseen by the other people in the castle until your hair and beard grow out. Then you can have the run of the castle disguised as someone other than a monk. Without a disguise you are not safe from being reported."

Luther pursed his lips, thinking. I could tell he didn't like giving up his freedom to come and go, to teach and preach. "But as whom could I be disguised?" he finally said.

I suddenly had an idea. "This is a castle where fighting men gather. Why not be a knight . . . like you always wanted to be? You could be Knight George!"

Doctor Luther chuckled. "But I wouldn't be real. I'd be a pretender."

"So what? You need some kind of a disguise. And what's more common in a castle than a knight?"

"Just one more thing," I said to Arlene, still feeling a hint of suspicion. "How did you happen to be in Wittenberg at Raven's Tavern last winter? And how did John Eck know about Luther burning the bull only moments after you ran into the tavern, having seen it yourself? Did you tell him?"

Arlene's face went white, and her mouth hung open as she turned toward her father. Finally she took a deep breath and turned back to face me. "That was my big mistake," she said, wringing her hands. "I was staying there—my cousin owns the tavern. And my father and I have always been very interested in Doctor Luther. I saw you the day you took the bull off the church door."

"I know you did. That was the first time I saw you, too."

"Well," she continued, "on the day that Doctor Luther burned the bull and those other papers, I ran back to the tavern and told it all to my cousin. I didn't realize who John Eck was and that he was sitting right there and heard everything I said." She turned to Doctor Luther. "When I realized what I'd done, I decided that I had to help you. So I followed you to Duben, then came on to meet with my father. I'm so very sorry . . ."

"No bother, my dear," interrupted Luther. "It was a public event. Eck would have known within an hour anyway. You did nothing wrong."

Arlene looked at me, and we smiled at each other.

The days passed, not too unpleasantly, and I served Doctor Luther in every way I could. The first thing he wanted me to do was track down what had happened to our wagon and retrieve his Greek Bible and his lute. He decided to use his time in confinement translating the New Testament into German so the common people could read God's Word.

"But there's another way for people to learn the Gospel," he said to me one day. "We need songs, songs that the people can sing, songs that will stay in their hearts long after they have forgotten Sunday's sermon. How about this one, Karl?" and he picked up his lute.

> *A mighty fortress is our God,*
> *A bulwark never failing;*
> *Our helper He, amid the flood*
> *Of mortal ills prevailing.*

"I'm not sure what should come next," he said as he strummed the cords and hummed the melody again. "It's just that this castle with all its strength is really nothing without God's power. Here, how about this verse:

> *Did we in our own strength confide,*
> *Our striving would be losing,*
> *Were not the right Man on our side,*
> *The Man of God's own choosing.*

"And who is that?" I asked. "The captain of the castle?"

"No, no. But that's a good line. Hmmm . . ."

> *Dost ask who that may be?*
> *Christ Jesus, it is He;*
> *La, la, la, . . .*

He stopped singing. "Oh, well. I don't know yet what should come next. But I'll work on it. Someday, Karl, I'm going to publish a book of songs for the people. The Devil doesn't stay long where there is good music."

By summer Luther's hair had grown over his head and he sported a square, black beard. The captain gave him the run of the castle as Knight George, a visiting knight from some un- named land. And, indeed, Luther had been through some fierce battles, fighting for a powerful  Lord, defeating at least some of the evil in the land.

But in spite of his translation work on the New Testament, he always made time to help me with my studies. "You'll be ready to enter regular university by the time we get back to Wittenberg," he told me one day.

I grinned. My dream was coming true. But a new one was growing alongside it. It was about Arlene. We saw each other every day in the castle and some- times went for walks in the forest.

However, though dreams may keep you going,

they always have their obstacles. And my dreams about Arlene were no exception. At the end of the summer the captain sent her off to stay with his sister, the Duchess of Ebernburg, to be trained as a noble lady. I should have kept my mouth shut about Arlene not being trained in the social graces.

Oh, well. When she returns and I have graduated from the university, then maybe . . . .

More About
Martin Luther

MARTIN LUTHER WAS BORN on November 10, 1483, in Eisleben in Saxony (part of Germany). Soon after Martin's birth, his peasant parents—Hans and Margarethe—moved to Mansfeld to find employment in the mines. His industrious father rented a forge where he could smelt copper ore into raw copper and thereby went into business for himself.

Luther attended school there, in Magdeburg, and in Eisenach, and finally entered university in Erfurt. One day when twenty-two-year-old Martin was returning to the university, he is said to have been caught in a severe thunderstorm and nearly struck by a bolt of lightning. In terror he cried out and pledged to become a monk if only his life would be spared.

Within two weeks he made good on his promise and entered a monastery. In the monastery he made another vow: "Henceforth I shall serve you God, you Jesus, you only." And he did. On April 3, 1507, Luther was ordained a priest. His superiors found him to be very bright and dedicated. In 1512 he earned his doctor of theology degree and became a professor in the University of Wittenberg.

But in spite of his professional success, Luther felt tormented by his sins and did not feel he had found favor with God. The harder he worked to be "good," the worse he felt until one day he was studying Romans 1:17: "For therein is the righteousness of God revealed from faith to faith: as it is written, The just shall live by faith."

Even though he was a teacher of religion, he had not realized that one cannot *earn* God's favor. It is a gift from God, received by faith alone. And Martin accepted God's gift.

This discovery transformed Luther's life.

His first question was, "Why didn't I learn this good news from my church?" He looked around. Common people everywhere who wanted to please God were told by priests to buy indulgences and obey the church's rules. The selling of indulgences (written pardons for sin) brought much money into the church treasury. Obeying all the rules gave the church leaders great power.

Luther was upset. These practices were a fraud, and he decided to oppose them. He began by trying to convince the church leaders that they had to teach the truth. He debated other church leaders and wrote booklets saying why the church's practices were wrong. He declared that the Bible was more important than the popes or the declarations of the church councils that made up the rules. They were not supreme. They had made mistakes, proven, in

Luther's opinion, by the fact that they reversed their rulings on various issues.

A few church leaders and some state rulers agreed with Luther. Duke Frederick of the state of Saxony was one of those who sympathized with Luther. But other church and state leaders saw that his ideas could greatly weaken their power over the people, and so they opposed him.

As the story in this book relates, the struggle came to a head with Luther's trial at the Diet of Worms where he refused to take back what he had written unless he could be proved by the Bible to have been wrong. After his rescue and confinement in the Wartburg Castle, Luther remained there, disguised as a visiting knight for almost a year, attended by a young page who constantly had to remind Luther to remain in character.

While there he completed many influential publications, the most significant of which was the translation of the New Testament into German.

The Reformation was gaining momentum, but in some quarters, even in his own university at Wittenberg, it took a violent and fanatical turn. Luther was unable to give guidance from a distance, so he finally left the protection of Wartburg Castle to speak from the pulpit in the City Church in Wittenburg. His calming leadership was effective in Wittenberg, but the spirit of reform was abroad in the land. And by 1524 peasant armies were on the march against the wealthy landowners all over Europe. "We are free—it says so in the Scriptures. And free we will be!" they demanded. This was none of Luther's doing, at least not directly, but his ideas nonetheless sparked their revolt.

At first their vast numbers overwhelmed the nobility, and forty cloisters and many castles were taken. The peasants called for and needed Luther's support, but he did not grant it. In fact, he wrote a pamphlet encouraging the nobility to put down the revolt. They did, slaughtering peasants by the thousands.

Luther died in 1546, with the new church firmly established in Europe.

Though there were many reformers, several elements contributed to Luther being the most influential. He was a powerful speaker and writer and succeeded in publishing and circulating many of his ideas *before* he was forcefully opposed. This enabled him to enlist many supporters—some of them very influential. That may have saved his life. Luther's timing and location in central Europe offered a convenient issue for politicians in the Holy Roman Empire to use in trying to wrestle some of the power away from the Roman Catholic Church for their own purposes. Luther was not seen to be the threat to the state that some Anabaptists were because of their pacifism.

Initially Luther had no intention of breaking away from the Roman Catholic Church. He simply wanted to correct its errors. Therefore, it came as a surprise and a disappointment to him to find that his practice of a "reformed" religion in Germany had founded a new and separate church. He also did not want this church to take its name from him, but Lutheranism remains the name of the beliefs and practices he originated.

Today the Lutheran church—like many other churches—is made up of subgroups that operate differently from one another. Some adhere strongly to Luther's teaching that the Bible is the Christian's only rule for faith and life. Others place less practical emphasis on its supreme importance. Some teach Luther's discovery that our sins are forgiven as a result of God's grace, through faith alone, and that each person must exercise faith in order to enjoy a relationship with God. Others do not teach this clearly and offer more of a religion of tradition and ritual into which one is born.

For Further Reading

Bainton, Roland H., *Here I Stand: A Life of Martin Luther* (New York: Abingdon-Cokesbury, 1950).

Cowie, Leonard W., *Martin Luther, Leader of the Reformation* (New York: Frederick A. Praeger, 1969).

Fife, Robert Herndon, *The Revolt of Martin Luther* (New York: Columbia University Press, 1957).

Friedenthal, Richard, *Luther: His Life and Times* (New York: Harcourt Brace Jovanovich, Inc., 1967).

Lilje, Hanns, *Luther and the Reformation, an Illustrated Review* (Philadelphia: Fortress Press, 1967).

Severy, Merle, "The World of Luther," *National Geographic*, Vol. 164, No. 4, Oct. 1983, pp. 418-463.

Thulin, Oskar, *A Life of Luther* told in pictures and narrative by the reformer and his contemporaries (Philadelphia: Fortress Press, 1966).

Series for Middle Graders* From BHP

ADVENTURES DOWN UNDER · by Robert Elmer
When Patrick McWaid's father is unjustly sent to Australia as a prisoner in 1867, the rest of the family follows, uncovering action-packed mystery along the way.

ADVENTURES OF THE NORTHWOODS · by Lois Walfrid Johnson
Kate O'Connell and her stepbrother Anders encounter mystery and adventure in northwest Wisconsin near the turn of the century.

AN AMERICAN ADVENTURE SERIES · by Lee Roddy
Hildy Corrigan and her family must overcome danger and hardship during the Great Depression as they search for a "forever home."

BLOODHOUNDS, INC. · by Bill Myers
Hilarious, hair-raising suspense follows brother-and-sister detectives Sean and Melissa Hunter in these madcap mysteries with a message.

GIRLS ONLY! · by Beverly Lewis
Four talented young athletes become fast friends as together they pursue their Olympic dreams.

JOURNEYS TO FAYRAH · by Bill Myers
Join Denise, Nathan, and Josh on amazing journeys as they discover the wonders and lessons of the mystical Kingdom of Fayrah.

MANDIE BOOKS · by Lois Gladys Leppard
With over four million sold, the turn-of-the-century adventures of Mandie and her many friends will keep readers eager for more.

THE RIVERBOAT ADVENTURES · by Lois Walfrid Johnson
Libby Norstad and her friend Caleb face the challenges and risks of working with the Underground Railroad during the mid–1800s.

TRAILBLAZER BOOKS · by Dave and Neta Jackson
Follow the exciting lives of real-life Christian heroes through the eyes of child characters as they share their faith with others around the world.

THE TWELVE CANDLES CLUB · by Elaine L. Schulte
When four twelve-year-old girls set up a business of odd jobs and baby-sitting, they uncover wacky adventures and hilarious surprises.

THE YOUNG UNDERGROUND · by Robert Elmer
Peter and Elise Andersen's plots to protect their friends and themselves from Nazi soldiers in World War II Denmark guarantee fast-paced action and suspenseful reads.

*(ages 8–13)